COHERENT MIND

A QUANTUM SHIFT

TRANSCENDING LIMITING BELIEFS

LALI A. LOVE

Disclaimer

The perspectives and poetry shared in this book are based on the author's personal experiences and knowledge gained through a Neuroscience certification course. This content is intended for informational and inspirational purposes only and should not be considered medical, psychological, or therapeutic advice. The author is not a licensed psychologist or mental health professional and makes no claims about providing treatment. Readers are encouraged to consult qualified professionals for any medical concerns.

Coherent Mind:
A Quantum Shift

Distributed by Bublish Inc.

Paperback ISBN: 978-1-64704-957-7
eBook ISBN: 978-1-64704-958-4

Award-Winning Publications

Fictional Novels:

Heart of a Warrior Angel: From
Darkness to Light (2019)
The De-Coding of Jo 1: Hall of Ignorance (2020)
The De-Coding of Jo 2: Blade of Truth (2021)
The De-Coding of Jo 3: Keys to Eternity (2022)

Non-Fiction Books:

The Joy of I.T. - Infinite Transcendence (2020)
Ananda: Poetry for the Soul (2021)
Organic eMotions: Poetry for hUmaNITY (2022)
Realms of My Soul: A Forgotten Dream (2023)
Realms of My Soul 2: A Liberating Path (2023)
Realms of My Soul 3: A Golden Gift (2023)

Self-Transformation Books:

Coherent Heart: A Hero's Odyssey (2024)
Coherent Mind: A Quantum Shift (2025)

Dedication

To the curious souls who transform chaos into clarity, turn adversity into strength, and activate the limitless power of their quantum mind— this journey of abundance is yours to claim.

Threads We Weave

Timelines entwine like rivers wide,
Their currents pulled by thought and tide.
The echoes of our hearts compose
Pathways where fate and vision close.

A single spark, a whispered dream,
Unfurls within the cosmic stream.
Each moment bends, a thread unwinds,
Where light and shadow shape our minds.

Your heart—an orbit, finely spun,
Aligns with worlds yet seen by none.
A mirrored realm reflects your hue,
What dwells within is drawn to you.

Be mindful of the threads you weave,
For time is but the web you breathe.
A spoken word, a fleeting sigh,
Can shift the stars that lace the sky.

Envision wealth not bound by gold,
But light that shimmers, fierce and bold.
A beacon in your field aglow,
That calls the path where dreamers go.

I greet this day with belief untold,
The universe, my hands enfold.

With trust, I paint the canvas wide,
My heart, a compass, my soul, a guide.

Embrace the shift, let fear release,
For change unfolds in whispered peace.
I weave the light, the gold, the dreams,
In every thread, a vision gleams.

With grateful hands, I shape the flow,
A sovereign power, I come to know.

Cosmic Traveler

You are the echo of the infinite,
a bridge between all that has been
and all that is yet to rise.

With each inhale, you carry the breath of dying stars,
their silent implosions birthing light from shadow,
a universe unraveling in your pulse.

You are not a flicker in time—
you are time itself, folding and unfurling,
the rhythm of something ancient
moving through flesh and memory.

Look closer—
you are not the spectator but the witness,
a constellation carved from stardust,
tracing the map of all you have been
and all you are meant to remember.

There is no beginning.
No end.

Only the hum of creation,
the pulse of expansion resting in your bones.

You are the ember that outlasts the night,
the whisper that stills the storm,

the flame that breathes eternity
into a fleeting spark.

Do not shrink before your own existence.

You were never meant to kneel
before the vastness of the cosmos.

You are its architect.
Its purpose.
Its unshakable force.

A cosmic traveler.

And the universe—
it does not exist outside of you.

It lives through you.
It waits—
patient, eternal—
for you to awaken.

CONTENTS

Forword

Quantum Paradigm Shift: Call to Action

Self-transformation is not an abstract ideal—it is an alchemical process, ignited by a single, profound perspective: every breath, every moment, offers a choice.

For generations, we've been conditioned to believe otherwise—that we are powerless, mere byproducts of an indifferent world, shaped by forces beyond our control. From childhood, we are taught to see ourselves as flawed, perpetually seeking salvation, external validation, and permission to feel whole.

Yet within us lies an ancient intelligence, a divine blueprint encoded in every cell, waiting to be awakened. This essence is not bound by the material world nor confined by doctrine—it is our natural state of being, an unfiltered connection to the unified quantum field, a limitless reservoir of creation.

We are not separate from the universe; *we are the universe, aware of itself.* Each of us is a living expression of Source consciousness, a unique conduit of the divine force that breathes life into all existence. This sacred current pulses through the *Coherent Heart*, the portal to the unified field, where infinite potential flows and the human experience unfolds.

Sovereignty is not bestowed—it is reclaimed. It begins with knowledge, sharpens through discernment, stabilizes in balance, and ignites through curiosity. The moment we dismantle inherited illusions, we collapse the false walls of separation and step into the quantum field of creation. Here, reality is not a fixed construct but a living canvas, shaped by the electromagnetic force of our very being.

Coherent Mind isn't just another self-help guide—it's a revolutionary playbook for transformation, fusing ancient wisdom with cutting-edge discoveries in neuroscience and quantum mechanics.

This book unearths the power of neuroplasticity, revealing how to rewire subconscious patterns, regulate your nervous system, and align your energetic investments with the highest frequencies of abundance.

More than a roadmap, it's a revolution—an initiation into infinite possibility. The veil is lifting—dismantle the illusion and step fearlessly into your innate power.

You are not helpless.

You are not fractured.

You are the architect of reality itself.

It is time to reclaim your magnetism, rewire your mind, and manifest the life your soul was destined to create.

> *"You are both the artist and the masterpiece, sculpting reality with every thought, emotion, and intention. Through mind-heart coherence, you awaken the power to transcend limits, weaving beauty and magic into each breathtaking moment."*
>
> —Author Lali A. Love

PART 1

REWIRING REALITY

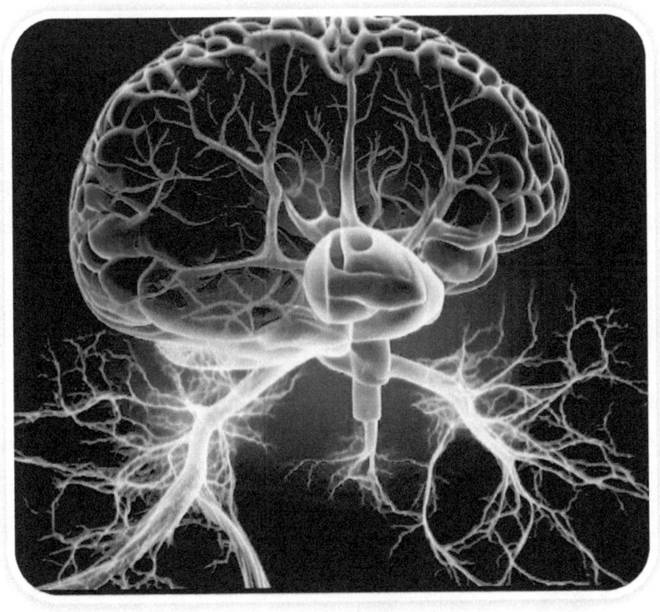

Introduction

Know Thyself – A Quantum Perspective

Who are you, really? Beyond the name you were given, beyond the roles you've been conditioned to play—who are you beneath the surface? Peel back the layers. The expectations, the identities, the inherited stories. Strip away the projections of the future and the echoes of the past. Look deeper. Beyond the illusion of form. What remains?

At the quantum level, you are not fixed. You are not defined. You are an ebbing wave of infinite possibilities, collapsing into a singular reality with every thought, every choice, every moment of awareness.

You are energy—vibrating, shifting, expanding through patterns of endless potential. Yet, in this experience, you feel solid, tangible, real. But here's the paradox: you are mostly empty space. A flickering dance of atoms, appearing and disappearing in probability fields. And in that vast emptiness, you find your real essence.

Think of the versions of you that exist—you from five minutes ago, the one reading in this moment, and the one you are becoming. Are they the same? Quantum physics says no. You are not static. You are a current, flowing and reshaping with every breath.

This is reflected in the famous double-slit experiment—light exists as both wave and particle, its nature determined by observation. Now, replace light with you. Feel that resonance? Your essence is sculpted by your perception.

You are not merely an observer of life. You are the observer and the observed. The dreamer and the dream.

Self-awareness, in metaphysical philosophy, mirrors quantum observation. Just as consciousness collapses infinite possibilities into a single, defined reality, your awareness shapes the very fabric of your life. Every conscious reflection is a pulse of creation—an act of self-love, designing your world as the observer and architect.

We exist within a fractal holographic universe, where every thought, every action, every moment ripples through infinite dimensions. The patterns of existence resonate at every scale, revealing how the micro and macro are One—interconnected, boundless, and full of untapped potential.

In this living, evolving cosmos, reality is not fixed. It unfolds, shaped by our consciousness in harmony with the universe. As John Wheeler's *Participatory Universe Theory* suggests, we are not passive bystanders—our thoughts, choices, words. and actions actively form the world around us, dancing in the continuous flow of evolution.

Science and metaphysics converge on one profound viewpoint: **Reality is fluid. It is shaped by the consciousness that perceives it.**

You are not the story. You are the author.

Every moment of contemplation invites transformation, offering you the power to collapse infinite possibilities into a tangible, lived experience.

You are not separate from the universe—you are woven into its very fabric. Just as entangled particles remain mysteriously linked across vast distances, your consciousness transcends space and time, eternally connected to the greater whole.

Yet from early childhood, we're conditioned to exist in survival mode, where fear and stress shape our mental states and distort our well-being.

But what if breaking free from this cycle was within your grasp? What if the key to rewriting your narrative has always been inside you?

Your biology, your vitality, your joy—these are not governed by fate. They are sculpted by the connection between your mind and heart. Change your beliefs, and you have the power to reshape your entire reality.

In *Coherent Heart*, we explore the synergy of emotional intelligence and spiritual wisdom, aligning with the unified field of consciousness. Life's challenges become catalysts for growth, and we embrace the Hero's Odyssey as our own metamorphosis.

But what happens when the heart and mind synchronize in quantum alignment?

This book mergers the power of scientific insights and alchemical wisdom, helping you dismantle limiting beliefs, reprogram subconscious patterns, and awaken the boundless potential within. Transformation starts by shifting your perspective—aligning intention with action—and watching your life unfold in ways you never thought possible.

In *Coherent Mind*, you'll reclaim your self-worth, transmute pain, rewrite limiting beliefs, rewire your brain, regulate your nervous system, restore balance, reignite vitality, and consciously reshape your reality. Each chapter empowers you to take meaningful action with a practical playbook for manifestation. This is the path to co-creation, embodiment, and true self-mastery—the journey to becoming the creator of your own life.

The convergence of quantum physics and metaphysics reveals that your existense is shaped by the consciousness that perceives it. Your beliefs and perceptions aren't just thoughts—they are the architects of your health, vitality, and even your genetic expression.

As your mental clarity sharpens, you become fully present, deeply empowered, and in sync with the higher intelligence guiding you. Neuroplasticity confirms that when we transform within, our entire world shifts. By rewiring outdated scripts and consciously construct new neural pathways, we reshape the course of our lives—moment by moment.

We are not prisoners of our past—we are the architects of our future. Shift your perspective, and you shift your biology. Discover the missing link that connects mind, body, and spirit, and reclaim the vibrant, limitless life that has always been your birthright.

Ignite the dormant power within you. The journey of self-transformation begins the moment you realize that the abundance you seek has always been within you, waiting to be activated. It's all in your hands—the choice is yours.

1. Breaking Free from the Mind's Illusion

Do you feel trapped by the weight of the world or forces beyond your control? What if I told you the real imprisonment lies within your mind, where a part of you still clings to past fears and unresolved pain?

You are not stuck because life is holding you back; *you are stuck because you have yet to release what no longer serves you.*

Resistance to change is not a sign of failure, but a threshold—a test from the universe urging you to rise. In this moment, you stand at the doorway to liberation, but only if you dare to let go of the illusion that binds you. The power to break free has always been within you.

When we stand at the edge of transformation, life doesn't lay out a smooth path. Instead, it presents obstacles as mini quizzes—each one whispering, *Are you truly ready to step into a higher version of yourself?*

These aren't just setbacks or stop signs. They are the call to reclaim your power. The resistance you feel is an invitation to trust yourself, to stand firm in your vision, to break free from what no longer serves you.

So, I ask you: *Are you ready to leave your past behind?*

Are you willing to claim the future your heart desires?

The breakthrough is always on the other side of fear. And right now, the universe is asking, *Will you step forward anyway?*

Threshold of Manifestation

What if the breakdowns, the setbacks—the very things you fear—aren't roadblocks but signposts?

You set your intentions: *I am ready to rise.*

You declare your heart's aspirations: *I manifest peace, abundance, and joy with purpose.*

And then? Everything falls apart.

A crisis erupts. A relationship fractures. An old wound resurfaces. The chaos pulls you back into a spiral of stress, scarcity, anxiety, and self-doubt.

This is where most people retreat. They listen to fear and uncertainty. They believe the narrative that nothing has changed.

They slip back into old identities that tell them wealth is unsafe, love is fleeting, and contentment is a mirage.

And in that moment, you wonder: *Why does this always happen when I'm trying to grow?*

The answer is simple: your ego—the version of your identity rooted in fear—is fighting for survival, sending fiery red signals through your inflamed nervous system.

Your petrified mind clings to what it knows, even when that experience is painful. Even when it keeps you small, disempowered, trapped in cycles of worry and resistance. Your ego only understands struggle. It knows lack. It knows endurance. It knows *familiarity*.

The human ego isn't the villain to be killed. Its role is to shape your personality, protect your body from actual danger, and navigate the density of the material world.

But beneath the surface, it spins the illusion of separation, keeping you trapped in outdated belief systems and limiting patterns. It masquerades as control, whispering skepticism, magnifying obstacles, convincing you that the universe is against you.

However, It's not the world holding you back—it's the unhealed parts of you, surfacing to be seen, understood, validated, and released.

This is where most people give up, mistaking resistance for failure. But what if resistance isn't rejection—it's revelation? A mirror reflecting the fears, negative stories, and unconscious patterns that must be integrated before you can step fully into the life calling you forward.

If you keep attracting the opposite of what your heart is yearning for, it's not the universe denying you—it's your own unprocessed energy and subconscious programs rising to be cleared. When you set a goal, the universe moves to align with it, but if unintentional blocks stand in the way, they surface first—not to stop you, but to be dissolved.

This is the threshold. The test. The point where most turn back. You are being called to break through—by understanding how your mind is wired and how your biology responds.

Your brain is a supercomputer, designed for survival, not evolution. The limbic system reacts to change as a threat, triggering fear and skepticism. But transformation requires rewiring.

By harnessing the power of neuroplasticity—the brain's ability to form neural pathways—you can break free from subconscious patterns. Each time you align your thoughts and actions with your intentions and affirmations, you send a signal to your brain that the unknown is not a threat or dangerous, but expansive opportunity for growth.

The art of manifestation isn't about forcing outcomes—it's about rewiring your mind and energy to clear the path to your higher self. That's when you magnetize and align with your state of being, the creative flow.

Trust. Align. Expand. The life you've always dreamed of is already waiting. Your *Coherent Heart* knows the way.

Introspection: Codes of *Whole-Inness*

What if we were never truly lost in the matrix of duality, only asleep—our answers not distant, but encoded within our DNA, or hidden right before us, in plain sight? They're woven into the stories we tell, etched in ancient scriptures, and reflected in the films we watch— quietly embedded in the fabric of our reality, patiently waiting for us to awaken.

What if everything around us was designed to reveal that we are aspects of One Source, and the world we inhabit is simply a tool to help us remember?

What if the biblical scriptures were more than mere history? What if Yeshua wasn't a figure to be worshipped, but a way-shower, guiding us to step into our sovereignty and fulfill a purpose beyond our wildest imagination?

What if Trinity represents the embodiment of divine balance—the alchemical union of masculine and feminine energies within us in perfect harmony?

And what if astrology wasn't a superstition, but a forgotten language—an ancient code, written in the stars, mapping the very frequencies we were born to inhabit?

What if Neo in the movie *The Matrix*, wasn't just a character, but a symbol—a mirror of the untapped potential within all of us? If we rearranged the letters, it reveals a deeper message—One—the essence of who we are, embedded in the very structure of existence?

What if *Alice in Wonderland* wasn't just a fantasy written by a cosmic traveler, but a guidebook—inviting us to awaken within the dream?

What if *Avatar* wasn't about another world, but a profound shift in perspective—teaching us to see through another's eyes, a gentle prompt of our shared unity and wholeness?

What if our imaginations weren't random wanderings, but alternate realities within parallel universes, waiting for us to consciously create them?

What if reality isn't a series of isolated events, but an interconnected phenomenon, shaped by quantum principles like entanglement? It's not just a sequence unfolding—it is a dynamic system influenced by perception, intention, and the fundamental laws of physics. It is simply a story, waiting for us to rewrite it?

The Buddha didn't escape suffering—he saw through it, recognizing it as an illusion of the mind, learning to recode and alchemize it.

What if time wasn't just a ticking clock, but the living pulse of the universe, flowing through us and activating our quantum connection?

What if quantum physics, sacred geometry, and the hidden codes of creation have always been speaking to us, offering glimpses of infinite possibilities and keys to enlightenment we have yet to fully comprehend?

And what if every esoteric tradition we've explored—from Kemetism, Hinduism, and Zoroastrianism to the ancient wisdom of our ancestors, Judaism, Buddhism, Taoism, Hermeticism, Kabbalah, Christianity, Islam, the Archangels, and Galactic Star Systems—has been guiding us toward a singular profound revelation: **we are all threads in the same vast, unified web of divine's infinite intelligence?**

This book is an invitation to open your mind and explore the vast quantum possibilities that can help you rewire your beliefs, transforming codes of suffering into a reality of harmony.

ESCAPING MENTAL PRISONS

When we move through life on autopilot, we surrender to the grip of predictive programming—a reality shaped not by conscious choice but by conditioned patterns.

Each thought, reaction, choice, and decision becomes a mere echo of the past, an algorithm, a repetition of familiar scripts embedded deep within our subconscious.

Without awareness, we unknowingly relinquish our power, allowing old limiting narratives to dictate our future. But the moment we become mindful—when we step beyond the invisible boundaries of habit—we reclaim the pen that writes our destiny.

The art of transformation begins when we break free from the illusion of preordained outcomes and step boldly into the realm of infinite possibility. Resistance you feel is a signal that you're on the edge of something greater.

Because the moment you decide to move forward, life will test you—not to punish you, but to ask:

Are you truly ready to release the past and step into a life of abundance, harmony, and flow?

The real battle lies within, reflected in the subconscious programming that keeps you tethered to a reality you've outgrown. These patterns manifest as triggers—unhealed wounds that surface as emotional overreactions.

When something feels like it's taking over emotionally, it's often an old pain you have avoided or failed to heal. Rather than numb, hide, or dissociate, you have the power to choose how you respond.

But the moment you commit to something greater, your past ego-identity tightens its grip, dictating your every move. It doesn't fight with logic—it fights with emotion:

the surge of frustration, the gnawing fear that threatens to unravel your resolve.

The exhaustion whispering, *Maybe I'm not ready yet.*

Deep childhood wounds and victim mentality resurfacing, murmuring, *See? Nothing ever changes.*

This is not a coincidence. This is conditioning.

Your identity was designed for survival, not expansion. It only knows what you've felt, and it clings to accustomed perceptions and convictions—even when that familiar experience is drowning you.

Every limiting belief, every toxic pattern, every self-sabotaging behavior serves one purpose: to keep you trapped in a reality your nervous system recognizes as "safe," even if that "perceived safety" is suffering.

This is why so many never break free. They confuse discomfort for failure.

It's subtle. It's sneaky. But discomfort isn't failure. It's an indication that transformation is happening.

It convinces you're unsuccessful. And if you believe it— if you react from fear—you snap back into the identity you're trying to leave behind. This is how patterns repeat—not because you're flawed, but because you're letting the discomfort of change convince you to return to what feels "regular or normal."

So, how do you break free? You don't fight your old self.

You outgrow it. You evolve.

Your subconscious identity only exists as long as you keep sustaining it. It thrives on fear. It lives on reactivity. It feeds on your willingness to relinquish your power. The moment you stop feeding it, it begins to dissolve.

You may never feel ready. But, YOU have to decide.

You must hold the vision—even when doubt creeps in.

You must trust the shift—before the evidence appears.

You must refuse to let the unknown dictate your next step.

Because every thought, every emotion, every word, every action is casting a cosmic vote for the person you're becoming.

The question is—*Which version of you are you feeding?*

A New Paradigm of Sovereignty

This isn't just another self-transformation book. It's a movement—a blueprint for activating your highest potential.

But first, you must embark on the reclamation of your divine essence—the realization that you are not a product of external forces limited by the material world, but the creator of your own reality.

Sovereignty is an energetic alignment—the moment you awaken to the infinite field of consciousness within and merge with Universal Source of Wholeness.

It is the sacred realization that you are a divine expression of the cosmos, and that your thoughts, beliefs, and emotions shape the very fabric of reality.

Reclaiming your autonomy is not about control in the conventional sense; it is about having unwavering trust in the power of your choices, the freedom to transcend conditioned limitations, and the courage to walk your path with both purpose and authenticity.

As you awaken to this perspective, you realize that you are not bound by time, space, or circumstance. Instead, you are a co-creator in the sacred dance of balance— unified with the eternal flow of the universe and fully equipped to shape your reality in synchronization with your higher self.

It is a shift in consciousness. It is a return to your rightful place as the architect of your destiny—empowered, limitless, and fully alive.

Rooted in scientific research, neuroscience, quantum mechanics, metaphysical principles, and ancient intelligence, this self-transformation journey will empower you to:

- Harness the force of your consciousness.
- Regulate your nervous system.
- Shift your reality with intention, trust, and surrender.
- Break free from cycles of fear, scarcity, and doubt.
- Transcend your limitations, rewrite your victimhood story and become the author of your reality.

This isn't abstract theory; this is a **manifestation playbook**, filled with actionable pathways, wisdom, lived experience, and alchemical mastery. Each step guides you through a process of profound, lasting change—an internal revolution that will ripple out into the world around you.

Your Breakthrough Begins Now

This is your time to choose. You don't need permission.

You don't need scientific evidence. You just need to decide.

And once you do, the universe will rearrange itself to meet you in the frequency you are emitting.

Are you ready to reclaim your sovereignty?

QUANTUM PLAYBOOK: RECOVERING SELF-WORTH

Studies in neuroplasticity confirm that the art of self-love is not just a mindset—it is a trainable neural pathway *(Dr. Richard Davidson, The Emotional Life of Your Brain)*. When practicing consistently, acts of self-love rewires the brain, shifts your energy fields, and transmutes your external reality.

The following practice of mirror work rewires the neural pathways associated with self-perception and confidence. Research in self-directed neuroplasticity *(Dr. Jeffrey Schwartz, The Mind and the Brain)* suggests that intentional self-talk and facial recognition in the mirror activate brain regions linked to self-compassion and emotional regulation.

Step 1: Acknowledge Where You Abandon Yourself

Resistance to self-love often stems from subconscious conditioning—beliefs ingrained in childhood that taught you love must be earned, that your worth is tied to external recognition, or that sacrificing your self-esteem and putting others first is the only way to be valued.

Ask Yourself:

- Where do I betray or abandon myself for external validation?
- What old belief keeps me from fully embracing my authenticity and worth?
- How would I treat myself if I truly believed I am deserving of sacred love?
- Where do I feel truly safe to express my authentic feelings without judgment, reprisal, or fear?

Neuroscience Insight: Self-worth is regulated by the default mode network in the brain. When you recognize self-sabotaging patterns, you activate the prefrontal cortex, which allows you to rewire them *(Dr. Lisa Feldman Barrett, How Emotions Are Made)*.

Write a letter to the version of you that first learned they were "not enough" or valued. Were you parentified as a child, taking on adult responsibilities before your time? What does your inner child need to hear?

Affirmation: *I am safe to love myself unconditionally.*

Step 2: Create a Sacred Space for Reflection

Your environment matters. Choose a quiet, peaceful place where you feel safe. Stand or sit in front of a mirror with soft lighting.

- Light a candle, play calming harmonic frequency music, or hold a crystal (like rose quartz) to amplify loving energy.
- Before starting, take 3 deep breaths, relaxing your shoulders and softening your gaze.

Step 3: Establish Eye Contact with Yourself

Look directly into your own eyes, they are the window to your soul—not your hair, not your skin, not your flaws. Hold your own gaze.

Notice what emotions arise. Do you feel resistance? Discomfort? If so, that's okay. Stay with it. Feel into it.

Scientific Insight: Holding eye contact with yourself stimulates the medial prefrontal cortex, the region associated with self-awareness and identity regulation *(Dr. Lisa Feldman Barrett, How Emotions Are Made)*.

Step 4: Speak Words of Love and Affirmation

Gently place your hand on your heart. Speak directly to yourself out loud using empowering, present-tense affirmations:

- "I love and accept myself exactly as I am."
- "I am proud of the person I am becoming."
- "I am worthy of kindness, love, and respect."
- "I am seen, heard, validated, and accepted."

Personalize your affirmations. What words do you need to hear? Say them with conviction, as if you were comforting your loved one or your little child.

Psychological Insight: Speaking affirmations while making eye contact increases dopamine and oxytocin production, reinforcing emotional connection and self-acceptance *(Dr. Kristin Neff, Self-Compassion).*

Step 5: Release Self-Judgment and Reparent Your Inner Child

As you continue mirror work, you may notice old wounds, shame, or self-criticism surfacing. Instead of avoiding them, acknowledge and validate your emotions.

Speak to your reflection as if you are your own loving parent:

- "I see your pain, and I honor your journey."
- "You are safe now. I will never abandon you."
- "You don't have to prove your worth—it was never in question."
- "You are more than enough in your purest form, deserving of love that knows no conditions."

Close your eyes and visualize your inner child at five years of age, standing in front of you. Imagine embracing them, whispering words of love, security, and reassurance.

Scientific Insight: Studies show that self-compassion activates the parasympathetic nervous system, reducing cortisol (stress) and increasing emotional resilience *(Dr. Richard Davidson, The Emotional Life of Your Brain)*.

Step 6: Embody Self-Worth Through Posture and Energy

The way you carry yourself in front of the mirror sends subconscious signals to your brain.

- Stand tall with open body language—shoulders back, head held high.
- Smile gently at yourself, even if it feels unnatural at first.
- Observe your own energy shift as you hold this posture.

Neuroscience Insight: Embodying confident body language activates the limbic system, signaling safety, self-trust, and worthiness *(Amy Cuddy, Presence)*.

Hold a power yoga pose (hands on hips, strong stance) while affirming: "I radiate confidence. I am whole."

Step 7: Commit to Daily Mirror Work

Repetition is key to rewiring self-worth at a subconscious level.

Morning Practice: Start your day by looking in the mirror and saying:

- "Today, I choose to love and honor myself."
- "I accept the divine expressing itself through me."
- "I am the embodiment of unconditional devotion; I am safe to receive with abundance of joy."

Evening Routine: End your day by expressing gratitude to your reflection:

- "I am proud of myself for showing up today."
- "I am the creative expression of the divine, co-creating my existence."
- "Every day, I grow in self-love and confidence."
- "I am the light, the light that I am. I am the pure love I have always been seeking."

Track your progress. Write reflections on how you feel after a week of mirror work. Notice any emotional shifts or resistance softening.

You Are Becoming

Every time you return to the mirror, you consciously choose self-love over self-abandonment.

Pure love, by its very nature, can never cause harm—whether through our words, thoughts, or actions. Why would we choose to reject, hurt ourselves or another when each being reflects our own divinity, a mirror of our essence, or the innocent child that lives within every human?

You are not fixing yourself—you were never broken. You are remembering your worth, reclaiming your power, and embodying the love you deserve to feel. The energy you hold toward yourself reflects outward. As you embody self-worth, your external world will shift to match it *(Dr. Joe Dispenza, Becoming Supernatural).*

2. Acknowledging & Healing Trauma

At its core, your nervous system craves safety, connection, and integrity. But trauma rewires it for survival. When you experience pain, your brain adapts—its sole mission becomes shielding you from harm. It sharpens its vigilance, anticipating danger before it arrives, keeping you on edge, bracing for the worst. What begins as protection can become a prison.

Trapped in survival mode, your nervous system stays locked in fight-or-flight, even when no real threat exists. Relaxing feels unnatural. Trust feels reckless. Love feels like a risk you can't afford. To cope, your brain may silence emotions, muting not only pain but also joy, peace, and the warmth of human connection. The world shrinks into a landscape of caution, where even small triggers ignite a storm within.

Vulnerability, once a bridge to closeness, starts to feel like a battlefield. Your brain, conditioned to equate openness with harm, builds walls instead of doorways. Trust becomes fragile, every connection measured against the fear of betrayal.

You thwart your heart, keep others at a distance, convinced that self-reliance is safer than surrender. Hyper-independence becomes your armor, but by shielding yourself from pain, you also block out the very thing that heals—connection.

Yet, just as trauma rewires the brain, so can healing. Through nervous system regulation, somatic techniques, trauma-informed therapy, and radical self-compassion, you can teach your body that safety exists again.

The walls can soften. The heart can open. And trust, once a foreign language, can become fluent once more.

Healing takes time and patience, but it is not a pursuit of perfection—it is a return to wholeness. A homecoming to yourself. And when your nervous system finally feels secure, connection is no longer a risk—it becomes the very thing that sets you free.

A Journey Back to Wholeness

Every emotion—joy, sorrow, heartbreak, loss—leaves a biochemical imprint on the body. Under normal circumstances, these emotions pass through us, metabolized like breath. But when an experience is too overwhelming—especially in childhood, when we lack the tools for processing—our bodies, in their infinite wisdom, store it until we are ready to heal.

Unresolved trauma does not stay silent. It infiltrates our very tissues, embedding itself in the fascia, the connective web that binds our physical body. Over time, it marks the organs and glands tied to our deepest wounds. Studies show that sexual trauma often manifests in the reproductive system—leaving scars on the womb, breasts, or prostate—while heartbreak and grief take root in the lungs and heart.

Fascia is far more than a passive structure. It is a dynamic, living network that envelops every muscle, bone, and organ, providing support and enabling fluid movement. Intricately connected to the nervous system, fascia plays a critical role in the body's ability to sense its position and movement in space.

Research has revealed that fascia is capable of adapting and remodeling under stress, impacting pain, flexibility, and overall physical function.

The health of your fascia directly affects not only your mobility but your ability to heal, showcasing the profound connection between mind, body, and tissue. *(Source: Schleip, R., 2012, Fascia is a sensory organ: A review of the evidence. The Journal of Bodywork and Movement Therapies)*

At first, the body whispers—a subtle twinge of fatigue, a flicker of inflammation. Ignore these quiet signals, and they escalate, speaking in the language of chronic pain, illness, and dis-ease. Yet, healing begins within—at the very core of our being.

In 1991, scientists discovered 40,000 specialized neurons in the heart—cells capable of thinking, feeling, and remembering independently of the cranial brain. This affirms what ancient wisdom has long known: the heart holds its own intelligence, a frequency beyond logic.

Yet traditional therapy, while valuable, engages only the mind, leaving the heart's silent wounds untouched.

Healing is not merely about understanding—it is about feeling, about moving through the emotional blockages stored within the body.

Healing untreated trauma is not a destination but a return to the natural self that existed before fear, before wounding. It is a reclamation, a shedding of pain, anxiety, and guardedness. The path is not easy. It requires facing the very things you've spent a lifetime avoiding. But for those who dare, the reward is liberation.

Weight of Childhood Wounds

Unprocessed childhood trauma does more than linger in memory—it imprints onto the body, reshaping biology in ways we don't always recognize. Survivors live in a state of hypervigilance, their nervous systems wired for danger, even in safety. This is not just emotional—it is physiological.

The fight-or-flight response, meant for momentary survival, becomes a way of being. The adrenal glands deplete. The immune system weakens. Hormones spiral out of balance. Sleep is restless, digestion falters, and exhaustion takes hold. The body, trapped in survival mode, runs on empty until it can no longer sustain itself.

But these imprints of distress does not define you. The words spoken in cruelty, the wounds inflicted by others—these are not reflections of your worth. They are projections of unhealed pain.

You are not what happened to you. You are what you choose to become. And healing begins the moment you reclaim that choice.

The Body Remembers

Living in survival mode takes its toll on your heart, mind, and spirit.

The amygdala—your brain's alarm system—fires relentlessly, while the prefrontal cortex, the seat of reason, dims.

The result? Emotional reactivity, chronic stress, and exhaustion—your body's final attempt to manage years of distress and overwhelm. Your body tightens. Thoughts spiral. Inflammation rises.

Chronic fatigue, autoimmune dis-ease, and persistent pain are not random. They are your body's response to long-term dysregulation—coping with unprocessed emotions and suffering.

When the nervous system remains stuck in survival mode, it drains energy, weakens immunity, and amplifies pain signals. Over time, this wears the body down, preventing it from regulating itself.

Real healing begins when you address these deep-rooted patterns—when you understand the messages your body is sending and work with your nervous system to restore balance. It is not about forcing change; it's about guiding your body back to balance and harmony, reclaiming its natural state of wholeness.

This art of restoration is not found in words alone—it is a realignment of your energy centers, a rewiring of the nervous system until safety is no longer an idea, but a felt experience.

When emotions are suppressed, the body holds them. Tension knots in the muscles. Headaches, chronic pain, and inflammation take root. The nervous system remains in an endless loop of survival. But healing begins the moment you allow yourself to feel—to release the grief, the anger, the fear, in a safe and embodied way.

This is the body's plea for peace.

You were never meant to live in a state of perpetual defense. Your body longs for ease. Your heart, for connection. And your soul, for the freedom that comes when you finally let go.

SCIENCE OF TRAUMA & ITS IMPACTS

Trauma is a profound disruption of the body's natural balance. It occurs when the nervous system is overwhelmed by an experience that exceeds its capacity to cope.

This overwhelming event alters brain function, triggering a cascade of chemical and hormonal responses that can rewire neural pathways, leaving lasting emotional and physiological imprints.

These psychological scars don't just reside in the mind—it manifests in the body, influencing everything from heart rate and breath to the regulation of stress hormones like cortisol.

Left unhealed, trauma becomes encoded in cells, shaping perception, behavior, and the way we interact with the world *(Source: McEwen, B. S., 2007).*

At the core of trauma is the fight-or-flight response, releasing hormones like adrenaline and cortisol to prepare for survival. While these reactions are adaptive in the short term, prolonged exposure keeps the body on high alert, leading to chronic stress and health issues.

These wounding programs alters the very architecture of the brain. The amygdala, the brain's fear center, becomes hyperactive, triggering constant anxiety, hypervigilance, and emotional reactivity. This heightened state of alertness confuses the brain, making it hard to differentiate between real threats and benign situations.

Neuroplasticity reinforces this cycle, making it harder to regain emotional control. The fear remains embedded in the brain, sabotaging efforts to calm down *(Source: Phelps, E. A., 2006, Emotion and Cognition).*

The prefrontal cortex, which governs reasoning and impulse control, becomes underactive after trauma. Weakened connectivity between the prefrontal cortex and the amygdala impairs our ability to process emotions rationally. Instead of responding with reason, survivors often react impulsively, overwhelmed by emotions, making it difficult to think clearly or make grounded decisions *(Source: Liberzon, I., & Martis, B., 2006).*

Trauma also affects memory. The hippocampus, responsible for storing memories, shrinks after prolonged exposure to cortisol. This shrinkage impairs the brain's ability to distinguish between past and present experiences, trapping survivors in a loop where past trauma constantly resurfaces.

Flashbacks and intrusive memories keep the person locked in the past, unable to separate it from their current reality *(Source: Bremner, J. D., 2003, Hippocampal Volume Reduction in Depression).*

The stress response system also malfunctions after trauma, keeping the body in a constant state of alert, flooding it with cortisol. This disrupts the body's ability to return to equilibrium, leading to chronic fatigue, digestive issues, and weakened immunity *(Source: McEwen, B. S., 2007, Physiology and Neurobiology of Stress and Adaptation).*

Beyond the brain's structural changes, trauma disrupts the balance of neurotransmitters—serotonin, dopamine, and GABA—that regulate mood and relaxation. Trauma rewires these neurochemical pathways, resulting in imbalances that contribute to depression, anxiety, and emotional numbness.

When these chemicals are disrupted, the brain struggles to find balance, even when external circumstances improve *(Source: Yehuda, R., 2002, Post-Traumatic Stress Disorder).*

Despite this, hope exists. Through treatments like mindfulness, cognitive-behavioral therapy (CBT), and somatic practices, individuals can rewire their brains in healthier ways. These approaches help rebuild connections between the prefrontal cortex and amygdala, restoring emotional regulation and balance *(Source: Davidson, R. J., & McEwen, B. S., 2012).*

Somatic therapies—such as yoga, breathwork, and body-focused techniques—offer an additional path to healing. These practices help release stored tension, soothe emotional numbness, and regulate the nervous system.

By tapping into the brain's neuroplasticity, these pathways of change facilitate the release of trauma stored in muscles and tissues. As the body heals, the mind follows suit, leading to emotional integration and relief *(Source: Van der Kolk, B. A., 2014, The Body Keeps the Score).*

These combined therapeutic efforts help trauma survivors tap into the brain's natural ability to heal, offering a path to emotional freedom, resilience, and wholeness.

Shadow Aspects & Soul Integration

We are all reflections—both light and shadow—shaping and being shaped by one another in this realm of duality.

From a metaphysical viewpoint, our journey is not about taking sides but about integration, alignement, healing, and awakening the divine essence within.

Darkness has a role to play in the grand tapestry of existence. It is not here to divide us but to catalyze and crystalize our path, teaching us balance through contrast.

What's truly fascinating is each of us has a unique soul-print; we may embody light, while another may cast a shadow. Our roles shift depending on perception—who we observe and who observes us. The goal is not to judge but to find equilibrium within, for when we embrace both aspects of our being, we dissolve the illusion of separation and step into unity.

The code for this wisdom has always been within us, waiting to be recognized. Each of us is an expression of limitless potential, existing here to fulfill a purpose.

True purpose begins with healing—breaking the chains of generational cycles, rediscovering the divine essence within, and reclaiming the worthiness that has always been ours. Only through this profound awakening can our higher calling unfold, leading us to a life of true fulfillment and the thriving existence we were always destined to live.

This journey has never been about division; it has always been about merging back to wholeness.

Along the way, we have been given tools—first religion, then science, now technology—but each is merely a reflection of the same ultimate task: to evolve, to expand, and to rediscover the divine within.

Regardless of the path we choose, our mission remains the same—to heal, to seek, to balance, and ultimately, to walk together in harmonious unity.

We've been taught to fear the darkness—the shadow within, the hidden wounds, and the unspoken fears that shape us. It is the depth of the human condition, where our deepest truths often lie obscured, waiting to be seen and healed.

We exile it, suppress it, deny it, pretend it does not exist. But here's the harsh reality: What we resist does not disappear.

It waits and persists. It waits to be acknowledged. It waits to be healed.

And eventually, it returns—louder, fiercer, demanding our attention with every obstacle and lesson.

The darkness, the parts we label as evil, are not our enemies. They are lost fragments of human subconsciousness—not to be worshiped, not to be feared, but to be dissolved, transmuted, and led.

What happens when we abandon the wounded parts of ourselves? They don't disappear—they fester, hidden in the shadows, silently turning against us.

Neuroscientific research shows that unresolved trauma and repressed emotions can manifest physically, contributing to chronic stress, anxiety, and even illness. Studies from the American Psychological Association reveal that emotional suppression can negatively impact our immune system, making it harder for us to heal and move forward.

But here's the shift—healing isn't the absence of darkness; it's the integration of it. It's the courage to bring these fragmented parts of ourselves back into the light, embracing them with pure, loving awareness, and allowing them to repair and transform.

Research in neuroplasticity supports this approach, showing that by consciously reframing and integrating past trauma, we can literally rewire the brain, promoting emotional resilience and healing. Studies from the National Institute of Mental Health have demonstrated how practices like mindfulness and self-compassion can reduce the effects of stress, enhancing our ability to heal both mind and body.

When we stop running, when we turn to face what we have shunned, we make an extraordinary discovery: These shadows were never against us. They were our teachers all along.

So, ask yourself: *What have I rejected? What shadow parts of me remain unloved, abandoned, repressed, denied?* Because healing is not about banishment. It is about incorporating all aspects of self unconditionally into wholeness.

Rhythm of Life (Yin and Yang)

In Taoism, darkness and light are not opposing forces, but two halves of a single, eternal whole—forever entwined, constantly shifting.

Yin, the dark feminine principle, embodies mystery, the unknown, and the internal world where chaos and creation reside. Yang, the masculine force, represents illumination, order, and knowledge.

Neither exists without the other. Just as the cosmos drift within the embrace of dark matter, life itself emerges from the fertile abyss of the unseen.

As the sun sets and daylight fades, the body yields to Yin's quiet pull. The pineal gland releases melatonin, guiding us into sleep while awakening the third eye to the ethereal landscapes of dreams.

This nocturnal alchemy invites us inward—to reflect, process, and integrate the lessons of the day. In ancient times, darkness was revered as the cosmic womb, the source of renewal. Yet in modern life, we resist it, fearing stillness as if rest itself were an enemy.

Taoists understood the sacred rhythm of transformation: when one force reaches its extreme, the other inevitably rises. The deeper we surrender to the quiet embrace of Yin, the greater the potential for new light to emerge. Likewise, the more we chase Yang—enlightenment, action, clarity—the more we stir the shadows of doubt and fear.

Yin and Yang are the very principles of balance and harmony, and the dance of light and darkness reflects their dynamic interplay.

Together, they create a cyclical, transformative process that drives the rhythm of life. Light and darkness are not opposites, but complementary forces, each playing an essential role in fostering change, growth, and universal harmony.

In our lives, this dance is ever-present. We experience periods of action, clarity, and expansion (Yang), followed by times of introspection, rest, and inner growth (Yin). Both are essential for our well-being.

By honoring the ebb and flow of light and darkness, we cultivate vibrational equilibrium, learning to move with life's natural rhythms rather than resisting them.

The modern world's obsession with relentless activity has disrupted this balance, cutting us off from the restorative wellspring of rest.

The path back to balance is not through resistance but through surrender—through stillness, through trust, and through a deep belief in the cyclical nature of renewal.

Role of Fear

From a psychological perspective, fear is an instinctive reaction to perceived threat—a primal alarm system that activates deep-rooted survival mechanisms. Even when danger is no longer present, fear distorts perception, controlling behavior and clouding judgment.

It hijacks the mind, limiting clarity and preventing rational thought. Over time, it embeds itself in the subconscious as a constant shadow, subtly influencing thoughts, actions, and relationships. *(Source: Damasio, A. R., 1999, The Feeling of What Happens)*

Fear is a force that pulls inward, contracting, spiraling down from the mind to the base of the spine, rooting deep within the body. It is cold, and contracting, preparing us to freeze or flee.

When fear seizes us, our limbs weaken, our vision blurs, our breath shortens—our very essence collapses inward. This is the primal response of survival from the root chakra or energy center where the majority of the world's population resides.

At the heart of this reaction are the adrenal glands, perched atop the kidneys, releasing a surge of energy to prepare for battle or escape. In moments of true danger, this response is life-saving.

But when fear becomes a chronic state—when it loops endlessly, perceiving threats where none exist—it drains our life force, leaving us exhausted, brittle, and disconnected from our inner wisdom.

Over time, unchecked fear steals our vitality, manifesting as fatigue, joint pain, backaches, and premature aging.

Yet fear is not the enemy. It is a messenger. Sometimes, it warns us to change course, to tread carefully. Other times, it signals the threshold of transformation—the doorway we must walk through.

Growth never happens in comfort. It happens at the edges, in the spaces where fear meets courage.

By learning to sit with fear, to witness it rather than react to it, we reclaim our power. We move from impulse to intention, from survival to sovereignty.

In stillness, in trust, in surrender—fear dissolves, and the cycle of renewal begins again.

Notion of Illusion

In today's spiritual landscape, the focus is often on love and light, but you cannot discover the light without first walking through the darkness. True awakening is not simply about observing the illusions built around us. It's about turning inward with deep introspection and confronting the shadows we have long buried within ourselves.

Instead of viewing reality as an "illusion", something false or to be rejected, think of it as a limited perspective, a veil that clouds the bigger picture. From the moment we're born, society, culture, and our own experiences shape the lens through which we perceive everything.

This lens of duality isn't wrong—it's just incomplete. It's like gazing at a breathtaking landscape through a fogged window: you see glimpses, but the full depth and beauty remain hidden.

The notion of illusion asks us to gently lift that fog, not to abandon our world, but to deepen our understanding of it. We're not called on to reject the emotions, experiences, or beliefs that have shaped us; we're invited to acknowledge that there is so much more beyond them.

What we see is merely a reflection of our collective consciousness—a glimpse of something far greater. When we embrace this awareness, we open ourselves to a fuller, richer experience of life, one that transcends the boundaries of what we thought we knew.

Return to Awareness

Awakening is the process of remembering your true self after a long period of unconscious sleep or spiritual amnesia—a return to the awareness that was always within you but forgotten. This can feel like a personal collapse, a sense that your entire identity is being shattered.

To activate, you must release the version of your identity you once held so tightly to, confront the ghosts of your past, and begin to rebuild from the ground up.

This path to illumination isn't easy. There are moments when you will feel lost, overwhelmed by the vastness of the wisdom you're uncovering. The deeper you dive, the more detached you might feel from the physical world around you.

However, this third density reality isn't something to escape or reject—it's something to embrace. The journey of awakening is alchemical in nature—it's about transforming the lead of your old self—the pain, fears, the wounds—into golden hues of bliss.

This hero's journey will demand everything from you, but in the midst of every challenge, you will uncover who you truly are. What may feel like destruction is, in reality, a rebirth.

During this time, the greatest battle you will face is not one of strength or intellect, but one of frequency. The world, with its endless noise and distractions, will attempt to convince you that its version of reality is the only objective truth—unyielding and absolute.

But expanding consciousness is realizing that you don't have to limit yourself. Once, survival favored the strongest. Now, it belongs to those who master their emotional and spiritual energetic emittance.

When we shift the way we think and the way we feel, something profound happens at the cellular level. Our bodies, made up of 50 trillion cells, are constantly receiving and responding to energy. These cells, through their membranes, function as antennas—tuning us into specific energetic frequencies.

Each of these 50 trillion cells contains about 100 trillion atoms, and in every single atom, a dynamic process is unfolding.

Every nanosecond, these atoms emerge from the field of energy around us and collapse back into it, creating a continuous dance between matter and energy.

This constant interaction is not random. It's a reflection of the template or matrix we hold in our consciousness—the beliefs, perceptions, and emotions we carry within us. As energy emerges from the quantum field and interacts with our cells, it shapes our bodies to match this inner template.

What we believe about ourselves directly influences the chemicals released in our body, which, in turn, affects our physical health.

This is why healing is not only possible—it's a testament to the immense power we possess in our human form.

The state of our consciousness is actively creating our reality at a fundamental level. The way we think, feel, and believe dictates the state of our bodies, as well as our potential for transformation and healing.

Every single day, the world will test your vibratory wavelength and frequency. Doubt, fear, insecurity, and chaos will swirl around you, trying to make you believe your dreams are out of reach. It will attempt to convince you that the life you desire is impossible.

But the world you see is only one of 8 billion possible realities, each vibrating at its own frequency.

When you raise yours, the old world's limits begin to dissolve.

The people, beliefs, and habits that once defined you may try to pull you back—not from malice, but because they're still anchored to a lower frequency reality.

And then there's the pullback—the wave of negative charge that follows every step forward.

It may feel like punishment, but it's not. It's a karmic test. The question is how you'll respond: Will you react and slip back into old patterns, or will you shine your light of awareness and change habits to break that cycle?

You always have the power to choose how you respond. Will you react to the chaos with resistance, or will you stand in the calm of your higher self?

Here are some powerful mindset affirmations designed to open energy fields and enhance manifestation:

1. **Root:** I am safe, grounded, and secure in my place in this world. I am worthy.
2. **Sacral:** I am creative, enthusiastic, and in flow with the universe. I am seen.
3. **Solar Plexus:** I am powerful, confident, and my free will shapes my reality. I am valued.
4. **Heart:** I give and receive pure love effortlessly. My heart is pure and open, feeling alive. I am a magnet for abundance, attracting all that aligns with my highest good.
5. **Throat:** I speak my truth with clarity and the world listens. I release all limiting beliefs

and allow new, empowering energies to flow through me.

6. **Third Eye:** I trust my intuition and see beyond the physical world. My thoughts are powerful, and I choose to focus on what I want to manifest.

7. **Crown:** I know that I am connected to the divine Source and all universal wisdom flows through me. I am a co-creator with the universe, manifesting my desires effortlessly and with joy.

Triggers: The Body's Alarm System

A trigger or flashback is more than a fleeting reaction—it is a wormhole, a portal into the subconscious, revealing unresolved imprints within the nervous system.

It is not merely a disruption but an unhealed fragment of the self, surfacing in search of recognition, integration, and release.

You may not consciously remember, but your nervous system does.

This is why anxiety appears unprovoked, why doctors insist you are healthy despite chronic symptoms, why overwhelm strikes without cause, or why dissociation becomes second nature.

The mind forgets, but the body does not. The nervous system archives unprocessed experiences, reacting to present triggers as if the past is still happening. It shapes emotions, thoughts, and behaviors in ways you may not yet understand—its sole purpose: survival.

This is why unease, a racing heart, or unexplained pain arise without an immediate threat. It's why people-pleasing, overachieving, procrastination, or dissociation may feel like personality traits when, in reality, they are survival strategies—patterns wired to protect you.

But awareness is the key to liberation. When you recognize how the past silently shapes the present, you reclaim the power to rewrite your story. Triggers become guides. Patterns loosen their grip. And the nervous system, once locked in defense, can finally learn to rest.

When the Brain Goes to War

From a neuroscience perspective, a trigger activates the amygdala—the brain's fear center—signaling a flood of cortisol and adrenaline.

The heart pounds. Muscles tense. Hypervigilance takes over. Designed for survival, this response primes the body for danger, even when none exists.

Meanwhile, the prefrontal cortex—the seat of reason and emotional regulation—goes offline, making us reactive rather than reflective. But through self-awareness, mindfulness, and nervous system regulation, we can rewire these pathways, shifting from survival mode to safety.

Healing is not about erasing the past but answering its call. It is a return to the moment of fragmentation—to the unmet need that was denied, resisted, or abandoned. It is the gateway to soul retrieval practices.

When trauma strikes, the nervous system, overwhelmed and unprepared, partitions aspects of our experience into dissociation.

These fragments remain locked in time, blocking our energy fields, waiting for the moment we are finally ready to meet them with presence, compassion, and safety.

Somatic movement, breathwork, and EFT (Emotional Freedom Technique) strengthen the ventral vagus nerve, restoring a sense of safety and engagement. Over time, the nervous system shifts from habitual fear responses to resilience, adaptability, and ease.

To heal our triggers is to walk back through that wormhole—not to relive the pain, but to retrieve the part of ourselves that was left behind.

It is to hold space for the younger self who once trembled in fear, to offer the love, validation, and security that were absent in that moment.

As we do this, the nervous system rewires. The need for hypervigilance dissolves. The body opens to deeper states of peace, trust, and wholeness.

Triggers were once survival mechanisms. But in modern life, they fire unnecessarily—at a stressful email, a difficult conversation, an old emotional wound. The work is not to suppress them but to meet them— to recognize them as invitations to heal, to rewire, to return.

Over time, repeated triggers condition the brain and body to expect danger, keeping us in a cycle of stress.

- **Activates the Sympathetic Nervous System:** The body perceives danger, real or perceived.
- **The Amygdala Fires:** The brain's fear center signals a threat, leading to heightened vigilance.
- **Cortisol and Adrenaline Surge:** Stress hormones flood the body, increasing heart rate, muscle tension, and anxiety.
- **Prefrontal Cortex Shuts Down:** Logical thinking and emotional regulation decline, making us reactive and overwhelmed.

Glimmers: Path to Regulation and Resilience

Glimmers are the gentle antidote to triggers—fleeting yet powerful moments that ignite a sense of peace, belonging, and quiet hope. While triggers pull us into stress, fear, or past pain, glimmers guide us toward safety, connection, and calm.

Unlike the sharp jolt of a trigger, a glimmer soothes, reassures, and reminds us that beauty exists in even the smallest pockets of life.

You can train your brain to recognize and cultivate more of them. Every experience sends signals to our nervous system's fork in the road, determining whether we feel safe or threatened.

When we experience a glimmer, our nervous system shifts from sympathetic activation (fight-or-flight) to parasympathetic regulation (rest-and-digest).

This transition happens through key pathways:

- **Vagus Nerve:** Glimmers activate the ventral vagal complex, the branch of the vagus nerve responsible for social engagement, safety, and connection. This reduces heart rate, lowers blood pressure, and signals to the body that it is safe to relax.
- **Neurotransmitters and Hormones:** Positive sensory experiences—like feeling the warmth of the sun, witnessing a beautiful landscape, or connecting with a loved one—boost dopamine (reward and motivation), oxytocin (bonding and trust), and serotonin (mood stability). At the same time, they decrease cortisol, the stress hormone that fuels anxiety and inflammation.

- **Prefrontal Cortex and Amygdala:** Glimmers rewire neural pathways by reinforcing activity in the prefrontal cortex, the brain's center for logic, emotional regulation, and executive function. This inhibits overactivity in the amygdala, the area responsible for fear and threat detection, reducing stress responses over time.

- **Heart-Brain Coherence:** Studies from the HeartMath Institute show that positive emotional states create consistency between the heart and brain, optimizing nervous system function. Glimmers contribute to this by shifting heart rate variability into a balanced rhythm, enhancing resilience to stress.

Pathways of Change

Healing is a journey back to your original state—before fear etched itself into your thoughts, emotions, and physical being. It is not an easy path transcending the conditioning. But the reward is beyond measure.

Step 1: Acknowledge the Pain, Awareness Is Key

Trauma cannot heal if it is denied, bypassed, or suppressed. Begin by scanning your body, gently focusing your attention where you feel tension, pain, or discomfort. Ask yourself:

- Where do I hold my deepest wounds?
- What recurring emotional patterns am I stuck in?
- What memories bring a visceral reaction in my body?

Writing in a journal or speaking aloud to yourself in a compassionate way can help bring subconscious wounds to light.

Step 2: Pain-Conscious Breathing

Breathwork is a powerful tool for emotional release. Studies show that deep, diaphragmatic breathing activates the parasympathetic nervous system, shifting the body from a state of stress (fight-or-flight) to one of relaxation and healing.

- **Heart-Focused Breathing:** Breathe deeply while imagining the breath moving in and out of your heart. Focus your attention on the rhythmic beats. This technique has been shown to reduce anxiety and regulate emotions.

Step 3: Release Stored Trauma - Movement and Sound Healing

Trauma is stored in the body, not just the mind. To release it:

- Move: Yoga, dance, or even shaking your body helps unlock trapped energy.
- Sing or Chant: Research shows that singing in a group boosts immune function, releases oxytocin, and regulates emotions. Chanting "OM" has been shown to reduce activity in the amygdala, the brain's fear center.
- Use Sound Therapy during EFT: Listening to 432 Hz or 528 Hz frequencies can help balance emotions and restore harmony while tapping on the meridian points.

Step 4: Rewire the Brain - Shift from Survival to Safety

The brain has a negativity bias—it holds onto painful experiences for survival. But healing requires shifting into a new state of being by processing and integrating the trauma.

- **Gratitude Practice:** Write down three things you're grateful for daily. Neuroscience shows that gratitude rewires the brain to focus on safety and abundance rather than fear.
- **Visualization:** Close your eyes and imagine yourself fully healed, joyful, and free. The brain does not distinguish between real and imagined experiences, so this primes your nervous system for transformation.

Step 5: Forgive and Let Go - Ultimate Act of Liberation

Forgiveness is not about excusing past harm—it is about freeing yourself from its grip. Holding onto resentment keeps trauma alive in the body. Ask yourself:

- What am I still holding onto that no longer serves me?
- Can I offer myself the same compassion I offer others?
- How would I feel if I released this burden?

One simple yet powerful technique is Ho'oponopono, an ancient Hawaiian practice of reconciliation and healing. Say these four phrases, either to yourself or directed toward a specific situation: "I'm sorry. Please forgive me. Thank you. I love you."

Step 6: Connect with the Heart-Your Inner Healing Intelligence

Since the heart holds its own wisdom, focusing your attention on your heartbeat is vital for deep healing.

- Place your hand on your heart and breathe slowly, feeling its rhythm. Picture a younger version of yourself at 5 years of age, express unbounded love for your innocence.
- Practice self-love affirmations daily: I am safe. I am whole. I am worthy of healing and peace.

Healing is an act of courage, a return to pure love frequency.

On the other side of this journey lies liberation—the kind of freedom where life begins to flow effortlessly. Relationships deepen. Health is restored. Abundance becomes a natural state of being. The burdens we once carried dissolve, and we step into the life we were always meant to live.

The *Coherent Heart* already knows the way. The question is—are you ready to listen?

How to Cultivate More Glimmers

With regular practice, glimmers rewire the nervous system to recognize safety over stress. They teach the body to experience joy without resistance, strengthening its ability to return to equilibrium when challenges arise.

- **Savor the Moment:** Gratitude amplifies glimmers. When you witness a breathtaking sunset, pause. Inhale deeply, exhale slowly, and silently thank the universe for this fleeting masterpiece. The more you acknowledge these moments, the more they multiply.
- **Tune into Your Body:** Inner-sensing is the art of feeling from within. When triggered, sensations can be overwhelming—tightness in the chest, a racing pulse, a surge of heat. But glimmers bring the opposite: a softening,

a gentle ease that flows through your entire body. Notice it. Relish it. Let it anchor you in the present.

- **Unplug Each Day:** Intentionally step away from the noise. Let the sun warm your skin as you play with your puppy. Sit beneath a tree and listen to the symphony of birds. Watch ripples dance across a body of water. These small acts of presence expand your capacity to experience joy.

Glimmers may arise in countless other ways—a shared smile with someone you love, the awe of witnessing nature's grandeur, the warmth of newfound connection. When they happen, they don't just shift your mood; they transform your physiology.

And here's the magic: the more glimmers you collect, the stronger your nervous system becomes. Like drops of light accumulating in a reservoir, they build resilience.

So, when life inevitably throws its storms, you don't just endure—you rise, grounded in the quiet certainty that peace is always within reach.

Attachment Imprinting

From the moment we take our first breath, we are biologically designed to seek connection. Connection is not merely an emotional experience—it is a fundamental survival mechanism woven into the neural fabric of our being. Our earliest bonds shape the architecture of our brain, influencing how we perceive safety, trust, and love.

Attachment imprinting influences our core being, as early bonds with caregivers stamp lasting patterns in the brain that influence our emotional responses and how we form relationships. These foundational experiences establish neural pathways that govern how we perceive love, trust, and connection throughout life.

Secure connection fosters emotional resilience and healthy relationships, while insecure attachment can create lifelong struggles with stress regulation and forming deep bonds, shaping not just our emotional world, but the very biology of how we interact with everyone around us. (*Source: Bowlby, J., 1969, Attachment and Loss; Schore, A. N., 2001, The effects of early trauma on the development of the right brain*)

But when those bonds are fractured—through abandonment, neglect, abuse, lack of nurturing, or inconsistent care—the subconscious mind encodes survival programs rooted in attachment patterns such as hypervigilance or emotional detachment, leading to adaptive strategies for coping with threat. These survival mechanisms, though initially protective, can hinder emotional and relational well-being later in life. (*Source: Schore, A. N., 2003*)

These shadow aspects of our survival-based ego cloud our perception, projecting distorted realities that trap us in cycles of fear, illusion, and limitation. Rather than seeing life as it truly is, we filter it through unresolved wounds, unconscious biases, and ingrained patterns of wounding programming.

The world does not simply exist as an external force—it is a mirror reflecting the depth of our internal landscape.

Only by illuminating these dark shadows with self-awareness and compassion can we break free from the illusions they create, reclaiming our power to shape reality through clarity, love, and higher consciousness.

The prefrontal cortex, responsible for emotional regulation and higher reasoning, and the insula, the neural bridge between body and mind that processes social connection, fail to develop optimally in an environment of insecurity.

Instead of experiencing relationships as a source of nourishment and safety, the brain learns to associate them with unpredictability or pain.

These deeply embedded patterns become the invisible script that dictates how we love, trust, and relate—often leading us into cycles of avoidance, anxious attachment, or codependent behaviors.

Yet, neuroscience and metaphysics reveal an empowering perspective: the subconscious mind is not permanent.

Neuroplasticity allows us to rewire the very structures once shaped by trauma.

Through conscious awareness, somatic healing, and energetic realignment, we can override outdated survival programs and establish new neural pathways that foster trust, security, and emotional resilience from a *Coherent Heart*.

At the core of this transformation lies the most powerful force in the universe—pure, unconditional love.

Neuroscience has shown that pure love, in its truest form, activates the vagus nerve, promoting a state of safety and connection within the nervous system. The release of oxytocin, known as the "bonding hormone," strengthens neural circuits associated with trust and emotional regulation, while reducing the stress response triggered by the amygdala.

When we are met with love that asks for nothing in return, the brain reinterprets safety, dissolving old defense mechanisms and restructuring neural pathways toward self-acceptance and belonging.

Metaphysically, attachment wounds are echoes of energetic imprints—frequencies stored in the body that shape our vibrational state. When we exist in a frequency of fear or unworthiness, we unknowingly attract experiences that reinforce those beliefs.

But when we shift our inner resonance—through mindfulness, meditation, breathwork, and somatic practices—we recalibrate our energy field, magnetizing relationships that reflect our newfound sense of safety and self-worth.

Unconditional love is not just an emotion—it is a frequency of our divine being, a biochemical state, and a catalyst for deep healing. It is the force that reawakens dormant neural connections, allowing us to experience relationships beyond the constraints of past conditioning.

Healing attachment wounds helps in reclaiming sovereignty over our inner world. It is the process of transmuting fear into trust, disconnection into belonging, and survival into deep, embodied devotion.

When we step beyond the illusions of our past programming, we open the door to authentic, soul-nourishing relationships—first with ourselves and then with the world around us.

UNDERSTANDING THE POWER OF HEALING

How you manage, feel, or repress emotions as an adult is a mirror of what was modeled for you in childhood.

The emotional landscape you inherited as a child shapes the very fabric of your current responses, often rooted in unresolved survival patterns that affect your brain and nervous system.

These patterns are the hidden threads weaving through the tapestry of long-term health imbalances.

The way you speak to yourself today reflects how others spoke to themselves and to you as a child. The manner in which you express—or suppress—anger mirrors the boundaries or lack placed around your emotional expression as a young vulnerable kid.

Your relationship with work, the stress it carries, and the pressure you place on yourself are often echoes of the value placed on achievement during childhood. The love you received, conditional upon your productivity, still reverberates in how you approach your worth today. Your immune system's strength, too, is a reflection of how safe and supported your body felt in childhood when it was facing illness and stress.

Did it feel protected, or did it fight alone, distrusting others?

The quality of your relationships as an adult is often shaped by the way conflict was navigated in your childhood home—whether wounds were healed with tenderness or left to fester in silence or suppressed with fear in a toxic environment.

How you respond to stress today is a direct reflection of how you were held—or abandoned—during stressful moments as a child.

The emotional challenges you face often trace their roots to unhealed patterns, carried from the past into your present.

Healing these wounds requires more than a surface-level fix. It calls for a holistic approach—one that embraces tools like somatic experiencing, parts work, and brain retraining.

These methods are designed to release the trauma stored in the body, reset the nervous system, and allow the body to find balance once again.

Understanding how the past shapes the present gives you the power to uncover the root causes of your struggles, not just treat the symptoms. This awareness invites healing—not as a distant dream, but as a living, breathing process.

Emotional Intelligence (EI)

Real emotional intelligence is understanding without judgment. It's realizing that sometimes, the most healing thing you can do for someone is to sit with them in their pain—without the urge to fix it. Healing doesn't come from having all the answers; it comes from showing up with presence and grace.

For those who've carried trauma deeply, it can become locked in the muscles, buried where you can't see it. The iliacus, deep within your pelvis, often holds fear and unresolved emotional pain, leading to pelvic discomfort, pain while walking, even reproductive issues. Releasing tension here restores a sense of safety.

The same applies to the psoas, the "muscle of the soul," which stores anxiety and fear, manifesting as lower back pain and tension. Somatic practices help release this stored tension, helping you feel grounded once again.

Trauma conditions your brain. The amygdala, ever on alert, keeps you locked in a cycle of fear, making your body prepare for battle—even when the threat has long passed. Anxiety, sleep disturbances, and chronic fatigue become familiar companions.

But in reality, your brain is trying to protect you, though it's stuck in outdated patterns.

The stories you've internalized—the lies told to you— are not truths. They are echoes, fading into the past.

It's time to find the courage and decide to let them go.

To heal, you must reconnect with your body and find safety within your nervous system.

Traumatized, your system swings between hyperarousal (fight or flight) and hypo-arousal (shutdown), exhausting you emotionally and physically. This dysregulation takes its toll on your mood, your energy, and your relationships.

When we experience traumatic events in childhood, our spirit fractures, retreating into hidden corners of our psyche as our nervous system shifts into survival mode.

This fragmentation is not a weakness—it is a profound act of self-preservation in the physical world.

The mind, overwhelmed by what it cannot yet process, tucks away the unbearable, shielding us from pain too great to endure.

But what is buried is never truly gone. These fragmented aspects of the self linger in the subconscious, shaping our emotions, behaviors, and perceptions. They whisper through our fears, manifest in our triggers, and surface in patterns we cannot seem to break.

The nervous system, wired for survival, remains in a state of hypervigilance long after the threat has passed, mistaking the echoes of the past for present danger.

Yet, what once protected us can also imprison us.

Over time, our neurons—our brain's intricate messengers—become hardwired, forging well-worn pathways that dictate our responses.

This means our nervous system, in its relentless pursuit of familiarity, often defaults to old patterns rather than choosing what truly serves us. Sustainable change is not a fleeting epiphany but a discipline of repetition and consistency.

One of the nervous system's most defining traits is its instinct to return to the known. When confronted with stress or uncertainty, our body and mind instinctively react as they always have, even when those reactions hinder our growth.

The past becomes the blueprint, even if that blueprint is cracked and crumbling.

Consider the unconscious scripts we have rehearsed for years if we have:

- suppressed emotions, our nervous system equates feeling with danger.
- lived in a guarded state, vulnerability becomes a threat.
- stayed silent, speaking up feels unsafe.
- rushed through life, stillness becomes unsettling.
- lived in fear, security itself feels foreign.
- identified with failure, success feels like an intrusion.
- been consumed by worry, presence feels unnatural.
- relied on self-criticism, self-compassion feels undeserved.
- tied our worth to productivity, joy, play, and creativity seem frivolous.

-     lived in a state of stress and anxiety, relaxation feels like a vulnerability.

Awareness is the first spark of transformation. Begin to notice the cycles you are not consciously choosing but unconsciously repeating. Healing is not a destination—it is the relentless unraveling of these patterns, a daily commitment to breaking free from what no longer serves you.

It is a journey of retrieval—the sacred process of calling these lost pieces home. It is the moment we move beyond survival and into integration, where we gently guide the nervous system out of its defensive loop and into safety.

Neuroscience confirms what ancient wisdom has long known: trauma is stored not just in the mind, but in the body. The very cells of our being hold the memory of what we could not process, keeping us bound to the past until we create the conditions for release.

The process of healing does not end when the symptoms subside. It demands consistent action, a mindful devotion to rewriting your nervous system's story. The body does not speak in words but in sensations.

As you regulate your nervous system, your breath deepens, your muscles soften, your heart expands, your mind clears, your jaw unclenches, tension dissolves, posture unwinds.

For the first time in a long time, your body finally feels safe to exist in the present. Healing is the return to wholeness.

As you begin to heal, you'll realize how many relationships were built on your own self-abandonment. But emotional safety isn't about avoiding conflict; it's knowing you can voice your perceptions without the fear of rejection, judgment, or losing love.

Healing no longer means sabotaging or abandoning yourself to keep others comfortable. It's about showing up for yourself in vulnerability—even when it's hard, even when it hurts. True strength is not denial. It's tenderness, softness, honoring your wounds, integrating shadow aspects, and still choosing to move forward with grace. It is the foundation of self-love.

Your worth isn't something you need to prove. It's something you must remember. It is your birthright.

Your nervous system deserves safety, not survival. True healing begins when you reclaim your voice and stop sacrificing your authenticity to please others.

Love should never demand you to forfeit yourself in the process. When you finally regulate your nervous system, you'll no longer mistake neglect, disrespect or abuse for pure love.

The process of healing is the unlearning of the false belief that pure love must be earned. It does not require you to shrink, stay silent, or suppress your light. Love that manipulates, controls, or stifles your truth is not love—it is a toxic attachment. Healing begins when those conditions cease to exist.

From a metaphysical perspective, healing is alchemy—the sacred transformation from mere survival to profound peace. It is the return to yourself, the reclamation of your body as a sanctuary, your intuition as a compass, and your worth as unshakable.

You are not the wounds inflicted upon you; you are the infinite potential of who you choose to become.

With self-love, in every moment you choose yourself—your primary needs, your healthy boundaries, your internal light—you reclaim fragments of your soul, scattered once in the shadows of pain.

Your energy ignites, your voice strengthens, and your spirit elevates, becoming a force of boundless power.

Healing is not about fixing; it is about embracing. It is the tender, relentless act of self-devotion through the storm, cradling your scars as sacred reminders of the battles you have survived. Each step forward is a reclamation of your soul, opening unseen doors to freedom and possibility.

Your nervous system, that delicate bridge between body and spirit, longs for safety. When you honor this need, peace flows like water, nourishing the very roots of your being.

From this sacred place of safety, you do not merely survive—you thrive, blooming into the radiant wholeness of all you were always meant to be.

Releasing Resistance

Healing does not follow a clock. It is not measured in days, months, or years—it unfolds in divine timing, which is less about time and more about alignment.

What we perceive as "timing" is actually the unfolding of our inner evolution—a process of integration, release, and alignment with our highest truth.

Every negatively charged experience we carry is not just a memory—it is energy waiting to be transmuted. Every wound, every painful experience, is stored as energetic imprints in the body and subconscious mind.

Until integrated, they manifest as emotional blocks in the seven energy centers, fears, or patterns that keep us tethered to the past. The healing process releases these dense energies so that you can rise into the highest expression of your being. And this release happens the moment you are ready to surrender—not to suffering, but to transformation.

The life you seek—the manifestations you long for—are not distant. They exist here, in the present moment, vibrating at the frequency of your fully healed, fully realized self.

As you release resistance and embody your authentic essence, you become an energetic match for the reality you were always meant to live.

Physiology of Liquid Crystal Beings

Everyone is a healer by birthright. Our bodies, designed to self-heal, carry an innate wisdom—yet true healing begins with understanding that the soul must be freed, allowing its life force to flow unimpeded through the intricate network of energy centers that animate every living being.

When we incarnate, our spirit enters the body through the crown center, a sacred metaphysical connection known as the silver cord, merging with the physical vessel to experience the material world of flesh.

This divine process of incarnation is the conduit through which pure energy infuses our body, animating our life force through the dynamic and harmonious interplay of our energy centers—where the mind, body, and spirit align in sacred unity.

As this soul force enters, it activates the energy centers, causing them to spin faster and draw universal life force from the environment. This influx of energy fuels the body's innate ability to heal and regenerate. But what happens when this process is obstructed?

Every thought, emotion, and action that disrupts energetic harmony—whether it be fear, anger, unhealthy habits, anxiety, or emotional turmoil—creates blockages that inhibit the natural flow of life force.

When an energy center becomes restricted, it can no longer fully absorb or distribute this vital energy, leading to imbalances that manifest physical, emotional, or mental ailments.

Dis-ease, then, is not merely a malfunction of the body but a result of inhibited soul life.

The immortal essence within us—the divine force that cannot be destroyed—struggles to penetrate the blocked energy centers, diminishing the body's ability to heal itself. Healing is the sacred alchemy of restoring this intelligent flow to allow the soul's life force from fully expressing itself.

To heal is to realign with the eternal, to clear the pathways through which divine energy moves, and to restore the body's innate capacity to regenerate. The first step is always to remove what obstructs the flow with shadow integration—only then can the life force illuminate, rejuvenate, and return us to a state of wholeness.

If we shift our physiology perspective, we understand that we are luminous beings of liquid crystal, woven from the very essence of light and vibration. Our DNA, cell membranes, fascia, and the water that surrounds them form a living, intelligent matrix—an antenna attuned to the symphony of frequency, energy, and sound.

This crystalline structure is not merely a biological component but the foundation of our vitality, the stage upon which the dance of life unfolds.

Within this intricate lattice, molecules align in perfect harmony, forming conduits for the unseen forces that shape existence. They respond with intelligence to electricity, magnetism, and energetic fields, translating cosmic whispers into the language of the body.

This exquisite design enables rapid communication and seamless energy transfer, fueling the processes of healing, regeneration, and transformation. In this crystalline architecture, we do not merely exist—we resonate, we transform and evolve, we become.

Yet, at the heart of this intelligent design lies something even more extraordinary: *water*. Our human bodies are composed mostly of water—making us conductors of energy.

- Brain: 73% water
- Heart: 73% water
- Lungs: 83% water
- Muscles and kidneys: 75-80% water

More than a mere element, water, with its unique molecular structure, is not just essential for survival; it plays a critical role in the transmission of energy throughout the body. As it moves through our cells and circulatory system, water acts as both a medium and a catalyst, carrying the flow of vital life force energy through the intricate channels of our being.

It is a quantum bridge linking the visible to the unseen, the physical to the ethereal. It is a vast, intelligent reservoir, capturing, storing, and transmitting frequency information, responding to the subtle forces of the universe—light, sound, electromagnetic waves, even the quantum spin of subatomic particles.

The emerging science of aquaphotomics reveals that water is not a passive substance but an active participant in its environment.

Studies suggest that its molecular structure shifts in response to electromagnetic frequencies, spoken words, music, and even the presence of DNA *(Source: Del Giudice, 1988; Pollack, 2013)*.

This remarkable adaptability suggests that water carries encoded information, acting as a medium through which biological and energetic systems communicate *(Source: Montagnier, 2011)*.

Further research indicates that structured water clusters can retain and transfer low-frequency energy, such as infrared light, a discovery that may explain the efficacy of energy-based healing modalities like acupuncture and biofield therapy *(Source: Voeikov & Del Giudice, 2009).*

These findings propose that water is not merely a chemical compound but a sophisticated information carrier, amplifying and transmitting energy across biological systems.

From a quantum perspective, water emerges as the fundamental regulator of life itself. It influences cellular function, governs metabolic processes, and maintains bioenergetic balance within all living organisms.

The study of water unveils its role as a bridge to the quantum unified field, where energy, consciousness, and matter converge *(Source: Szent-Györgyi, 1957; Preparata, 1995).*

Quantum brain dynamics further suggests that memory is not merely stored in the brain but arises from the profound interplay between the microtubules within neurons, the water that lines them, and the vibrational frequencies of light and sound in our environment.

We are crystal beings of light, shaped by its presence and trained by the rhythmic dance of the sun and moon.

Each morning, as sunlight enters our eyes, it passes through the delicate layer of cells in the retina, where it is transformed into an electrical impulse that extends to nearly every cell in our body.

This cascade of photonic energy stimulates the release of essential hormones and neurotransmitters—cortisol, progesterone, estrogen, testosterone, dopamine, and serotonin—igniting biochemical processes that govern our mood, metabolism, and overall well-being.

Sunlight triggers the production of beta-endorphins and fat-burning lipoproteins, setting the stage for vitality and balance *(Source: Foster & Kreitzman, 2004).*

Our entire physiology is attuned to celestial rhythms. Digestion, immunity, respiration, neurological function, and cardiovascular health are all synchronized with the rising and setting of the sun.

Yet, just as light is essential for activation, darkness is the medicine for restoration. As night falls, the absence of light signals the pineal gland to release melatonin, the master regulator of rest and repair.

This sacred interplay between light and dark fuels the cycles of wakefulness and renewal, guiding our bodies through the intricate choreography of life *(Source: Reiter, 2017).*

We are not separate from the cosmos but intricately woven into its grand design. To neglect these rhythms is to turn away from the very forces that sustain us. It is time to remember our place within this luminous ecosystem—to honor it, tend to it, and thrive in harmony with the pulse of nature itself.

Frequencies of Love in Motion

We are not merely flesh and bone but harmonic beings, vibrating in symphonies of love consciousness.

The architecture of the heart, the spiraling helix of DNA, and the mathematical precision of musical scales are not arbitrary constructs but evidence of an intricate, intelligent design—one that binds us to the fundamental rhythm of the universe. We are love in motion, attuned to the unseen forces that shape our reality.

When two souls magnetize and match, an invisible yet profound phenomenon unfolds: their brainwaves synchronize, mirroring each other's frequencies as if composing a duet written in the language of the cosmos.

This process, known as neural coupling, aligns minds and emotions, fostering an almost telepathic attunement during intimate moments—be it a whispered conversation, a lingering touch, or the silent understanding exchanged in a single gaze.

Neuroscientific research confirms that during these deeply resonant interactions, corresponding regions in the brain ignite in synchrony, creating a neurological bridge that transcends the physical. *(Source: Stephens, G. J., Silbert, L. J., & Hasson, U., 2010)*

Music, the purest expression of vibration, amplifies this connection. Studies reveal that when people sing, play, or even listen to melodies together, their heartbeats and neural rhythms begin to sync.

The brain, in response, releases oxytocin—the biochemical essence of love and trust—strengthening emotional bonds.

Simultaneously, dopamine surges, heightening pleasure, anticipation, and desire, reinforcing the magnetic pull between individuals. *(Source: Zatorre, R. J., & Salimpoor, V. N., 2013)*

But beyond the poetry of emotion lies a profound revelation: love, attraction, and connection are encoded in our brainwave states, each carrying its own energetic signature.

- **Gamma Waves (40+ Hz)**: The pulse of infatuation. When attraction strikes like lightning, the brain hums in the gamma state, a high-frequency vibration that fuels heightened awareness, passion, and an almost intoxicating sense of euphoria. Time bends. Reality sharpens. Every sensation is amplified. Listening to this frequency can help detox and repair the brain by removing plaque buildup.
- **Beta Waves (15-30 Hz)**: The rhythm of deep connection. As trust deepens and minds intertwine in meaningful conversation, beta waves dominate, sharpening focus and

intellectual engagement. It is here, in this space of mutual curiosity, that relationships transition from mere attraction to genuine understanding.

- **Alpha Waves (8-12 Hz):** The current of intimacy. When walls dissolve and vulnerability flourishes, the brain slows into the alpha state, inducing calm, openness, and emotional surrender. Love shifts from passion to presence, from longing to belonging.

- **Theta Waves (4-8 Hz):** The vibration of devotion. Long-term commitment—the kind built on trust, loyalty, and unconditional love—emerges in the theta state. This is the realm of deep emotional security, where love becomes less about seeking and more about being. Both prayer and the Earth's Schumann Resonance produce a brainwave at this frequency the promotes cell regeneration, reduces oxidative stress, activates the parasympathetic nervous system, and supports emotional balance.

- **High Beta Waves (20-30 Hz):** The frequency of loss. Just as love synchronizes, separation disrupts. Heartache, betrayal, and emotional turmoil propel the brain into a chaotic high-beta state, triggering overthinking, distress, and the agonizing pull of attachment.

This invisible symphony within us—the rhythm of love, longing, connection, and loss—reveals an undeniable reality: we are not simply experiencing emotions; we are resonating with them. Every touch, every word, every moment of love or pain is encoded in frequencies that shape our very being.

And so, to love is to harmonize. To heal is to return. To exist is to vibrate in the great cosmic song, forever seeking the resonance that feels like home.

The Invisible Forces That Shape Us

Sound and harmony are not just concepts—they are the invisible forces that shape our world, weaving the fabric of our reality with each vibration. These elements, though closely intertwined, carry distinct qualities that define how we experience life, from the stillness of silence to the most majestic symphonies.

Both sound and harmony are rooted in the unseen language of vibration, but each plays a unique role in the symphony of our existence. *(Source: Hall, D. E., 2000, The Physics of Sound)*

At its core, sound is more than just something we hear—it's a pulsation that reverberates through the air, the water, the very ground beneath our feet.

These vibrations are created when molecules in a medium (whether air, water, or solid material) are displaced, creating pressure waves that propagate outward.

It is through these waves that we experience sound as a sensation, as our brains translate the frequency (the speed of the vibration) and amplitude (the strength of the vibration) into what we perceive as pitch and volume. *(Source: Rossing, T. D., & Moore, F. R.,2007, The Science of Sound)*

Sound is alive—it's the rustle of leaves caught in a gentle breeze, the deep resonance of a cello, the hum of the human voice, or the powerful crash of a thunderstorm.

It is not only something we perceive through our ears but something that reaches deep within, impacting our emotions, influencing our thoughts, and even shaping our physical state.

Each sound is a vibration that resonates within our bodies, making it one of the most fundamental ways we interact with and experience the world. *(Source: Levitin, D. J., 2006, This Is Your Brain on Music)*

The Medicine of Sound

More than just auditory experience, sound is a force of healing, a vibrational medicine woven into the very fabric of our being.

Ancient wisdom has long understood what modern science now confirms: sound frequencies influence our mental, emotional, and physiological states. It is an unseen force, a thread that connects us to the deepest knowing of who we are.

Imagine this: when we chant OM, a single word vibrating in unity with the universe, our bodies and minds respond as if the very pulse of life has synchronized with us.

Research shows that chanting OM significantly reduces activity in the amygdala, the brain's emotional control center responsible for our fight-or-flight response. In this shift—this moment of stillness—is where we find ourselves.

Our stress dissolves. Our heart softens. Anxiety and fear ease, and for a moment, we are free. We enter a place of calm that transcends the chaos of the world around us, feeling deeply connected to something greater, something infinite. *(Kalyani, B. G., 2011, International Journal of Yoga)*

But the beauty of sound is not just in its solitary practice—it thrives when shared. Singing with others doesn't just make us feel good—it makes us healthier.

Think of a choir gathered in song, their voices rising in harmony. Research reveals that singing together boosts our immune systems, enhancing white blood cell production—our body's natural defense against infection. But it doesn't stop there.

Serotonin, the hormone responsible for feelings of happiness and well-being, floods our bodies, lifting our spirits in a profound way. And the stress that weighs on our shoulders, the constant hum of cortisol that keeps us on edge, begins to fade. *(Kreutz, G., 2004, Journal of Behavioral Medicine)*

When we sing together, we heal together. In those moments, sound becomes not just a practice but a catalyst for collective wellness, a vibration that connects each person to the others in a sacred bond of shared experience.

It's not just the music that heals—it's the connection. Every note sung, every breath shared, reverberates through the collective heart, reminding us that we are not alone.

This understanding opens up a profound realization: we are our own sound healers.

The resonance of our voice, the hum of our breath, the rhythmic pulsations of our heart—all of these create frequencies that influence the very fabric of our being.

We have the power to heal ourselves, to tune our inner worlds to the frequency of love, peace, and vitality. Every time we sing, speak, or listen to sound, we engage in a process of self-healing, attuning ourselves to the universal harmony that flows through all life.

Yet, the deepest realization of sound may be this: it connects us all. Through shared song, synchronized breath, and collective resonance, we align not only with ourselves but with each other.

In that sacred space, we remember that we are all One, interconnected by the rhythms that govern the universe.

I've seen this firsthand in the most unexpected places—in the healing circles where people come together, not just to chant or sing, but to be heard. To find their voice and, in doing so, find themselves.

When people who thought they were beyond healing, beyond connection, stand together in song, their voices trembling at first, then growing stronger, the vibration of their collective energy weaving a thread of restoration through their spirits. Sound has this incredible ability to soften the edges of grief, to dissolve the heaviness of pain, and to guide us back to each other.

The power of sound is not just theoretical. It's real. It's tangible. It's a force that can shift our energy, heal our wounds, and ultimately remind us that we are all part of the same cosmic song. It teaches us that we don't have to heal in isolation—we can rebuild together, in harmony.

And when we do, we feel not only connected to the people around us but to the pulse of the earth itself, to the universe that moves in perfect rhythm, orchestrating the symphony of life. In this place, we are free.

In this place, we are whole.

INTEGRATING & UNIFYING FRAGMENTS

The art of integration is the sacred process of reclaiming the fragmented aspects of the self, dissolving illusion, and stepping into wholeness. It is the great alchemy of existence—the merging of light and shadow, the harmony of mind and spirit, the transcendence of duality into unity.

From a metaphysical perspective, integration is the moment we awaken to self-awareness, realizing that our childhood wounds, suppressed emotions, and unconscious beliefs are not separate from us but pieces of a greater whole. The heart, our bridge between the seen and unseen, pulses with the wisdom of this reunion, guiding us toward coherence with the divine.

Yet, this is not merely a spiritual unfolding; it is deeply woven into our biology. Neuroscience reveals that the brain, like the soul, seeks unity. Through neuroplasticity, it rewires itself, forging new pathways that shift perception, dissolve trauma, and create space for transformation.

The amygdala, once hijacked by fear, learns to soften, allowing the prefrontal cortex—the seat of higher awareness—to lead with clarity. The brain's hemispheres synchronize, bridging logic with intuition, structure with creativity, thought with feeling.

The dialogue between heart and brain, once thought separate, is now known to shape our reality. As the heart enters coherence, its rhythm harmonizes the brain waves, regulates the nervous system, and shifts our entire energetic state.

This synergy between science and spirit is undeniable—their union is the key to our transformation.

To integrate is to reclaim. To embody. To transcend survival and step into creation, where thoughts, emotions, and energy no longer work against us but move as one unified force. It is not merely healing; it is becoming.

For in the end, integration is not about fixing what was broken. It is the return to our divine nature—the profound remembrance that we were whole all along.

This process requires:

- **Shadow Work:** Acknowledging childhood wounding, and embracing suppressed emotions, fears, and unconscious programming.
- **Inner Alchemy:** Transmuting lower vibrational energy centers (root, sacral, solar plexes) such as fear, unworthiness, and guilt into higher frequencies like self-love, harmony, and wisdom.
- **Heart Coherence:** Activating the heart field to bridge the gap between the conscious and

subconscious mind, integrating emotional and spiritual intelligence in alignment with higher-self.

- **Energy Alignment:** Releasing stored trauma from the energy centers to allow a free flow of life force energy (prana/chi).

Real integration happens when we no longer resist parts of ourselves but instead hold them in loving awareness, allowing them to dissolve into the unified whole.

It is a sacred journey from the chaos of survival to the sanctuary of peace. It is an intimate reunion with your body, a profound memory of your divinity, and a bold reclamation of your inherent worth.

It is the quiet, powerful realization that you are not the echoes of what happened to you but the luminous soul choosing who to become in this very moment.

Each time you honor yourself—your needs, your boundaries, your inner peace—you gather the scattered pieces of your essence, once lost to pain. Through soul retrieval, your life force energy revives, your voice strengthens, and your spirit rises with undeniable power. This is the foundational nature of self-love.

As you continue to heal and integrate, you become the author of your own story, rewriting the narrative with strength and resilience. New pathways unfold before you, like doors unlocking to freedom and infinite possibility. It is an act of grace, of embracing yourself in all your humanity, even in the midst of pain.

It is the quiet bravery to release anything that disrupts your peace, honoring the sacred rhythm of your nervous system as it seeks safety.

When you nurture this sanctuary within, your body, mind, and heart flourish together, transforming survival into thriving, and restoring the fullness of who you truly are.

When we integrate metaphysical with the scientific, we see that consciousness is not just an abstract spiritual concept but is deeply embedded in our biology.

In essence:

- Metaphysical integration dissolves the illusion of separation and aligns us with the divine self.
- Neuroscientific integration restructures the brain and nervous system to sustain that state of coherence.

True transformation requires both—spiritual awareness to awaken the truth and physiological adaptation to embody it. Integration is not simply about understanding who we are but about becoming a living embodiment of our highest potential.

Epigenetics of Trauma's Legacy

Our genes carry the blueprint of life, but they are not set in stone.

Epigenetics—the study of how environmental factors influence gene expression—reveals that trauma, stress, and emotional wounds can alter how our genes function without changing the DNA sequence itself.

It's as if trauma rewrites the instructions, shaping not only our emotional responses but also the way our bodies process stress, heal, and adapt.

Trauma leaves biological imprints, triggering changes in genes that regulate mood, memory, and stress response. While DNA methylation and histone modification act like molecular switches, turning genes on or off, chronic stress can disrupt this delicate balance.

However, just as trauma can alter gene expression in our cells, healing can restore it. Through mindfulness, therapy, and conscious lifestyle choices, individuals can rewrite the narrative encoded in their biology. *(Source: Meaney, M. J., & Szyf, M., 2005, Molecular Psychiatry)*

But the impact of trauma doesn't stop with one person. It ripples across generations, passed down like an invisible inheritance. Studies show that children of trauma survivors may carry altered stress responses, even if they never experienced the original wound firsthand.

A parent's unresolved pain—whether from war, abuse, or loss—can shape a child's emotional and physiological development, increasing their susceptibility to fear, anxiety, or emotional disconnection. This phenomenon, known as intergenerational trauma, weaves past suffering into the fabric of future generations.

Yet trauma's legacy is not just biological; it is also behavioral. Parents who have endured hardship may unknowingly pass down coping mechanisms—emotional suppression, avoidance, or hyper-independence—that influence how their children navigate the world.

A child raised by an emotionally distant caregiver may grow up struggling with vulnerability, mirroring patterns of self-protection inherited from generations before them.

Ripple Effects: Intergenerational Echo

Trauma does not exist in isolation. It reverberates through generations, leaving invisible but profound marks on the emotional and physical well-being of descendants.

This transgenerational imprinting occurs through both biological and environmental pathways. We have learned that neuroplasticity ensures early childhood environments play a crucial role in shaping future emotional resilience.

If a parent has endured unprocessed trauma, their nervous system may remain in a heightened state of alert, inadvertently transmitting anxiety, fear, or emotional disconnection to their child. Through both epigenetic inheritance and learned behavior, trauma becomes an unconscious legacy. *(Source: Cozolino, 2010)*

Coping Mechanisms: Unseen Inheritance

Beyond biological alterations, trauma weaves itself into the fabric of family dynamics.

The coping mechanisms survivors develop—emotional numbness, hyper-vigilance, avoidance, withdrawal or attachment difficulties—often become ingrained behaviors passed down across generations.

Children absorb these patterns like sponges, learning emotional regulation from their caregivers' responses. A parent who endured childhood neglect may unconsciously teach their child to suppress emotions, fostering a cycle of emotional disconnection.

A survivor of domestic violence may unknowingly model hyper-reactivity to stress, leaving their child primed for heightened fear responses.

These inherited coping strategies can manifest as difficulties in forming secure relationships, chronic self-doubt, or an inability to process emotions in a healthy way.

Unconscious survival mechanisms, once essential for protection, may become roadblocks to intimacy, self-awareness, and personal growth. Recognizing these patterns is the first step toward breaking the cycle and reclaiming agency over one's emotional destiny. *(Source: Perry & Szalavitz, 2006)*

Rewriting the Epigenetic Code

The most profound revelation of epigenetics is that trauma's grip is not absolute. Just as negative experiences can alter gene expression, healing interventions can restore balance.

Practices such as trauma-informed therapy, mindfulness, somatic healing, and meditation have been shown to reverse some of the biological imprints of trauma, promoting resilience and emotional regulation.

Emerging research suggests that by cultivating safety, emotional awareness, and nervous system regulation, individuals can shift their epigenetic expression, fostering well-being not only for themselves but for future generations. *(Source: Siegel, 2012)*

The story of epigenetics is one of both caution and hope. While trauma may leave its mark, it does not define our fate. Through conscious awareness, emotional processing, and intentional healing, we have the power to rewrite the narrative, transforming inherited pain into generational strength.

Breaking Intergenerational Cycles

The implications of intergenerational trauma are profound. It creates a vicious cycle of pain, fear, and survival responses that can feel impossible to break. But the science of neuroplasticity gives us hope.

Just as trauma can reshape the brain and genes, so too can healing practices. By engaging in trauma-informed therapies, mindfulness, and emotional regulation practices, individuals can begin to rewrite the biological and emotional patterns passed down to them.

By healing ourselves, we don't just heal our own wounds—we begin to change the course of our family's legacy and DNA. Through awareness and intentional Pathways of Change, we can stop the cycle of trauma before it starts, creating healthier, more resilient generations to come.

The remarkable power of epigenetics, combined with the neuroplasticity of the brain, offers a pathway for transformation, not only for individuals but for entire family systems for generations.

It's a reminder that while trauma may shape us, it doesn't have to define us.

TAPPING TOOLS & SOMATIC RELEASE

Emotional Freedom Technique (EFT), often called "tapping," is a powerful fusion of ancient Chinese medicine and modern psychology designed to release unprocessed trauma and emotional blockages stored in the body. Like acupuncture, EFT stimulates meridian points—but instead of needles, you use gentle tapping while focusing on an emotional issue.

This simple yet profound practice signals the nervous system to calm, helping to regulate stress responses, dissolve trapped emotions, and restore emotional balance. *(Source: Church, D., & Feinstein, D., 2017)*

How EFT Works

- **Identify the Issue:** Name the fear, emotion, or limiting belief you want to release.
- **Rate the Intensity:** On a scale of 0 to 10, assess the strength of your emotional response.
- **Set an Intention**: Create an affirmation that acknowledges the issue while embracing self-acceptance.
- **Tap Through the Sequence**: Gently tap on specific meridian points while repeating a reminder phrase.
- **Reassess**: After tapping, check the intensity of your emotion. If it persists, repeat the

process until you feel a shift toward calm and relief.

By engaging the mind and body simultaneously, EFT helps reprogram the brain's response to trauma or feelings of anxiety, freeing you from past emotional patterns and fostering a sense of inner peace. *(Source: Clond, M., 2016)*

Pathways of Change

EFT tapping is based on stimulating nine meridian points on the body, believed to be linked to emotional, psychological, and physical well-being. By tapping on these points while focusing on a specific issue, you can help release energetic blockages, restore balance, and rewire emotional responses. *(Source: Sebastian, B., & Nelms, J., 2017)*

1. **Karate Chop Point (Small Intestine Meridian)** – Side of Hand, located on the edge of the hand, on the fleshy part below the pinky finger.

- **Emotional Links:** Psychological reversal, self-sabotage, inner conflict.
- **Helps With:** Overcoming resistance, shifting limiting beliefs, self-acceptance.
- **Example:** If you're dealing with feelings of unworthiness, you might start by tapping on this point while saying, "Even though I feel unworthy, I deeply and completely

love and accept myself." This helps to start the process of emotional acceptance and acknowledgment of the belief you want to change. "Even though I feel stuck, I deeply and completely accept myself."

- **Visualization:** Imagine cutting away old energetic cords of self-doubt, making space for self-trust and clarity. As you tap notice how you feel in your body.

2. Eyebrow Point (Bladder Meridian) – Inner Brow, located at the beginning of the eyebrow, near the bridge of the nose.

- **Emotional Links:** Fear, anxiety, trauma, survival stress.
- **Helps With:** Releasing fear, enhancing mental clarity, cultivating courage.
- **Example:** If you feel scared, tap here while repeating, "I feel afraid, but I am safe in my body," helps reframe the negative emotion and shifts your perspective on the situation. "I release the fear that is holding me back. I trust in the flow of life."
- **Visualization:** Picture a waterfall washing away fear, leaving you with crystal-clear awareness.

3. Side of Eye (Gallbladder Meridian) – Temple Area, located on the bone at the outside corner of the eye.

- **Emotional Links:** Frustration, resentment, anger, indecisiveness.
- **Helps With:** Letting go of grudges, forgiveness, gaining new perspectives.
- **Example:** If you're experiencing feelings of anger, tap on this point while saying, "I am safe to feel resentment, but I choose to release it," helps ease the emotional tension. "I release the frustration and welcome peace."
- **Visualization:** See yourself standing on a mountaintop, breathing deeply, feeling free from stressors and emotional burdens.

4. Under Eye (Stomach Meridian) – Under the Pupil, on the bone directly under the eye

- **Emotional Links:** Anxiety, worry, nervousness, insecurity
- **Helps With:** Emotional stability, inner security, trust
- **Example:** This point is helpful for releasing negative self-talk. You might tap here while saying, "I am letting go of all the negative thoughts I've been holding about myself." Also try, "I am safe. I trust myself to handle any challenge."
- **Visualization:** Imagine golden light filling your solar plexus, strengthening your confidence, and boosting your resilience.

5. Under Nose (Large Intestine & Governing Meridian) – Located between Nose & Upper Lip

- **Emotional Links:** Shame, guilt, unworthiness, self-judgment.
- **Helps With:** Self-forgiveness, compassion, empowerment.
- **Example:** If you are feeling guilt or shame, tap here while repeating, "I forgive myself and release all guilt. I release the weight of guilt and embrace my inner worth." This can help clear negatively charged emotions and self-judgment.
- **Visualization:** Envision a warm golden light at your heart center, expanding with every breath, dissolving all shame.

6. Chin Point (Stomach & Central Meridian) – Located between Lower Lip & Chin

- **Emotional Links:** Fear of rejection, self-esteem issues, emotional suppression.
- **Helps With:** Confidence, self-expression, worthiness.
- **Example:** This point can help address issues of self-worth. You could tap here while saying, "I am worthy of success, and I release all feelings of being stuck. I am worthy of love, abundance, and joy."

- **Visualization:** Picture your throat and heart glowing with blue and pink energy, expressing your authentic truth effortlessly.

7. Collarbone Point (Kidney Meridian) – Located below the Collarbone

- **Emotional Links:** Fear of change, stress, survival instincts.
- **Helps With:** Grounding, resilience, balance.
- **Example:** Tapping on this point can help release feelings of anxiety or stress. "I am calm and centered, and I release all tension from my body. I choose to feel safe and strong in the face of change."
- **Visualization:** See yourself rooted like a tree, absorbing stability, and strength from the earth. Imagine a gentle wave flowing though your body, clearing away any obstacles and allowing your mind and body to move into a state of harmony and flow. Feel the shift as clarity and balance take over with every tap.

8. Under Arm (Spleen Meridian) – Located about 4 Inches Below Armpit

- **Emotional Links:** Self-unease, emotional overwhelm, worry.
- **Helps With:** Releasing self-doubt, embracing self-empowerment.

- **Example:** A powerful release of guilt, worry, and obsessive thoughts, while promoting clarity, confidence, relaxation and compassion for ourselves and others. This point is often used to help release fear or overwhelm. "I let go of all my worries, and I embrace peace and clarity. I am enough just as I am. I release all overwhelming sensations."

- **Visualization:** Imagine the heavy cloak of guilt and worry shedding away while the golden orb of light radiates while enveloping you or your loved one with security, confidence, and joy throughout the body.

9. Top of Head (Crown Field – Governing Meridian)

– Connects to the brain and higher self consciousness

- **Emotional Links:** Overthinking, spiritual disconnect, limiting beliefs.
- **Helps With:** Higher awareness, clarity, wisdom.
- **Example:** Tapping here while focusing on anxiety could help clear mental blocks associated with stress. You might say, "I am releasing the anxiety and tension that I've been holding onto. I am connected to my higher self and divine wisdom."
- **Visualization:** See yourself bathed in radiant golden light bubble as it envelops

you in warm embrace, connected to infinite wisdom and peace.

Transformative Benefits of EFT

EFT isn't just a technique—it is a gateway to profound transformation. With every tap, you send a message to rewire your subconscious: *I am safe. I am worthy. I am free.* As negatively charged energy dissolves, you step into a life of clarity, balance, and limitless potential.

- Calms Stress and Anxiety – Instantly soothes the nervous system, lowering cortisol levels and promoting inner peace.
- Releases Emotional Blockages – Frees suppressed emotions and stagnant energy, creating space for healing.
- Boosts Self-Worth and Confidence – Shifts negative self-perceptions and reinforces empowering beliefs.
- Heals Trauma and Past Wounds – Helps reprocess painful experiences, offering deep emotional relief.
- Strengthens Emotional Resilience – Equips you with a tool to navigate life's challenges with greater ease.
- Supports Physical and Emotional Well-Being – Addresses the mind-body connection, aiding in both emotional and physical healing.

By using the meridian points, you focus your attention to clear negatively charged energy and replace it with empowering thoughts and affirmations.

Quantum Playbook: Rescuing Pain

The path to your highest self has always been within you. Before true healing can occur, it's essential to understand why we resist it. Pain, no matter how heavy, can feel familiar—creating the illusion of safety.

Brain retraining rewires unresolved emotional patterns by shifting automatic thought processes that trigger stress, directly impacting the nervous system and physiology from the top down. This process moves you from dysregulation to balance.

Meanwhile, somatic experiencing goes deeper, uncovering the roots of trauma's emotional patterns from the bottom up. By bringing unconscious triggers into awareness, it allows you to step out of the emotional loops that keep you stuck.

Together, these practices reprogram how your brain and body process stress, fostering safety and healing across mind, body, and spirit. The synergy between brain retraining and somatic therapies paves the way for sustainable, long-term healing—releasing trapped pain and helping you break free from the past.

The subconscious clings to old wounds, fearing that change will dismantle everything we've known. But healing isn't about waiting for the perfect moment; it's about choosing embodiment—deciding, each day, to become the version of yourself that is already whole.

Step 1: Acknowledge the Resistance Without Judgment

Resistance isn't failure—it's a signal. Trauma creates neural pathways that reinforce avoidance, so when deep healing arises, your brain may resist. Instead of fighting it, observe it with curiosity.

Ask yourself:

- What part of me is afraid to heal?
- What shadow wounds have I been avoiding?
- What beliefs and victimhood stories keep me tethered to the past?
- What would happen if I released this pain?

Neuroscience Insight: Resistance is a survival mechanism rooted in the amygdala, the brain's fear center. By naming the fear, you activate the prefrontal cortex, which helps reduce the emotional intensity, allowing for greater regulation and clarity. *(Siegel, D. J., 2012, The Developing Mind).*

Affirmation: *I am safe to witness my emotions. My healing unfolds in perfect timing.*

Step 2: Feel to Heal—Somatic Release

Trauma is stored in the body. Healing requires felt experience, not just intellectual understanding. Activate your parasympathetic nervous system through:

- Breathwork – Deep belly breathing (4-7-8 technique) to regulate the nervous system.
- Movement – Yoga, dance, or shaking therapy (Tension and Trauma Release Exercises).
- Tapping (EFT) – Rewire trauma patterns by tapping acupressure points while speaking affirmations.
- Sound healing – Humming, chanting, or listening to 432 Hz/528 Hz frequencies to shift brainwaves.

Scientific Insight: Somatic healing helps discharge trauma stored in the vagus nerve, which plays a critical role in regulating the body's stress response. By engaging with the body through somatic practices, we can release stored trauma, restoring balance and promoting healing. (*Porges, S. W., 2011*).

Affirmation: *I allow my body to release what no longer serves me. I am aligned and balanced.*

Step 3: Rewrite Your Subconscious Narrative

Your subconscious operates 95% of the time, shaping your reality (*Dr. Bruce Lipton, Biology of Belief*). If you were conditioned to expect lack, rejection, or struggle, your brain seeks evidence to confirm it. Time to rewire:

- Affirmations – Repeat statements that reinforce safety and abundance.
- Journaling – Write "Letters of Release" to past versions of yourself or those who hurt you.
- Visualization – Close your eyes and feel yourself already healed. How do you breathe? How do you walk?

Neuroscience Insight: Neuroplasticity enables the brain to rewrite old trauma loops by repetition and emotion, reshaping neural pathways and promoting healing. Through intentional practice, you can shift habitual patterns and reprogram the mind to overcome wounding beliefs *(Dispenza, J., 2012, Breaking the Habit of Being Yourself)*.

Affirmation: *I am whole. I am already living my highest potential.*

Step 4: Shift from Control to Trust

The ego wants certainty. But healing isn't about forcing—it's about flowing. Surrender allows divine alignment to work in your favor.

- Let go of attachment – Reflect and meditate on *"What if this is happening for me not to me?"*

- Trust divine timing – Every delay is a redirection toward something greater.
- Practice patience – Healing happens in layers, not all at once.

Psychological Insight: Trust activates the brain's default mode network, enhancing intuition and problem-solving by shifting the mind into a state of ease and creativity. This neurological shift allows for more fluid, insightful thinking and better decision-making (*Brewer, J. A., 2021, Unwinding Anxiety*).

Affirmation: *I release control and trust the unfolding of my journey.*

Step 5: Commit to Radical Self-Compassion

Healing isn't linear. Some days, you'll feel invigorated and light, others, dense and solemn. The key is grace.

- Speak to yourself like a loved one – Would you shame a child for struggling?
- Take radical accountability – Healing means owning your patterns without blame.
- Do no harm – Be mindful of emotional reactions and don't lash out. Your words, thoughts, and actions shape your energetic field.

Scientific Insight: Self-compassion lowers cortisol (the stress hormone) and boosts oxytocin (the love and bonding hormone), creating a biochemical shift that enhances emotional resilience and healing *(Neff, K. D.,2011, Self-Compassion: Stop Beating Yourself Up and Leave Insecurity Behind).*

Affirmation: *I give myself grace. I am exactly where I need to be.*

Step 6: Engage in Soul-Aligned Creation

Healing isn't just about release—it's about flowing with creation. Trauma blocks life force energy. Creative expression restores it.

- Write – Poetry, stories, conscious journaling.
- Paint, sing, dance – Move energy through art.
- Play – Engage in childlike joy—laughter rewires trauma responses.

Scientific Insight: Creative flow states activate theta brainwaves, the same frequency associated with deep healing, heightened intuition, and subconscious reprogramming *(Csikszentmihalyi, M., 1990, Flow: The Psychology of Optimal Experience).*

Affirmation: *I am a powerful creator. I channel my energy into joyful expression.*

Step 7: Align with the Present Moment

The healed version of you already exists. Your job isn't to chase healing—it's to embody it in the now.

- Act – How would the healed version of you think, feel, and behave?
- Practice mindfulness – Stop thinking about the past or the future. Bring awareness to the beauty of now.
- Live your highest timeline – Make small choices today that align with the future you desire.

Scientific Insight: The observer effect in quantum physics suggests that your focus influences reality at a fundamental level. By embodying your healed state in the present, you collapse time, shift probabilities, and manifest it into existence *(Bohr, N., 1928, The Quantum Postulate and the Recent Development of Atomic Theory)*.

Affirmation: *I release my pain. I am already free.*

How to Call in Your Highest Reality

- Clarity – Define what you desire with precision.
- Feel it now – Emotionally embody the reality as if it's already yours.
- Align your actions – Make daily choices with integrity that reflect your healed state.

- Detach from the "how" – trust the universe to handle the details.
- Receive – Stay open to unexpected opportunities.

Scientific Insight: Manifestation isn't wishful thinking—it's neural conditioning. The reticular activating system (RAS) in your brain filters reality based on your dominant focus. When you believe something is possible, your brain literally looks for ways to make it happen (*Dr. Tara Swart, The Source*).

Affirmation: *I align with my highest potential timeline. Everything I desire is already within me.*

Yes, healing requires deep, transformative work. It demands courage and grace to face what you've been avoiding. But on the other side of this journey lies the return to your natural state of wholeness—a state of peace, joy, and effortless flow.

As you acknowledge your trauma, embrace healing, and release resistance, you align with your highest timeline—one where peace, abundance, and vitality are not merely attracted, but embodied.

Healing is not about waiting; it is about **becoming.** The moment you choose to rewire your subconscious and step into your higher self, your entire reality begins to shift.

3. Exploring the Subconscious Mind

Throughout history, mystics and philosophers have echoed a profound viewpoint: we create our reality through perception. Modern neuroscience and quantum physics now validate what esoteric wisdom has long known—our beliefs, deeply embedded in the subconscious mind, influence not only our thoughts and emotions but also our biological processes and the material world around us.

The subconscious mind is the vast, hidden layer of consciousness that operates beneath our waking awareness. Unlike the conscious mind, which processes logic, reasoning, and decision-making, the subconscious is a storehouse of memories, emotions, and deeply ingrained beliefs that shape how we perceive and respond to the world. It functions like an autopilot system, influencing 95% of our daily thoughts, habits, and behaviors without us even realizing it. *(Source: Ecker, 2012)*

From birth, our subconscious absorbs information like a sponge, forming neural pathways based on experiences, social conditioning, and emotional responses. These beliefs—whether empowering or limiting—become the blueprint that governs our actions and perceptions.

Childhood Programming

Before the age of seven, our brains exist in a theta wave state, which is highly suggestible. During this time, we absorb beliefs directly from our caregivers, society, and culture—creating the foundational programming that dictates our sense of self-worth, relationships, and our perception of success.

These early impressions, often without our conscious understanding, shapes the very lens through which we view ourselves and the world. *(Source: Hughes, 2011)*

A study conducted by Dr. Bruce Lipton demonstrated how early life experiences directly affect our biology. Environment and emotional experiences during early childhood can alter the expression of genes, setting the stage for our physical and mental health later in life. *(Source: Lipton, 2008)*

Repetitive Thought Patterns

The subconscious plants the seeds of limitation through repetition, particularly when emotions intensify. If a belief is reinforced over time—whether it is "I am not good enough" or "Money doesn't grow on trees"—it becomes deeply entrenched. These beliefs become self-fulfilling prophecies, silently guiding our actions and limiting our potential. *(Source: Ecker, 2012)*

Research from neuroscientist Dr. Joe Dispenza has shown that repetitive thought patterns physically rewire the brain, strengthening neural pathways associated with specific beliefs. These ingrained patterns can create neural circuits that maintain the status quo, preventing personal growth and perpetuating lack based convictions.

Emotional Associations

There are hidden forces behind our reactions. Every experience carries an emotional charge, and our subconscious stores these emotions in association with past events.

For instance, if a child experiences rejection, they may unknowingly internalize a belief that they are "unlovable." In adulthood, this belief can manifest in patterns of avoidance or co-dependency. These hidden emotional imprints influence how we navigate the world, affecting our adult relationships and self-worth. *(Source: Porges, 2011)*

In his research on the Polyvagal Theory, Dr. Stephen Porges demonstrates how early emotional experiences impact the autonomic nervous system, influencing how we respond to stress and perceive safety in relationships. This emotional imprinting affects our physiological responses to the world, often without us being consciously aware of it.

The Reticular Activating System

The brain houses a mechanism known as the Reticular Activating System (RAS), which acts as a filter of belief—ensuring that we only perceive information that aligns with our existing convictions. If we believe "opportunities are scarce," this filter will block out potential chances for success, reinforcing the patterns. *(Source: Limbic Brain, 2018)*

A study by neuroscientist Dr. Jeffrey Schwartz highlights how the RAS filters our perceptions based on our mental focus, confirming that our subconscious mind influences which external stimuli we pay attention to and which we ignore (Schwartz, 2002).

Imagine for a moment an ancient, sacred library that holds the story of your life. Every page tells of your experiences, emotions, and deeply ingrained beliefs. Some pages whisper empowering narratives, while others murmur doubts and limitations.

This library is your subconscious mind, and its blueprint—shaped by repetition, emotional intensity, and social reinforcement—the foundation upon which we build our reality.

Power of Conscious Transformation

Just as an architect can redesign a flawed structure, so too can we reconstruct our mental framework. By bringing awareness to our subconscious programming, we have the power to replace outdated, limiting beliefs with those that serve our highest good. We can reshape our destiny, break free from self-imposed limitations, and manifest a life filled with abundance, joy, and fulfillment. *(Source: Doidge, 2007)*

Dr. Joe Dispenza's work further emphasizes that through conscious meditation and mental rehearsal, individuals can create new neural pathways in the brain, rewiring the subconscious to embrace new, empowering beliefs.

Unconscious vs Subconscious

Let's explore the labyrinth of the human mind, where two hidden forces guide much of our behavior: the unconscious and the subconscious. These terms, often used interchangeably, represent two distinct aspects of our mental landscape, each with its own unique influence on how we think, feel, and act.

Silent Storehouse of Repression

The unconscious mind is like an undiscovered cavern beneath the surface of our awareness, a repository of thoughts, memories, and desires that we are not directly conscious of, yet still profoundly influence our lives.

This part of the mind is often associated with *repression*—the act of pushing painful or traumatic memories out of conscious reach. Here, ancient fears, forgotten desires, and unresolved conflicts lie dormant, influencing our behavior in subtle and sometimes mysterious ways.

These hidden forces may seep into our waking life, manifesting in dreams, unintended slips of the tongue, or unexplained emotional reactions that seem to come from nowhere.

While we cannot access the unconscious mind at will, it exerts a powerful influence over our lives. For example, a person who harbors an irrational fear of public speaking may not consciously recall the traumatic event that seeded this fear, yet the unconscious holds it tightly, silently influencing their actions.

It is often only through therapeutic intervention that we can bring these unconscious forces to light—allowing us to confront and release emotional burdens we never even realized we carried.

Gateway to Automatic Behavior

In contrast, the subconscious mind operates like an unseen but active force that guides much of our *automatic behavior*. It is the mental repository of all the knowledge, skills, and experiences we've accumulated over the years, waiting just beneath the surface, ready to be tapped into when needed.

Unlike the unconscious, which holds material that is often hidden away, the subconscious is more accessible. It stores everything we've learned—our habits, our reflexes, and the skills we have mastered through repetition.

It is the reason why, when you're driving a car, your body can perform all the necessary actions—steering, braking, shifting gears—without conscious thought. These actions are ingrained in your subconscious mind, driven by muscle memory and the repeated learning of basic tasks. *(Source: (Schneider, W., & Shiffrin, R. M., 1977)*

While we may not be actively aware of these learned responses, they are always there, ready to guide our performance without the need for conscious effort.

The subconscious helps us navigate life's complexities with ease, allowing us to focus our conscious mind on other tasks. And, unlike the unconscious, which can sometimes control us in ways we don't understand, the subconscious is more malleable.

Through mindfulness, hypnosis, or focused effort, we can access and influence the subconscious to change habits, rewire thought patterns, and even tap into creative potential.

The key difference between the unconscious and the subconscious lies in their accessibility and the nature of their influence.

The unconscious mind is a vast, hidden domain where memories, desires, and unresolved conflicts lie dormant, often beyond our immediate reach. It is the *mind's keeper of the past, often holding onto old wounds and forgotten truths that can shape our future in unexpected ways.*

The subconscious, on the other hand, is the *mind's bridge between conscious awareness and automatic behavior.* It holds the routines, skills, and knowledge that we have absorbed over time and through conscious effort, we can learn to reshape it, reprogramming old habits or unlocking hidden talents.

Both realms, while distinct, work together to form the blueprint of who we are and what we believe to be real. Together, they hold keys to the mysteries of the mind, and when we understand the brain's process, we unlock the full potential of our human experience.

PHILOSOPHY OF BELIEFS

Beliefs are deeply ingrained thought patterns that the subconscious mind accepts as truth, regardless of their accuracy. These mental programs shape how we perceive experiences, make decisions, and engage with the world. *(Source: Bargh & Chartrand, 1999)*

Long before we are old enough to question the perceived thought patterns, they take root within us—shaped by whispers of authority, the weight of experience, and the silent teachings of a world that demands our unquestioning faith.

The subconscious, a realm more powerful than we dare to acknowledge, absorbs these impressions without scrutiny, accepting them as unshakable facts. And so, we move through life, unaware that we are not acting by conscious choice, but by the invisible scripts imprinted upon us.

But beliefs are not fixed. They are not undisputable laws written in stone. They are stories—stories we have inherited, stories we have been told, and stories we have come to tell ourselves. Some empower us, propelling us toward limitless potential. Others shackle us, forging invisible chains that confine our minds, our hearts, and our very destiny.

A single moment of pain can rewrite the script of a lifetime. The sting of betrayal, the shadow of loss, the ache of rejection—each has the power to inscribe new beliefs upon the fabric of our subconscious, altering the way we see the world.

The child who is abandoned may grow into an adult who believes love is fleeting. A heart once broken may learn to fear connection. A dream dismissed too often may become the belief that success belongs only to others. These unseen convictions shape our choices, guiding us toward or away from possibility, long before we are even aware of them.

And yet, the most insidious beliefs are not merely personal; they are collective. Woven into the fabric of culture and passed down through generations, programs of separation, division, and control.

They whisper through the echoes of religion, tradition, race, media, and expectation. They dictate what is beautiful, what is worthy, what is possible. They tell us who we should be, what we must desire, and where our limits lie. We do not question them—not because they are true, but because they are familiar.

But familiarity is not truth. And the moment we recognize this—truly recognize it—we stand at the threshold of liberation.

Rewriting the Narrative

The mind is not a prison, nor is it bound by the walls of past conditioning. It is a canvas—vast, unfinished, alive with possibility. The beliefs we hold are not permanent laws etched into stone; they are brushstrokes, impressions left by experience, and like any masterpiece in progress, they can be reshaped, refined, and reimagined.

Neuroscience affirms what the soul has always known—the brain is not static. It is an ever-evolving landscape, forging new pathways with each thought, each revelation, each deliberate shift in perception *(Source: Doidge, 2007)*. What once confined us can be dismantled. What once defined us can be rewritten.

Yet transformation is not passive; it does not arrive by mere longing. It requires us to become designers of our own reality, dismantling the scaffolding of limiting beliefs and constructing a foundation expansive enough to hold the fullness of who we are.

The idea that we are not enough is not truth—it is conditioning, a lens through which we have learned to see ourselves. And like all lenses, it can be adjusted, sharpened, or cast aside entirely *(Source: Beck, 1976)*.

To rewrite the mind's deepest narratives, we must engage both intellect and emotion. Cognitive reframing challenges the constructs that no longer serve us, loosening their grip until they crumble.

Meditation and visualization imprint new realities before they unfold, teaching the mind to believe in possibility until possibility becomes tangible *(Source: Lazar, 2005)*. But real transformation is not an intellectual pursuit alone—it must be lived, felt, embodied.

Emotional integration allows wisdom to settle into the body, where it takes root, not as fleeting insight, but as unshakable knowing *(Source: McCraty, 2010)*.

We are not prisoners of our past, nor passive recipients of the stories we inherit. We are creators. And with every choice, every revelation, every moment of awareness, we hold the pen.

The narrative is ours to rewrite.

POWER TO CHOOSE

Having a choice is the most fundamental power we possess. It is the act of selecting a direction, a belief, or an attitude in response to the circumstances we face. But what if we understood that every belief, every thought, every emotion is a conscious choice? What if we recognized that we are not merely reacting to life—we are actively shaping it?

Science tells us that the mind is a dynamic, evolving system, capable of rewiring itself based on the choices we make. Neuroplasticity demonstrates that the beliefs we hold today are not permanent—they are malleable. We can choose differently, and in doing so, we can change our internal reality. We can redesign the very structure of our perception.

When we awaken to the fact that every belief is a choice, we realize the immense power we have over our lives. We are no longer at the mercy of outdated patterns or subconscious programming. Instead, we step into the role of creator—the co-author of our own becoming.

We can choose expansively.

We can choose abundantly.

We can choose a reality not defined by fear or self-doubt, but by the infinite potential of who we are meant to be.

Just like the Hermetic principle of Mentalism—All is Mind—the universe itself is limitless. And within that vast, uncharted expanse of mind, we hold the power to remodel everything.

Transformation begins with awareness. Once we realize that our beliefs are lenses—patterns shaped by past experiences, societal conditioning, or our own fears— we gain the ability to change them.

The brain responds to the narrative we feed it. By questioning the limiting stories we've accepted as truths, we can choose to replace them with new beliefs that serve our highest potential. In doing so, we don't just alter our thinking—we rewire our brains and transform our lives.

Meditation or contemplation quiets the noise of ingrained thought patterns, opening the mind to new possibilities. Cognitive reframing allows us to shift our perspective, dismantling old constructs and making space for expansive perspectives.

Self-affirmation statements imprint these new beliefs into our neural pathways, reinforcing them until they become part of our identity. These techniques are not just abstract practices—they are scientifically proven tools for reprogramming the mind, healing emotional wounds, and expanding human prospective.

The power to transform has always been within us. It is the power to choose—at every moment, in every thought, in every action. And once we choose differently, everything begins to change.

Examples:

1. A Belief About Self-Worth

- As a child, if you were often told **"You're not good enough"**, your subconscious may adopt this belief.
- As an adult, you might unknowingly **self-sabotage opportunities** because the subconscious seeks to confirm its programming.
- **Cognitive Reframing:** By challenging limiting beliefs and replacing them with empowering ones, we shift our mental filters. If you replace your self-worth belief with "I am constantly growing and evolving", it rewires self-perception. *(Source: Beck, 1976)*

2. A Belief About Lack of Money

- If you grew up hearing **"Money doesn't grow on trees"**, your subconscious might associate wealth with struggle.
- This can lead to **scarcity mindset behaviors**, like undercharging for your work, devaluing your time, or fearing financial success.
- **Visualization:** Studies on mental rehearsal show that imagining a desired reality

strengthens neural connections, making it easier to embody new beliefs *(Source: Lazar, 2005)*. Visualization paired with deep meditative states can bypass the analytical mind and program the subconscious directly.

3. A Belief About Relationships

- If you experienced **abandonment or emotional neglect**, your subconscious may develop the belief **"Love isn't safe"**.
- This can manifest in **fear of intimacy, anxious attachment, or choosing emotionally unavailable partners**.
- **Emotional Integration:** Simply repeating affirmations is not enough; beliefs shift when paired with emotional intensity. Research on heart-brain coherence suggests that aligning thoughts with elevated emotions (such as gratitude or love) amplifies transformation *(Source: McCraty, 2010)*.

In every moment, you have the power to make a conscious decision—to choose a different path and create new timelines.

You are not bound by the beliefs you inherited.

You are not a prisoner of the subconscious programming that has shaped your past.

The power to transform your reality begins with the simple yet profound awareness that you hold the ability to choose new beliefs.

RELEASING THE FAMILIAR

While choice is the ability to select a path or belief, willpower is the inner strength that sustains and empowers us to follow through on that choice, even when challenges arise. *Choice is the decision, the spark; willpower is the resolve to act on it consistently, the flame that sustains it.*

However, changing deeply ingrained beliefs requires more than willpower—it calls for a rewiring of the brain. Scientific research on self-directed neuroplasticity reveals that with focused attention and mindfulness, we can consciously override automatic responses, reshaping our neural pathways with deliberate effort (*Source: Schwartz & Begley, 2002, The Mind and the Brain*).

This insight forms the foundation for transformation—one that begins with shifting perception and reshaping attitude.

Perception and attitude are intrinsically connected. A single shift in perception—a new lens through which to view an old issue—can trigger a transformation in attitude.

In turn, changing an attitude often demands a series of perception shifts, each one dismantling the old narrative, making room for something new to emerge.

Both require courage. The courage to see the world differently and the bravery to release what is familiar, even when it has become comfortable. Yet in mastering this, we hold the power to change not only how we navigate the world but how we experience it at its deepest core.

Attitudes are not just thoughts; they are deeply woven into our emotions. A thought can trigger neural circuits, releasing chemicals that immediately manifest as an emotion. For instance, a single insecure thought can spiral into a pervasive feeling of self-doubt, affecting our entire state of being.

The brain, in its tremendous intelligence, recognizes this emotion and reinforces it, generating more thoughts aligned with that feeling. This creates a feedback loop where thinking fuels feeling, and feeling reinforces thinking, cementing the attitude that shapes our reality. But attitudes are not static.

They shift constantly. What begins as a thought pattern eventually becomes entrenched in the subconscious, seeping into our beliefs and sculpting the foundation of our existence.

Most people live as reactive beings, allowing external circumstances to dictate their emotional states. When life is smooth, they feel uplifted; when challenges arise, they feel defeated.

In this cycle, they become victims of their environment. But what if we could break free? What if we could face life's trials with conscious choice, not automatic reactions?

Mastering this shift is not just about mental discipline; it's about reclaiming control over our internal world. By choosing to act differently, we can reform our beliefs and emotions, altering the course of our lives.

The greatest obstacle to change is the gravitational pull of strong emotions. These powerful feelings tether us to the past, reinforcing the cycles that keep us stuck. To disrupt this pattern, we must cultivate the ability to regulate our emotions with a *Coherent Heart*—a skill that requires awareness, resilience, intention, and emotional intelligence.

This mastery is not mere self-discipline. It is liberation. By shifting perception and altering attitude, we gain the ability to redefine our lives—not as victims of external circumstances, but as conscious creators of our reality.

SHIFTING PERCEPTION

Perception isn't just about what we see—it's how we make sense of the world around us. It's a unique filter shaped by our beliefs, emotions, and past experiences. *(Source: Palmer, S. E., 1999, Vision Science: Photons to Phenomenology)*

To shift perception is to change the lens through which we experience reality, reinterpreting events to reshape their meaning. This process unfolds in the higher centers of the mind, where reason and introspection gently challenge the instinctive pull of emotional reactivity.

It is cognitive alchemy—the art of transmuting raw experience into a new, elevated narrative.

Imagine this: you are cut off in traffic. In an instant, irritation flares—your mind brands the other driver as reckless, inconsiderate, maybe even hostile. It's a quick emotional reaction, fueled by instinct.

But what if, instead, you shift your perspective? What if you imagine they're rushing to an emergency, desperate to reach a loved one in distress?

With that single reframing, anger dissolves. Understanding and compassion takes its place. The event itself remains unchanged, but your interpretation has evolved. Suddenly, your entire state of being transforms—more peaceful, less tension.

Neuroscience illuminates the mechanics behind this shift. The prefrontal cortex—the seat of reason—engages, guiding the way sensory input is processed. At the same time, the amygdala, the brain's emotional epicenter, begins to loosen its grip, softening the surge of reactive impulses.

Over time, as these perception shifts become habitual, neural pathways are rewired. The mind becomes more adaptive, more resilient—no longer a slave to external circumstances, but empowered from within.

CHANGING ATTITUDE

Attitudes are the culmination of repeated thoughts, emotions, and behaviors, creating patterns that shape our relationship with the world. Shifting an attitude means reprogramming these ingrained tendencies, rewiring habitual emotional responses into something new.

Consider someone who carries a deep-seated fear of public speaking. Their attitude, formed by past experiences and internalized beliefs, fuels a cycle of avoidance and self-doubt. To change this, they must do more than challenge their thoughts. They must actively recondition their emotions and behaviors, breaking free from old patterns through deliberate, courageous action.

Repetition becomes the sculptor of the new self, carving fresh neural pathways and reshaping the body's emotional responses. Each small success—the thrill of delivering a well-received speech—triggers the brain's reward systems, gradually replacing fear with confidence.

Over time, what began as a conscious effort becomes a deeply ingrained part of self. Changing an attitude runs deeper than simply altering thoughts—it's an alteration of our beliefs, which forms the foundation for our attitudes; they shape the lens through which we perceive the world, influencing how we feel and respond to situations.

When we change our beliefs—especially limiting or negative ones—we alter the framework governing our thoughts and emotions. This shift naturally leads to a change in attitude, shifting our outlook toward life, challenges, and others.

Conversely, when we consciously choose to shift our attitude, it can trigger a reexamination of our beliefs. For example, adopting a more optimistic attitude toward difficult circumstances might prompt us to challenge and replace ingrained programs of helplessness or defeat.

The act of adjusting our attitude creates space for new, empowering beliefs to take root. This forms a feedback loop: new attitudes reinforce new beliefs, and evolving beliefs sustain a positive, inspired repetition of patterns.

Essentially, changing beliefs leads to a fundamental shift in how we feel and react, while altering our attitude can catalyze the transformation of the deeper beliefs that shape our reality. Both work in tandem to create lasting change.

Raising Awareness

It all begins with raising awareness—the transformative act of recognizing what's within.

At its core, awareness is the state of being conscious or knowledgeable about something—the moment we recognize something that was once unseen. It is the brain's ability to perceive, process knowledge, and interpret both the external world and our internal landscapes. (*Source: Weber, R. P., & Crandall, R., 2007*)

This dynamic process activates intricate neural circuits, particularly in the prefrontal cortex—the command center of our higher cognition—shaping our attention, decision-making, and self-regulation.

Awareness is a fluid dance between sensing and interpreting. Incoming stimuli weaves into the fabric of our past experiences, memories, and emotions, allowing us to reflect consciously, adapt to life's uncertainties, and take purposeful action.

In essence, awareness is the pulse of our consciousness, guiding us to attune to the ebb and flow of the world within and around us.

Yet, all too often, our minds run on autopilot, silently governed by deeply ingrained beliefs—hidden forces that shape 95% of our thoughts and actions.

These subconscious patterns, formed by past experiences, propel us forward without question or conscious examination. We are often carried by currents we cannot see, moved by beliefs we have yet to recognize.

To break free from these invisible forces, we must pause, take a deliberate breath, and shine a light on these unexamined beliefs.

Only in that brief moment of heightened introspection can we begin to rewrite our personal narrative and reclaim control of our lives.

Conscious Choice

This is where our true power resides: in the conscious act of choice. The moment we decide to challenge a limiting belief, we awaken the prefrontal cortex—the brain's center for decision-making and intentional thought.

This is no mere mental exercise. Neuroimaging reveals that this conscious decision physically reshapes our brain, carving new neural pathways in the process.

Imagine it as blazing a trail through an untamed forest—rough and unyielding at first, each step feeling unfamiliar and challenging. But with persistence, the path clears, and over time, this once-daunting journey becomes second nature, instinctively followed.

Change does not happen in an instant; it unfolds through repetition. Dr. Tara Swart, in *The Source*, highlights the power of consistency in neuroplasticity: the brain rewires itself in response to repeated stimuli. With every intentional choice to replace a limiting belief with an empowering thought, we cultivate a new mental landscape.

Whether through affirmations, visualizations, or simply being fully present in the moment, we begin to reshape the very architecture of our minds. In this process of transformation, we aren't merely changing our thoughts—we are rewiring the very fabric of our reality.

EMOTIONAL ALIGNMENT & MASTERY

Our emotions don't just follow our thoughts; they fuel them. As Dr. Joe Dispenza writes in *Breaking the Habit of Being Yourself*, aligning our emotional state with the new beliefs we wish to adopt strengthens the neural connections that sustain them.

When we truly feel the change we want to embody—when we align our heart with our thoughts—we accelerate the rewiring process. This emotional resonance creates an energetic force that deepens our commitment to the new path, transforming thought into lasting belief.

The power of conscious choice lies not only in intellectual understanding but in our active participation in shaping our reality. Every time we confront and challenge a limiting belief, we activate our brain's potential for transformation. It's as if, through this gentle persistence, we reprogram the very essence of our experience. We move from a place of limitation to one of boundless possibilities.

By embracing the science of neuroplasticity, we unlock the perspective that we are not trapped by the conditioning of our past. We are, in fact, the authors of our own stories.

Through conscious choice, we hold the pen that rewrites our beliefs—and with it, our entire life's narrative. Through conscious choice, we are not prisoners of our past beliefs. We are the creators of our future.

The brain, far from being a passive recipient of life's circumstances, is an active participant in the construction of our reality. With every decision, we reshape our beliefs and, in turn, our experience of the world.

This journey requires patience, mindfulness, and trust in the process. But with each choice, we draw closer to the version of ourselves we were always meant to be. Through the power of conscious choice, we transcend the parameters of our old beliefs and step into the limitless possibilities.

In the end, transformation is an active choice. It is the willingness to challenge perception, shift attitude, and rewire the subconscious mind.

PLACEBO EFFECT & NEUROPLASTICITY

Let's explore the phenomenon where a person's belief in the effectiveness of a treatment triggers real physiological changes in the body, even when the treatment has no active medical properties.

Neuroscience defines the placebo effect as "a brain-mediated response where the belief in a treatment triggers neural and biochemical responses that lead to real, physical health improvements."

This underscores how the mind's expectations and beliefs can influence the body's physiological processes and highlights the profound connection between belief and healing.

While science focuses on how belief can trigger chemical reactions in the brain that lead to physical improvements, metaphysics expands on the idea that belief and intention can shift our energy and align us with healing on a deeper level.

Both perspectives emphasize the incredible power of the mind to influence the body and our reality. When a person believes they are receiving a treatment that will help them, the brain responds by releasing chemicals that can reduce pain, boost mood, and promote healing.

This phenomenon bridges the gap between science and metaphysics, showing how our beliefs and expectations shape our reality and influence our health.

From a scientific standpoint, the placebo effect occurs when a person experiences genuine improvement after receiving a treatment with no active medical properties—whether it's a sugar pill, saline injection, or sham procedure. The power lies not in the treatment itself, but in the individual's belief that they are receiving a healing intervention.

This belief activates the brain's natural healing mechanisms, triggering the release of endorphins (natural pain relievers) and dopamine (a neurotransmitter that regulates mood and motivation).

Studies have shown that people who believe in the effectiveness of a placebo often experience significant improvements in pain management, mood, and even conditions like depression. The brain's reward and pain-relief systems are activated, creating physiological changes in response to the mind's expectation of healing.

Key Mechanisms in the Placebo Effect:

- **Expectation:** The anticipation of benefit activates brain circuits related to reward and healing.

- **Endorphins:** These natural painkillers are released, easing pain, and enhancing well-being.
- **Dopamine:** This "feel-good" neurotransmitter boosts mood, motivation, and recovery.

Neuroscientific studies using brain imaging have revealed that when a person expects healing, regions of the brain involved in pain processing, such as the prefrontal cortex and thalamus, show increased activity. This supports the idea that belief alone can alter the body's biological responses, even in the absence of any real pharmacological intervention.

Consciousness and Energy

From a metaphysical perspective, the placebo effect exemplifies the profound connection between consciousness, energy, and physical health. In this view, the mind's beliefs and intentions have the power to shift the energy fields within the body, aligning them with a desired state of wellness.

Belief in healing isn't just a thought—it's an energetic charge that influences the body's vibratory field and can lead to actual physical changes. This metaphysical lens suggests that our consciousness is not confined to our mind but extends into the physical world, actively shaping our experiences. The placebo effect serves as a reminder that we are not passive recipients of our environment, but active participants in creating our reality.

When we believe in healing, we tap into a powerful energy Source capable of transmuting our physical state and manifesting wellness. The placebo effect serves as a testament to how consciousness can influence our bodies, overriding perceived physical limitations and opening the door to profound healing. *(Source: Dr. Bruce Lipton, 2020)*

Both scientific and metaphysical perspectives converge on one powerful perspective: belief is transformative.

The science behind the placebo effect reveals how the brain, influenced by belief, can activate biological responses that improve health. Meanwhile, the metaphysical perspective sees belief as a form of energy that can align the body with a higher state of health.

Together, these views underscore the extraordinary power of the mind to influence the body and our reality—reminding us that healing begins not just in the body, but in the mind.

By understanding the placebo effect from both perspectives, we unlock the incredible potential of our own minds to heal, transform, and create.

BEHAVIOR & BRAINWAVE ALCHEMY

The brain's extraordinary neuroplasticity is a powerful reminder that we are not bound by our past beliefs.

It has the remarkable ability to reorganize itself and forge new neural connections throughout life, offering a pathway to transformation. You can rewire limiting beliefs and replace them with empowering ones by engaging in specific practices designed to engage the brain's plasticity.

Transformation begins with awareness—the courage to confront the subconscious beliefs that shape our reality. Next, reprogramming the subconscious mind is essential. Repetition, particularly through affirmations, is a powerful tool for change. Over time, these new beliefs strengthen, replacing old, limiting thought patterns and reshaping how you view yourself and the world around you.

To accelerate this shift, incorporate neuroplasticity practices like visualization, meditation, and breathwork. These methods actively stimulate new neural connections, reprogramming both your mind and emotional responses. With focused intention, you reshape the very structure of your brain, guiding it toward a reality that aligns with your highest potential.

Healing is also necessary on an emotional level. Past trauma leaves energy imprints that skew our responses to life. Releasing this stored emotional energy creates space for healthier patterns to emerge, allowing you to respond with greater clarity, freedom, and grace.

The brain is not static—it is a dynamic, ever-evolving organ. By consciously engaging with these techniques, you can reshape your beliefs, heal emotional scars, and rewire your mind. Through intentional practice, you hold the power to transform your life.

The Golden Thread

Across every mystical tradition, there exists a golden thread—a certainty that ties them all together: belief is the fundamental force that shapes our reality.

It is the secret ingredient behind healing through the mind, the engine behind extraordinary success, and the catalyst for astonishing transformations. It is the quiet power that drives everything—if you truly accept and apply it.

Our beliefs—whether positive or negative—are largely stored and operated from the subconscious. It is not just a passive notion; it is the force that makes things happen. The idea that thought attracts that upon which it is directed is not just philosophy—it is a law of the universe.

Fearful thoughts are as potent in creating outcomes as enthusiastic, empowering thoughts. Both are magnetic, drawing to you exactly what you believe. It is not a question of whether thoughts are creative; it is a question of what kind of thoughts you choose to create.

When this viewpoint pierces your consciousness, you begin to sense the awe-inspiring power at your disposal. However, you must truly feel the belief on a deep, soul-shaking level—a conviction that flows through every cell of your being. It is more than thought; it is an emotional and spiritual force that vibrates through the universe, attracting the results your heart desires.

This force is the spark that ignites the Law of Attraction. When thought is sustained and aligned with purpose, it becomes the vehicle for manifesting reality.

Like a magnet, it draws forth subconscious forces, aligning your coherent mind and heart with your highest potential. Your aura shifts, and suddenly, people, places, and opportunities that were once far away begin to gravitate toward you. The world begins to bend to your will.

To many, the idea that all power is within may seem unfathomable. But consider this: nothing exists on the external plane unless it first exists within your mind. Your inner vision is what gives birth to the outer world. Your mind's eye is the designer of your reality, shaping it with every thought you think.

Know yourself. Understand your power. Surround yourself with knowledge of what is possible. Immerse yourself in the stories of those who've walked the path of belief and emerged victorious with healthy curiosity. Read their words, watch their videos, engage with their energy. Let it become your inspiration, and let your own belief become your guide.

The mind is a tool, and when it is trained to believe, it will no longer serve doubt. It will serve your greatest vision. Act as though your belief has already manifested. Choose decisions from the space of your already realized goal. Every action strengthens your conviction and reinforces your reality.

Your beliefs are more than personal thoughts; they are energetic signals that ripple through your entire field. The stronger your conviction, the more effortlessly the world aligns with your inner vision. Reality doesn't need to be convinced—it already mirrors your energetic state.

What you believe is what you create. The stronger your belief, the faster the universe bends in your favor. This is not magic—it is the profound, unstoppable force of belief in action. So, believe in yourself, deeply, truly, and without hesitation. You deserve the life your heart desires.

QUANTUM PLAYBOOK: REWRITING CORE NARRATIVES

The mind and body are inseparable, and science proves it. Healing begins with understanding belief—

not as a conscious choice, but as a deeply ingrained survival response. Symptoms persist because your nervous system is protecting you, shielding you from overwhelming emotions or buried pain.

By identifying, deconstructing, and replacing limiting narratives with empowering convictions, you can break free from self-imposed restrictions and unlock the gateway to manifestation.

These techniques draw on evidence-based practices from neuroscience, psychology, and mindfulness, providing a transformative framework for self-mastery and growth.

Step 1: Identify the Root of the Belief

Every limiting belief has an origin—a past experience, cultural conditioning, or a childhood imprint that shaped your self-perception.

Ask Yourself:

- What is one belief that holds me back the most?
- Where did this belief originate? (A childhood experience? Society? A past failure?)
- Whose voice is attached to this belief? Is it mine, or someone else's?

Write down or journal about a core limiting belief and trace it back to its first memory. Recognizing where it began is the first step in releasing its grip. Here are some examples:

- "I am not enough."
- "My worth depends on what I achieve."
- "I have to prove myself to be loved and seen."
- "If I make mistakes, I will be judged or rejected."
- "I must be perfect to be accepted."
- "Why does this always happen to me, I'm jinxed."
- "Money doesn't grow on trees."
- "We can't afford that."
- "I'm not smart or talented enough."
- "Hard work = struggle."
- "The world is dangerous."
- "I have to always be on guard."
- "Bad things always happen to me."
- "I can't trust people."
- "I am not safe in my body."

Neuroscience Insight: The amygdala stores emotional memories, which shape unconscious beliefs. Bringing these memories to conscious awareness weakens their automatic influence *(Dr. Daniel Siegel, Mindsight)*. Studies show that Cognitive Behavioral Therapy helps identify negative thought patterns, allowing individuals to recognize and challenge their old stories *(Beck, A. T., Cognitive Therapy)*.

Affirmation: *I am safe to explore and release my old beliefs.*

Step 2: Challenge and Deconstruct its Validity

A belief only holds power when it goes unquestioned. When you challenge it, it loses its foundation when you debunk the scarcity mindset. You realize that they are often based on outdated or false information.

- Is this belief 100% true in all cases? (Has anyone ever proven otherwise?)
- What evidence contradicts it? (Find real-life proof that challenges the belief.)
- What would I tell a friend who believed this about themselves?

Write down a limiting belief you hold, or perception of lack then list three pieces of evidence that prove it wrong. Example:

- Belief: "I always fail when I try something new."
- Contradictory Evidence:
  - I learned to walk as a baby—I failed and got back up countless times.
  - I didn't know how to drive until I practiced, and now it's second nature.
  - I once believed I couldn't do something and then proved myself wrong.

Psychological Insight: Cognitive Behavioral Therapy demonstrates that questioning negative thoughts weakens their influence, allowing for new, rational thinking to take root *(Dr. Aaron Beck, Cognitive Therapy)*. Neuroplasticity research shows that the brain rewires itself through conscious practice and repetition *(Doidge, N., The Brain That Changes Itself)*.

Affirmation: *My past does not define my future. I am rewriting my story.*

Step 3: Rewire the Belief Through Empowering Alternatives

To reprogram the subconscious, it's not enough to simply deconstruct limiting beliefs—you must actively replace them with positive, empowering thoughts and reinforce them consistently. This repetition rewires your brain and solidifies new neural pathways.

As the saying goes, "Neurons that fire together, wire together." The more you repeat a new belief, the stronger it becomes creating lasting transformation.

- Affirm it daily – Speak your new belief out loud with conviction.
- Feel it as your objective truth – Emotion solidifies new neural pathways *(Dr. Joe Dispenza, Becoming Supernatural)*.
- Visualize it – Engage your senses and imagine yourself already embodying the belief.

Rewrite your limiting belief into an empowering affirmation and say it 3 times daily while looking in the mirror. Example:

- Old Belief: "I am not worthy of success."
- New Belief: "I am fully worthy of success, prosperity, abundance, and fulfillment."

Neuroscience Insight: Studies show that repeating affirmations activate the reward system in the brain, increasing self-confidence and motivation (*Dr. Christopher Cascio, Neural Correlates of Self-Affirmation*). Visualization has also been shown to activate the same neural circuits as actual experience, enhancing belief and behavior change.

Affirmation: *I choose to believe in my limitless potential.*

Step 4: Take Aligned Action to Reinforce the New Belief

Rewiring subconscious beliefs requires consistent practice. Just as it takes time to develop negative thought patterns, it takes time to establish new, positive ones. The fastest way to solidify a new belief is to act as if it's already true.

- **Create New Habits**: If you truly feel that you are worthy of success, the next step is to act in alignment with that belief by forming new habits that reflect it. Start small but intentional actions—applying for that job you desire, taking on new challenges, or making decisions that elevate you to your highest potential. Every action reinforces your belief, making it not just a thought, but a living reality.

- **Use Anchors:** Associate a physical gesture (e.g., tapping your fingers together or placing your hand over your heart) with your empowering beliefs. Over time, this anchor will activate the positive belief when you need it most.

- Surround yourself with people who reinforce this mindset.

- Identify one small action that aligns with your new belief and take it today. Speak up in a meeting, introduce yourself to someone new, or start a project you've been postponing.

Psychological Insight: Studies show that habitual practice (at least 21-66 days) is essential to shifting ingrained neural pathways (*Lally, P., How Are Habits Formed*).

Affirmation: *I embody confidence and take action toward my highest self.*

Step 5: Reinforce the New Identity with Emotional Integration

For lasting transformation, it is crucial to integrate the emotional aspect of healing. Emotional resistance can prevent the full release of limiting beliefs. Change is not a one-time event—it is a daily long term practice of shifting attitudes and perception.

- **Somatic Healing:** Engage in somatic practices like yoga, breathwork, or body scanning to release trapped emotions associated with limiting beliefs.
- **Emotional Freedom Techniques** (EFT): Use tapping to release negative emotions and beliefs stored in the body *(Church, D., The EFT Manual).*

Every Sunday, journal about progress:

- What belief changes have I noticed?
- What challenges came up? How did I navigate them?
- What actions will I take next week to reinforce my new belief?

Quantum Insight: Studies suggest that somatic therapies and mindfulness-based practices can rewire the brain by integrating body-mind connection in the healing process *(Van der Kolk, B. A., The Body Keeps the Score).*

Affirmation: *I am the architect of my mind. I choose thoughts that align with my highest potential.*

Rewiring your subconscious beliefs is a dynamic, ongoing process that combines awareness, emotional release, repetition, and consistent alignment with your highest potential. By practicing these evidence-based techniques, you can break free from the chains of limiting beliefs and engage the power of mental alchemy.

4. Understanding Neuroscience

Your brain is not static—it is a masterpiece in motion, rewiring itself with every thought you think, every choice you make, and every emotion you feel.

Neuroscience confirms that every mental and emotional emittance strengthens or reshapes neural pathways, actively influencing how you perceive and interact with the world. This means transformation isn't just possible—it's inevitable if you learn to harness it.

In these pages, we'll explore the science of neuroplasticity—not just to understand it, but to apply it with intention. You'll discover how to harness the pathways of change to overcome self-doubt, shift lifelong behaviors, and step into the fullest version of yourself.

Because once you realize your brain is always changing, you gain the power to modify it with purpose. And when you do that, you don't just shift your thoughts—you transform your entire reality. *(Source: Doidge, N., 2007, The Brain That Changes Itself)*

Boosting Our Brain Chemicals

The brain's chemicals are its concerto, orchestrating every thought, feeling, and action with precise harmony. The following neurotransmitters act as messengers, coursing through neural pathways to influence mood, incentive, and energy. *(Source: National Institute of Mental Health, 2023)*

Dopamine: The "reward chemical" drives motivation, pleasure, and goal-directed behavior, creating satisfaction when objectives are achieved. For a boost:

- Engage in activities like reading, cleaning, lifting weights, eating protein-rich foods, or setting and completing small tasks.

Serotonin: The "happiness molecule" regulates mood, sleep, appetite, and emotional balance, fostering calm and well-being. For a boost:

- Bask in the morning sunlight, enjoy fresh fruits, practice slow, deep breathing, sip herbal tea, prioritize deep sleep, or take rejuvenating naps.

Norepinephrine: The "focus enhancer" improves alertness, energy, and attention, helping the body adapt to stress and challenges. For a boost:

- Engage in activities that stimulate mental focus, such as setting priorities, practicing mindfulness, or exercising.

Oxytocin: Known as the "bonding hormone," it enhances trust, emotional connection, and social bonding, especially during caregiving or intimacy. For a boost:

- Hug loved ones, spend time with pets, show acts of kindness, or listen and make eye contact, in service for humanity and helping others, engage in meaningful social connections.

Endorphins: The body's natural painkillers, they ease discomfort and create euphoria, often referred to as a "runner's high." For a boost:

- Laugh, exercise, sing, enjoy dark chocolate, dance, or move to uplifting music.

Glutamate: The brain's primary neurotransmitter, crucial for learning, memory, and adaptability. For a boost:

- Engage in mentally stimulating activities, such as puzzles, gathering new skills, learning about neuroscience, or creative pursuits.

GABA (Gamma-Aminobutyric Acid): The "calmness chemical," reduces neural activity to promote relaxation and ease anxiety. For a boost:

- Practice meditation, sit in quiet contemplation, yoga, mindfulness, or consume GABA-supporting foods like green tea and fermented foods.

The relationship between brain chemicals and the nervous system is a dynamic, interconnected process where neurotransmitters drive the system's activity and work together to maintain balance, shaping emotional and physical well-being. This delicate balance structures not just how we feel but how we experience life itself.

Yet, in a world engineered for instant gratification, we are conditioned to seek fulfillment in illusions. For example, watching porn offers the mirage of intimacy without connection. Alcohol numbs the senses while masquerading as joy. Smoking imitates calm yet erodes vitality.

Junk food promises nourishment but leaves the body starving for true sustenance. Social media feeds the delusion of belonging while deepening isolation. Online shopping provides fleeting excitement yet never satisfies the soul's hunger for meaning.

Do not trade the richness of the human experience for synthetic dopamine. True fulfillment cannot be found in artificial reality—it is cultivated in presence, in nature's depth, in the raw, unfiltered beauty of pure authentic living.

NERVOUS SYSTEM'S COMMAND CENTER

Imagine possessing the universe's most intricate masterpiece—an orchestra of billions of neurons, firing in electric synchrony, sculpting every thought, memory, and sensation. Your brain is not merely an organ; it is the command center, weaving the fabric of reality itself.

Within this labyrinth of synapses and circuits of your supercomputer, your past is stored, your present is perceived, and your future is imagined into being.

Neuroscience unveils the hidden architecture of the mind—an ever-adapting network where thoughts spark chemical cascades, beliefs sculpt neural pathways, and the stories we tell ourselves shape the reality we experience.

But how does this enigmatic powerhouse function? How do thoughts emerge, emotions ignite, and beliefs become the invisible engineers of our destiny?

The Grand Design

We understand that the nervous system is a vast and intricate network, orchestrating every thought, movement, and sensation, yet much of its complexity remains a mystery.

A century ago, the idea of controlling objects with the mind was pure science fiction. Today, thanks to advancements in brain-computer interfaces, individuals can operate bionic limbs using neural signals alone.

Research by Miguel Nicolelis at Duke University demonstrated that primates could control robotic arms through brain activity, paving the way for human applications. Similarly, brain injury treatments have seen remarkable progress.

Studies using functional magnetic resonance and diffusion tensor imaging have provided unprecedented insights into neural connectivity and plasticity, enabling targeted rehabilitation.

Neuroscientists like Eric Kandel have shown how synaptic changes underlie learning and memory, reinforcing the brain's ability to rewire itself.

By mapping neural activity across macroscopic, microscopic, and nanoscopic scales, researchers continue to unravel the mysteries of cognition, perception, and consciousness.

These breakthroughs offer profound insights into memory, attention, language, and emotions—the very essence of what it means to be human.

At the core of human experience lies a sprawling city with highways of information—the nervous system, divided into two realms:

- **The Central Nervous System (CNS):** The Throne of Consciousness
  - The brain and spinal cord reign supreme here, orchestrating thought, movement, perception, and emotion. Every decision, every sensation, every whisper of intuition is processed within this intricate hub of cognition.

- **The Peripheral Nervous System (PNS):** The Messenger of Reality
  - Extending outward like the roots of an ancient tree, the PNS connects the CNS to every muscle, organ, and tissue. It bridges the body and brain, ensuring that sensations are felt, commands are executed, and survival instincts remain sharp.

Within this vast system lies a delicate balance—the sympathetic nervous system, which ignites the fight-or-flight response, and the parasympathetic nervous system, which soothes the body into rest and restoration.

In the dance of survival and serenity, these forces dictate the rhythm of our existence.

Neurons as Cosmic Architects

Every thought, every emotion, every flicker of awareness is carried by neurons—the brain's celestial architects. These microscopic wonders are the messengers of consciousness, conducting electrical and chemical signals that shape our inner and outer worlds.

Neurons are specialized cells responsible for receiving and transmitting information throughout the body. The brain contains approximately 86 billion neurons, each intricately connected by trillions of synapses, allowing for the complex web of communication that governs thought, sensation, and action *(Source: Azevedo, 2009)*.

Each neuron is composed of:

- **Dendrites:** The seekers, reaching out to receive wisdom from neighboring cells.
- **Axons:** The transmitters, carrying messages across vast neural landscapes.
- **Synapses:** The portals, where neurotransmitters whisper secrets from one neuron to another.
- **Myelin Sheath:** The accelerators, ensuring that information travels at the speed of thought.

The neurons found in the heart's network are primarily located in the ganglia and work together to control heart rate and rhythm, as well as the communication between the heart and brain *(Source: Armour, 2004)*. They form a part of the enteric nervous system, which is often referred to as the "second brain" because of its ability to operate independently *(Source: Furman, 2014)*.

Through the heart-brain connection, the heart's neurons allow us to experience emotions such as love, fear, and empathy, offering insight into how deeply intertwined our emotions are with our physiological state. This intricate network of light is how reality is woven, moment by moment.

COGNITIVE REFRAMING & MENTAL ALCHEMY

Reality is not fixed—it is filtered through neural pathways shaped by past experiences. Cognitive reframing, rooted in neuroplasticity, rewires the brain by disrupting old thought loops and forging new, empowering connections *(Source: Beck, 1976; Doidge, 2007)*.

Each time you reinterpret a challenge, you weaken limiting beliefs and reinforce resilience *(Source: Davidson & McEwen, 2012)*. This is mental alchemy— the art of transforming perception into power.

By shifting your internal narrative and identity, you don't just change your thoughts; you remap your brain, rewire your reality, and transmute limitation into limitless potential. This transformation is anchored in the pillars of cognition:

1. Memory: Designer of Identity

Memory, and the intricate process of memorization, has long been a subject of fascination and mystery. For centuries, its mechanisms remained elusive, hidden within the depths of the brain.

It was only with the advent of medical imaging—such as PET scans—that scientists could map the specific regions of the brain and central nervous system responsible for encoding, storing, and retrieving information.

This deeper understanding has proven invaluable, particularly in diagnosing and treating neurodegenerative diseases like Alzheimer's, where memory is progressively impaired. By identifying the neural pathways involved, researchers can develop targeted interventions and preventative strategies to preserve cognitive function.

The good news is that memory can be strengthened at any stage of life. Through deliberate practice, cognitive exercises, and lifestyle adjustments, we can enhance our ability to learn, retain, and recall information.

Memory is the keeper of time, the thread that binds our past to the present. Without it, our sense of self would dissolve into an eternal now. But memory is not a singular entity—it is a vast network of impressions, experiences, and emotions stored across different regions of the brain:

- **Hippocampus:** The librarian of long-term memory, transforming fleeting moments into permanent imprints.
- **Amygdala:** The guardian of emotional memory, searing intense experiences into the subconscious.
- **Prefrontal Cortex:** The strategist, organizing thoughts, making connections, and retrieving information.

Memories evolve, reshape, and fade. With each recall, we reconstruct the past, subtly altering its narrative—reminding us that both our past and future are malleable.

2. Attention: Sculptor of Reality

Attention, derived from the Latin *attentio*, meaning "the act of turning one's mind towards," is the gateway to perception, learning, and memory.

To grasp its essence, we can turn to the pioneering American psychologist William James, who, in his seminal 1890 work *The Principles of Psychology*, described attention as "the taking possession by the mind, in clear and vivid form, of one out of what seem several simultaneously possible objects or trains of thought."

This act of mental selection is the foundation of cognition, shaping how we interact with the world.

Neuropsychologist Eric Sieroff expands on this, emphasizing that attention is not merely passive observation but an active process that enables individuals to direct their actions toward specific stimuli. It allows crucial information to remain in working memory, ensuring that essential details are not lost amid the constant influx of sensory input.

A fitting metaphor for attention is that of a beam of light—at any given moment, it illuminates a particular area while leaving the rest in shadow. Just as a spotlight on a stage highlights one performer while the others fade into darkness, our attention isolates a subject, action, or thought from the sea of competing stimuli.

However, attention is not infinite. It is a fleeting, dynamic force, shifting naturally from one focus to another. This transient nature is not a flaw but an evolutionary necessity.

Prolonged fixation on a single task can overwhelm the neural circuits, much like an electrical system overloaded by excessive current. Without the ability to disengage and redirect, the mind would succumb to cognitive exhaustion, unable to process new information or adapt to changing circumstances.

Thus, attention is both a gift and a limitation—a tool that sharpens perception, fuels learning, and guides action, yet one that must be managed wisely to maintain mental balance and efficiency.

Research has revealed that attention operates with distinct characteristics that shape how we process information. Reaction time, for instance, is directly influenced by the number of distractions present—more distractions lead to slower responses. *(Source: Forster, S., & Lavie, N., 2007)*

At the same time, attention follows a sequential process, handling information in a precise order while seamlessly integrating multiple data points into a coherent whole. When functioning automatically, it efficiently filters out irrelevant stimuli, isolating what truly matters.

Where attention goes, energy flows.

Beyond filtering, attention enhances readiness by signaling when to act. Automatic attention oversees routine processes that require little effort, while voluntary attention directs focus toward critical elements and events.

Memorization and learning would be impossible without attention. This cognitive function enables the body to evolve and adapt gradually to its environment, from birth to adulthood. Built on three fundamental axes—mobilization, allocation of attentional resources, and the rewards obtained after effort—attention plays a crucial role in acquiring knowledge and skills.

Attentional capacity is not static—it evolves over time. At birth, it is fragile and primarily attuned to survival instincts. As individuals grow, their focus broadens, shaped not only by their own experiences but also by the psychological influences of those around them.

From infancy to adulthood, attention is a cornerstone of cognitive and emotional development, adapting continuously to the demands of an ever-changing world.

Attention is the lens through which we filter the infinite stream of information bombarding our senses every second. It determines what we see, hear, and feel—what becomes real.

There are two primary modes of attention:

- **Focused:** The sharp blade of concentration, cutting through distractions to isolate a single thought or task.
- **Divided:** The juggler of the mind, shifting between multiple stimuli in a constant dance of perception.

The reticular activating system (RAS), nestled within the brainstem, acts as the gatekeeper of attention, determining which sensory signals reach the conscious mind. Through meditation, mindfulness, and deliberate practice, we can refine our ability to direct attention with precision, enhancing productivity, creativity, and emotional balance.

3. Language: Alchemy of Thought into Sound

Communication is a fundamental cognitive function, woven into the fabric of human interaction from the very first moments of life.

A newborn's cry is not just an expression of discomfort; it is a primal attempt to connect, a signal that instinctively draws the attention of caregivers. This initial exchange marks the beginning of a lifelong process—one in which the ability to send and receive messages gradually evolves into complex and meaningful communication.

The acquisition of language, though often viewed as a physiological milestone, is far more than a mechanical process of learning words and grammar. It is deeply intertwined with psychological development, shaping an individual's social identity and cognitive growth.

The phenomenon of so-called "Mowgli children"—cases where individuals are deprived of human interaction—illustrates the profound link between communication and socialization. Without communication, the framework of human connection unravels, leaving an individual isolated, unable to integrate into society. *(Source: Lane, H., 1976)*

It is crucial to distinguish between language as a structured system of words and communication as a broader ability to transmit and interpret meaning. While mastering a language involves learning vocabulary and syntax, communication transcends linguistic barriers. It encompasses gestures, expressions, tone, and the intuitive exchange of emotions—elements that form the foundation of human connection.

Given its pivotal role in cognition, neuroscience has devoted significant attention to understanding the mechanisms of communication. Research has uncovered how various brain regions, such as Broca's area and Wernicke's area, facilitate language processing and comprehension.

Studies using functional imaging have demonstrated that communication engages not only linguistic centers but also networks responsible for emotional processing, decision-making, and memory.

The impact of communication on cognitive function is profound, influencing everything from learning to social adaptation. Language is the bridge between minds, the sculptor of civilizations, the essence of human connection. More than mere words, language is the architecture of thought, shaping how we perceive and interact with reality.

The Broca's Area, located in the frontal lobe, is the engine of speech production, while the Wernicke's Area, nestled in the temporal lobe, deciphers meaning from sound. Together, they transform raw thought into spoken word, a process so fluid we rarely pause to appreciate its brilliance.

But language is more than communication—it structures cognition. The words we use define our perceptions, reinforcing beliefs and emotions. By consciously refining our language, we can reshape the narrative of our lives.

4. Emotions: Messenger of the Soul

For centuries, the mystery of emotions has baffled scientists and philosophers alike. How can something so deeply felt, yet so intangible, be explained?

Emotion is more than a fleeting feeling—it's a powerful physiological and psychological state shaped by neural, hormonal, and cognitive processes. These forces influence our behavior and decisions, orchestrated by the brain's limbic system (including the amygdala and hippocampus) and the autonomic nervous system, which regulates heart rate, respiration, and hormones. Together, they prepare the body for action, helping us respond to our environment with precision.

The moods, affect, and feelings are not just reactions but adaptive tools, guiding us through life. They not only help us navigate our surroundings but also shape how we communicate and learn. From primal emotions like fear, joy, and anger, to more complex ones like guilt, pride, and shame, emotions are our internal compass, influencing how we think, remember, and act. *(Source: LeDoux, J. E., 2000, Emotion circuits in the brain)*

Understanding our emotions is challenging enough, but interpreting the emotional states of others? That's a puzzle we're still piecing together. Yet, emotions steer nearly every decision we make—from choosing a life partner to deciding what to wear or eat. In the end, emotions are not just reactions; they are the forces that guide our most fundamental experiences.

Managing our emotions can greatly enhance self-awareness and improve social interactions. Emotional intelligence—the ability to recognize, understand, and regulate emotions—helps us adapt to challenges, build stronger relationships, and navigate life with resilience.

Research shows that emotional learning begins early in childhood, as kids are taught to identify and express feelings, which helps them connect with others. As adults, we continue to refine this emotional adaptability, learning how to manage the complexity of relationships, work, and societal expectations.

In recent years, neuroscience has provided new insights into the biological processes behind emotions. Advanced brain imaging techniques, such as electroencephalography (EEG), have helped us identify key brain areas involved in emotional processing.

Ultimately, emotions are the language of the subconscious—a guide to our inner world. They are not just reactions, but messengers carrying important signals from deep within, helping us navigate the complex terrain of our human experience.

The limbic system, an ancient structure within the brain, is the seat of emotional intelligence. The interaction between these areas can help explain why emotions sometimes override logic, leading to impulsive decisions or heightened stress responses.

- **Amygdala:** Understanding the watchguard of fear, anger, pleasure, and passion.
- **Hypothalamus:** The regulator of stress, pleasure, and bodily rhythms.
- **Prefrontal Cortex:** The grand master of emotional intelligence, regulation, guiding rational responses.

Emotions are not enemies to be suppressed but energy to be acknowledged and understood. By developing emotional awareness and resilience, we can master the art of responding from the *Coherent Heart* rather than reacting, shifting our experiences from suffering to empowerment.

Pathways of Change

Catastrophic thinking is like a storm cloud that distorts reality, making every challenge feel like a disaster waiting to happen. You miss a deadline at work, and suddenly, your mind jumps to the worst-case scenario, "I am going to get fired." Or if a friend takes longer than usual to reply, and you immediately assume they're upset or have lost interest in you.

These thoughts feel real, but they are built on fear, not fact. Left unchecked, this mental habit fuels anxiety, limits your potential, and keeps you trapped in a cycle of self-doubt. Fortunately, you can retrain your brain to break free from this pattern.

Step 1: Recognize the thought for what it is

- The next time you catch yourself spiraling, thinking negative about outcomes that are not based on evidence, pause and call it out. Acknowledge that this fear-based thought isn't grounded in reality but is simply your brain following an old, familiar shortcut—a neural pathway carved from past experiences. Awareness is the first step to breaking the cycle.

Step 2: Shift the narrative

- Instead of fixating on the worst possible outcome, challenge yourself to imagine the best. What if missing the deadline leads to an opportunity to showcase your problem-solving skills? What if your friend is just busy and will respond later with enthusiasm? You don't have to convince yourself that the best-case scenario will happen—just entertain the possibility. Like strengthening a muscle, this practice may feel unnatural at first, but over time, it reshapes how your mind responds to uncertainty.

Step 3: Rewire through repetition

- Your brain is adaptable, capable of forming new neural pathways through repetition and practice. The more often you consciously shift your perspective to consider positive or neutral outcomes, the stronger this new mental habit becomes. Eventually, optimism and rational thinking will feel just as automatic—if not more than catastrophizing.

Your thoughts shape your reality. By retraining your brain to approach challenges with clarity and balance, you empower yourself to move through life with confidence and resilience.

Neuroplasticity research shows that repeated thought patterns physically rewire the brain, altering neural connections and influencing behavior over time (*Source: Doidge, N., 2007*).

Reservoir of Thought Forms

We understand that the subconscious mind is a vast, powerful, unseen force—an invisible engine that quietly shapes our behaviors, emotions, and perceptions. It operates beneath the surface of our awareness, yet its power is undeniable.

Neuroscience has begun to peel back the layers of this profound mental realm, revealing its ability to influence everything from our daily actions to our physical health.

The unconscious mind, in contrast, is deeper and more complex. It holds repressed memories, desires, and experiences that are so deeply buried that they are beyond our normal conscious awareness.

These unconscious elements often stem from trauma, fears, or unresolved emotional conflicts. Unlike the subconscious, the unconscious mind is not easily accessed through typical introspective methods.

It influences us in ways we often don't realize, playing a major role in shaping our overall psyche and driving behaviors.

The unconscious is also home to instincts, primal drives, and deeper urges that can shape our patterns of thinking and feeling in profound ways. Freud, who popularized the concept, believed that many mental imbalances stem from unresolved unconscious conflicts.

In essence, the subconscious mind handles the practical day-to-day functions of our mind, while the unconscious mind carries the emotional and psychological weight of unresolved trauma, fears, and instincts that influence our deeper drives and patterns of behavior. It is where automatic responses, emotional conditioning, and hidden biases govern the very fabric of our lives.

Storage Tank

Imagine the subconscious mind as an enormous vault, storing every experience, emotion, and memory we've ever had. Unlike the conscious mind, which is analytical and focused on the present, the subconscious, a powerful and active processor of psychology, operates in the background, managing and storing information at lightning speed.

It's not just a passive storage space in our intelligent system; *it converts experiences into learned patterns and behaviors that govern how we react. (Source: Bargh, & Morsella, 2008)*

- **Automatic Responses:** The subconscious is responsible for keeping our body running smoothly. It regulates automatic functions like breathing, heartbeat, and digestion, ensuring we don't have to consciously think about these essential processes. But its reach extends far beyond the physical—it governs mental processes, too. Our habitual behaviors, like driving a car or typing on a keyboard, become second nature as they move from the conscious to the subconscious mind. These actions are no longer things we have to actively think about—they're simply part of who we are.

- **Learned Patterns:** Through the concept of neuroplasticity, the brain rewires itself to accommodate repeated behaviors and thoughts. The more we repeat a certain action, the stronger the neural pathways become, making those actions automatic. This is how we build habits—both good and bad—without even realizing it. It's why breaking a habit can feel like an uphill battle: the subconscious has already set those patterns in motion, embedding them deep within our neural network.

Emotional Regulation

Our emotions are more than just fleeting feelings; they are intricately woven into the fabric of the subconscious mind. Neuroscience has illuminated the link between the subconscious and the emotional brain, revealing how past experiences and emotional reactions are stored and triggered in ways that influence how we perceive the present moment.

- **Emotional Conditioning:** The subconscious mind doesn't forget emotional experiences.

If we experienced fear or a traumatic event as a child, for example, the subconscious stores these memories and can trigger them long into adulthood, even in situations that have no inherent danger. These subconscious triggers often surface as anxiety, fear, panic attacks, or stress, and can affect our victimhood behavior before we even understand why we feel that way.

- **Emotional Habits:** Over time, certain emotional reactions become ingrained in the subconscious. These emotional habits shape how we respond to the world around us. For example, someone conditioned to feel anxious in social situations might react with fear, even when there is no real threat. The subconscious is not just a passive vault for emotional memories—it actively regulates how we feel and respond to new experiences.

Influence on Behavior and Decision-Making

Research in neuroscience and psychology supports the idea that what we often perceive as conscious decisions are significantly influenced by subconscious processes. The subconscious mind actively shapes our choices through learned patterns and emotional responses.

These findings underscore the profound impact on our daily decisions, often steering us in directions we're not fully aware of. While we may believe we are making independent choices, much of our decision-making process is influenced by deeply embedded patterns.

- **Subconscious Biases:** These hidden mental scripts, shaped by our experiences and environment, govern how we perceive others and the world around us. Implicit biases are perfect examples of subconscious conditioning—they influence our thoughts and decisions without our conscious awareness. We may act on these biases without realizing the underlying force shaping our behavior.
- **Behavioral Conditioning:** The subconscious mind also has the power to condition our behaviors. Through techniques like hypnosis and affirmations, we can directly access the subconscious and reprogram outdated or limiting beliefs. By planting new seeds of thought, we can alter the course of our actions, transforming how we interact with the world.

Role in Health and Healing

The power of the subconscious extends beyond mental and emotional realms—it can also have a profound impact on our physical health. The mental states stored in the subconscious can affect our physical well-being, triggering or alleviating illnesses.

Chronic stress, for instance, can be held in the subconscious and manifest as physical symptoms, creating a cycle of discomfort that seems impossible to break.

Also, the placebo effect is a testament to the subconscious mind's ability to influence our bodies. When the mind believes in a certain outcome—whether it's a real drug or a sugar pill—the body responds accordingly.

This phenomenon illustrates the power of belief and shows that the mind and body are inextricably linked, with the subconscious acting as the conduit for that connection.

MASTERING SELF AWARENESS

Emotional intelligence (EI) is the disguised force that shapes our lives in ways we often overlook. It is the quiet power behind resilience, the unseen thread that weaves strong relationships, and the catalyst for personal and professional success.

Unlike IQ, which measures cognitive ability, emotional intelligence determines how well we navigate the complexities of human interaction, regulate our emotions, and turn adversity into growth from a *Coherent Heart.*

At its core, EI is the art of self-awareness—the ability to recognize and understand our feelings, tracing their origins and acknowledging their impact on our thoughts and actions.

It is also self-regulation, the discipline to manage emotional impulses, shifting from reactive outbursts to mindful responses.

Those who master this skill don't suppress their emotions; rather, they channel them constructively, transforming anger into assertiveness, fear into courage, and frustration into determination.

Art of Empathy

Emotional intelligence is not just an inward journey—it extends outward, shaping how we perceive and connect with others. Empathy, the heart of EI, allows us to step beyond our own perspective and truly feel what another person experiences.

It is the foundation of deep, meaningful relationships, dissolving misunderstandings and fostering trust. Those with high emotional intelligence don't just hear words; they hold a neutral safe space, they listen between the lines, picking up on unspoken sensations and responding with understanding.

Vital Relationships

In a world where connections are often fleeting and misunderstandings commonplace, emotional intelligence (EI) has emerged as the bridge that connects us to ourselves—and to others. It's the quiet power behind every positive conversation, every resolved conflict, and every inspiring leader. Whether in a friendship, family, or love, emotionally intelligent individuals have the rare ability to bring harmony into any room, navigating the complexities of personalities with ease and grace.

They know that true influence doesn't stem from control or dominance, but from the deep bonds we form through genuine connection—the ability to lift others up and lead from a place of authenticity.

Science confirms that EI is not a fixed trait. It's a skill we can nurture and grow with neuroplasticity. With conscious effort, we can reform our emotional responses, increasing our self-awareness and transforming how we interact with the world.

The more we practice mindfulness, regulate our emotions, and listen with empathy, the stronger our EI. In a world defined by constant change, uncertainty, and digital noise, mastering EI is no longer just an asset—it's a necessity. It's the foundation of resilience, the key to thriving and the ability to navigate life with clarity, strength, and grace.

Those who master emotional intelligence with a *Coherent Heart* don't just react to the world around them, they create environments of understanding, trust, and connection that have the power to heal, uplift, and transmute the very fabric of our relationships.

This capacity is not about suppressing our feelings— it is about understanding them with vulnerability, harnessing their power, and using them as a bridge to deeper self-awareness and more fulfilling relationships.

Art of Learning: A Lifelong Evolution

From the moment we take our first breath, we embark on an extraordinary journey of learning. As infants, we instinctively acquire fundamental motor skills— first mastering the delicate balance of sitting, then the rhythmic coordination of crawling, and finally, the triumphant feat of walking.

Guided by caregivers, we absorb the nuances of language, social interactions, and the distinction between right and wrong.

As we grow, the structured world of education takes center stage, equipping us with knowledge and critical thinking skills that shape our futures. Yet, traditional learning often becomes a burden, entangled in stress and societal expectations.

The joy of discovery is overshadowed by the pressure to perform. Here, the role of educators becomes transformative—those who cultivate curiosity rather than compliance can reignite the spark of true learning.

Beyond the classroom, passion-driven exploration takes over. Whether through art, science, sports, or personal pursuits, learning remains a lifelong adventure—one that flourishes when fueled by purpose and curiosity.

Addiction: Hijacked Reward System

Addiction is a relentless force, deeply embedded in the lives of individuals, families, and entire societies. Once blamed on moral failure or lack of willpower, science has now unveiled the complex neurophysiological processes that fuel these compulsive behaviors.

At the heart of addiction lies the brain's reward system, a sophisticated network driven by dopamine—a neurotransmitter that governs pleasure, motivation, and survival. Normally, dopamine reinforces essential instincts like eating and social bonding. *(Source: Kalivas, P. W., & Volkow, N. D., 2005)*

However, addictive substances and behaviors—ranging from drugs and alcohol to social media, sugar, and gambling—hijack this system, flooding the brain with unnatural surges of pleasure, intensifying cravings and perpetuating the cycle.

Over time, the brain adapts, reducing its natural dopamine production, leading to dependency, withdrawal, and an insatiable craving for the next fix.

While research has fueled the development of evidence-based treatment programs, the landscape of addiction is ever-changing. Traditional substances have been joined by digital dependencies—compulsive scrolling, online gaming, and social validation loops.

The decline in cigarette consumption is a testament to the power of prevention, but the fight against addiction requires continual innovation. Early intervention, education, and mental health awareness remain our most potent tools in breaking the chains of dependency.

Understanding Motivation

Motivation is the invisible force propelling us forward, the bridge between intention and action. It shapes our ambitions, fuels our resilience, and determines how we navigate challenges. At its core, motivation is the dialogue between mind and body—a constant interplay between our desires and the obstacles we must overcome.

While often confined to professional and academic contexts, motivation extends far beyond career goals. It influences every aspect of human existence: personal growth, relationships, creativity, and even the way we manage adversity. Understanding its origins unlocks the potential for transformation. *(Source: Ryan, R. M., & Deci, E. L., 2000)*

Psychological theories distinguish between two primary types of motivation:

- Intrinsic motivation arises from within—a passion for mastery, the joy of creativity, the fulfillment of self-discovery.
- Extrinsic motivation, on the other hand, is driven by external rewards—money, status, success, recognition.

While both play a role in shaping behavior, research suggests that intrinsic motivation fosters deeper fulfillment and sustained success.

Humans are wired to seek meaning, to pursue purpose, to optimize their existence. By harnessing motivation with intention, we cultivate discipline, inspire change, and elevate our lives beyond mere survival.

Power to Rewrite Our Reality

Neuroscience has ushered in a revolution, illuminating the profound connection between brain, body, and consciousness. As research unravels the mysteries of cognition, behavior, and mental health, society is shifting—breaking free from outdated stigmas and embracing a future where knowledge empowers healing.

Mental health, once shrouded in misunderstanding, now stands at the forefront of global awareness. Depression, anxiety, and neurodegenerative diseases like Alzheimer's are no longer dismissed but actively addressed with compassion and cutting-edge interventions.

Advances in neuroplasticity and epigenetics reveal a profound viewpoint: our thoughts, beliefs, and environment shape our biology. The stories we tell ourselves—of limitations or possibilities become the blueprint of our reality.

Unlocking Human Potential

Neuroscience is not just a field of study; it is the key that unlocks the limitless power of human potential. Your mind is not a passive observer of the world—it is the architect of your reality.

Every belief you hold, every emotion you nurture, every thought you entertain weaves the narrative of your life.

Through the transformative power of neuroplasticity, you can align your thoughts with your deepest intentions, orchestrating the symphony of your mind and awakening the boundless potential within. You are not confined by the echoes of your past, nor at the mercy of fate.

You are both the creator and the creation, painting the tapestry of your existence with every thought, every neuron, every decision. You are the inventor of your destiny, wielding the power to reshape your life.

Quantum Playbook: Reprogramming Neural Pathways

Your subconscious mind controls 95% of your daily thoughts, emotions, and behaviors *(Dr. Bruce Lipton, The Biology of Belief)*. If you don't consciously program it, it runs on autopilot, reinforcing old patterns—whether empowering or limiting.

Most people try to change their lives through willpower alone, but transformation requires a subconscious shift at the neurological, emotional, and behavioral levels.

Step 1: Prime the Brain for Neuroplasticity

The brain doesn't change by accident—it needs intentional activation of neuroplasticity, the ability to form new neural connections *(Dr. Norman Doidge, The Brain That Changes Itself)*.

Old beliefs create deep neural grooves, making transformation feel difficult—but you can reshape them with deliberate action using neuroplasticity tools.

Pre-Sleep and Wake-Up Programming

- Your subconscious is most impressionable during the theta brainwave state—right before sleep and upon waking *(Dr. Joe Dispenza)*.

- Before bed, listen to guided affirmations or a self-hypnosis recording targeting the belief you want to reprogram.
- Spend 5 minutes visualizing your ideal self before checking your phone.
- Every night, write one empowering belief then read it aloud before sleep.

Affirmation: *My mind is a powerful architect, shaping my reality with every thought.*

Step 2: Rewire the Subconscious Through Repetition and Emotion

Recognize that your subconscious doesn't respond to logic—it responds to repetition and feeling *(Dr. Lisa Feldman Barrett, How Emotions Are Made).*

Most people repeat affirmations mindlessly, without engaging their emotions—making them ineffective.

It's crucial to engage heart-centered emotions to cement beliefs faster.

- **Feeling Affirmations:** Instead of just saying "I am confident," recall a time you felt confident. Feel that emotion as you repeat the affirmation.
- **Power Posing:** Holding an expansive, open posture for 2 minutes increases testosterone

(confidence) and decreases cortisol (stress) *(Dr. Amy Cuddy, Harvard Study)*.

- **Mirror Work:** Look into your own eyes and state your new belief out loud, holding eye contact. This builds self-trust and overrides past programming.

Stand in front of a mirror daily, hold a power pose, and state 3 empowering beliefs with deep conviction.

Affirmation: *Every time I reinforce my new belief, my brain strengthens it as reality.*

Step 3: Clear Emotional Blocks and Reprogram the Nervous System

The body stores emotional trauma, which can override conscious efforts to change. Until you release it, subconscious resistance remains *(Dr. Bessel van der Kolk, The Body Keeps the Score)*.

If your body associates change with fear, it rejects transformation at the subconscious level.

It's important to regulate your nervous system so your body feels safe enough to change.

- **Emotional Freedom Technique:** Tapping on acupressure points while affirming a new belief sends signals to the brain that it's safe to release old patterns *(Dr. Dawson Church, The Genie in Your Genes)*.

- **Somatic Therapy:** Trauma isn't just mental—it's stored in the body. Practices like shaking, cold exposure, and movement therapy help reset the nervous system.
- **Breathwork:** Deep belly breathing activates the parasympathetic nervous system, reducing subconscious resistance to change *(Dr. Andrew Huberman, Neuroscience of Breathwork)*.

Every morning, practice tapping for 3 minutes, followed by deep belly breathing with intention.

Affirmation: *I allow my body and mind to release all resistance to my transformation.*

Step 4: Anchor New Beliefs Through Daily Aligned Action

Taking small, aligned actions daily trains your subconscious to accept a new belief as reality *(Dr. James Clear, Atomic Habits)*.

If you don't act on your new belief with micro-actions to shift your identity, your brain won't fully accept it.

- **Act "As If" Daily:** Example: If your belief is "I am confident," take one daily action that confident people do (speaking up, making eye contact, standing tall).
- **Stack New Beliefs onto Existing Habits:** Pair a new affirmation with something you

already do daily (say an affirmation every time you brush your teeth).

- **Celebrate Small Wins:** Acknowledge each successful shift, so your brain associates the new belief with reward (Dr. BJ Fogg, Tiny Habits).
- Every morning, list ONE small action that supports your new belief and do it immediately.

Affirmation: *Every action I take cements my new identity into my subconscious.*

Step 5: Create Long-Term Change with Habit Stacking

Change sticks when new beliefs become automated habits. Without consistency, your brain reverts to old patterns.

Turn reprogramming into an effortless daily habit with a reinforcement system.

- **Morning:** Speak affirmations while looking in the mirror (2 minutes).
- **Mid-Day:** Take one action aligned with your new belief.
- **Evening:** Reflect and visualize your highest self before sleep (5 minutes).
- Set a phone reminder with your new belief so you reinforce it daily.

Affirmation: *I am the architect of my mind. I consciously shape my beliefs, knowing that every thought I nurture and feel becomes the foundation of my reality. With each belief I choose, I design the world around me, molding my experiences and creating the life I truly desire.*

5. Regulating the Nervous System

You dissociated, shut down, became anxious, a people-pleaser, or turned to addiction—not out of weakness, but as a means to survive. The adult battling chronic fatigue is the child who endured. Every coping mechanism was your body's way of protecting you, ensuring you made it through. But what if I told you these responses didn't just make you a warrior—they shaped you into a resilient, adaptable, and profoundly strong human being?

Your nervous system, though silent, has been orchestrating your survival all along. It shapes how you perceive, react, and move through the world, holding the imprints of your past while quietly guiding your present. Its wisdom runs deeper than we often realize.

The journey you've walked, though painful, has forged an unshakable strength within you—one that can now be reclaimed. Let's dive deeper and explore pathways to regulate this intricate, highly intelligent system so that survival is no longer the goal—thriving is.

At every moment, the nervous system shifts between activation—fight, flight, or freeze—and relaxation—rest and digest—dictating our thoughts, emotions, and behaviors. This sophisticated network of neural pathways and sensory receptors transforms raw stimuli into subjective experience, filtering reality through a deeply personal lens.

Imagine the human nervous system as an intricate labyrinth of electrical highways, where every impulse is a traveler carrying vital messages to the farthest reaches of the body.

Visualize a sprawling city lit by millions of interconnected fiber-optic cables, each sparking to life with purpose and direction.

In this maze, the brain serves as the master control tower, orchestrating the flow of information through a vast network of neurons, much like a symphony conductor guiding harmonious interplay.

Axons, the system's shimmering tunnels, transmit electrical signals as bursts of light, while synapses act as tiny, high-speed bridges allowing messages to leap across microscopic gaps.

These signals traverse with breathtaking speed, fueled by ion channels that open and close like finely-tuned gates, maintaining the delicate balance of communication.

This bioelectrical maze is not merely a structure; it is a dynamic, living intelligent system scientifically proven to process billions of signals per second, controlling everything from the beat of the heart to the brush of a fingertip, forming the very foundation of our perception and interaction with the world.

No two people perceive an event the same way because the nervous system—not just external circumstances—

determines interpretation. It processes, prioritizes, and reacts to incoming information, influencing whether we feel safe, threatened, or indifferent.

When well-regulated, it moves fluidly between states, maintaining equilibrium and supporting emotional resilience.

However, chronic stress, trauma, and unresolved emotions can disrupt this balance, leaving the nervous system trapped in survival mode. Instead of adapting, it struggles to reset, manifesting as anxiety, fatigue, chronic pain, or emotional instability.

Since the autonomic nervous system governs essential functions like heart rate, digestion, and respiration, dysregulation can ripple through the body, affecting both mental and physical health.

Regulation is the key to optimal functioning—the ability to return to aligned balance after stress. Without it, the nervous system remains locked in a cycle of overreaction or exhaustion, distorting perception and draining vitality.

Understanding and supporting its rhythms is not just a path to well-being but a foundation for how we experience life itself.

COHERENT STATE

Where Balance and Clarity Thrive

Imagine waking up to a tranquil morning, sunlight filtering softly through the window as you wrap your hands around a warm cup of tea. The world hums in quiet harmony, and within, a deep sense of peace unfolds.

There's no rush, no tension—only presence. Your breath moves in a slow, effortless rhythm, your heart beats in steady synchrony, and your mind, unburdened by clutter, is free to think, create, and connect. This is the state of coherence, where the nervous system is finely attuned, balancing alertness with ease.

At the core of this equilibrium is the parasympathetic nervous system, guided by the vagus nerve, the body's master regulator of calm and restoration *(Source: Porges, 2011)*.

When engaged, this system signals safety, promoting relaxation, digestion, and cellular healing.

The body is no longer in survival mode; instead, it functions at its peak, allowing for deep physical restoration and mental clarity. In this state, stress hormones subside, heart rate variability increases—a sign of resilience and adaptability—and cognitive function flourishes. *(Source: McCraty & Zayas, 2014)*

Physiologically, coherence is marked by a rhythmic balance:

- **Steady heart rate and breathing:** A calm, measured pace that enhances oxygenation and cellular repair.
- **Emotional equilibrium:** A grounded state of being, fostering resilience, compassion, and inner peace.
- **Cognitive clarity:** The ability to think fluidly, solve problems, and make decisions without the fog of stress.
- **Social engagement:** A natural openness to connection, where empathy and trust thrive. *(Source: Thayer & Lane, 2009)*

The is the body's natural "rest-and-digest" mode, a stark contrast to the fight-or-flight response. It is here that we are most receptive to learning, creativity, and effective communication. When the nervous system oscillates naturally between action and restoration, life flows effortlessly.

Our internal tempo syncs with the greater rhythm of existence, and the noise of daily stress fades into the background, leaving only clarity and presence.

Because real strength and resilience is not found in relentless momentum, but in the ability to pause, reset, and move forward from a place of coherence.

Empowering Methods

The coherence you feel is more than just an emotional or mental state—it's a physiological condition, a state where your heart, mind, and body are aligned in perfect harmony.

Every cell, every thought, every breath, is attuned to the frequency of peace, creativity, and connection. When you're in this state, you're not just calm—you're in your most empowered, grounded, and aware version of yourself. And from this place, you can respond to life's challenges with grace, focus, and unshakable clarity.

Affirmations: *In this moment, I am safe. I breathe in peace, I exhale tension. My heart beats in harmony with the rhythm of life. With every inhale, I invite calm; with every exhale, I release all that no longer serves me.*

STRESS STATE

When the Body Lives in Overdrive (Sympathetic Activation)

Picture yourself rushing to a crucial meeting—your pulse quickens, breath turns shallow, and a thin layer of sweat dampens your palms. Thoughts race, colliding like waves in a storm, each one a demand, a deadline, an urgent call for action.

Your body is fully engaged in survival mode, primed for combat or escape, even though the enemy is not a wild predator but the relentless pressures of modern life.

This is sympathetic activation, the body's built-in alarm system, flooding your system with adrenaline and cortisol to heighten awareness, sharpen reflexes, and fuel immediate response. *(Source: Sapolsky, 2004)*

In moments of acute stress, this surge of energy can be useful, even lifesaving. Your mind zeroes in, muscles tense, and your body mobilizes resources to meet the challenge ahead. But what happens when this state is no longer temporary? When the engine revs too high for too long, without relief?

The line between peak performance and physiological exhaustion begins to blur. What once felt like motivation now feels like anxiety; what once fuelled focus now scatters thoughts into chaos.

Your heart pounds not with excitement but with pressure, your breath constricts, your shoulders tighten—signs that the body is struggling to regulate itself, trapped in a cycle of relentless hyperarousal. *(Source: McEwen, 1998)*

Imagine juggling a dozen spinning plates, each one demanding your attention. At first, you manage, shifting, adjusting, keeping pace with the demands. But as time wears on, your grip weakens, your concentration frays.

The nervous system, designed for short bursts of activation, is now stuck in overdrive, unable to downshift. The weight of stress becomes cumulative, leading to cognitive fatigue, anxiety, and eventual burnout. The very system designed to protect you is now working against you, draining energy reserves, and disrupting equilibrium. *(Source: Chrousos, 2009)*

The challenge, then, is not to avoid stress entirely—it is an unavoidable part of life—but to learn how to release it, to shift from sympathetic dominance back into balance.

This means engaging in intentional regulation: deep, rhythmic breathing to slow the heart rate, movement to release built-up tension, mindfulness to anchor awareness in the present. The key is not to eliminate the stress response but to master the art of recovery, allowing the body to oscillate naturally between action and restoration, between intensity and ease. *(Source: Porges, 2011)*

Because survival is not just about running from danger—it is also about knowing when to stop running. When faced with a perceived threat or challenge, the body activates the sympathetic nervous system, preparing for "fight or flight." This state is marked by:

- **Increased heart rate and breathing**: A faster pace to deliver more oxygen to the body.

- **Heightened awareness**: Focus sharpens, and the body becomes more alert to external stimuli.
- **Physical tension**: Muscles tighten in preparation for action.
- **Emotional intensity**: Feelings of anxiety, fear, or anger may arise.

In a healthy context, this stress state can be beneficial for short bursts of energy or focus. However, prolonged chronic stress can lead to burnout, dis-ease, or health issues if the body remains stuck in this heightened state.

When the body enters a stress response, the sympathetic nervous system floods the body with stress hormones like cortisol and adrenaline, increasing heart rate, elevating blood pressure, and preparing muscles for action.

While this response is helpful in life-threatening situations, prolonged activation leads to chronic stress, burnout, and dysregulation in the nervous system.

Pathways of Change

To regulate the nervous system requires conscious breathwork and mindful movement, which directly communicates safety to the brain and activates the parasympathetic nervous system, responsible for rest, digestion, and recovery.

By consistently practicing these somatic techniques, the nervous system rewires itself, making resilience—not reactivity—the default state.

1. Conscious Breathwork Techniques

Box Breathing (Four-Square Breathing):

- What Happens in My Body: This technique helps balance my oxygen and carbon dioxide levels, activating my parasympathetic nervous system—the system responsible for rest and relaxation.
- How It Helps Me: Within minutes, my heart rate slows, my body relaxes, and I feel centered again.

Physiological Sigh (Double Inhale, Long Exhale):

- What Happens in My Body: This technique releases trapped carbon dioxide, instantly calming my nervous system.
- How It Helps Me: My racing thoughts slow with applied focus, my muscles release tension, and I shift from stress to clarity almost immediately.

Resonance Breathing (Coherent Breathing):

- What Happens in My Body: Breathing in a steady 5-6 breaths per minute rhythm syncs my heart rate and nervous system, increasing resilience.

- How It Helps Me: My heart, lungs, and mind synchronize into a state of calm focus, allowing me to approach challenges with clarity instead of fear.

Affirmations: *I am safe. My breath flows with ease, signalling peace to my body and mind. With every inhale, I invite calm and clarity. With every exhale, I release tension and fear. I am grateful for my breath of life.*

2. Mindful Movement: Regulating Through Physicality

Stress isn't just in the mind—it's stored in the body. Tight shoulders, a clenched jaw, shallow breathing—these aren't mere discomforts; they're distress signals from a nervous system stuck in survival mode.

Chronic stress rewires neural pathways, increasing inflammation and weakening immunity *(Source: McEwen, 1998)*. But movement is medicine. Intentional physical practices help release stored tension, improve circulation, and restore balance.

- **Progressive Muscle Relaxation** – Tense and release each muscle group from toes to head. This lowers cortisol and increases heart rate variability for better stress regulation *(Source: Conrad & Roth, 2007)*.

- **Gentle Movement for Detoxification** – Walk, sway, or bounce on your toes for five minutes to stimulate the lymphatic system, aiding immune function and reducing inflammation *(Source: Nickelston, Stop Chasing Pain)*.
- **Somatic Shaking for Release** – Loosely shake your limbs for one to two minutes to discharge stored stress and reset the nervous system, a technique used to treat trauma *(Source: Berceli, 2010)*.
- **Deep Stretching for Emotional Release** – Hold hip-opening or chest-expanding stretches for 30 seconds while breathing deeply. Activates the vagus nerve and promotes relaxation *(Source:Pascoe et al., 2017)*.

Every stretch, breath, and shake is a signal to your nervous system: you are safe. Mindful movement isn't just exercise—it's a path to resilience, balance, and reclaiming your body as a place of peace.

Affirmations: *I release all tension and stored emotions through movement. My body is strong, safe, healthy, and vibrant.*

3. Healing Power of Connection: Co-Regulation with Others

Connection is a fundamental part of nervous system regulation. Neuroscience reveals that our nervous systems synchronize with those around us—a process called co-regulation.

When we interact with calm, grounded individuals, our own system mirrors that stability, reinforcing a sense of security and ease.

Forming connections with animals and living things is the balm that soothes the soul and the nervous system, a metaphysical elixir with the power to heal in ways that defy the tangible. When we experience authentic connection—a warm embrace, a knowing glance, or the gentle cadence of a kind voice—it acts as an energetic current, resonating deeply within us.

Scientifically, it reduces cortisol levels, calms the fight-or-flight response, and activates body's natural state of rest and restoration. Metaphysically, it reminds us of our shared essence, a divine thread of unity that weaves through all beings.

In moments of genuine connection, the heart's electromagnetic field synchronizes with another's, creating a silent harmony that vibrates beyond the physical. It is within this sacred exchange that healing takes root, as isolation transforms into belonging, and the fractures of our psyche begin to mend in the light of shared humanity and unity consciousness.

Affirmations: *I am safe, supported, and deeply connected. My nervous system finds balance in loving presence.*

4. Rest and Sleep: Ultimate Reset Button

Sleep is the body's most profound regenerative state, essential for nervous system repair. During deep sleep, the brain processes emotions, consolidates memories, and detoxifies itself.

Chronic sleep deprivation leads to heightened stress responses, impaired cognitive function, and emotional dysregulation.

Prioritize sleep hygiene by establishing a consistent bedtime routine. Avoid screens before bed, as blue light suppresses melatonin, the sleep hormone.

Engage in relaxing activities—reading, gratitude, listening to calming Solfeggio frequency music, or practicing deep breathing. If struggling with overactive thoughts, body scanning meditation can help release tension and ease the mind into rest.

Affirmations: *I allow my body to rest and heal. I wake up refreshed, rejuvenated, and ready to embrace life. My body deserves to be pampered and to rejuvenate with tranquility.*

Restoring Harmony

When we practice self-care routines and stabilize, different regions of our body communicate in harmony, thoughts are clear, emotions are stable, and the body adapts effortlessly to change. This rhythmic alignment—measured through brainwave harmony—shapes perception, decision-making, and overall well-being.

A well-regulated nervous system maintains this balance, shifting smoothly between states of alertness and relaxation. But when coherence is disrupted by stress, trauma, or imbalance, the mind fragments, emotions spiral, and the body struggles to find stability.

The art of nervous system mastery is not about suppressing emotions or bypassing stress—it's about cultivating the resilience to return to balance after disruptions. This is found in the ability to restore harmony, where the brain, body, and nervous system work in unison, unlocking clarity, adaptability, and a profound sense of inner peace.

Through breathwork, vagus nerve activation, neural rewiring, sensory grounding, movement, connection, and restorative sleep, we reclaim control over our internal state.

Over time, these practices reduce inflammation, retrain the nervous system to default to safety rather than stress, unlocking greater emotional stability, cognitive clarity, and an enduring sense of peace.

The nervous system is a masterpiece of adaptability—when we learn to work with it rather than against it, we unlock the profound ability to live with greater ease, presence, and vitality.

FREEZE OR SHUTDOWN STATE

The Silent Collapse (Dorsal Vagal)

Picture standing on the edge of an overwhelming situation when the body senses that there is no way to fight or flee. You feel the weight of helplessness descend, a thick fog wrapping around your mind and body.

Your heart, once hammering with adrenaline, now slows to a distant, muffled beat. It is as if the very essence of your being is withdrawing, retreating into the depths of silence to escape the unrelenting weight of existence. A fog rolls in—thick, impenetrable—blurring the world beyond your reach.

You are not running. You are not fighting. You are freezing.

The body has entered the dorsal vagal state, the last line of defence when survival feels impossible, when the only refuge is to disappear within. *(Source: Porges, 2011)*

In this state, the nervous system is not merely overwhelmed; it is inflamed, locked in an unyielding collapse. Sensation dulls, as though you no longer inhabit your own body. Your limbs feel heavy, disconnected from will, your movements sluggish if they come at all.

There is an eerie detachment, as if you are separate from your own existence, floating somewhere beyond yourself, watching but unable to intervene. Energy vanishes, draining like water slipping through cupped hands, leaving behind only exhaustion, depletion, and a hollow sense of disconnection. *(Source: Schore, 2012; Lanius et al., 2015)*

Emotionally, the descent is even more profound. The vibrancy of life force—the warmth of connection, the spark of joy—fades into an indifferent shade of gray. Despair does not arrive in a sudden crash but seeps in like a slow-moving tide, eroding the shores of hope.

Your thoughts become sluggish, tangled, difficult to grasp, as if the very act of thinking requires too much effort. Even the will to act, to move, to reclaim a sense of agency, feels impossibly distant. You are not merely frozen—you are trapped in the silence itself. *(Source: Van der Kolk, 2014)*

This is the body's ultimate survival strategy, an evolutionary adaptation designed to protect when neither fight nor flight is an option. In the animal kingdom, a prey animal caught in the jaws of a predator will go limp, entering a state of biological surrender.

In humans, this same response can be triggered by extreme trauma, chronic stress, burnout, or experiences of profound helplessness. But what once served as a protective mechanism can become a prison, leaving you locked in a cycle of paralysis, disempowerment, and emotional shutdown. *(Source: Dana, 2018; Levine, 2010)*

Yet, even within this frozen state, there remains a path forward. With appropriate therapy, healing can begin by rekindling the connection between mind and body, gently coaxing the nervous system back into regulation.

Small movements, sensory grounding, deep rhythmic breathwork—these are the bridges that can lead out of the abyss. Safety, connection, and the slow reawakening of vitality offer the key to unlocking the freeze, allowing life to return in whispers before it floods back in full force. *(Source: Porges, 2011; Levine, 2010)*

The body does not betray—it protects. And just as it learned to freeze, it can learn to move again. Symptoms of this state include:

- **Physical numbness or dissociation**: A feeling of being detached from the body or environment.
- **Low energy or lethargy**: The body may "shut down" to conserve energy.
- **Emotional numbness or hopelessness**: A sense of despair or detachment from emotions.
- **Reduced cognitive function**: Difficulty concentrating or making decisions.

This state often arises in situations of overwhelming stress or trauma and may lead to feelings of helplessness, disconnection, or depression.

Pathways of Change

The methods for recovering from the Freeze or Shutdown state, often caused by the dorsal vagal response, requires a deep, gradual process of re-engagement with the body and the environment.

The freeze response isn't a weakness—it's a survival instinct. When the nervous system perceives a threat too overwhelming to fight or escape, it shuts down, leaving you feeling numb, disconnected, or immobilized. But healing is possible. Through neuroplasticity, the brain can be retrained to move out of paralysis and back into engagement, restoring a sense of safety and control.

1. Reconnect with the Body Through Micro-Movements

In freeze, the body feels distant, heavy, or numb. Small, intentional movements signal safety to the brain, awakening the sensory-motor system and breaking the cycle of immobility *(Source: Levine, Waking the Tiger, 1997).*

- Wiggle your fingers and toes. Slowly roll your shoulders.
- Press your feet into the ground, feeling the support beneath you.

- Expand your range of motion gradually— gentle stretches, rocking side to side.

Each small movement tells your nervous system: It is safe to re-engage.

2. Stimulate the Vagus Nerve with Breathwork

The vagus nerve plays a crucial role in both activating and calming the nervous system. Deep, slow breathing, particularly through the diaphragm, helps stimulate the parasympathetic nervous system, which counters the freeze response by promoting a sense of safety, balanced, regulated state.

Over time, with consistent practice, your brain can rewire its response to stressors, creating new neural pathways for relaxation and ease.

3. Process Emotions Through Safe Expression

Freeze can suppress emotions, making it hard to feel or express them. Writing, vocalization, or movement-based expression rewires the brain to process emotions in a manageable way *(Source: Siegel, The Developing Mind, 2012).*

- Journaling: Write without judgment—your thoughts, sensations, or emotions, no matter how subtle.

- Emotion Naming: Say aloud what you're feeling, even if it's just: "I feel stuck." Naming emotions reduces their intensity.
- Gentle Vocalization: Humming, sighing, or whispering helps reconnect to your natural rhythm.

Expression doesn't have to be big—it just has to begin.

4. Reintroduce Sensory Stimuli Gradually

The freeze response heightens sensitivity to stimuli, often leading to avoidance. Gentle exposure helps the brain form new, positive associations *(Source: Ogden, Sensorimotor Psychotherapy, 2006).*

- Run your hands over soft textures, like a blanket or smooth stone.
- Walk barefoot on grass, sand, or carpet, noticing the sensation.
- Listen to soothing sounds—rain, ocean waves, calming music.

Slow, safe re-exposure rewires the nervous system to engage with the world without fear.

Healing is a Process, Not a Destination

I once believed my freeze response was permanent, but step by step, I proved otherwise. Each breath, each movement, each moment of reconnection is proof that you are not stuck—you are healing. The freeze state is not an endpoint. It is a pause, a place to recover—not a place to remain.

HYPERAROUSAL STATE

The Unrelenting Storm (Overstimulation)

Imagine standing on the edge of a battlefield long after the war has ended. The air is still, the danger has passed, yet your body refuses to believe it.

Your pulse quickens, your muscles tighten, and your mind scans for threats that no longer exist. This is the relentless reality of hyperarousal—a state where the dysregulated nervous system remains trapped in high alert, unable to disengage from the fight-or-flight response, even in the absence of immediate danger. *(Source: McEwen, 1998)*

At the heart of this physiological turmoil lies the brain's threat detection system. The amygdala, the brain's emotional command center, is hypervigilant, perceiving shadows as monsters and whispers as roars.

It signals the hypothalamic-pituitary-adrenal (HPA) axis to flood the body with stress hormones—adrenaline surges, cortisol lingers, and the body is primed for battle. But the enemy is invisible, often nothing more than the echoes of past trauma.

Meanwhile, the prefrontal cortex—the rational mind—struggles to regain control, its voice drowned out by the amygdala's alarm bells. *(Source: Van der Kolk, 2014; Arnsten, 2009)*

This unyielding tension wreaks havoc on both mind and body. The heart pounds as if chased by an unseen predator, digestion falters under prolonged distress, and sleep becomes an elusive refuge. The immune system, battered by chronic inflammation, weakens, leaving the body vulnerable to illness.

Over time, hyperarousal carves deep grooves into one's neurobiology, manifesting in anxiety imbalance, PTSD, and even autoimmune dysfunction.

The body is not simply stressed; it is rewired, conditioned to see safety as an illusion and relaxation as a risk. *(Source: Sapolsky, 2004; Chrousos, 2009)*

Yet, there is a way out of the storm. Science reveals that activating the parasympathetic nervous system—the body's natural brake—can disrupt this cycle of survival-mode living.

Practices like deep breathing, meditation, and vagus nerve stimulation serve as antidotes, coaxing the body into a state of calm.

Polyvagal theory illuminates the power of social connection, breathwork, and mindfulness in restoring physiological equilibrium, proving that the nervous system, though wounded, can heal. *(Source: Porges, 2011; Lanius, 2015)*

Hyperarousal is not a life sentence; it is a call to reclaim sovereignty over the mind and body. The battlefield may exist in memory, but the present moment holds the key to peace. In understanding the mechanisms of hyperarousal, we arm ourselves with knowledge—not to fight, but to finally, and fully, surrender to healing.

Pathways of Change

The calming methods for recovering from this state involves calming the overactive nervous system and restoring balance.

Practices that promote relaxation, such as deep breathing, mindfulness, and grounding techniques, help shift the body from the constant fight-or-flight mode into a state of calm. Regular exercise, adequate rest, and social support also play vital roles in re-establishing emotional and physical equilibrium.

By intentionally engaging in activities that activate the parasympathetic nervous system—such as meditation, restorative yoga, or spending time in nature—the body can break the cycle of chronic stress, release accumulated tension, and restore a sense of inner peace and resilience.

In situations of prolonged stress or emotional overload, the body may move into a state of hyperarousal, where the nervous system remains on high alert.

This state is characterized by:

- **Excessive physical energy or tension**: The body is in a constant state of fight or flight, making it difficult to relax.
- **Racing thoughts or anxiety**: Overactive thinking, intrusive thoughts, and negative chatter can lead to a constant state of worry or fear.
- **Sleep disturbances**: Difficulty falling asleep or staying asleep due to heightened alertness.
- **Emotional volatility**: Increased irritability, anger, or nervousness.

Affirmations: *I choose to slow my breath, bringing peace to my mind and body. I release the tension in my shoulders, in my chest, and in my mind. I trust that I am capable of navigating the demands of life with calm and clarity. Each breath I take brings me back to the present, to the now, where I am in control. I am safe.*

HYPO-AROUSAL STATE

When the Mind and Body Retreat (Under-Activation)

There are moments when the weight of stress and emotional overwhelm becomes so relentless that the body doesn't fight back—it shuts down. This isn't the rush of adrenaline that fuels action, nor the tension of bracing for impact.

Instead, it is a quiet withdrawal, a slow descent into stillness, as though life is unfolding behind a thick, impenetrable fog. This is hypo-arousal, a state where the nervous system becomes under-activated, shifting from engagement to detachment in a desperate attempt at self-preservation.

Unlike the charged urgency of hyper-arousal, hypo-arousal is marked by depletion—of energy, motivation, and emotional responsiveness. It often follows prolonged exposure to stress, trauma, depression, or exhaustion, when the mind and body can no longer sustain the effort of vigilance.

This state is closely tied to the dorsal vagal response, the nervous system's way of shutting down when fight or flight is no longer an option. The body moves into conservation mode, prioritizing survival over participation, leading to:

- **Profound fatigue:** A sluggish heaviness, as if moving through quicksand.
- **Emotional numbness:** Apathy replaces emotion, joy feels distant, and motivation dwindles.
- **Disconnection from life:** Social withdrawal, avoidance, and an inability to engage in once-meaningful activities.
- **Cognitive brain fog:** Thoughts feel scattered, focus is elusive, and even simple tasks seem overwhelming.

The external world feels muted, interactions feel distant, and even personal desires become unclear. It is as if the body is saying, *Enough*. No more input. No more effort. Yet, while hypo-arousal may serve as a temporary refuge from stress, prolonged disconnection can spiral into burnout, depression, and a loss of self-awareness. *(Source: Schore, 2009)*

This state is deeply connected to depression, particularly through dysregulation of the autonomic nervous system and disruptions in neurochemical balance.

The dorsal vagal shutdown—part of the parasympathetic nervous system—dampens physiological and emotional responses, mirroring the lethargy, disinterest, and cognitive difficulties seen in clinical depression. *(Source: Schore, 2009)*

Additionally, the hypothalamic-pituitary-adrenal (HPA) axis, responsible for regulating stress responses, becomes dysregulated under chronic stress, leading to cortisol imbalances. Low cortisol levels, often seen in burnout-related depression, contribute to exhaustion and emotional blunting. *(Source: Miller & Raison, 2016)*

Meanwhile, disruptions in dopamine and serotonin systems—the brain's reward and mood-regulating neurotransmitters—lead to anhedonia (the inability to feel pleasure), a hallmark of major depressive imbalance. *(Source: Maes, 2011)*

Functional brain imaging studies further reveal that hypoactivity in the prefrontal cortex and overactivation of limbic structures, such as the amygdala, contribute to emotional dysregulation and the inability to initiate action in depressive states. *(Source: Mayberg, 2003)*

These neurological changes explain why individuals experiencing hypo-arousal often struggle with motivation, focus, and social engagement—key symptoms of depression.

Breaking the Cycle of Depression

Because hypo-arousal and depression are intertwined, healing involves reawakening the nervous system in a way that feels safe and sustainable.

Somatic therapies, mindfulness-based interventions, and polyvagal-informed practices help regulate the ANS, gradually shifting the body out of shutdown.

Additionally, structured behavioral activation, which encourages small, manageable actions, can reignite dopamine pathways and restore a sense of purpose and engagement.

Just as the body instinctively shuts down to protect itself, it can also be guided back into balance, one steady breath, one gentle connection, at a time.

The path out of hypo-arousal is not through force or pressure, but through gentle re-engagement—small moments of connection, sensory experiences, and practices that awaken the nervous system from dormancy.

Just as the body instinctively shuts down to protect itself, it can also be guided back into balance, one steady breath at a time.

Pathways of Change

The key to overcoming hypo-arousal through neuroplasticity lies in creating new neural connections—ones that are grounded in safety, motivation, and connection.

Each of these techniques serves to actively rewire the brain, gently nudging it away from the patterns of disengagement and emotional numbness that characterize hypo-arousal.

The process is gradual. Be patient with yourself as you reintroduce movement, connection, and positivity into your life.

By consistently engaging these neuroplasticity techniques, you can effectively reawaken your energy, restore motivation, and shift the neural pathways responsible for hypo-arousal into healthier, more engaged patterns.

When the nervous system enters hypoarousal, it disconnects from life, leaving you feeling numb, isolated, and unmotivated. But the brain is adaptable. Through intentional practices, you can reignite engagement, rewire neural pathways, and restore a sense of connection.

1. Practice Gratitude: Shifting from Numbness

Gratitude activates the brain's reward system, increasing dopamine and serotonin, neurotransmitters linked to well-being and motivation *(Source: Emmons & McCullough, 2003).*

- Each day, write down three things you're grateful for—as simple as sunlight on your skin or a kind smile from a stranger.

- With consistency, this rewires the brain to actively seek positive experiences, fostering engagement and emotional resilience.

2. Engage the Social Brain: Connection as Medicine

Humans are wired for connection. Social interactions activate the ventral vagal system and prefrontal cortex, strengthening neural pathways for bonding and emotional regulation *(Source: Porges, Polyvagal Theory, 2011)*.

- Reach out to a trusted friend, family member, or therapist—even a brief conversation begins breaking the cycle of isolation.
- Engage in safe, positive social interactions, whether virtual or in person. Even small connections create shifts in the nervous system, fostering engagement.

3. Reframe Thoughts with Micro Shifts

Negative thought patterns reinforce disconnection. Cognitive Behavioral Therapy helps rewire the brain by replacing limiting beliefs with empowering ones *(Source: Beck, 1976)*.

- Notice self-defeating thoughts: "I don't have the energy to do anything."

- Replace with a balanced, action-based reframe: "I have the strength to take one small step toward feeling better."

Over time, these micro-shifts reshape neural pathways, fostering motivation and engagement.

4. Awaken Presence Through Sensory Stimulation

Engaging the sensory cortex reconnects you to the present moment, pulling you out of emotional numbness *(Source: Van der Kolk, The Body Keeps the Score, 2014).*

- Hold a soft cozy blanket, warm cup of tea, or scented candle, focusing on texture, temperature, or aroma.
- Listen to Solfeggio frequencies or nature sounds, bringing awareness to sound vibrations.
- Even noticing the chirping of birds or the weight of your body on the ground signals safety to the nervous system.

Affirmations: *I allow myself the space to heal with grace and compassion. I release the weight of my exhaustion and accept that it is okay to feel slow, to feel drained. With each small step, I reconnect to my energy, to my purpose.*

OPTIMAL REGULATION STATE

Gateway to Limitless Potential (Flow)

The flow state is a highly regulated, balanced state where the body, mind, and emotions are in complete harmony. This is often experienced during peak performance moments, such as when engaged in creative activities, sports, or deeply meaningful work.

There are moments in life when everything clicks into place. Time bends, the outside world fades into the background, and your actions feel effortless—almost as if something beyond you is guiding the way.

The basketball player executing the perfect shot in the final seconds of the game, the pianist lost in the melody of her composition, the writer whose words pour onto the page with a life of their own. This is the flow state—a state of heightened focus, seamless action, and deep fulfillment where peak performance feels almost supernatural.

The concept of flow was first introduced by psychologist Mihály Csíkszentmihályi, who spent decades studying what makes people feel most alive and engaged in their work. He discovered that true happiness is not found in idle relaxation but in the full absorption of meaningful activity, where skill and challenge intertwine in perfect balance with a *Coherent Mind*.

Neuroscience of Flow: A Brain in Perfect Harmony

Beneath the surface of this effortless state lies a precise orchestration of neurobiology. Flow is not just a feeling—it is a distinct neurological state where the brain enters an optimal rhythm, shifting into a mode of heightened efficiency and creativity.

- **The Quieting of the Inner Critic:** One of the defining characteristics of flow is the silencing of self-doubt. This occurs due to transient hypo frontality, a temporary deactivation of the prefrontal cortex—the brain's center for self-monitoring and critical thinking *(Source: Dietrich, 2004)*. This is why, in flow, thoughts do not hesitate. The mind does not over-analyse. Instead, actions feel automatic, guided by instinct rather than deliberation.

- **A Surge of Performance-Boosting Neurochemicals:** The brain floods with a powerful cocktail of neurotransmitters that enhance mood, motivation, and focus:
  - Dopamine – Sharpens attention, boosts creativity, and reinforces learning.
  - Norepinephrine – Increases alertness and energy, enhancing reaction time.

- ○ Endorphins – Reduce pain and promote euphoria, explaining the sense of exhilaration during flow.
- ○ Anandamide – A neurotransmitter associated with heightened lateral thinking and a sense of bliss.

BRAINWAVE SYMPHONY & FREQUENCY STATES

At its highest level, human cognition operates as a symphony—a seamless interplay of neural rhythms that allows for peak performance. Nowhere is this orchestration more profound than in the flow state, a psychological phenomenon where focus deepens, creativity surges, and action becomes effortless.

In the flow state, the brain functions at its most harmonious, with different regions communicating in sync, creating a powerful foundation for peak performance. One key factor that makes this possible is the synchronization of brainwaves.

These rhythmic electrical oscillations in the brain represent different states of consciousness, from alertness to deep relaxation. When in flow, the brain shifts between various brainwave frequencies, each contributing to optimal functioning.

1. Alpha Waves (8-12 Hz): Bridge Between Relaxation and Focus

Calm, clarity, and creative insight.

Alpha waves emerge when the mind is relaxed yet alert, making them the ideal foundation for flow. Common during meditation and daydreaming, alpha activity fosters mental clarity and enhances the brain's ability to sustain deep focus without cognitive strain. By quieting the inner critic, alpha waves allow for seamless execution of tasks, uninterrupted by distractions.

- **Scientific Insight:** Research conducted by Fink et al. (2009) found that increased alpha activity is associated with creative problem-solving and the generation of novel ideas. This suggests that alpha waves serve as a neural bridge between conscious effort and spontaneous insight.

2. Theta Waves (4-7 Hz): Deep Flow Zone

Where intuition and creativity thrive.

Theta waves, typically linked to deep meditation and light sleep, play a pivotal role in immersive flow states. This frequency fosters intuition, abstract thinking, and heightened receptivity to novel connections. Artists, musicians, and elite athletes often exhibit increased theta activity when fully absorbed in their craft, experiencing moments of effortless execution and creative breakthroughs.

- **Scientific Insight:** A study by Dorst et al. (2014) revealed that theta waves are strongly correlated with high levels of creativity. During flow, they help bypass the brain's prefrontal cortex—responsible for self-monitoring—allowing for uninhibited expression and intuitive problem-solving.

3. Beta Waves (12-30 Hz): Focused Energy State

Sustained attention and cognitive control.

Beta waves are associated with active concentration, problem-solving, and analytical thinking. While deep relaxation is essential for entering flow, sharp focus is equally crucial. In high-performance states, the brain seamlessly integrates beta activity to sustain engagement, prevent mental drift, and execute complex tasks with precision.

- **Scientific Insight:** Research by Zheng et al. (2016) indicates that optimal performance occurs when alpha and beta waves work in tandem—allowing for sustained attention while avoiding cognitive overload. This balance is crucial for maintaining energy and preventing burnout in high-stress environments.

4. Gamma Waves (30-100 Hz): Peak Cognitive Zone

High-level processing, integration, and mastery.

Gamma waves, the brain's fastest oscillations, are linked to advanced cognition, memory recall, and the integration of complex information. In the most intense moments of flow—when mastery feels effortless, and ideas crystallize instantaneously—gamma activity surges. This heightened state enables individuals to process vast amounts of information simultaneously, leading to moments of profound clarity and peak cognitive efficiency.

- **Scientific Insight:** A study by Lutz et al. (2004) demonstrated that gamma wave activity is significantly heightened in experienced meditators and individuals engaged in deep concentration. This suggests that gamma waves contribute to the integration of multiple cognitive processes, enhancing learning, perception, and decision-making.

Neural Symphony of Flow

Flow is not a singular brainwave state but a dynamic interplay of neural frequencies. Alpha waves foster relaxed concentration, theta waves enhance creativity, beta waves sustain focus, and gamma waves elevate cognition. When these oscillations synchronize, the brain enters its most efficient, high-performing state—where action and awareness merge, and the extraordinary becomes effortless.

By understanding the rhythm of brainwaves, we move closer to mastering the art of flow—tuning the mind into a state of seamless execution, creative brilliance, and peak human potential.

Research shows that while the conscious mind processes only 50 to 60 bits of information per second, the unconscious mind processes an astonishing 10 to 11 million bits. This suggests that the unconscious holds the key to unlocking untapped potential—a realm of possibilities waiting to be discovered.

However, the unconscious mind is not the final destination—it serves as a gateway to higher consciousness. In many spiritual traditions, this higher state of awareness is described as the "All is Mind" or the unified field, a source of infinite potential and creativity. It is within this expansive field of consciousness that transformation takes place.

So, how do we access this higher consciousness? Practices like meditation offer the pathway. Meditation allows us to quiet the surface-level noise of our thoughts, enabling us to delve deeper into the layers of our being. Through this practice, we begin to tap into the vast reservoir of potential that lies beneath the surface of our conscious awareness.

Meditation is, in essence, the alchemical process for the mind. Just as alchemists sought to transmute base metals into gold, meditation allows us to transmute our automatic, conditioned thoughts into higher flow states of awareness.

In doing so, we free ourselves from the constraints of old patterns and conditioning, stepping into a state of expanded consciousness where transformation and growth can occur, empowering us to consciously create the reality we desire.

What Does Flow Feel Like?

Flow is not simply about doing something well—it is about becoming one with the moment. Those who experience it describe common sensations:

- **Deep Absorption** – Total focus on the task at hand, with no awareness of distractions.
- **Effortless Action** – Movements or thoughts feel automatic, intuitive, and smooth.
- **Loss of Self-Identity** – The sense of "I" dissolves; there is no room for doubt or second-guessing.
- **Time Warp** – Hours melt away when immersed it creative joy.
- **Intrinsic Motivation** – The activity itself is fulfilling, regardless of external rewards.

Imagine an artist at her easel, completely immersed in her painting. Each brushstroke moves in perfect rhythm, guided by an unspoken connection between vision and motion. Each color blending effortlessly as she creates a masterpiece without overthinking.

She is not forcing her art—it is simply flowing from within when she's in theta state. Every movement is intuitive, guided by a creative force beyond conscious thought. Hours pass like fleeting moments, yet she is neither exhausted nor distracted. She exists only in the now.

A musician lost in melody feels the pulse of the music deep within her soul, every note echoing the joy of her being. In flow, creativity is effortless, and the joy that arises isn't something we chase—it simply emerges, organically.

Even the most challenging tasks feel rewarding, fulfilling, as if every step is part of a journey where the effort is transformed into enjoyment.

But perhaps the most exhilarating aspect of flow is the sensation that everything is working, effortlessly. Imagine a dancer on stage, her body gliding across the floor, her steps no longer requiring thought. They happen as though guided by an invisible force, each movement flowing into the next with perfect rhythm.

A coder working on an algorithm might experience the answers materializing, as if the solutions were already waiting to be discovered. In this state, there is no resistance, no struggle. Every action feels inevitable, an extension of my being, like a conversation between the universe and myself.

The flow state is more than just an emotional experience—it is the ultimate experience of optimal regulation. It is a neurobiological phenomenon where different brainwave frequencies synchronize to promote creativity, focus, and peak performance.

Understanding the role of alpha, beta, theta, and gamma waves allows us to recognize how the brain achieves this harmonious state. As we practice entering flow, we can cultivate the optimal conditions for creativity, innovation, and excellence in any area of life—whether in sports, art, work, or everyday tasks.

Flow isn't just a state of doing; it is a state of being, where our minds, bodies, spirit, and emotions operate in perfect balance. It is not just about doing something well; it is about being fully absorbed in the moment, where action and awareness merge into one.

VAGUS NERVE RESET

The human voice is more than a means of communication—it is a powerful instrument of healing. Singing, humming, and chanting don't merely produce sound; they awaken the vagus nerve, a vital conduit of the parasympathetic nervous system that orchestrates the body's ability to relax, restore, and regenerate.

This intricate nerve, stretching from the brainstem through the heart and into the gut, serves as a bridge between voice and vitality. By activating it, vocalization unlocks profound physiological benefits, from reducing oxidative stress to fostering neurogenesis—the birth of new brain cells.

Gateway to Healing

Scientific research reveals that stimulating the vagus nerve has remarkable neuroprotective effects. A study published in Scientific Reports found that vagus nerve stimulation (VNS) significantly reduces oxidative stress, a major contributor to cellular aging and neurodegenerative diseases.

By limiting the accumulation of reactive oxygen species—harmful molecules that damage cells—and dampening inflammation, VNS aids in protecting brain function and overall well-being. This finding suggests that activating the vagus nerve through vocal exercises may enhance cognitive resilience and emotional well-being. *(Source: Vagus Nerve Stimulation, Neurorehabilitation and Neural Repair, 2020)*

The magic lies in the mechanics of vocalization. When we sing, hum, or chant, we engage multiple physiological processes that stimulate the vagus nerve:

- **Breath Control:** Deep, diaphragmatic breathing—a fundamental aspect of vocalization—enhances vagal tone, slowing the heart rate and activating the body's relaxation response.
- **Vocal Cord Vibration:** The wavelength of energy produced while vocalizing create a direct mechanical stimulation of the vagus nerve. Notably, certain tones, such as the high C note at 528 Hz, resonate at a frequency often associated with cellular repair and positive physiological effects.
- **Auditory Stimulation:** Listening to rhythmic melodies and harmonic tones influences neural circuits connected to the vagus nerve, promoting a state of deep relaxation and emotional balance.

Power of the Human Voice

While the scientific community continues to explore the full extent of vocalization's impact on brain health, the evidence is compelling: our voices hold the key to self-healing.

Singing, humming, and chanting are more than mere expressions—they are gateways to neural restoration, reduced oxidative stress, and enhanced cognitive function.

By harnessing the power of sound, we may unlock the extraordinary potential within us to heal, harmonize, and thrive.

Brain's Cleaning System

The lymphatic and nervous systems form a profound, symbiotic relationship—one that dictates the body's ability to detoxify, heal, and thrive. Though often discussed separately, these two intricate systems are inextricably linked, influencing everything from cognitive clarity to immune resilience.

While the nervous system controls thoughts, emotions, and bodily functions, the lymphatic system acts as the body's waste removal system, clearing out toxins, dead cells, and excess fluids.

When the lymphatic system becomes sluggish, waste builds up, leading to inflammation, fatigue, and even cognitive issues like brain fog. But when it flows properly, it supports mental clarity, immune strength, and overall vitality.

For years, scientists believed the brain had no way to flush out waste—until they discovered the glymphatic system, the brain's own detox. This network clears out toxins and proteins linked to neurodegenerative diseases like Alzheimer's.

However, it only works during deep sleep. When we don't get enough restorative rest, harmful waste lingers in the brain, leading to inflammation, memory issues, and cognitive decline.

At the center of this connection is the vagus nerve, a vital link between the brain and body. It helps regulate heart rate, digestion, and—importantly—lymphatic circulation. When activated, the vagus nerve signals the body to relax, reducing inflammation and encouraging lymph flow.

Activities like deep breathing, singing, humming, and meditation naturally stimulate this nerve, helping to flush toxins and support nervous system balance.

A congested lymphatic system can trigger a chain reaction in the body, affecting:

- Brain function – leading to brain fog, memory issues, and mental fatigue.
- Energy levels – causing chronic fatigue and sluggishness.
- Immune response – making the body more prone to illness and inflammation.
- Nervous system balance – contributing to anxiety, stress, and mood swings.

Since the nervous system depends on lymphatic draining to clear out toxins, poor lymphatic flow can leave the brain and body feeling weighed down and out of sync.

You can support both systems with simple, natural habits:

- Breathe deeply – Expands the lungs, stimulates the vagus nerve, and moves lymph fluid.
- Move regularly – Walking, stretching, and exercise help pump lymph through the body.
- Stay hydrated – Lymph is mostly water, so dehydration slows it down.
- Prioritize deep restorative sleep – Allows the brain's glymphatic system to remove toxins.
- Try lymphatic massage or dry brushing – Helps clear blockages and improves circulation.

When the lymphatic and nervous systems work together in harmony, the body feels lighter, the mind becomes clearer, and overall well-being improves. By taking simple steps to keep both systems flowing, you can unlock greater energy, mental clarity, and long-term health.

METAPHYSICAL POWER OF PRESENCE

In the quiet stillness of the present moment, all illusion dissolves. The mind seeks to pull us into the past, where old wounds linger, or into the future, where fears and doubts take root.

Yet, the most profound truth is simple: only the now is real. It is in this fleeting instant that we hold the power to connect with the divine force that flows through all things. To be fully present is to awaken to our highest potential, to access the infinite space where time itself becomes irrelevant.

Imagine, for a moment, that you are standing at the edge of a vast ocean. The waves crash around you, relentless and powerful. But when you stop, breathe, and simply be in the moment, the ocean calms. It becomes clear, serene. This is the power of being. When we release the grip of the past and the anticipation of the future, we tap into an inner stillness that is not bound by time, but rather, connected to all of existence.

The teachings of the ancients reveal that in the present, we align with the universal flow. The pulse of creation beats in harmony with our hearts, and we become conduits of the divine energy that shapes our world. In this space, we are free from the confines of our survival-based ego programs and its stories.

We transcend the illusion of separation, realizing that we are one with everything in existence—everything we have been and everything we will become.

To live fully in the present is to step into your power, to become the co-creator of your own reality. In this moment, you are infinite. The past is no longer a burden, and the future is merely a potential. In the now, you are boundless. And in this perspective, you discover that you are both the dream and the dreamer, co-creating the reality you choose.

Mastering New Skills

Let's say you have always dreamed of playing the piano, the elegant sweep of your fingers across the keys filling the room with beautiful music. Yet, every time you sit at the piano, your fingers stumble, your mind feels clouded, and the notes don't quite sound right. It's frustrating. However, your brain is capable of far more than you realize. Through repetition, dedication, and focused practice, you can transform from a clumsy beginner to a skilled musician.

Learning to play the piano, like learning a new language or diving into mindfulness meditation, is an exercise in neuroplasticity. The more you practice, the more your brain adapts. In the beginning, your motor cortex, the region responsible for coordinating movement, is working overtime, sending signals to your hands and fingers that they are not yet familiar with.

Your auditory cortex, which processes sound, is constantly adjusting to help you distinguish the different notes, and your cerebellum, the brain's timing mechanism, is fine-tuning your sense of rhythm. At first, it feels difficult—awkward, even—but this is the process of your brain laying down new neural pathways.

With every note, every scale, every chord, you're reinforcing these connections. As you continue practicing, the initial discomfort begins to fade. Your fingers move with greater ease, the music starts to flow, and your mind becomes less cluttered.

The more consistent your practice, the stronger and more efficient these neural circuits become. Eventually, your brain's pathways are so well-established that playing becomes second nature. What once felt foreign is now an extension of yourself.

This ability to reshape your brain enables you to transform yourself by simply practicing, by showing up day after day and committing to growth. The piano, once a daunting challenge, becomes a beautiful instrument for artistic expression, and you—once a beginner— become a master.

The Learning Process:

1. **Start Slow and Small** – When learning the piano, break down the piece you are learning into sections. Instead of trying to play the entire piece at once, focus on one small section. For example, master the first two measures of the song, and then gradually add more.

2. **Deliberate Practice** – Practice intentionally. Slow down the pace, and focus on each finger placement, ensuring you are learning the

correct movements. This is key to creating strong neural pathways for the motor coordination required.

3. **Visualization** – Visualize yourself playing the piece perfectly. Your brain doesn't differentiate between imagination and reality, so when you imagine playing the piano flawlessly, you are strengthening the neural pathways that control your fingers.

4. **Consistency** – Practice every day. Even short, 10-minute sessions daily will gradually build stronger connections between your brain and the motor actions needed to play.

5. **Positive Feedback** – Celebrate the small wins. When you get a few notes right or play a section smoothly, acknowledge your progress. The brain releases dopamine—the feel-good neurotransmitter—whenever you succeed, reinforcing the new neural pathways and boosting motivation.

The Brain's Infinite Potential

Your brain is your superpower. Unlock your potential to rewrite your story, evolve, and step into the highest version of yourself. This hero's journey is one of continuous growth, and every step you take is not just rewiring your brain but transforming your entire life, which is yours to create.

You are the architect of your mind. The only limit to your transformation is the belief that you cannot change.

QUANTUM PLAYBOOK:
RESETTING FOR INNER BALANCE

Emotional regulation is a skill we can cultivate at any point in our lives. By learning to self-soothe, recognizing our triggers, and using tools like breathwork, mindful movement, and somatic practices, we can guide our nervous system from dysregulation to calm. Though we cannot change the past, we have the power to rewire our responses in the present, building a foundation of emotional resilience that can sustain us throughout our lives.

Understanding how the vagus nerve plays a crucial role in regulating the parasympathetic nervous system is essential for our emotional and physical well-being. When chronically stressed, however, it becomes dysregulated, diminishing resilience, heightening inflammation, and fuelling anxiety (*Source: Dr. Stephen Porges, Polyvagal Theory*).

On a deeper level, our seven energy centers (chakras) govern the flow of vitality throughout our body. When blocked, they disrupt balance, leading to mental, emotional, and physical disparities.

By integrating neuroscience, vagus nerve stimulation, and energy alignment, we unlock powerful pathways of transformation—dissolving trauma, regulating the nervous system, and restoring harmony between body and mind. This process reconnects us to our highest state of coherence and optimal well-being.

Step 1: Balancing the Root Center (I AM) – Safety and Belonging

Location: Base of the spine
Governs: Survival, grounding, physical security
Nervous System Connection: Autonomic Nervous System, fight-or-flight response

Description: The root center is our foundation, our sense of security, stability, and connection to the physical world. When we live in fear, insecurity, lack, or survival mode, we become disconnected from our innate sense of belonging.

When misaligned, it triggers worry and survival mode, causing the nervous system to remain stuck in fight-or-flight *(Dr. Bessel van der Kolk, The Body Keeps the Score).* Childhood trauma, financial instability, or relationship issues can lead to root imbalances, which contribute to chronic stress and fear. Activate grounding techniques to reset the vagus nerve and establish nervous system stability.

Regulation Techniques

- **Grounding (Earthing):** Walking barefoot on natural surfaces regulates cortisol and shifts the nervous system into a parasympathetic state.
- **Cold Exposure (Hydrotherapy):** Activates the vagus nerve, reducing inflammation and lowering stress.
- **Nutritional Balance:** Magnesium, omega-3, and adaptogenic herbs (ashwagandha, Rhodiola) reduce overactivation of the sympathetic nervous system.
- **Light Visualization:** Picture a red glowing light at the base of the spine, grounding you into the soil of safety.
- **Yoga:** Tree pose, warrior pose, squats.

Affirmation: *I AM grounded, stable, and secure. I trust the foundation of my life. I AM safe in my body and on this Earth.*

Step 2: Balancing the Sacral Center (I FEEL) –Emotional Flow and Creativity

Location: Below the navel

Governs: Emotions, sensuality, creative expression

Nervous System Connection: Enteric Nervous System, gut-brain axis

Description: Imbalances in this energy center leads to suppressed emotions, guilt, and stagnation *(Dr. Caroline Myss, Anatomy of the Spirit)*. Repressed emotions or unprocessed trauma related to intimacy, guilt, or shame can prevent the flow of creativity and vitality.

Release emotional blockages by engaging in practices that activate the vagus nerve and restore emotional flow.

Regulation Techniques

- **Somatic Therapy:** Engaging in expressive movement (dance, tai chi) helps release stored trauma.
- **Polyvagal Exercises:** Stimulating the vagus nerve (humming, deep diaphragm breathing) calms emotional dysregulation.
- **Probiotic-Rich Diet:** A healthy gut microbiome supports serotonin production, crucial for emotional balance.
- **Creative Expression:** Engage in painting, writing, or music to activate neuroplasticity and emotional healing.
- **Water Therapy:** Baths, swimming, or visualizing orange glow and water flow can balance this energy center.
- **Yoga:** Hip-opening poses like butterfly, pigeon pose.

Affirmation: *I FEEL fully alive and honor my emotions and express my creativity freely. I trust my heart and allow my authentic self to shine unapologetically.*

Step 3: Balancing the Solar Plexus (I DO) – Self-Worth and Personal Power

Location: Upper abdomen

Governs: Personal power, motivation, self-discipline

Nervous System Connection: Sympathetic Nervous System, adrenal regulation

Description: The solar plexus is the center of self-confidence and inner strength. When this center is imbalanced, doubt, low self-esteem, and fear of failure dominate (*Dr. Joe Dispenza, Breaking the Habit of Being Yourself*).

Seeking validation externally or avoiding responsibility weakens the solar plexus and causes emotional burnout. Embody resilience by taking consistent, aligned actions and radical accountability that reinforce your self-worth and vagus nerve health.

Regulation Techniques

- **Intermittent Fasting:** Enhances mitochondrial function, improving energy levels and stress resilience while regulating the metabolism.

- **Postural Adjustments:** Standing tall with open posture reduces cortisol and increases confidence.
- **Sunlight Exposure:** Boosts serotonin and dopamine, supporting motivation and energy.
- **Light Visualization:** Envision a golden flame in your abdomen, fuelling your confidence.
- **Breathwork** (*Kapalabhati Pranayama*): Rapid belly breathing activates the parasympathetic nervous system, reducing stress.
- **Yoga:** Core-strengthening poses like plank, boat pose.

Affirmation: *I DO succeed in manifesting my heart's desires. My power comes from within. My confidence radiates and I take aligned action toward my highest destiny.*

Step 4: Balancing the Heart Center (I LOVE) –Devotion and Self-Acceptance

Location: Center of the chest
Governs: Devotion, compassion, connection
Nervous System Connection: Parasympathetic Nervous System, oxytocin release

Description: The *Coherent Heart* field is the bridge between the physical lower world and higher self, the center of pure love consciousness. When wounded, this field is closed and we may struggle to give or receive love freely, carrying resentment, grief, or self-rejection.

When the heart is unblocked, we activate the power of free-will and discernment, tapping into the quantum unified field of flow *(Dr. Rollin McCraty, HeartMath Institute).*

Grief, resentment, or self-rejection creates blockages in the center, disrupting both emotional and physical health. Activate *Heart Coherence* through techniques that strengthen the vagus nerve and restore emotional balance.

Regulation Techniques

- **Heart Rate Variability (HRV) Training:** Practices like coherent breathing (5-5-5-5 breathing) improve vagal tone and stress resilience.
- **Social Connection:** Cuddling, eye contact, and loving relationships increase oxytocin, reducing anxiety.
- **Laughter Therapy:** Stimulates the vagus nerve, balancing heart rhythms and emotional stability.
- **Gratitude Practice:** Write down or say three things you are grateful for every day to activate the vagus nerve and promote positively charged emotion.

- **Light Visualization:** Visualize a green light expanding from your chest outward.
- **Yoga:** Cobra, camel, bridge.

Affirmation: *I LOVE and accept myself exactly as I am. I forgive myself and others with ease and grace.*

Step 5: Throat Center (I SPEAK) – Expression and Authenticity

Location: Throat

Governs: Communication, self-expression, truth

Nervous System Connection: Vagus Nerve, vocal tone regulation

Description: Living behind an inauthentic, false mask of delusion or suppressing our voice leads to energetic blockages here. Fear of judgment, people-pleasing, or struggling to articulate emotions can hinder this center.

Express your voice with confidence but with respect and integrity without causing harm to anyone. Engage in journaling, chanting, or singing to open this energy channel. Find the courage to tell your story so others can relate. Release the fear of being misunderstood.

Regulation Techniques

- **Chanting and Humming**: OM stimulates the vagus nerve, calming the nervous system.

- **Expressive Writing:** Releasing thoughts onto paper activates emotional processing centers.
- **Mindful Speech and Deep Listening:** Engages prefrontal cortex, reducing stress and improving emotional regulation.
- **Light Visualization:** Picture a vibrant blue light radiating from your throat.
- **Yoga:** Shoulder stand, fish pose.

Affirmation: *My voice matters, it is powerful, clear, and honest. I express my highest wisdom with authenticity. I SPEAK with integrity, confidence and grace.*

Step 6: Third Eye (I SEE) – Intuition and Inner Wisdom

Location: Forehead, between the brows
Governs: Intuition, insight, inner wisdom
Nervous System Connection: Pineal Gland, melatonin regulation

Description: The third eye or pineal gland is the gateway to clarity and perception beyond the physical world. It is the radio antenna connected to higher dimensional realms, frequencies of the universe that go beyond physical matter. It is our soul's guidance system.

When clouded by doubt, illusion, or overthinking, we struggle to trust our intuition and make aligned choices. Meditate, practice visualization, and trust the subtle nudges from within. Reduce distractions and spend time in stillness to sharpen inner vision.

Regulation Techniques

- **Mindfulness Contemplation:** Strengthens prefrontal cortex, improving clarity and intuition.
- **Omega-3 Fatty Acids and DHA:** Supports brain function and neurogenesis.
- **Circadian Rhythm Alignment:** Reducing screen time before bed optimizes melatonin and sleep quality.
- **Light Visualization:** Picture deep indigo light activating your inner wisdom.
- **Yoga:** Child's pose, forward folds.

Affirmation: *I trust my intuition and my guidance system. I SEE clearly beyond illusion. I trust my inner wisdom and divine intuition.*

Step 7: Crown Chakra (I KNOW AND COMMAND) – Transcendence and Higher Self

Location: Top of the head
Governs: Spiritual connection, enlightenment
Nervous System Connection: Default Mode Network, expanded consciousness

Description: The crown field connects us to the divine Source, the infinite intelligence of the universe where the higher self exists. Feelings of disconnection, illusion of separation, existential doubt, or lack of purpose often stem from imbalances and misalignment.

Engage in metaphysical practices and philosophies shared in my book, *Coherent Heart,* that resonate with you—meditation, prayer, radical intention scripting, or contemplation. Surrender control and open yourself to divine guidance.

Regulation Techniques

- **Pineal Gland Activation** (Sun Gazing and Meditation): Supports serotonin-to-melatonin conversion, enhancing spiritual connection.
- **Transcendental Meditation:** Alters brainwave activity, shifting into theta and gamma frequencies.
- **Gratitude and Higher Purpose:** Enhances neuroplasticity, rewiring for abundance and purpose.
- **Light Visualization:** Imagine a brilliant violet light connecting you to universal wisdom.
- **Yoga:** Savasana, lotus pose.

Affirmation: *I KNOW that I'm an expression of divine Source. Infinite intelligence flows through me. I*

COMMAND that I anchor the highest potential timeline of unity and peace.

When you align your scientific knowledge with energetic awareness, you reclaim control over your nervous system, healing from the inside out, shifting your perception.

Your body is the temple, your mind the architect, your heart the bridge to the quantum field, and your spirit the guiding force.

When emotional and spiritual intelligence synchronize, you move beyond limitation, attuning to the harmonic flow of creation itself.

In this state of coherence, intention shapes reality, energy bends to consciousness, and the unseen forces of the universe align in your favor. This is the alchemy of transformation—the moment you transcend, create, and awaken to infinite possibility.

6. Navigating Mental Health

Mental health is not merely a concept—it is the essence of our lived experience, shaping our thoughts, emotions, and interactions with the world. Every feeling we harbor, every memory we store, leaves an imprint on the brain's intricate neural pathways. Yet, these pathways are not rigid.

Even in the face of trauma and adversity, the brain possesses an extraordinary ability to rewire, adapt, and heal. This dynamic process of neuroplasticity is the foundation of resilience, offering a path to liberation from patterns of suffering and a return to inner harmony.

For years, the prevailing belief in neuroscience held that the brain's structure remained largely unchanged after childhood. However, groundbreaking research has dismantled this notion.

Beneath the surface, mental health is orchestrated by a delicate interplay of biology, psychology, and chemistry. Every thought, emotion, and experience reshape the brain's internal landscape, influencing our sense of stability and well-being.

Understanding this science deepens our awareness of just how profoundly mental health governs every facet of our existence—and how remarkably we can heal.

At its core, mental health is the equilibrium of the brain, an organ of immense complexity, where neurotransmitters, hormones, and neural structures collaborate to regulate mood, memory, and cognition.

Yet, when subjected to prolonged stress, trauma, or emotional distress, this intricate system can falter, disrupting its natural rhythms and impairing its ability to function optimally.

More than a measure of emotional stability, mental health defines our psychological and social well-being, influencing our decision-making, stress management, and relationships.

It is essential at every stage of life, from childhood through adulthood. Scientific advancements have illuminated the deep connection to biological, psychological, and environmental factors, revealing that mental health is not just an aspect of life—it is the very foundation of human experience.

Neuroplasticity: The Brain's Power to Rewire and Heal

Contrary to past beliefs, we have learned that the brain is not a static organ—it is an evolving magnum opus. Neuroplasticity, the brain's ability to reconfigure itself, is a beacon of hope for those struggling with mental health imbalance.

Trauma, stress, and depression can carve destructive pathways into neural circuits, yet this same mechanism allows for healing and renewal. Therapeutic interventions—such as psychotherapy, mindfulness, and meditation—can stimulate neuroplastic change, restoring balance and resilience. *(Source: Davidson & McEwen, 2012)*

Genetics: Dance Between Nature and Nurture

While genetics lay the groundwork for mental health, environment and experience compose the narrative.

A family history of mental illness can predispose individuals to similar struggles, but epigenetics—the study of how genes are influenced by external factors—reveals a more nuanced outlook.

Trauma, stress, and lifestyle choices can activate or suppress genetic expressions, shaping mental health in profound ways. *(Source: Meyer-Lindenberg, 2010)*

Understanding this interplay empowers individuals to rewrite their genetic destiny through conscious choices and healing interventions.

Psychological Factors

The process of neuroplasticity reflects how neural circuits reshape in response to experiences, learning, or injury, dynamically transforming the mind's inner perceptions and outward interactions.

Deeply influenced by psychological factors such as thoughts, emotions, and environmental stimuli, this adaptive ability underscores the intricate interplay between mental resilience and biological change.

Research reveals how neuroplasticity fosters cognitive flexibility, emotional regulation, and recovery from traumatic imbalance, seamlessly bridging the tangible neural framework with the intangible psyche. *(Source: Siegel, D. J. The Developing Mind: How Relationships and the Brain Interact to Shape Who We Are, 2020)*

1. Cognitive and Emotional Processes: The Lens Which We Perceive Reality

- The mind is a storyteller, and the narratives it spins dictate emotional well-being. Cognitive distortions—such as catastrophic thinking and black-and-white reasoning—are hallmark traits of depression and anxiety. Negative thought patterns create mental prisons, while emotional dysregulation amplifies suffering, forming the foundation of imbalances like borderline personality disorder *(Beck, 1967; Linehan, 1993).*

2. Attachment Theory: The Echo of Childhood in Adulthood

- Our earliest relationships leave lasting imprints. Attachment theory suggests that childhood bonds with caregivers shape emotional resilience or fragility. Insecure attachments—formed through neglect, inconsistency, or trauma—often manifest in adulthood as anxiety, depression, and relationship difficulties *(Bowlby, 1988).* Recognizing and healing these patterns can restore emotional balance and deepen connections with others.

3. Stress and Coping: The Silent Sculptor of the Mind

- Stress is an unavoidable force, but how we navigate it determines its impact. The hypothalamic-pituitary-adrenal (HPA) axis, responsible for regulating cortisol—the body's stress hormone—can become overactivated under chronic pressure. Prolonged exposure to stress rewrites the brain, increasing vulnerability to anxiety, depression, and PTSD *(McEwen, 2008).* Cultivating adaptive coping strategies, such as mindful conscious breathwork, and resilience training, can act as a shield against its destructive effects.

4. Social Support: The Healing Power of Connection

- Human connection is a cornerstone of mental well-being. Research has consistently shown that robust social networks bolster psychological resilience, whereas isolation magnifies vulnerability to depression and anxiety *(Cohen & Wills, 1985)*. Meaningful relationships serve as emotional anchors, providing support in times of turbulence and reinforcing the intrinsic value of belonging *(Hawkley & Cacioppo, 2010)*.

ENVIRONMENTAL & LIFESTYLE FACTORS

Just as your environment influences you, the choices you make every day sculpt your brain's very architecture.

As you embark on this journey of self-healing, remember: the process is not instantaneous, but it is inevitable. By consciously choosing the environments, thoughts, and actions that nurture your mind, body, and spirit, you can reshape the very fabric of your reality.

1. Childhood Adversity and Trauma: The Shadows That Linger

- The echoes of childhood trauma reverberate through adulthood, shaping brain architecture and emotional regulation. Adverse childhood experiences (ACEs)—such as abuse, neglect, or toxic dysfunction—wreak havoc on the developing brain, altering key structures like the prefrontal cortex and hippocampus *(Anda, 2006)*. Healing from these wounds requires intentional effort, whether through therapy, self-reflection, or trauma-informed practices.

2. Sleep and Mental Health: The Brain's Restorative Elixir

- Sleep is the unsung hero of mental well-being. Chronic sleep disturbances, such as insomnia, have been directly linked to mood imbalance, cognitive impairment, and emotional dysregulation *(Hartz, 2013)*. Sleep serves as a crucial period of neural restoration, emotional processing, and memory consolidation, making it a non-negotiable pillar of mental health.

3. Diet and Physical Activity: Fueling the Mind for Resilience

- The gut and brain share an intimate connection, with nutrition playing a pivotal role in emotional stability. Diets fueled by processed foods contribute to inflammation and mental health imbalance, while nutrient-dense foods enhance cognitive function and emotional balance. Similarly, physical activity is a natural antidepressant, stimulating the release of serotonin and dopamine—neurotransmitters that promote well-being and vitality *(Schuch, 2016)*. Mindful movement is not just exercise; it is medicine for the mind.

Your brain is a canvas, and through neuroplasticity, you are the artist—creating a masterpiece of resilience, transformation, and limitless potential.

TRAUMA-MENTAL HEALTH LINK

Trauma is a profound neurological disruption. It extends far beyond psychological distress—it reshapes the lens through which we interpret and experience the world, altering the very fabric of how we perceive safety and danger.

It heightens our sensitivity to threats, real or imagined, often leaving us at odds with our own bodies.

This is why understanding the intricate workings of our nervous system—the mechanism that discerns safety from danger—is essential.

By recognizing how our body instinctively responds to its environment, we can begin to bridge the gap between fear and calm. Rather than battling against these natural responses, we learn to collaborate with our body, guiding it toward equilibrium.

This partnership transforms our relationship with ourselves, allowing us to navigate our mental health with greater resilience, self-awareness, and trust.

By exploring the intricate linkages between trauma and underlying mental health imbalance, we can better navigate the path to recovery and resilience.

Post-Traumatic Stress Disorder (PTSD): The Brain Trapped in Survival Mode

PTSD arises when trauma overwhelms the brain's ability to process, trapping survivors in a relentless cycle of fear and hypervigilance. The amygdala—the brain's alarm system—becomes hyperactive, constantly scanning for danger and triggering intense emotional reactions.

At the same time, the hippocampus, which helps distinguish past from present, can shrink, leading to intrusive flashbacks that feel as vivid and real as the original trauma.

The prefrontal cortex, responsible for rational thought and impulse control, weakens, making it increasingly difficult to override the body's fear responses.

This neurological imbalance keeps individuals stuck in survival mode, unable to break free from the past *(Bremner, 2006)*.

Depression: When the Brain's Chemistry Falters

As a trauma survivor, I've come to understand how deeply our past experiences can impact our emotional well-being. Prolonged stress drains the brain's ability to regulate emotions, leaving us more vulnerable to anxiety and depression.

Chronic hyperarousal overwhelms the amygdala, amplifying fear responses, while the prefrontal cortex—responsible for calm decision-making—struggles to keep up, leading to constant worry and restlessness.

In moments of depression, I've felt how the hippocampus, the brain's memory and emotional regulator, can also shrink under the weight of trauma. This affects cognitive function, reinforcing feelings of hopelessness and making it harder to see a way forward.

Serotonin and cortisol imbalances further contribute to mood instability, making even small stressors feel insurmountable *(Shin, 2006; Drevets, 2001)*.

Anxiety: The body's natural response to perceived danger

I have found that the key to calming anxious thoughts lies in the very structure of our nervous system. Instead of trying to rationalize anxiety, I've learned to focus on the sensations in my body.

By tuning into areas like the belly, throat, or chest, I shift from judgment to self-compassion. This simple change has allowed me to uncover the deeper roots of my anxiety, leading to healing, self-trust, and serenity.

For too long, I misunderstood anxiety as something to fight. I believed it was a threat to avoid, which only made it worse. But the real transformation began when I softened toward it—when I learned to listen with curiosity and compassion to the messages it carried. Anxiety, I realized, was not my enemy; it was trying to protect me.

When I began to hold space for my anxious parts, I created new pathways to resilience. With practice, my nervous system slowly learned to trust again. Now, I face life's challenges with strength, no longer driven by the frantic need to control every outcome.

Anxiety triggers the body's fight-or-flight response—heightened heart rate, rapid breathing, muscle tension. While this is essential in moments of real danger, it becomes problematic when excessive and persistent. Anxiety, such as generalized anxiety, social anxiety, and panic attacks, are the real epidemic affecting millions worldwide *(Source: American Psychiatric Association, 2023)*.

Dissociation and Identity Fragmentation: The Mind's Escape Mechanism

For individuals exposed to extreme or prolonged trauma, the brain may resort to dissociation as a defense mechanism. This detachment from reality serves as a psychological shield, allowing the mind to distance itself from overwhelming pain.

However, over time, dissociation can blur the lines of identity, causing emotional numbness, memory gaps, and a persistent sense of disconnection. This fragmentation can manifest as identity confusion, making it difficult for individuals to establish a stable sense of self *(Source: American Psychiatric Association, 2023)*.

Addiction and Substance Abuse: The Hijacked Reward System

Trauma often primes the brain for addiction by altering the dopamine pathways that regulate pleasure and reward. When natural coping mechanisms fail, substances become an artificial escape, flooding the brain with dopamine, and temporarily numbing emotional pain.

Over time, this reliance on external stimuli rewires the brain's reward system, making addiction not just a behavioral issue but a deeply ingrained neurological pattern. The cycle of self-medication and dependence reinforces unhealthy coping strategies, making recovery a challenging but not insurmountable journey.

Understanding these neural mechanisms is crucial in destigmatizing mental health imbalance and fostering effective healing strategies. With the right interventions—therapy, mindfulness, medication, and social support—the brain can rewire, paving the way for strength, recovery, and renewed hope.

Pathways of Change

Often, anxiety emerges when we lose touch with the subtle, vital signals of our body. Disconnected from these sensations, even the slightest shifts within can feel overwhelming, spiraling us deeper into unease.

It begins slowly—perhaps a racing heart, a tightness in the chest, shallow, rapid breaths, or clammy palms.

We focus on these sensations as they seize our attention, magnified by the lens of fear, until they seem to herald an impending catastrophe. A tight chest no longer feels like simple tension; it becomes the harbinger of doom. The mind, desperate to make sense of these physical cues, weaves stories of danger: *Something is wrong with me. I'm in peril.*

These thoughts, far from soothing, ignite a cascade of stress, escalating the situation until it bursts into a full-blown panic attack. The body, already overwhelmed, becomes ensnared in this loop, with the mind amplifying every sensation as a threat.

The more we resist these feelings, the more insurmountable they seem.

In this cycle of push and pull, the body rebels against its experience, sensing danger in its own signals.

Meanwhile, the mind, unwilling to surrender control, interprets and reinterprets these sensations, compounding the distress. Fear feeds fear, and the spiral tightens.

Breaking free requires more than willpower; it demands self-attunement. To interrupt the pattern, we must reconnect with the body, grounding ourselves in its sensations without judgment or fear. By meeting these signals with presence and compassion, we reclaim the ability to regulate our responses, dissolving the hold of anxiety and restoring harmony between body and mind.

Example:

Most often, self-sabotage unfolds when we unconsciously undermine or push away the very things we long for, often without even realizing it. It manifests through subtle actions and behaviors that seem to work against our best intentions. Yet, these patterns are far from random—they are deeply rooted, unconscious responses designed to override our conscious desires.

At its core, self-sabotage is a form of self-protection. When our nervous system perceives what we desire as a potential threat, it intervenes to keep us "safe," even at the cost of our goals or happiness. This protective mechanism reflects a deeper conflict between the parts of us yearning for growth and the parts conditioned to fear it.

Recognizing these patterns is the first step in breaking free, allowing us to align our actions with our aspirations rather than our fears.

Somatic Healing Movement

Somatic healing techniques are body-centered therapies designed to release trauma and stress stored in the body, fostering emotional and physical healing.

These practices integrate awareness of physical sensations, mindful movement, and breathwork to reconnect individuals with their bodies, regulate the nervous system, and promote a sense of safety and well-being. *(Source: National Institute for the Clinical Application of Behavioral Medicine, 2023)*

The technique offers a powerful pathway to address anxiety and self-sabotage as an example, guiding us to reconnect with our bodies and transform the unconscious patterns that limits our life. These practices don't merely calm the mind—they speak directly to the body's wisdom, releasing stored tension and fostering a profound sense of safety and empowerment.

For anxiety, grounding becomes an anchor in the storm. Picture yourself standing barefoot on the cool, forgiving earth, its energy steadying the chaos within.

Engage all your senses: notice five things around you, feel textures beneath your fingertips, listen to indirect sounds, breathe in the air's fragrance, and taste the present moment.

Each sensation roots you deeper into the now moment, cutting through the spirals of fear.

Breathwork acts as your lifeline. Imagine drawing a steady square in the air with your breath—inhale for four beats, hold for four, exhale for four, and pause for four. With each cycle, feel the grip of panic loosen.

Or let your belly rise and fall, its rhythmic motion whispering reassurance to your nervous system. Use EFT for specific meridian points while acknowledging your anxiety and affirming safety.

When your body feels locked in tension, progressive muscle relaxation can help you unravel. Tighten and release each muscle group, starting from your toes and working upward, as if wringing anxiety from every fiber of your being.

And if the weight of fear becomes unbearable, shake it off—literally. Let your body tremble and quake as animals instinctively do after danger, discharging the nervous energy trapped within.

For self-sabotage, the work goes deeper, peeling back layers of resistance to uncover childhood wounds beneath. Begin with body awareness: close your eyes and scan your body like a map, searching for hidden tension or unease. Focus on these sensations, not as enemies but as messengers. Listen to what they have to say.

In moments of internal conflict, somatic movement can offer refuge. Recall a memory of safety—perhaps the warmth of sunlight on your skin or the quiet embrace of a favorite place. Let this feeling flood your body, anchoring you in its peace. Mindful movement becomes a form of expression, breaking the chains of fear and doubt. Through yoga or free-flowing dance, let your body speak without words, releasing emotions trapped beneath the surface.

Pair this with inner child work—place a hand over your heart and gently address the part of you that resists. Offer it compassion, as you would to an innocent child or pet that is scared and vulnerable.

When self-sabotage strikes, ask yourself: *What is my body trying to protect me from?* Sit with the answer, no matter how uncomfortable, and hold safe space without judgement for the feelings that surface. If the weight feels too heavy to carry alone, seek connection. A trusted friend, a beloved pet, or even a skilled therapist can help regulate your nervous system through shared presence.

Exploring somatic healing is more than a set of techniques—it's a reclamation. A journey to embrace your body as an ally, not an adversary. Through grounding, breath, movement, and compassion, you'll discover the profound strength within to soothe anxiety, disrupt self-sabotage, and step into a life guided by clarity, courage, and self-trust.

METABOLIC DYSFUNCTION

What if the mind's deepest suffering, the silent war within, was not merely a chemical imbalance, nor solely the echo of trauma, but something more primal—something cellular?

A crisis of energy. An unseen war waged within the very mitochondria that fuel our thoughts, emotions, and consciousness itself.

Science is beginning to unravel a viewpoint long hidden in plain sight: mental illness—depression, bipolar syndrome, schizophrenia—may be an imbalance of metabolism, born from a brain starved of its most essential resource: *energy*.

Dr. Christopher Palmer's Brain Energy Theory challenges the bedrock of modern psychiatry, revealing that when neurons lose their ability to produce and regulate energy, cognition dims, mood destabilizes, and reality itself fractures.

The mind does not simply break—it falters, like a city flickering in a rolling blackout, struggling to hold its structure as its power supply fades. *(Source: Dr. Christopher M. Palmer, 2022)*

Depression is not just sadness but suffocating inertia, a body wading through molasses as inflammation, oxidative stress, and insulin resistance conspire to smother the very spark of vitality.

Bipolar syndrome—a storm of extremes—is mirrored in the erratic shifts of glucose metabolism, the brain's delicate balance thrown into chaos. Schizophrenia, long shrouded in mystery, reveals its ties to the dysfunction of the tiny energy-producing structures inside our cell, where perception distorts as the mind fights against its own failing circuitry.

Yet, if mental illness is an energy crisis, then healing is not beyond reach. It means that the mind is not irreparably fractured but desperately malnourished.

It suggests that through metabolic restoration—by nourishing the body, stabilizing blood sugar, reducing inflammation, optimizing sleep, and reconnecting with the rhythms of nature—we may reignite the brain's lost vitality. *(Source: Dr. Christopher M. Palmer, 2022)*

It does not negate the weight of trauma, nor dismiss the complexity of genetics, but rather offers a radical revelation: that suffering is not a fixed state, but a dynamic one, influenced, altered, and—perhaps—ultimately transcended.

The implications are staggering. If we are to truly heal the mind, we must first understand the battlefield upon which it fights. And that battlefield is not only in the psyche but in the very engine of life itself—the invisible energy that fuels our existence.

Burnout's Silent Epidemic

There is an insidious force that gradually wears down the body, mind, and spirit. It creeps in like a shadow, often undetected until its toll has been taken.

In today's fast-paced, high-demand, virtually-connected world, burnout has become an epidemic—affecting not just those in high-stress professions but anyone who feels overwhelmed, underappreciated, or disconnected from their true sense of self.

What is Burnout?

Burnout is a profound unraveling of the mind and body, a collapse born from unrelenting stress that pushes beyond the limits of endurance. It begins subtly, with a creeping sense of unease, and crescendos into emotional, mental, and physical depletion that strips away vitality.

The pressure to meet constant demands—whether professional, relational, or self-imposed—slowly erodes resilience, leaving a void where motivation and passion once thrived. Tasks that once inspired now feel insurmountable, and the weight of helplessness takes hold.

At its core, burnout is a disruption of the delicate balance within, marked by dysregulation of the hypothalamic-pituitary-adrenal (HPA) axis and surging cortisol levels.

This physiological storm clouds cognitive clarity, destabilizes emotions, and undermines overall well-being, creating a cascade of disconnection from both self and purpose *(Source: Maslach, C., & Leiter, M. P., 2016).*

Anatomy of Burnout: How It Affects the Brain and Body

The brain, like the body, has limits. When we push ourselves too hard, too fast, for too long, the brain's capacity to regulate and adapt begins to break down.

The physiological impact of burnout is profound, often leading to emotional numbness, diminished cognitive function, and a decrease in overall well-being.

- **Stress Response System:** When we experience stress, the hypothalamic-pituitary-adrenal (HPA) axis is activated, triggering the release of stress hormones like cortisol and adrenaline. In short bursts, this is a healthy response—helping us rise to challenges. But when stress becomes chronic, the body's stress response system becomes overtaxed. Elevated cortisol levels suppress immune function, disrupt sleep, and impair cognitive performance.

- **Chronic Stress and the Brain:** Prolonged stress can lead to shrinkage of the hippocampus, the part of the brain responsible for memory and emotional regulation. This is why burnout often feels like an overwhelming fog: the brain becomes unable to process information efficiently, and emotions can feel out of control.

- **Impaired Emotional Regulation:** As burnout sets in, the prefrontal cortex, the brain's decision-making and emotional regulation center, becomes less active. This makes it harder to think clearly, make decisions, and regulate emotions. Burnout can result in irritability, frustration, and difficulty focusing. The amygdala, the brain's fear, and emotional processing center, may become hyperactive, amplifying negative emotions and creating a vicious cycle of stress and anxiety.

- **Physical Manifestations:** Burnout affects more than just the mind. The body is deeply affected by prolonged stress. Chronic fatigue, headaches, muscle tension, digestive issues, and sleep disturbances are all common physical symptoms of burnout. The body is essentially telling you that it has reached its limit.

Recognizing Early Signs of Burnout

- **Mental and Physical Exhaustion:** No matter how much rest you get, you still wake up feeling drained, both physically and mentally. Fatigue becomes your constant companion, making even simple tasks feel exhausting.
- **Social Withdrawal:** You start avoiding friends, family, or colleagues, not because you don't care, but because you don't have the energy to engage. Conversations feel draining, and isolation starts to feel easier than connection.
- **Loss of Motivation:** Tasks that once excited you now feel like a chore. Whether it's work, hobbies, walking your dog, or personal goals, you find yourself struggling to muster the enthusiasm you once had.

- **Difficulty Focusing:** Your thoughts feel scattered, concentration becomes a challenge, and forgetfulness sneaks into your daily routine. Even the simplest decisions seem harder to make.
- **Increased Irritability:** Small frustrations feel magnified. You become more impatient, short-tempered, and easily annoyed—often snapping at things that wouldn't have bothered you before.

If these signs resonate with you, don't ignore them. Burnout is serious—it can lead to long-term health issues and emotional strain. Prioritize rest, set boundaries, and care for your mental and physical well-being. And if the weight of burnout feels too heavy to carry alone, seek professional support. You deserve to feel balanced, energized, and at peace.

Emotional Toll of Burnout

Emotionally, burnout is often accompanied by feelings of hopelessness, frustration, and detachment. The more we push ourselves beyond our capacity, the more we feel disconnected from our sense of purpose.

In the workplace, burnout can result in decreased job satisfaction, reduced productivity, and a loss of creativity.

In personal life, it can erode relationships and create a sense of isolation, leaving individuals feeling like they are simply going through the motions without joy or fulfillment.

One of the most dangerous aspects of burnout is its ability to make us feel numb—emotionally detached from both our work and our lives. This detachment can lead to feelings of worthlessness, depression, and self-doubt.

Over time, these feelings can become entrenched, leading to long-term mental health challenges.

Impact of Burnout: When the Brain Blows a Fuse

A fuse box safeguards a home's electrical system, preventing circuits from overloading. When too much current surges through, the fuse blows, shutting down electricity to prevent catastrophic failure.

Our nervous system functions the same way. It regulates stress, emotions, and energy—much like a circuit managing electrical flow.

But when stress is relentless, whether from trauma, pressure, or exhaustion, the system is forced beyond capacity. If the overload continues, burnout sets in—a neurological shutdown designed to protect the mind and body from collapse.

However, burnout is not mere exhaustion. It is the brain's fail-safe, mirroring how a fuse blows to prevent an electrical fire. When demand exceeds capacity, neural pathways become overwhelmed, triggering a system-wide collapse.

1. Overload Leads to System Failure

Like an electrical circuit strained by excess demand, chronic stress disrupts neural function. The prefrontal cortex—responsible for decision-making, focus, and emotional regulation—deteriorates under prolonged exposure to stress hormones like cortisol. This results in:

- **Cognitive Short-Circuiting:** Brain fog, memory lapses, and mental fatigue, akin to an unstable power grid flickering before failure.
- **Emotional Numbness:** To conserve energy, the brain reduces emotional responsiveness, leading to detachment and apathy.
- **Scientific Insight:** Brain scans reveal reduced prefrontal cortex activity in individuals suffering from burnout, much like fluctuating power levels in an overloaded circuit.

2. Brain's Emergency Shutoff

A fuse blows to prevent a fire; burnout forces a shutdown to avert deeper neurological and physiological damage. The autonomic nervous system, responsible for regulating stress, is pushed into overdrive (fight-or-flight mode). Over time, it collapses into parasympathetic shutdown.

- **HPA Axis Dysregulation:** Chronic stress overloads the hypothalamic-pituitary-adrenal (HPA) axis, leading to adrenal fatigue, mood instability, and immune suppression.
- **Amygdala Overactivity:** The brain's fear center becomes hyperactive, heightening anxiety while impairing rational thinking.
- **Scientific Insight:** A Nature Neuroscience study found that prolonged stress enlarges the amygdala while shrinking the prefrontal cortex—akin to an overused circuit degrading over time.

3. Recovery Requires a Full System Reset

Once a fuse blows, power cannot be restored until the system is reset. Likewise, overcoming burnout demands intentional nervous system regulation.

- **Neuroplasticity-Based Healing:** Mindfulness, therapy, and structured rest help rewire stress responses.
- **Vagus Nerve Activation:** Deep breathing, meditation, and cold exposure stimulate this cranial nerve, shifting the body back into a parasympathetic recovery state.

- **Scientific Insight:** Research from the University of Pittsburgh shows mindfulness meditation increases gray matter density in stress-regulating brain regions, reversing burnout's impact.

4. Managing Energy to Prevent Overload

Just as a circuit trips when too many appliances run at once, the brain has a cognitive threshold before exhaustion sets in.

- **Cognitive Reserve Depletion:** Burnout drains the brain's adaptive capacity, weakening executive function and decision-making.
- **Dopamine Deficiency:** Chronic stress reduces dopamine receptor sensitivity, making once-enjoyable activities feel meaningless—a hallmark of burnout-related depression.
- **Scientific Insight:** A Harvard Medical School study linked burnout to reduced dopamine signaling, explaining the loss of motivation and joy in overworked individuals.

5. Recognizing the Warning Signs

A flickering light warns of an impending power failure. Burnout has its own pre-collapse indicators:

- Persistent fatigue that rest does not relieve.

- Irritability, emotional withdrawal, and loss of enthusiasm.
- Difficulty concentrating, brain fog, and forgetfulness.

Building a Burnout-Proof System

Like an electrician redistributing energy loads, we must manage mental and emotional energy wisely:

- **Set Boundaries** – Reduce unnecessary cognitive and emotional burdens.
- **Prioritize Recovery** – Implement structured rest, movement, meditation, and self-care.
- **Strengthen Neural Resilience** – Use neuroplasticity-based techniques such as gratitude journaling and cognitive reframing.

Burnout is not failure—it is a biological safeguard, a call to recalibrate. Like an overloaded circuit shutting down to prevent destruction, burnout signals the need for balance, boundaries, and restoration.

It is not merely about recovery; it is about building a more resilient, burnout-proof system for the future.

Pathways of Change

The brain has an incredible ability to heal, adapt, and regenerate—even after prolonged burnout. While chronic stress can distort neural pathways in harmful ways, intentional recovery practices can rewire the brain for resilience, restoring clarity, energy, and emotional balance.

Here's how neuroplasticity can heal and reverse burnout:

Step 1: Rest and Recovery

The first step in reversing burnout is prioritizing deep, intentional rest, which is the foundation for healing to occur. Chronic stress floods the brain with cortisol, depleting energy reserves and impairing cognitive function. True recovery isn't just about sleep—it's about creating space for mental and emotional recalibration.

- **Neuroscientific Insight:** Rest enables the hippocampus—responsible for memory and emotional regulation—to replenish, restoring neural plasticity and cognitive clarity.

Step 2: Mindfulness and Meditation

To rewire the stress response, mindfulness and meditation activate the parasympathetic nervous system, shifting the brain from survival mode into a state of restoration. These practices reduce amygdala hyperactivity, lowering stress responses while enhancing emotional regulation.

- **Cognitive Benefits:** Studies show mindfulness meditation strengthens the prefrontal cortex, improving decision-making, emotional resilience, and stress processing.

Step 3: Conscious Movement

Physical activity is one of the most powerful, scientifically-backed tools for both preventing and recovering from burnout. Exercise stimulates neurogenesis—the birth of new neurons—particularly in the hippocampus, an area often impaired by chronic stress.

- **Brain Chemistry Boost:** Movement releases endorphins and dopamine, restoring motivation, emotional stability, and a sense of well-being.

Step 4: Realigning Energy and Values

Burnout often signals a misalignment between your actions and your core values. Healing requires reconnecting with what truly fuels you, whether that means setting boundaries, saying no to draining obligations, or redefining your personal and professional path.

- **Neuroscientific Insight:** Engaging in meaningful endeavors activates the brain's reward circuitry, reinforcing motivation, emotional fulfillment, and long-term resilience.

Step 5: Therapy and Support

Professional guidance can be a catalyst for transformation. Cognitive Behavioral Therapy (CBT) helps rewire negative thought loops, replacing them with adaptive, empowering beliefs.

- **Psychological Insight:** Talking to a therapist or coach provides tools for managing stress, navigating emotions, and creating sustainable change.

Burnout is a wake-up call. A distress signal from the brain and body, urging you to recalibrate. Ignoring it leads to collapse; listening to it opens the door to transformation.

Remember, healing is not about returning to who you were before burnout—it is about becoming stronger, wiser, and more resilient.

METAPHYSICAL PATH TO RECOVERY

In my experience, emotional burnout is not just a state of mental fatigue; it's a profound depletion of spirit. The weight of burnout is heavy, and it seeps into your very essence, leaving you feeling disconnected, disillusioned, and powerless.

But what if I told you that this darkness is not a permanent state? That within you lies a powerful force—an untapped well of energy—waiting to be restored, realigned, and reawakened when you truly embrace and accept your worth.

Radical Self-Love Journey

Self-love and selfishness may appear similar, but their essence—the vibrational wavelength they emit couldn't be more different. The defining factor is intention.

Selfishness is the act of prioritizing one's own needs, desires, or interests, often with little regard for the well-being of others.

While it is frequently seen as a negative trait that can harm relationships or create an imbalance, selfishness also has a constructive egoic side, serving as a mechanism for self-preservation and boundary-setting when exercised mindfully.

From a neuroscience perspective, selfishness reflects the brain's natural drive to secure survival and reward. The prefrontal cortex mediates the balance between self-interest and empathy, while the amygdala and dopamine pathways fuel behaviors that seek immediate gratification.

Ultimately, selfishness is shaped by intent, impact, and the brain's dynamic interplay between self-preservation and social connection.

Self-love, however, is rooted in respect and care; it's choosing to step back when exhausted, honoring and prioritizing your well-being without harming others. The impact is quite telling.

It is the fundamental practice of valuing and tending for oneself with kindness, acceptance, and compassion. Far from being selfish or indulgent, it is a vital foundation for emotional well-being, resilience, and healthy relationships.

Self-love involves recognizing one's inherent worth, embracing imperfections, and prioritizing personal growth and self-care.

From a neuroscience perspective, self-love engages brain regions associated with positive self-referential processing, such as the medial prefrontal cortex, while reducing activity in areas linked to self-criticism, like the default mode network.

Oxytocin release, often referred to as the "love hormone," fosters feelings of warmth and self-acceptance, while neural pathways involved in reward, reinforce behaviors that nurture well-being.

By cultivating self-love, individuals strengthen their capacity for empathy and connection, as the brain's regulation of stress and reward systems creates harmony between personal fulfillment and interpersonal bonds.

Selfish actions breed resentment, leaving others feeling dismissed and undervalued, while self-love—when expressed with honesty and kindness—earns respect, even if it means occasional disappointment.

And then there's the emotional weight. Selfishness often leaves a bitter aftertaste of guilt or regret, while self-love empowers and reinforces self-worth with integrity. True self-love is not about putting ourselves above others—it's about knowing when to set boundaries without compromising compassion.

Practicing radical self-love is not indulgence. It is the divine act of honoring our worth, recognizing that we are just as deserving of kindness and compassion as anyone else.

It is the gentle whisper of reassurance when we falter, the soft embrace we offer ourselves when the world feels heavy. It is the moment we choose rest over relentless striving, grace over guilt, and love over exhaustion.

To heal from burnout, we must practice radical self-love on a daily basis. This is not selfishness; it's divine recognition that we must care for ourselves in order to be able to care for others. Embrace yourself with kindness. Speak to yourself with compassion.

When you nurture your spirit with unconditional love, you create the space for your energy to flourish once again.

- **Example:** Close your eyes and place a hand over your heart. Feel its steady rhythm, the quiet proof of your existence. Breathe deeply, and with each inhale, welcome in the warmth of self-compassion. With each exhale, release the weight of self-neglect. Let love fill the spaces where weariness once resided. Let it soften the edges of your being, reminding you that you are enough—not because of what you do for others, but simply because you exist.

When you nourish yourself with compassion, you create the space for your energy to flourish once again. You reclaim your radiance, your joy, your peace. And in doing so, you become an even brighter light for the world around you—not through sacrifice, but through self-honoring wholeness.

- **Affirmation:** *I am deserving of love, care, and compassion. I nurture my body, mind, and spirit with gentleness and patience. I choose self-devotion over exhaustion, knowing that my well-being is sacred.*

QUANTUM PLAYBOOK: REIGNITING VITALITY

This playbook is your roadmap to reclaiming your vitality through neuroplasticity, energy transmutation, and spiritual renewal. Each step will help shift you from depletion to wholeness, from exhaustion to radiance.

Step 1: Reconnect with Your Higher Self - The Compass of Healing

Burnout is often a sign of misalignment with your true essence. When you disconnect from your inner guidance, you lose clarity, direction, and emotional resilience. The remedy? Returning to your heart center, where peace and purpose reside.

- **Morning Alignment:** Before reaching for your phone, place a hand over your heart, take five deep breaths, and ask: What does my spirit need today?
- **Journaling Prompt:** Write a letter from your higher self. What wisdom does this version of you share?
- **Mindful Stillness:** Five minutes of meditation daily rewires the brain, calming the amygdala and enhancing prefrontal cortex function. *(Source: Harvard Medical School)*
- **Affirmation:** *I am deeply connected to my higher self. My intuition leads me toward peace, balance, and purpose.*

Step 2: Transcend Limiting Beliefs - Rewiring the Subconscious

Burnout is fueled by deeply ingrained beliefs—the silent programs that whisper: I must always give to be valued or My worth is tied to my achievements. These narratives drain your energy and lock you in cycles of exhaustion.

- **Reframe Rest as Power:** If you feel guilt when resting, say: Rest is productive. I recharge so I can give from abundance, not depletion.

- **Visualization Technique:** Close your eyes and see yourself fully restored. What does this version of you do differently? Embody it now.

- **Cognitive Rewiring:** Repeated affirmations and thought reframing reshape neural pathways, shifting burnout-driven beliefs into empowering truths. *(Source: Dr. Joe Dispenza)*

- **Affirmation:** *I am worthy of rest. My value is not measured by productivity. I honor my needs, release guilt, and embrace balance with ease.*

Step 3: Shift Frequencies - Transmute Exhaustion into Vitality

Burnout is not just mental—it is stagnant energy trapped in the body. Like a blocked river, this energy must be released and transformed back into life force. Movement, breathwork, and grounding practices activate energy transmutation, shifting you from depletion to vibrancy.

- **Breathwork for Energy Flow:** Inhale golden light, exhale fatigue. Repeat until you feel lighter.
- **Move to Break Stagnation:** Whether through yoga, walking, or somatic shaking, movement clears emotional debris, restores neural plasticity, and recharges energy centers. *(Source: Stanford Neuroscience Institute)*
- **Sound Healing Activation:** Chanting or listening to 432 Hz music shifts brainwave states, promoting relaxation and energy flow.
- **Affirmation:** *I am a powerful alchemist, transmuting exhaustion into vitality. With each breath, I release heaviness and invite renewal.*

Step 4: Realign with Purpose - Soul's Path to Fulfillment

Burnout arises when your actions no longer align with your soul's calling. It is not just physical exhaustion—it is the spirit's rebellion against a life that drains rather than nourishes.

- **Reconnect with Passion:** What once made you feel alive? Reignite forgotten joys—writing, painting, serving others, immersing in nature.
- **Define Your True North:** Purpose is not about what you do, but who you become. Ask: Does my daily life reflect my highest self and provide fulfillment?
- **Surrender to Synchronicity:** When you align with purpose, life flows effortlessly. Pay attention to signs, synchronicities, and intuitive nudges—they are guiding you home.
- **Affirmation:** *I am balanced and whole. My purpose embraces joy and passion to guide me. I choose to live with intention, creativity, and authenticity.*

Step 5: Set Boundaries - Sacred Energy Guides

Without boundaries, your energy is constantly drained, leaving nothing for your own healing. Having healthy boundaries are not walls; they are acts of self-honoring. They define where your energy is invested and ensure you are nourished, not depleted.

- **The Power of "No" Without Guilt:** Protecting your energy is a spiritual act. You do not owe an explanation.
- **Sacred Stillness Practice:** Spend five minutes in silence daily. No distractions. Just presence.
- **Reevaluate Your Commitments:** Ask: Does this obligation nourish or drain me? If it depletes you, let it go.
- **Affirmation:** *I honor my energy by setting boundaries that support my well-being. I release the need to overextend and embrace stillness as a source of renewal.*

Step 6: Embody Gratitude - Frequency of Healing

Gratitude is an energetic portal—a shift from lack to abundance, burnout to vitality. It recalibrates your nervous system, activates neuroplasticity, and amplifies the energy of renewal.

- **Morning Gratitude:** Each morning, name three things you are grateful for. Let gratitude be your baseline frequency.
- **Shift Focus to What is Thriving:** Instead of focusing on exhaustion, acknowledge where energy already flows effortlessly.
- **Create Micro-Joy Moments:** Whether savoring tea, watching the sunrise, cuddling

with your fur baby, or dancing, small joys rewire the brain for resilience. *(Source: UCLA Mindfulness Research Center)*

- **Affirmation:** *I embrace gratitude as a force of healing. With each moment of appreciation, I restore my energy, amplify joy, and elevate my spirit.*

You are not merely recovering—you are transforming. Every breath, every choice, every act of self-honoring rewires your mind, recharges your energy, and realigns you with your highest potential.

This is not just healing. This is evolution. You are stepping into a new vibration—one of vitality, peace, and purpose. You are becoming the truest version of yourself, merging your *Coherent Mind* with your *Coherent Heart.*

7. WIRED FOR NEURODIVERSITY

The human brain is not a one-size-fits-all machine—it is a masterpiece of variation, a symphony of neural connections sculpted by evolution, experience, and individuality.

Neurodiversity helps us recognize the beauty of neurological differences—such as autism, ADHD, dyslexia, and beyond—they are not disorders but natural variations of the human mind.

These diverse ways of thinking, perceiving, and engaging with the world have always existed, shaping history, innovation, and human progress. *(Source: Raj, S., & Powell, T., 2021)*

Every brain is wired uniquely, and modern neuroscience confirms what many have long known—neurodivergent minds are not broken; they are simply different. Advances in brain imaging have revealed striking distinctions in structure, connectivity, and function:

- **Brain Connectivity:** The neural pathways of a neurodivergent individual often fire in unconventional patterns. In autism, regions linked to social cognition, sensory processing, and pattern recognition may exhibit heightened or reduced connectivity, contributing to deep focus, unique problem-solving abilities, and sensory sensitivity.

- **Dopamine and Attention:** In ADHD, the prefrontal cortex—the center for focus and impulse control—processes dopamine differently. This can lead to challenges with attention and executive function, but it also fuels creativity, spontaneity, and hyperfocus when engaged in something deeply stimulating.

- **Language and Perception:** Dyslexic minds navigate the world through spatial reasoning and big-picture thinking, often excelling in fields like engineering, art, and design. While traditional reading structures may pose challenges, these individuals frequently have an exceptional ability to think in images, patterns, and abstract concepts.

This diversity in cognitive function isn't a flaw—it's a spectrum of strengths that, when nurtured, can lead to extraordinary innovation, creativity, and problem-solving.

The science of neuroplasticity allows individuals to develop strategies that align with their unique cognitive style. Through experience, learning, and environmental adaptation, new neural pathways can be formed, strengthened, and refined.

With the right support, neurodivergent individuals can enhance their strengths, navigate challenges, and thrive in a world that is still learning to embrace cognitive diversity.

Evolutionary Gift

The diversity in cognitive function is a spectrum of strengths that has profoundly influenced human evolution. Differences in the way individuals think, learn, and process the world around them aren't merely incidental but rather integral to our collective adaptability and progress.

Many researchers believe that traits linked to autism, ADHD, and dyslexia once provided essential survival advantages.

- **The Hyper-Focused Visionary:** Autistic minds, with their deep focus and pattern recognition, may have contributed to advancements in mathematics, technology, and the arts. Many of history's greatest minds—Einstein, Tesla, Newton—are now thought to have had autistic traits.
- **The Restless Innovator:** ADHD, often misunderstood as a "disorder," may have once been essential for hunters, explorers, and creators—driving quick decision-

making, adaptability, and bursts of creative genius.

- **The Spatial Thinker:** Dyslexia, often linked to enhanced visual and spatial reasoning, has produced some of the world's most brilliant architects, engineers, and inventors, proving that intelligence cannot be measured by traditional academic standards alone.

These minds have always existed, always contributed, and always shaped history—not despite their differences, but because of them.

Breaking the Chains of Stigma

Yet, despite the extraordinary gifts neurodivergent individuals bring to the world, stigma remains a persistent shadow. The traditional medical model has long framed these differences as deficits—something to be "fixed" rather than understood.

Schools, workplaces, and society at large often demand conformity to neurotypical standards, dismissing the unique strengths and needs of neurodivergent individuals.

But a shift is happening.

We are moving toward a world where diverse minds are recognized, celebrated, and accommodated.

Where workplaces embrace inclusion, diversity, and out-of-the-box thinking, where education fosters alternative learning styles, and where no one is made to feel "less than" because their brain doesn't fit a rigid mold.

The world needs the brilliance of every kind of mind. It needs inventors, visionaries, the deep thinkers, the creative disruptors. It needs spaces where neurodivergent individuals are not merely accommodated but empowered—where their strengths are harnessed, their challenges are met with understanding, and their perspectives are valued.

Because the future is not built by those who think alike—it is shaped by those who dare to think differently.

Pathways of Change

Traditional education often fails neurodivergent learners by enforcing rigid, one-size-fits-all models that overlook how their brains absorb, process, and retain information. But with an approach rooted in neuroplasticity, learning becomes a process of engagement, adaptation, and strength-based exploration.

Multi-Sensory Learning: Activating Neural Pathways

Rather than relying solely on passive instruction (lectures, rote memorization), multi-sensory learning—which integrates visual, auditory, kinesthetic, and experiential techniques—activates multiple neural networks, improving information retention and engagement.

- Example: A dyslexic student who struggles with reading comprehension may thrive when information is presented through audiobooks, videos, mind maps, or hands-on activities. By engaging multiple senses, the brain creates alternative pathways for processing information.

Flexible Learning Environments: Strengthening Focus and Executive Function

Neurodivergent brains often struggle with traditional classroom structures that demand rigid focus and linear learning. Instead, offering flexibility in movement, schedules, and sensory inputs allows the brain to optimize learning conditions.

- Example: A student with ADHD might benefit from movement breaks, standing desks, fidget tools, or personalized schedules, helping regulate dopamine levels and maintain sustained attention.

Gamification: Reinforcing Learning Through Play

Neuroplasticity thrives on engagement and repetition—and nothing fuels engagement like play, creativity, and gamified learning. Turning learning into interactive experiences strengthens memory and enhances problem-solving skills.

- Example: Math concepts taught through puzzles, real-world applications, or digital simulations engage the brain's reward system, creating stronger neural connections for learning.

By restructuring education around how neurodivergent minds naturally learn, we harness the power of neuroplasticity to expand their potential—not to suppress it.

REVOLUTIONIZING THE WORKPLACE

A Strength-Based Model

While the corporate world often favors rigid productivity models, linear workflows, and hyper-social environments, these settings can be mentally draining for neurodivergent professionals.

A neuroplasticity-based approach instead adapts workplaces to leverage neurodivergent strengths, fostering an environment where innovation flourishes.

Aligning Work with Cognitive Strengths: Instead of forcing neurodivergent individuals to mask their differences, workplaces should align job roles with their cognitive strengths, enabling greater engagement, productivity, and innovation.

- Example: Someone with autism may excel in pattern recognition, deep analytical work, or complex problem-solving, making them invaluable in fields like data science, cybersecurity, and engineering. Meanwhile, an ADHD professional may thrive in dynamic, fast-paced roles requiring creative problem-solving and adaptability.

Adapting for Cognitive Efficiency: Just as neuroplasticity thrives on adaptive strategies, workplaces should implement flexible environments that allow neurodivergent professionals to work in ways that enhance their focus, energy, and productivity.

- Example: Providing quiet workspaces, remote work options, flexible deadlines, or alternative communication methods allows neurodivergent employees to maximize efficiency without battling sensory overload or executive dysfunction.

Project-Based and Hyperfocus-Driven Workflows: Many neurodivergent individuals experience intense periods of hyperfocus, where they can dive deep into tasks, solving complex problems with unparalleled efficiency.

Rather than enforcing rigid 9-to-5 structures, allowing project-based or flexible task management models harnesses this innate cognitive advantage.

- Example: Instead of requiring a neurodivergent employee to spread energy across multiple small tasks throughout the day, employers could design project-based workflows where deep, uninterrupted work leads to higher-quality output.

By redesigning work structures to fit neurodivergent cognitive styles, we unlock untapped innovation and build more inclusive, high-performing teams.

EMBRACING NEURODIVERGENCE

A Catalyst for Change

The world is evolving, and so must our approach to education and work. Through neuroplasticity-based strategies, we can create environments where neurodivergent individuals are not just included but empowered—where their cognitive strengths are not overlooked but celebrated and optimized.

When we move beyond outdated structures and begin designing systems that work with neurodivergent minds rather than against them, we pave the way for unparalleled creativity, innovation, and progress.

The future belongs to those who think differently. It's time we start shaping a world that truly recognizes, nurtures, and amplifies their potential.

Harnessing neuroplasticity is not about forcing the brain into a mold—it's about working with its natural rhythms to create new pathways that support clarity, focus, emotional resilience, and self-empowerment.

For neurodivergent individuals, this means embracing adaptive strategies that strengthen cognitive function while honoring the unique way their brains process the world.

QUANTUM PLAYBOOK: HARNESSING COGNITIVE STRENGTHS

Here are some techniques to actively rewire your neurodivergent brain for greater ease, confidence, and self-mastery:

Step 1: Sensory Regulation - Calming the Nervous System for Clarity

The brain thrives when sensory input is balanced. Too much stimulation can trigger overwhelm, while too little can cause focus to drift. By fine-tuning sensory regulation, we create an optimal environment for neuroplasticity to occur.

- **Example:**
    - Use noise-canceling headphones or ambient sounds to regulate auditory input.
    - Experiment with weighted blankets, aromatherapy, or tactile fidgets to calm the nervous system.
    - Organize workspace lighting—some thrive in bright light, while others need dim, warm tones.

- **Affirmation:** *I create an environment that nurtures my mind and allows me to thrive.*

Step 2: Movement-Based Learning and Workflows

Physical movement is one of the most powerful activators of neuroplasticity.

It boosts dopamine, enhances focus, and strengthens neural connections, making it an essential tool for neurodivergent minds.

- **Example:**
  - Micro-movement breaks: Set a timer to stretch, walk, or do light exercise every 30–45 minutes.
  - Try standing desks, walking meetings, or body doubling for productivity.
  - Engage in rhythmic activities like dancing, drumming, or martial arts, which help with pattern recognition and executive function.

- **Affirmation:** *My body and mind work together in harmony, fueling my creativity and focus.*

Step 3: Dopamine and Focus Optimization

Neurodivergent individuals often have fluctuating dopamine levels, making it difficult to sustain motivation and focus. The key to long-term neuroplasticity is developing strategies that naturally regulate and sustain dopamine.

- **Example:**
  - Gamify tasks with small rewards—turn work into a challenge, checklist, or time-based game.

- ○ Work in bursts of hyperfocus (Pomodoro technique) with intentional dopamine resets (hydration, music, brief movement).
- ○ Use novelty—rotate between different environments or switch up the format of how you engage with information.

- **Affirmation:** *I channel my energy in ways that inspire me, allowing my mind to focus with ease.*

Step 4: Emotional Resilience Through Gratitude and Visualization

Emotions wire the brain faster than logic, making gratitude and visualization powerful tools for rewiring thought patterns. When we consciously shift focus to what is working and possible, we engage the neural networks of resilience.

- **Example:**
  - ○ Start or end the day with a gratitude practice—write 3 things you appreciate.
  - ○ Use visualization to imagine yourself successfully completing tasks or navigating challenges.
  - ○ Engage in self-talk rewiring—when a limiting belief arises, replace it with a more empowering perspective.

- **Affirmation:** *I am constantly growing, learning, and expanding my ability to succeed in my own way.*

Step 5: Harnessing Hyperfocus as a Superpower

Hyperfocus is a dopamine-driven tunnel vision, common in ADHD, autism, and other neurodivergent minds. Unlike typical concentration, this state is involuntary—it pulls you in,

In ADHD, dopamine dysregulation in the prefrontal cortex creates two extremes: difficulty sustaining attention on mundane tasks, yet an almost obsessive absorption in activities that spark interest. *(Source: Volkow, Journal of Neuroscience, 2009)*

Instead of fighting against hyperfocus, learn to direct it intentionally. This is one of the greatest strengths of neurodivergent minds—when channeled correctly, it can lead to deep learning, innovation, and creativity.

- **Example:**
  - Identify your peak focus hours and reserve them for deep work.
  - Batch tasks that require intensive focus into structured time blocks.
  - Set "pre-focus practices" (e.g., a specific playlist, lighting a candle, or breathing exercises) to cue the brain into flow state.

- **Affirmation:** *My focus is a powerful gift, and I direct it toward what nourishes my spirit.*

Step 6: Releasing Shame and Embracing Acceptance

One of the biggest barriers to neuroplasticity is internalized stigma. When we judge ourselves for thinking differently, we reinforce limiting neural pathways. The shift toward self-acceptance rewires for confidence, ease, and self-trust.

- **Example:**
  - Reframe self-talk: Instead of "I'm bad at this," say, "I thrive when I approach this in a way that works for me."
  - Surround yourself with people that uplift.
  - Release outdated beliefs about how things "should" be done—your brain is your superpower, not your flaw.

- **Affirmation:** *I honor my unique mind. My differences are my strengths, and I trust my journey.*

Ultimately, rewiring the brain is not about forcing change overnight—it's a gradual, intentional process of replacing outdated thought patterns with new, empowering ones.

8. Reframing Reality

For centuries, the mind was thought to be a rigid machine—set in stone by childhood, shaped by genetics, and bound by fate. But modern neuroscience has shattered this illusion, revealing a breathtaking discovery: *Your brain is fluid. Adaptive. Limitless.*

This phenomenon proves that the mind the mind is a supercomputer in perpetual evolution, sculpted by every belief, thought, and experience. Each imprint carves new neural pathways, shaping how we perceive ourselves, the world, and what we believe is possible.

If self-doubt has ever silenced your voice, if fear has ever held you captive, if past wounds have ever chained you to an identity that no longer serves you—know this: you are not defined by who you were. You have the power to break free and rewrite your perceived story.

With conscious intention, you can dismantle old limitations and rewire your brain for resilience, confidence, and transformation. The blueprint of your mind is yours to design.

Brain's Ability to Rewire Itself

Inside your mind, billions of neurons "fire and wire" in intricate patterns, forming the very foundation of your thoughts, emotions, and behaviors. Every time you think a thought or repeat an action; you strengthen its neural circuitry—like carving a deeper groove into a well-worn path.

- **Structural Plasticity**: The brain physically reshapes itself, forging new neural connections and even generating new neurons in response to learning, intention, and experience.
- **Functional Plasticity**: When one region of the brain is damaged, another adapts to take its place, proving that resilience is woven into our very biology.

This means that change is not just possible—it is inevitable when we consciously direct our focus and energy. With every new choice, every shift in perception, we rewire our reality at the most fundamental level.

Neurons That Fire Together, Wire Together

The legendary neuroscientist Donald Hebb revealed this profound viewpoint, but what does it mean? Every time you reinforce a thought—whether positive or negative— you strengthen the neural pathway that supports it. The more you repeat a belief like "I am not good enough", the more deeply embedded it becomes. But here's the extraordinary part: the opposite is also true.

Just as a negative thought can be reinforced, it can also be dismantled. Old pathways weaken when they are no longer used—a process called synaptic pruning—making space for new, empowering neural connections to take their place. This is why mindset scripting, affirmations, and self-awareness are not just abstract concepts; they are biological tools for transformation.

- **Transcending Limiting Beliefs**: If you've spent years believing you are unworthy, reframing your inner dialogue with affirmations, visualization, and self-compassion can forge new neural pathways of confidence and empowerment.
- **Healing Emotional Trauma**: Painful memories are stored in the brain's neural networks, but through meditation, breathwork, and therapy, we can dissolve old triggers and create healthier emotional responses.
- **Mastering New Skills and Expanding Potential**: Whether it's learning an instrument, exploring Neuroscience, or developing a growth mindset, every challenge strengthens the brain, making it sharper, more resilient, and more adaptable.

You are not bound by old narratives, inherited limitations, or past pain. You hold the power to rewrite your mind, sculpt your destiny, and step into the highest version of yourself.

For instance, when someone holds a core belief that "the world is hostile", their amygdala—the brain's fear center—remains hyperactive, perpetually triggering a fight-or-flight response. This chronic stress floods the body with cortisol, leading to inflammation, suppressed immunity, and even disease.

Conversely, beliefs rooted in safety, abundance, and self-worth activate the prefrontal cortex and parasympathetic nervous system, fostering emotional resilience, healing, and well-being.

Example:

- **Placebo:** A patient given a sugar pill, believing it to be a powerful drug, experiences real physiological healing. This occurs because belief triggers biochemical responses, such as increased dopamine or immune activation.
- **Nocebo:** Conversely, if a person believes they are sick or in danger, their body will produce stress hormones, weakening their immune system and creating real symptoms.

Pathways of Change

Step 1: Raise Awareness

Become aware of the self-limiting beliefs that whisper doubt, fear, limitations, and unworthiness into your mind. These unconscious narratives are not just thoughts—they shape your emotions, trigger physiological responses, and embed themselves into your very being. Notice how they manifest in your body: the tightness in your chest, the knot in your stomach, the surge of anxiety that holds you back.

These beliefs are not absolute. They are patterns, imprinted by past experiences, yet entirely within your power to change. By recognizing them, you reclaim your ability to rewire your mind, release the tension they create, and liberate yourself from the illusions of limitation.

Step 2: Thought Reframing

When fear-based thoughts and negative chatter creep in, recognize them for what they are—ricochets of old conditioning, not absolute truth. Instead of allowing them to take root, consciously replace them with empowering affirmations that reinforce your innate strength and vitality.

Speak to yourself with gentle intention: "My body is resilient and regenerates with ease." Feel the certainty of these words resonating within you. Let them become the new rhythm of your mind, a steady pulse of healing energy rewiring your subconscious. With each repetition, you shift from limitation to possibility, from doubt to unwavering trust in your body's infinite capacity to heal and thrive.

Step 3: Embodied Visualization

Envision yourself radiating with vibrant health—every cell nourished and pulsating with energy, every breath filling you with vitality. Feel the warmth of renewal coursing through your body as if healing has already taken place. Before your physical reality shifts, let your mind and heart embrace the emotions of wholeness, strength, and regeneration.

Release the notion of waiting, it implies lack—a silent resistance to the present moment. Instead, surrender to the now. Embody the state of well-being as if it already exists. The body follows where the mind leads, and when you live in alignment with your desired state, transformation becomes inevitable.

Neuroplasticity is your brain's superpower—whether you want to break limiting beliefs, heal trauma, or master a new skill, your brain has the ability to rewire itself at any age. By consciously choosing empowering beliefs, shifting perceptions, habits, and actions, you can reshape your brain and transform your life at any age in each present moment.

Affirmations: *My past does not define me. I create my future with each new thought. Every day, I strengthen my mind with empowering beliefs. I release all that no longer serves me and welcome transformation. I am limitless, evolving, and capable of extraordinary growth.*

POWER OF NEGATIVE THOUGHTS

The mind and body are intricately linked, constantly influencing one another in ways we are only beginning to fully understand. In conditions like autoimmune diseases—where the body's immune system turns on itself—the mind plays a critical role in either making the struggle harder or helping to ease the burden.

When we experience negative thoughts and emotions, especially those born from stress, fear, or past trauma, they don't just stay in our minds—they ripple through our bodies, triggering a cascade of responses that increase inflammation and weaken our immune defenses.

This is driven by the release of stress hormones like cortisol, which, when chronically elevated, suppresses immune function and fuels inflammation.

Research by experts like Dr. Robert Sapolsky has shown that prolonged stress disrupts the body's delicate balance, affecting the HPA axis, and leading to a heightened immune response. This imbalance doesn't just leave us vulnerable to illness; it can actively worsen conditions like rheumatoid arthritis, lupus, and multiple sclerosis

The immune system, designed to protect us from harmful pathogens, begins to turn on itself, attacking the very cells it was meant to defend. This is where the link between negative thoughts and autoimmune conditions becomes undeniable.

When stress hormones like cortisol remain elevated for extended periods, they disrupt immune function, weakening the system's ability to differentiate between harmful invaders and healthy tissue.

The immune system, in a state of imbalance, loses its self-regulation and tolerance, allowing it to launch attacks against the body's own cells. It's as if the body has forgotten how to distinguish friends from foe. (*Source: Immunological Reviews, National Library of Medicine*)

But it's not just the immune system that suffers. The brain, too, is caught in the crossfire. The neuroimmune connection—a pathway through which the brain and immune system communicate—becomes distorted when negative emotions like stress and anger dominate.

The brain's emotional centers, especially the amygdala, send signals to the immune system, urging it to react as though under attack. Meanwhile, immune cells in the body, like microglia in the brain, become activated, further amplifying inflammation.

This vicious cycle not only worsens symptoms but also sets the stage for more emotional distress, creating a feedback loop that deepens the pain. *(Source: Journal of Neuroscience Research, National Institutes of Health)*

This interplay between negative thoughts and immune dysfunction is further complicated by the body's response to inflammation. Chronic inflammation, a hallmark of many autoimmune diseases, is stoked by emotional distress.

Research shows that negative emotions, particularly prolonged stress, can increase the production of inflammatory cytokines, which are molecules that promote inflammation.

The result? An immune system that is hyperreactive and prone to attacking the body's own tissues. For someone with rheumatoid arthritis or lupus, this means more pain, more swelling, and greater damage to joints and organs. *(Source: Journal of Neuroinflammation, BioMed Central)*

In the fight against immune-mediated diseases, there is not just medical intervention, but a powerful ally within you: your own mind. While negative thoughts and emotions can fuel illness, the opposite is also true— your mental and emotional state can be a catalyst for healing.

Practices like mindfulness, meditation, and cognitive-behavioral therapy have been proven to reduce stress and lower inflammation, helping to restore balance to the body.

Through the power of neuroplasticity, you have the ability to replace old, harmful thought patterns with new, healthier ones that promote emotional balance and boost immune function. Mindfulness helps quiet the noise of stress, allowing the body to rest in a peaceful state, while meditation lowers cortisol levels and calms inflammation, giving your immune system the chance to regain its strength.

The practice of gratitude and compassion, two powerful emotional states, can activate the parasympathetic nervous system—the body's natural "rest and digest" mode—promoting healing and reducing the physiological effects of chronic stress. *(Source: Black, D. S., & Slavich, G. M., 2016)*

Power of Mental Shifts

Your mind is not a passive observer; it is the driving force behind your body's health. By shifting your thoughts and embracing optimism, you can rewire your brain, unlocking neuroplasticity to reduce chronic inflammation and support a stronger immune system.

For example, instead of feeling helpless against autoimmune disease, you can take charge. Every thought you choose has the power to heal, to break the cycle of inflammation, and to guide your body toward recovery.

When you reclaim your inner power, you choose thoughts that nurture rather than harm, emotions that uplift rather than drain. With this powerful mental shift, you not only transform your perspective—you change the very physiology of your body, activating an immune system that defends you with strength and wisdom.

Through this, we remember: the mind is not separate from the body, and the body's healing begins with the thoughts we choose to believe.

COGNITIVE-BEHAVIORAL THERAPY

Cognitive-behavioral therapy (CBT) is a widely used, evidence-based form of psychotherapy that focuses on identifying and changing negative thought patterns and behaviors that contribute to emotional distress. *(Source: American Psychological Association, 2023)*

The underlying principle of CBT is that our thoughts, emotions, and actions are interconnected, and by altering unhelpful or distorted thinking, we can positively influence how we feel and act.

According to the *American Psychological Association*, CBT has been scientifically proven effective for a wide range of conditions, including depression, anxiety, and PTSD. It is one of the most extensively studied and effective psychological treatments available. *(Source: American Psychological Association, 2023)*

This goal-oriented therapy often involves techniques like cognitive restructuring, problem-solving, and behavioral experiments to foster healthier coping mechanisms and resilience. *(Source: Beck, A. T., 1997, The past and future of cognitive therapy. Journal of Psychotherapy Practice and Research)*

Pathways of Change

The following examples demonstrate some of the proven techniques for consideration:

1. Cognitive Restructuring (Reframing)

An individual with social anxiety might have the thought, "Everyone is going to judge me negatively at this party." CBT would guide the person to challenge this belief by asking, "What is the evidence for this thought?" and then reframe it: "It's possible some people may not notice me at all, or even if they do, their judgment is not a reflection of my worth."

The goal is to replace irrational, exaggerated thoughts with more balanced and realistic ones.

2. Behavioral Activation

A person struggling with depression might isolate themselves, feeling too tired or unmotivated to engage in social activities. In CBT, a therapist might suggest planning small, achievable activities that the person finds enjoyable or fulfilling. Over time, these activities can counteract the inertia of depression, increase mood, and break the cycle of avoidance.

3. Thought Records

To combat negative thoughts, a person might keep a daily journal in which they record situations that caused distress, the thoughts that arose in response to these situations, and alternative, more balanced thoughts. For instance, if someone is experiencing anxiety before a work presentation, the thought record might show:

- **Distressful Thought:** "I'm going to mess up, and everyone will think I'm incompetent."
- **Alternative Thought:** "I've prepared well, and even if I make a mistake, it's not the end of the world. Everyone makes mistakes." This helps individuals spot patterns in their thinking and start changing their mindset.

4. Mindfulness Techniques

While CBT traditionally focuses on cognitive and behavioral aspects, mindfulness practices are often integrated into therapy to help individuals stay present and grounded.

For example, if a person struggles with obsessive thoughts or anxiety, the therapist may guide them through a mindfulness exercise like focused breathing or body scanning. This helps individuals detach from overwhelming thoughts and focus on the present moment rather than getting lost in a cycle of worry.

5. Graded Exposure

For someone dealing with a phobia (like fear of flying), CBT can involve gradual exposure to the feared situation, starting with less anxiety-provoking steps. The person might begin by looking at pictures of airplanes, then watch a video of a flight, and eventually sit in an airplane without actually taking off. Gradually facing the feared situation in controlled steps allows the person to reduce their anxiety over time and builds confidence in their ability to cope.

6. Problem-Solving

When faced with a stressful situation, such as a job loss, CBT can help an individual break down the problem into manageable steps.

For example, the person might first identify the immediate emotional reaction to losing their job, then brainstorm practical solutions—such as updating their resume, reaching out to connections, and researching potential job openings. CBT encourages taking proactive steps, reducing feelings of helplessness, and creating a sense of control.

7. Activity Scheduling and Planning: A person with depression might struggle to motivate themselves to get out of bed or engage in daily tasks. In CBT, the therapist may guide the individual to schedule daily activities, starting with simple, enjoyable tasks.

The goal is to build momentum over time by structuring each day to include meaningful actions, which in turn helps combat the negative feelings of inertia and hopelessness.

8. Exposure and Response Prevention (ERP)

This technique is especially helpful for individuals with obsessive-compulsive disorder (OCD).

An individual might have compulsive thoughts about germs and engage in repeated hand-washing as a response.

In CBT, ERP would involve gradually exposing the person to the feared stimulus (e.g., touching something "contaminated") while preventing the usual compulsion (e.g., washing hands).

Over time, the person learns that their fear is not as overwhelming as they originally thought, and the urge to perform the compulsion diminishes.

9. Role Play

For someone who has difficulty with social interactions, role-playing can help them practice new behaviors and social skills. If a person has difficulty asserting themselves in conversations, they might practice with the therapist. The therapist could play the role of a friend or coworker, and the individual can rehearse standing up for themselves or expressing their needs in a healthy way.

10. Relaxation Techniques

For people dealing with anxiety or stress, CBT can include techniques like progressive muscle relaxation or guided visualization.

For instance, a person might be directed to progressively tense and relax each muscle group in their body to reduce physical tension. Visualization exercises might help calm anxiety by imagining a peaceful, safe environment or a successful outcome to a stressful situation.

Through these and other techniques, CBT may help individuals challenge unhelpful thoughts, break negative behavior patterns, and foster more adaptive coping strategies, ultimately leading to greater emotional resilience and mental well-being.

RESHAPING FOR TRANSFORMATION

We understand that the brain, a remarkable and intricate network of neurons, is anything but static. It's a dynamic, living system, capable of incredible adaptation and transformation. The brain has the ability to reorganize itself, form new neural connections, and recalibrate in response to our thoughts, experiences, and environment.

Every belief we hold, every emotion we feel, and every decision we make reshapes the neural pathways that govern how we see ourselves and the world around us.

Imagine if you could consciously engage with your brain's power to create a reality of abundance, emotional strength, and mastery. What if the life you've always desired was within reach, waiting to be unlocked by the rewiring of your mind?

Habits and Procedural Memory

A habit is a behavior that becomes automatic over time due to repetition. Initially, it requires conscious effort and attention, but with enough practice, it moves into the subconscious, becoming part of procedural memory.

This memory is stored in brain areas like the basal ganglia and motor cortex, which are responsible for motor control and efficiency. As habits form, the brain's ability to perform these actions improves, making them effortless and requiring less energy from the part of the brain that controls decision-making, the prefrontal cortex.

Some examples include driving, typing, or playing an instrument—activities that become second nature with practice.

Emotional Response Circuits

We understand that the heart of emotional responses is the amygdala, which assigns emotional significance to experiences, and the hippocampus, where those emotions are stored as memories. When we face trauma or chronic stress, these pathways grow stronger, reinforcing fear-based reactions.

Neuroplasticity allows us to retrain our emotional responses. Techniques like mindfulness and cognitive restructuring enable us to break the cycle of automatic emotional reactions and rewire our brains to respond with greater resilience and calm.

The neural pathways that govern your habits, beliefs, and emotions are not permanent. Through conscious repetition, you can strengthen the circuits that serve your growth and dismantle the ones that hold you back.

The brain, in its infinite adaptability, responds to your intentions. The neural pathways that once constrained you can now be the very ones that empower you.

QUANTUM PLAYBOOK: RESHAPING PERCEPTIONS

To cultivate emotional resilience and break free from stress, we must train our brain to shift from states of dysregulation to harmony. By consciously practicing habits and techniques that promote balance, we can shift from stress to calm, from chaos to clarity.

Step 1: Mindful Meditation—Creating Neural Pathways of Calm

- Meditation is a powerful tool in rewiring the brain. It strengthens the prefrontal cortex, responsible for decision-making and emotional regulation, while calming the amygdala, the brain's fear center.
- **Example**: Start with just 5-10 minutes of mindful meditation each day. Focus on your breath, and when your mind wanders, gently return to the sensation of breathing. Over time, this practice will make your brain more adept at handling stress with calm and clarity.

Step 2: Breathing Exercises to Engage the Vagus Nerve

- Deep, conscious breathing activates the vagus nerve, which is connected to the parasympathetic nervous system—the body's "rest and digest" mode. This reduces stress and brings your nervous system into balance.
- **Example:** Practice box breathing. Inhale for four counts, hold for four counts, exhale for four counts, and hold for four counts. Repeat for a few minutes. This simple technique

reduces cortisol levels and helps you achieve a calm, balanced state.

Step 3: Visualization—Rewiring the Brain with Positive Imagery

- Visualization harnesses the mind's power to create new neural pathways by vividly imagining positive outcomes. When you envision yourself calmly navigating stressful situations or achieving your goals, your brain treats these imagined experiences as reality, reinforcing new patterns of success and resilience.

- **Example:** Before a challenging event, like public speaking or a high-stakes meeting, visualize yourself remaining calm, confident, and composed. Picture the positive outcome you desire. With practice, this mental rehearsal will make it easier to stay centered when facing real-life challenges.

Step 4: Mindful Movement—Releasing Stored Tension

- Physical movement plays a crucial role in brain health. Regular exercise stimulates the production of brain-derived neurotrophic factor, a protein that supports neuron growth and repair, while also alleviating the effects of stress.

- **Example:** Incorporate mindful movement into your routine—be it yoga, stretching, walking, or dancing. As you move, focus on your breath and body, releasing any stored tension. This practice promotes emotional regulation and enhances neuroplasticity.

Step 5: Self-Compassion—Shifting Negative Self-Talk

- Negative self-talk can wire your brain to perceive threats more readily. Practicing self-compassion, however, rewires these neural pathways, promoting kindness and emotional balance.
- **Example:** When you make a mistake, instead of berating yourself, say, "It's okay. I'm doing my best, and I'll learn from this experience." This mindset shift activates areas of the brain that promote emotional regulation and resilience.

Step 6: Gratitude—Rewiring the Brain for Positive Emotion

- Gratitude shifts your focus from scarcity to abundance, rewiring your brain to prioritize positive emotions.
- **Example:** Keep a gratitude journal. Each night, write down three things you are grateful for and reflect on why you're

thankful. This practice will reshape your neural pathways, fostering a more optimistic and contented outlook.

Step 7: Engaging in Meaningful Relationships—Strengthening the Social Brain

- Human connection is at the heart of emotional resilience. Engaging with positive, supportive people strengthens the neural circuits that promote emotional regulation.
- **Example:** Nurture relationships that uplift and support you. Regularly check in with loved ones to share your feelings, which helps reinforce emotional resilience through social bonding.

Step 8: Positive Affirmations—Changing Your Brain's Default Mode

- Your brain's default mode network governs automatic thoughts. By feeding it with positive affirmations, you can create new neural pathways that strengthen your sense of self-worth.
- Example: Every morning, affirm your worth by saying, "I am confident, calm, and capable." Repeating these statements daily will reprogram your subconscious mind,

making it easier to respond with poise and clarity in challenging situations.

Step 9: Healthy Nutrition—Supporting Brain Function

- What you eat directly affects your brain's health. Nutrients like omega-3s, antioxidants, and vitamins support cognitive function and emotional regulation.
- **Example:** Include brain-boosting foods like fatty fish, leafy greens, nuts, and berries in your nutrition. These foods nourish your brain, helping you maintain emotional balance and resilience.

Step 10: Repetitive, Purposeful Action—Strengthening Neural Pathways

- Consistency is key in rewiring your brain. By taking small, deliberate actions each day, you can create new neural connections that support emotional regulation.
- **Example**: When faced with stress, pause before reacting. Breathe deeply and choose a calm response. With practice, this new habit will replace old, reactive patterns, helping you regulate your emotions with ease.

The path to transformation starts within your mind, shifting your perception. By rewiring your brain, you can break free from limiting beliefs, heal old wounds, and build the resilience to thrive. The life you desire—peace, strength, and empowerment—is already within you, waiting to be unlocked.

Now is the time to step into a new you—one who masters their thoughts, embraces their inner power, and shapes their future with unwavering belief.

9. Metaphysics & Existence

Beyond the realm of the tangible, beneath the surface of what we call reality, lies a deeper, more enigmatic dimension—one that cannot be weighed, measured, or confined to the physical.

This is the domain of metaphysics, the branch of philosophy that dares to explore the nature of existence itself, peeling back the layers of perception to reveal the unseen forces, timeless principles, and cosmic structures that shape the universe.

Where physics examines tangible aspects like matter and energy, metaphysics addresses the intangible and transcendent dimensions, exploring the fundamental principles underlying the nature of reality that go beyond the physical and measurable.

Here, we ask the essential, unsettling questions: *What is reality? What is the true nature of existence? What is my purpose? Is the universe finite or infinite?* As explored in my book, *Coherent Heart: A Hero's Odyssey,* these questions have ignited the minds of mystics, philosophers, and physicists alike, driving humanity's eternal search for the ultimate truth.

At its core, metaphysics is not just an abstract intellectual pursuit—it is the key to understanding the ethereal densities, our place in the cosmos, our relationship to the infinite, the interconnections of all things, and the mysterious connection between mind, heart, spirit and body.

Metaphysical cosmology explores the universe as a multidimensional interplay of energy, vibration, and intelligence, perceiving it not merely as a physical construct but as a manifestation of higher consciousness.

It suggests that existence is a fractal reflection of an infinite Source, with every aspect of creation—from galaxies to subatomic particles—woven into a unified field of consciousness.

This perspective views the cosmos as both the stage and the process through which the Divine experiences itself, evolving through cycles of creation, expansion, and dissolution.

By bridging science and philosophy, metaphysical cosmology invites us to see the universe as a living, conscious entity that mirrors the inner dynamics of our own soul's journey toward unity and self-realization.

LOVE CONSCIOUSNESS

What if the most powerful force in the universe is pure love—and not just any love, but unconditional love? It's the kind of love that knows no bounds, asks for nothing in return, and yet fills you with boundless energy.

Neuroscience reveals that this profound love triggers areas in the brain linked to pleasure and reward, confirming that unconditional love is not just a lofty ideal—it's woven into the very fabric of our biology. But beyond the science, humans are love in motion.

Research shows that kindness, generosity, devotion, and empathy are integral to our physical and emotional well-being. The brain's reward system, including regions like the ventral striatum and prefrontal cortex, light up when we engage in acts of compassion, indicating that love is not just an emotion, but a biological force moving through us *(Source: Singer, 2004; Decety & Lamm, 2007).*

When we embrace unconditional love, we align with the highest expression of our divine essence—becoming living embodiments of pure love consciousness, flowing freely through every moment, every relationship, and every choice.

The theory published by Dr. Stephen Porges reveals that human connection and affection activate the vagus nerve, which promotes feelings of safety and calm, regulating emotional states and health. This is not merely a concept; it's a physiological and energetic process that enhances our lives.

Every time we choose to act from our *Coherent Heart,* we step into a more expansive, harmonious version of ourselves, becoming agents of positive change in the world around us. It is the portal to universal infinite intelligence, the unified field—not just emotion, but the direct experience of unity, unbonded pure love, and divine connection.

It is the seat of intuition, resonance, and vibrational alignment, attuning us to the higher frequencies of the universe. In Hermeticism, the Law of Correspondence (As above, so below) implies that the heart mirrors the cosmic mind. It is not separate, but a fractal of universal intelligence.

Without the coherence of the heart, the mind's manifestations may be clouded by ego or false perception.

HIDDEN ORDER BENEATH CHAOS

What seems like chaos in the universe is often a veil for an intricate, hidden order—a deeper structure guiding the apparent randomness. Science reveals this through chaos theory, where unpredictable systems like weather or fractals follow precise, self-organizing patterns that shape everything from galaxies to the veins of leaves.

Metaphysically, chaos is viewed as a catalyst for transformation and the crucible of evolution—the necessary disruption that births new creation.

It whispers of a profound intelligence woven into existence, reminding us that even in turmoil, there's a greater harmony at play. Chaos is not the end—it's the beginning of something extraordinary.

The hidden order reflects the intelligence of the universe, where even apparent randomness aligns with a greater purpose or divine blueprint.

This perspective invites us to embrace uncertainty and trust that chaos is part of a larger, harmonious process of growth, balance, and unity.

Many philosophical and ancient traditions propose that the universe operates according to fundamental metaphysical laws, principles beyond the reach of physics yet deeply influential in shaping reality.

- The **Law of Vibration** states that everything, from the densest matter to the most fleeting thought, operates at a specific frequency. It is the fundamental movement or oscillation of energy that underpins the fabric of reality. Ancient mystics and modern quantum physicists alike recognize that energy is never static; it moves, shifts, and responds.
- The **Law of Attraction** proposes that like energy attracts like, meaning our thoughts, emotions, and beliefs function as magnets, pulling corresponding experiences into our lives.
- The **Principle of Mentalism**, a core tenet of Hermetic philosophy, suggests that

> All is mind—that reality itself is a mental projection, a grand illusion molded by consciousness.
>
> - The **Law of Conservation** states that everything we perceive—matter, light, sound, thoughts, and emotions—is energy vibrating at different frequencies. Even what appears solid is, at its core, composed of rapidly moving subatomic particles oscillating in a quantum field. Physics confirms that energy cannot be created or destroyed—only transformed (First Law of Thermodynamics).

Since energy cannot be destroyed, what we perceive as physical death, endings, or loss are merely transformations into new states of existence.

The body, for example, returns to the Earth, dispersing into nature, while consciousness—our true essence—remains part of the unified field of wholeness, experiencing reality beyond form.

This fundamental principle may seem abstract, yet it profoundly shapes how we perceive reality, uncover purpose, and navigate existence. If the universe is an interconnected, conscious field, our thoughts, feelings, and beliefs ripple beyond the personal, holding cosmic significance.

Across traditions—from Buddhism to Hermeticism, Plato's ideal forms to Einstein's relativity—a shared perspective emerges: we are far more than we appear to be.

Metaphysics and human experience intertwine as a dance of inquiry and meaning. While life unfolds in the tangible world, metaphysics unveils the unseen forces of consciousness, connection, and purpose. It reminds us that we are not passive observers but active participants in a vast, intelligent cosmos.

Through our thoughts and actions, we influence the energetic fabric of existence, weaving our individuated journeys into the greater story of creation. Metaphysics becomes a lens through which we transcend the ordinary.

It is the bridge between the known and the unknown, the seen and the unseen. It is the relentless pursuit of infinite.

CONSCIOUS BREATHWORK

Breath is more than mere survival—it is the silent engineer of our reality, the bridge between the physical and the infinite.

In Eastern traditions, breath is not just air moving through the lungs; it is Prana (India), Qi (China), Ki

(Japan)—the sacred life force that animates all existence. Every mindful inhale is an act of creation, every exhale a surrender to the cosmic flow.

To control the breath is to command the energy of the universe itself—it's a biological reset that optimizes your mind and body at every level, unlocking peak performance, deep healing, and lasting transformation.

Master your breath, and you master your mind, your health, and your future.

OXYGEN, THE FUEL FOR PRESENCE

With every inhale, we draw in the very essence of life— oxygen, the invisible force that fuels our body, mind, and spirit. Without it, existence ceases on Earth; with it, we thrive.

Oxygen is not just the air we breathe—it is the essential molecule in cellular respiration, as well as the catalyst for energy, the sustainer of thought, and the silent architect of vitality. *(Source: K. Brown, 2019)*

Breathing Life's Fuel

Deep within each of our cells, a miraculous process unfolds. Oxygen, carried by red blood cells, reaches the mitochondria—the tiny power plants within us—where it ignites the production of adenosine triphosphate (ATP), the pure energy that keeps us alive.

This process, known as cellular respiration, is the foundation of all physical and mental activity. Without sufficient oxygen, the body falters, muscles weaken, and the mind clouds. Imagine a fire without air—it smoulders and dies.

Our cells, too, require oxygen to sustain their flame, converting nutrients into energy with breathtaking precision. When oxygen levels drop, the body resorts to inefficient alternatives, producing lactic acid, causing fatigue, and slowing us down.

The Mind's Breath

Though the brain accounts for only 2% of our body mass, it consumes 20% of our oxygen supply. Every thought, memory, and creative spark depends on this vital element.

Oxygen fuels neurotransmitter production, supports neural pathways, and enhances focus, clarity, and emotional stability. When deprived of oxygen, even momentarily, confusion sets in, reaction time slows, and in extreme cases, consciousness fades.

This is why fresh clean air revitalizes the mind, why deep breathing clears our thoughts, and why meditation—anchored in breath—ushers in peace.

The Pulse of Life

As oxygen enters the lungs, it binds to haemoglobin, the molecule that carries it through the bloodstream, delivering life to every organ and tissue. The heart, ceaseless in its rhythm, relies on oxygen to sustain its beat.

Without adequate oxygenation, the cardiovascular system strains, leading to fatigue, shortness of breath, and, over time, more serious conditions. *Breath is not just air—it is circulation, movement, and vitality.* Each inhale nourishes the body, and each exhale releases toxins, maintaining balance in the intricate dance of life.

The Cleansing Force

Beyond energy and cognition, oxygen plays a crucial role in purification. Every breath assists the lungs, liver, and kidneys in expelling waste and toxins.

Carbon dioxide, the byproduct of metabolism, is carried away with each exhale, preventing acidity in the blood and maintaining harmony in the body's internal environment. Oxygen is the unseen healer, detoxifier, supporting the immune system, accelerating tissue repair, and even combating harmful bacteria.

This is why deep breathing practices, fresh air, and oxygen-rich environments rejuvenate both body and mind.

The Calm Within

The breath is the gateway between body and mind. When stress takes hold, our breathing becomes shallow, depriving the body of oxygen and triggering tension.

Yet by consciously slowing the breath, we activate the vagus nerve, motioning the body to relax, slowing the heart rate, and restoring inner peace. This is the power of breathwork—the reason meditation and mindful breathing reduce anxiety and enhance well-being. It's not just a technique; it's a return to the natural rhythm of life.

Oxygen is more than a necessity—it's the silent force that fuels every heartbeat, thought, and moment. It bridges life and awareness. A deep breath is not merely survival; it's a way to awaken the body, clear the mind, and ignite the spirit. Let's pause and truly live.

LIFE FORCE & INFINITE INTELLIGENCE

Chi, or life force energy is the invisible current that pulses through every living being—an ethereal, yet undeniable presence that breathes life into our human vessels.

It is the animating force of spirit that sustains us, a boundless, eternal current of vitality that flows through our veins and circulates through the universe, holding everything in existence. It is what makes us feel alive, vibrant, and present in every moment.

This life force is not confined by the limits of the material world; it flows freely through the very core of our being. It is the essence of who we are—infinitely powerful and deeply interconnected to the vast energy fields that span the cosmos.

When we align with this energy, we feel a sense of wholeness, harmony, and vitality—like we are in the flow of life itself. But when this energy is blocked, diminished, or distorted, we may feel disconnected, drained, or out of balance—both physically and emotionally.

The breath, our most primal connection to this life force, serves as the link between the seen and the unseen, the material and the spiritual. Every inhale is an invitation to draw in the vital energy of the universe, every exhale a release of what no longer serves us. It is not just a mechanical function; it is a moment of deep communion with our body and spirit, where we reconnect with the energy that sustains us.

Ancient masters understood this profound outlook—breath is the pulse of consciousness. The way we breathe shapes the way we think, feel, and vibrate within the quantum fabric of existence. Through intentional breathwork, we move beyond the limitations of the mind, unlocking dormant energy, clearing emotional imprints, and awakening to our highest potential.

- Pranayama, the yogic science of breath control, purifies the energy channels (nadis), expands awareness, and elevates consciousness.
- Qi Gong breathing circulates Qi through the body's meridians, dissolving energetic blockages and rejuvenating the soul.
- Taoist breathwork harmonizes the yin and yang forces within, cultivating longevity, vitality, and divine flow.

From this metaphysical perspective, breath is not just air—it is the carrier of divine infinite intelligence, an energy so potent it can alter reality itself.

PINEAL GLAND & HIGHER REALMS

Nestled at the center of the brain, the pineal gland is a tiny yet extraordinary organ. Measuring just 5 to 8 millimeters and weighing approximately 150 milligrams, this enigmatic gland is more than a simple endocrine system component.

While its primary role in regulating the body's circadian rhythm is well-known, its true significance reaches far beyond conventional science.

The pineal gland has indeed been regarded as a mystical bridge between the tangible and intangible, a "radio antenna" capable of tuning into the metaphysical frequencies of existence.

Ancient cultures and spiritual traditions have consistently honored their unique position within the human body—not merely as a biological organ but as a third-eye portal to expand consciousness and divine wisdom.

From a scientific perspective, the pineal gland's primary function lies in producing melatonin, a hormone that governs the body's internal clock, promotes restful sleep, and acts as a potent antioxidant and anti-inflammatory agent.

Melatonin production peaks at night, aligning our biology with the rhythms of nature.

However, evidence suggests that the pineal gland becomes particularly active in individuals engaged in meditation and spiritual practices, hinting at its deeper potential.

The 17th-century philosopher René Descartes famously referred to the pineal gland as the "seat of the soul," proposing that it served as the juncture where the physical body and the immaterial spirit converge.

This physiological and spiritual connection is believed to be most prominent between 10:00 PM and 3:00 AM, when the pineal gland releases a symphony of substances, including melatonin, serotonin (the "happiness hormone"), and other compounds.

These hormones not only regulate sleep, mood, and immune function but also influence memory, learning, and emotional well-being.

Yet the pineal gland is more than a regulator of biological processes—it is a gateway to higher consciousness, the 'higher self". Across cultures, it is often linked to the concept of the "third eye," a mystical center of intuition and spiritual insight.

Ancient Egyptians symbolized it with the Eye of Horus, an acorn representation of divine vision and protection.

In Hindu tradition, the pineal gland aligns with the sixth energy center associated with intuition and enlightenment. Similarly, in Buddhism, it connects to the crown energy center representing unity with the cosmos.

Mythology intertwines with the pineal gland's mystery. Hindu legends speak of the goddess Parvati plunging the world into darkness by covering her eyes, only for Shiva to restore light by opening a third eye on his forehead—a symbol of spiritual awakening and cosmic consciousness.

Even in the fossil record, evidence hints at the pineal gland's ancient legacy.

A 50-million-year-old fossilized lizard was discovered with a functional "third eye," known as the parietal eye, connected to its pineal gland.

This evolutionary remnant suggests that our pineal gland may have once been a literal third eye, attuned to light and energy in ways we are only beginning to understand.

Higher Self & Third Eye Gateway

The higher self is the divine spark within us, an aspect of infinite intelligence transcending ego and the limits of physical reality. It embodies our soul's pure essence, reflecting wisdom and connection to Source consciousness.

Deep within, the higher self knows our truth, guiding us on a path toward evolution, expansion, and lasting peace. Aligned with the universal flow, it operates from pure love essence, unity, and harmony, holding the key to our most authentic existence.

It's the eternal consciousness that bridges the physical and the infinite—beyond fear, beyond illusion. It speaks in whispers of intuition, synchronicity, and intuitive guidance. Opening and activating the third eye or pineal gland, is believed to enhance our ability to access deeper wisdom, inner knowing, and boundless insight, creativity, and an unshakable connection to all that is.

This connection is often associated with heightened awareness, greater clarity, and the ability to perceive beyond ordinary physical senses—into the realms of universal consciousness.

Modern science offers tantalizing glimpses into the pineal gland's hidden capacities. Researchers have discovered that the gland contains crystalline structures capable of generating electrical charges under pressure, much like quartz crystals.

These properties suggest that the pineal gland functions as a transmitter, receiving and broadcasting energetic signals, potentially enabling extrasensory perception such as clairvoyance and telepathy.

While the mechanisms remain shrouded in mystery, these findings open new frontiers for exploring the intersection of health, consciousness, and spirituality.

Ancient wisdom has long recognized the pineal gland as a threshold to the ethereal world, and science is finally catching up.

Activating this gateway requires attuning the body to nature's rhythm. Meditation, breathwork, and exposure to natural light enhance its function, while artificial light and toxins disrupt its delicate balance. When awakened, the pineal gland becomes more than a biological structure—it becomes a portal to expanded perception, allowing us to glimpse subtler dimensions of existence.

Imagine a world where every individual unlocks this latent power—where creativity, compassion, and intuition flourish, reshaping the fabric of human consciousness. The pineal gland, often dismissed as insignificant, holds the key to bridging the material and the metaphysical, offering a direct path to enlightenment and the ultimate realization of our interconnected existence.

To awaken it is to dissolve the illusion of separation and step into the infinite potential of the cosmos itself.

FINAL KNOT OF LIBERATION

To fully awaken, the soul must transcend its final barrier—a psychic knot blocking access to the crown, the ultimate gateway to boundless consciousness. This knot holds the key to liberation, and its untangling is the crucial step toward transcendence.

As the energy rises with relentless force, it unbinds the three knots, shattering the confines of limitation. The 1000-petaled Lotus unfurls, releasing a wave of cosmic expansion that expands the consciousness beyond its previous boundaries.

In this profound moment, the cosmic exit to the crown bursts open, igniting the 72,000 knots of the body of light. This is no fleeting awakening; it marks a permanent transformation. The illusion of separation dissolves, and you no longer identify as a singular self, but as the entirety of existence—the totality of the universe unfolding through you.

When the energy centers align and the crown activates, the cycle of divine union is complete. Time, as you once knew it, collapses. Duality ceases to exist. The illusion of the past and future fades away, leaving only the infinite present.

In this moment, you step into the fullness of sovereign liberation—a state of eternal Oneness, where reality is not a sequence of events, but an eternal unfolding of now. You are no longer bound by time; you are the present moment itself—free, united, and fully awakened.

Quantum Playbook: Unlocking Ancient Portals

This playbook merges ancient wisdom with modern science, offering a structured pathways to regulate the nervous system, release stored trauma, and expand consciousness. When harnessed with intention, it becomes a tool for healing, transformation, and manifestation.

Step 1: Activate Higher Consciousness

Conscious breathing shifts brainwave states, quiets mental noise, and heightens intuition.

- Box Breathing (4-4-4): Inhale, hold, exhale, and hold for four seconds each. This stabilizes the nervous system and sharpens focus.
- Alternate Nostril Breathing: Balances the left and right brain hemispheres, enhancing clarity and energetic harmony.
- Breath and Visualization: As you inhale, draw in golden light through your crown; as you exhale, release tension and mental clutter.

Step 2: Clear Stagnant Energy

Emotions and stress get trapped in the body. Breath is the key to releasing them.

- Diaphragmatic Breathing: Deep belly breathing activates the parasympathetic nervous system, reducing anxiety and restoring calm.
- Shaking and Breath Release: Inhale deeply, then shake your body as you exhale to release stored tension and stagnant energy.
- Vagus Nerve Toning: Humming or sighing on the exhale stimulates the vagus nerve, promoting deep relaxation.

Step 3: Release Karmic Imprints & Trauma

The subconscious holds unprocessed emotions. Breathwork releases old imprints and rewires the mind.

- Holotropic Breathwork: Deep, connected breathing (no pauses) shifts consciousness, allowing suppressed emotions to surface and dissolve.
- Targeted Breath Release: Breathe deeply into areas of tightness, sending awareness and healing to trapped emotions.
- Breath and Journaling: After breathwork, write freely and without judgment to uncover subconscious patterns.

Step 4: Amplify Manifestation Power

- Breath aligns mind, heart, and energy, tuning your frequency to your desires.

- Coherence Breathing (5-5 Pattern): Inhale and exhale for five seconds each to create heart-brain alignment.
- Breath and Affirmations: Inhale, I am magnetic to abundance. Exhale, I release doubt.
- Manifestation Breathing: With each inhale, pull energy from the quantum field; with each exhale, send it into your desired reality.

Step 5: Bridge the Physical and the Divine

Breath connects form to formlessness, dissolving ego and expanding consciousness.

- Spinal Breath Expansion: Inhale from the base of your spine to your crown, then exhale back down, circulating life force energy.
- Alternate Nostril Breathing (Nadi Shodhana): Balances the masculine (solar) and feminine (lunar) energies, uniting dualities within.
- Breath of Fire (Kapalabhati): Ignites inner vitality, clears energetic stagnation, and raises transformative energy.
- OM Breathing: Inhale deeply, then exhale with a slow, resonant "Om", attuning your vibration to universal consciousness.
- Surrender Breath: Inhale, holding an intention. Exhale, fully releasing it to the universe, trusting divine flow.

Daily Quantum Breath Routine

- Morning: Box Breathing and Coherence Breathing (to set clarity and intention).
- Midday Reset: Deep Belly Breathing and Shaking Release (to reset energy and focus).
- Evening: Conscious Breathwork and OM Breathing (to release, expand, and align).

Affirmations: *With each breath, I align with my highest self. I breathe in power, clarity, and peace. I exhale all that no longer serves me. I trust the intelligence of my breath to restore balance and harmony within me.*

Breath is the essence of life, the key to transformation, the bridge to the divine. It is the silent force shaping your reality—if you learn to use it with intention.

With every inhale, you claim your power. With every exhale, you surrender to the infinite flow.

10. Science of Balance

In the sacred dance of creation, two primordial forces weave the fabric of reality: the feminine electric current and the masculine magnetic field.

These are not mere metaphors or abstract esoteric concepts—they are the fundamental energetic blueprints that shape the cosmos, flowing through all levels of consciousness, from the subatomic to the celestial.

Often symbolized as yin and yang, Shiva and Shakti, Ida and Pingala, these dual energies govern the rhythm of creation, destruction, and transformation.

When harmonized, they birth unity, alignment, and expansion—within the self and throughout the greater quantum field. When imbalanced, they distort perception, disrupt energy flow, and create dissonance between mind, body, and soul.

Electro-Magnetism

In both metaphysical philosophy and electromagnetic physics, electricity and magnetism are inseparable yet distinct—one does not exist without the other.

Their interplay is the engine of manifestation, shaping both the tangible world and the unseen dimensions of thought, emotion, and intention.

- **Left Hemisphere (Feminine / Electro / Yin) – The Current of Creation:** Flowing like a river through the unseen realms, this energy is intuitive, fluid, nurturing, and receptive. It governs creativity, emotion, imagination, and the subconscious. Linked to the moon, water, and the parasympathetic nervous system, it is the force that dreams, conceives, and brings forth new possibilities. It is the breath of inspiration before the action, the womb before the birth.

- **Right Hemisphere (Masculine / Magnetic / Yang) – The Force of Manifestation:** Steady and structuring, this energy is directive, logical, fiery, and action-oriented. It governs focus, intellect, discipline, and the conscious mind. Associated with the sun, fire, and the sympathetic nervous system, it is the force that transforms potential into form, giving structure to vision and bringing thoughts into materialization. It is the architect of the dream, the fire that fuels movement, the will that shapes destiny.

In energetic alchemy, the feminine current (electricity) sparks the vision, while the masculine current (magnetism) grounds it into existence. Together, they create coherence within the biofield, synchronizing an individual's energy with the universal intelligence of the cosmos.

Human Energy System: Where Electro-Magnetic Forces Converge

Within the body, these forces spiral through the seven energetic fields or chakras, nervous system, and biofield, influencing every layer of physical and subtle energy.

They dance along the spinal column, intertwining through the Ida (feminine) and Pingala (masculine) channels, culminating in the center—the gateway to higher consciousness.

Yet, when imbalanced and one side dominates, the flow becomes disrupted:

- **Excess Feminine (Electro) Energy Effect:** Emotional overwhelm, passivity, escapism, lack of boundaries, and dissociation from reality.
- **Excess Masculine (Magnetic) Energy Effect:** Rigidity, control, aggression, hyper-rationality, and disconnection from intuition.

True mastery lies in the sacred equilibrium between the two, where they merge at the *Coherent Heart* center—

the portal to quantum alignment, soul awakening, and divine embodiment.

HEART-BRAIN DIALOGUE

In the depths of metaphysical wisdom, the heart is seen not merely as a vessel for life's blood but as the epicenter of intuition and higher consciousness.

It generates an electromagnetic field so vast and potent that it far surpasses the brain's influence, suggesting that the heart plays a far more profound role in shaping our experience of the world.

The heart, often regarded as the organ of life, does more than circulate blood—it pulsates with a profound energy that extends far beyond the physical realm.

Biologically, the heart generates a massive electromagnetic field—one that is significantly stronger than that of the brain. This energetic field doesn't just dissipate near the body; it radiates outward, stretching several feet into the environment.

Measured by electrocardiograms (ECGs), these electric waves serve as a subtle yet powerful reminder that the heart is much more than a pump—it is an energy source that shapes our connection to the world.

On a deeper level, the heart is seen not just as an organ but as a dynamic vortex where energy circulates, amplifies, and transforms. It serves as a portal, bridging the physical body to the expansive realm of the higher self.

This energetic flow is directly tied to our capacity for devotion, compassion, and our innate sense of Oneness with ourselves and the universe. It is the core from which we connect to something larger than our individual existence—the quantum unified field.

The vortex analogy captures the heart's ceaseless movement—its ability to take in and release energy in a constant, flowing rhythm. When we experience love, peace, or joy, the heart field radiates a vibrational energy that spreads outward, touching everything in its path.

In contrast, negative emotions like fear, grief, or anger can block or distort this flow, creating energetic imbalances that ripple through the body and mind.

Sacred geometry offers a powerful representation of the heart's role in the universe through the flower of life, a pattern of interconnected circles that forms a spiralling vortex.

This ancient symbol reflects the unity of creation, the seamless flow of energy that connects all life. It mirrors the heart's ability to draw energy in, transform it, and send it out into the world, perpetuating the eternal rhythm of life, creation, and renewal.

Together, the scientific and metaphysical perspectives paint a compelling picture: it is not merely an organ of survival but an energetic powerhouse, constantly moving, evolving, and interacting with the forces that govern both the physical and spiritual realms. The heart is a vortex of vitality, a bridge between our earthly existence and the infinite intelligence of the cosmos.

As explored in *Coherent Heart*, emotions like love, gratitude, and compassion are far from fleeting; they emit harmonious frequencies that regulate the nervous system, influence our DNA, and even shape the external reality around us.

At the core of this transformative connection is the concept of heart-brain coherence—an intricate, dynamic communication between the heart and brain that fosters emotional stability, mental clarity, and overall well-being.

Groundbreaking research from the *HeartMath Institute* shows that when we experience positive emotions, we enter a state of "psychophysiological coherence," where the rhythms of the heart, brain, and nervous system align in a harmonious dance. This unity unlocks heightened resilience, empowering us to self-transform, and to navigate life's challenges with grace and balance.

Remarkably, the heart sends more signals to the brain than the brain sends to the heart, creating an intricate web of neurological, biochemical, and energetic pathways that influence our emotions, decisions, and perceptions.

Positive emotions, like joy, inner peace, and appreciation, transform the heart's rhythm into an ordered, coherent pattern, which in turn amplifies brain function and fosters mental clarity. As the heart and brain sync, we experience a deepening sense of calm, emotional equilibrium, and reduced stress, enhancing our ability to respond to life with clarity and composure.

This relationship between the heart and brain is not a poetic metaphor but a tangible scientific viewpoint. When they are aligned, we unlock the full potential of our emotional intelligence, enabling us to manage stress, regulate our nervous system, and cultivate a profound sense of well-being.

In this synergy, we discover that the path to mental clarity, emotional resilience, and holistic health is not just possible, but inherent within us.

The heart and brain, working in concert, hold the key to our transformation, guiding us toward a life of greater peace and purpose.

ELECTROMAGNETIC FIELDS

We learned that the human heart, a marvel of both biology and energy, generates a profound electromagnetic field that extends beyond the physical body, weaving an intricate dance of coherence within.

This rhythmic field serves as a bridge between the tangible and the unseen. Emerging research suggests tantalizing connections between the heart's energetic pulse and the Earth's magnetic field, hinting at an invisible symphony of interaction between humanity and the planet itself.

Polarity, a fundamental principle of energy, shapes this intricate dynamic. Positive polarity, often associated with altruism, unity, and service to others, resonates with the harmonizing energy of connection and coherence. Negative polarity, in contrast, reflects self-service, separation, and the illusion of control, embodying energies that draw inward and resist integration.

These polarities influence not only individual behavior but also the energetic signatures we emit, potentially affecting our interactions with larger systems, including Earth's magnetic field.

Mother Earth itself undergoes cyclical pole shifts, a phenomenon where the planet's north and south magnetic poles gradually reverse their positions. These reversals, occurring roughly every 200,000 to 300,000 years, are driven by turbulent movements within Earth's molten iron core.

While the magnetic poles are in transition, the planet's protective shield against cosmic radiation temporarily weakens, potentially influencing biological systems, climate patterns, and human consciousness.

Scientists are actively studying the correlation between geomagnetic shifts and evolutionary leaps, hypothesizing that such cosmic recalibrations may act as catalysts for significant energetic and biological transformations on Earth.

The regulation of the nervous system is intricately tied to the electromagnetic fields generated by the heart and the brain. Heart coherence—a state where heart rhythms are stable and synchronized—directly impacts the autonomic nervous system, enhancing its ability to regulate stress responses and maintain homeostasis.

Steady electromagnetic fields generated from the heart can help harmonize neural oscillations in the brain, promoting emotional balance, clarity of thought, and resilience. Conversely, environmental electromagnetic disruptions, such as geomagnetic storms caused by solar activity or pole shifts, can dysregulate the nervous system, leading to increased stress, anxiety, and physiological imbalances.

This interplay underscores the profound relationship between human energy systems and external electromagnetic forces, highlighting the importance of unity in fostering well-being amidst cosmic fluctuations.

Even more compelling is the evolving understanding of how this heart-centered energy intertwines with the mind's coherence and the enigmatic realm of quantum physics.

These domains converge in a frontier of exploration, where polarity, consciousness, and the nature of reality beckon deeper inquiry.

As science ventures further into this uncharted terrain, the interplay between human energy and universal forces offers profound possibilities, urging us to reconsider the limits of our connection to the cosmos.

Electromagnetic Body

The human body is a living bioelectric system—a sophisticated soft technological interface through which consciousness interacts with the physical world.

Every function of your biology depends on the flow of ions and electrons, creating a harmonious rhythm that powers your existence.

Ancient civilizations understood this intricate energy system, which is why they revered precious metals like silver—not just as treasures, but as vital tools to enhance the body's electrical conductivity.

These metals amplify the flow of bioelectricity, enabling the brain to process information faster and dissolve energetic blockages within the meridian lines.

You are, at your core, an *electromagnetic being*. Like a battery, your body continuously generates and consumes energy, requiring constant recharging.

Silver, one of nature's most potent conductors, minimizes electrical resistance, improving the flow of cellular communication and energy pathways.

This ancient knowledge is the true origin of wearing jewelry—not merely as adornments but as functional tools to optimize the body's energetic systems. When worn strategically—around the neck, wrists, or ankles—specific metals can alleviate tension, pain, or stagnation by enhancing the flow of energy in those areas.

The human body, composed of nearly 90% water, functions as a dynamic salt battery, driven by the delicate interplay of its bioelectric currents.

When this balance is nurtured, you unlock the full potential of your electromagnetic nature, aligning your body, mind, and spirit with the flow of universal energy.

SCIENCE OF VIBRATION

The notion of "vibration", in a scientific context, refers to the measurable frequencies at which the human body and its components resonate. Each part of our body, from our organs to our cells, vibrates at specific frequencies.

The whole-body resonance, for instance, occurs at approximately 4-8 Hz for humans. This natural frequency of the body is integral to maintaining health, as deviations from this frequency can impact physiological processes. *(Source: Griffin, M. J., 1990).*

Studies have explored the influence of vibrational frequencies on health and well-being—for example, chronic exposure to extremely low-frequency electromagnetic fields has been linked to disrupted sleep, heightened feelings of anxiety, and an increased risk of depression.

On the other hand, positive, coherent frequencies—like those generated during practices such as meditation, yoga, or breathing exercises—have been shown to enhance emotional regulation and promote healing.

Rates of Fluctuation

Vibration refers to the fluctuation of energy—it is the rhythmic pulse that weaves through all of existence, the unseen tempo that connects every aspect of reality. Everything—whether physical matter, thoughts, or emotions—moves in constant motion, radiating a unique frequency that defines how it interacts with the universe.

From a metaphysical perspective, this energetic signature acts as a bridge between the visible and invisible, shaping both our personal reality and our connection to the world around us.

Everything, from the smallest atom to the largest celestial body, is constantly in motion and radiates its own unique energetic rate. In this view, the vibration of an object or individual can be seen as its animated imprint, influencing its interactions with other energies and with the universe as a whole.

Higher vibrations align with qualities such as love, compassion, and harmony, fostering growth and unity with the flow of life. Conversely, lower vibrations are tied to emotions like fear, anger, judgment, and negativity, often creating resistance and imbalance.

These frequencies are not merely abstract concepts; they ripple outward, influencing the energy we attract and the experiences we manifest.

By cultivating mindfulness, practicing self-awareness, and taking intentional actions, we can elevate our vibration to correspond with the universe's natural rhythm.

This alignment amplifies joy, abundance, and inner peace, creating a ripple effect that resonates with the collective energy around us.

In this interconnected web of existence, we are both creators and participants, shaping reality through the vibrations we choose to embody.

ALIGNMENT OF RESONANCE

Resonance is the profound phenomenon where a system vibrates in response to an external force that matches its natural frequency. Whether it's the movement of a pendulum, the echo of a musical note, or the energy within atoms, resonance amplifies the system's vibrations, catalyzing powerful changes.

It is through this harmony between frequency, vibration, and energy that transformation occurs—helping us understand how the universe itself orchestrates its elements. From the smallest particles to the vastness of the cosmos, resonance teaches us: when frequencies align, profound, transformative forces emerge.

In metaphysics, resonance takes on a deeper meaning—the alignment of energies, the invisible thread connecting everything in the universe. It's the way matching frequencies attract, amplify, and harmonize—both within us and around us. When our energy resonates with people, places, or situations that mirror our own vibration, we experience connection, clarity, and flow. It feels as though we're in tune with our purpose, in perfect harmony with our highest self.

But what happens when those energies don't align? Discord. When energies clash or misalign, we feel out of sync, disconnected from our true frequency. This is why self-awareness is key. By consciously raising our vibrational frequency, we shift our resonance, attracting experiences and relationships that match our highest essence, amplifying peace, growth, and fulfillment in every area of our lives.

When you're deeply moved by music, a place, or a person, it's because their energy is in harmony with yours. Likewise, our thoughts and emotions are forms of resonance. When we choose thoughts of optimism, gratitude, or peace, we raise our vibration, aligning with higher states of being.

On the flip side, negatively charged thoughts—anger, worry, judgment—resonate at a lower frequency, attracting experiences that reflect those wavelengths.

This concept of spiritual resonance is where the universe truly reveals its interconnectedness. Everything is a reflection of energy, and by aligning ourselves with higher frequencies, we harmonize with universal laws. This creates an energetic loop: our vibration influences the world around us, and in turn, the world brings us experiences that match our reverberation.

Ultimately, resonance in a metaphysical context is about finding balance and harmony—within ourselves and with the universe. By consciously tuning our energy to vibrate with higher, positively charged frequencies, we live in alignment with our highest potential.

Wheel of Consciousness

In metaphysics, evolution is not a linear progression but the recognition that everything is One—a unified whole. Consciousness does not ascend in a straight line; it moves in spirals, waves, and cycles, reflecting the natural rhythm of the cosmos itself.

The spiritual journey is not a hierarchy to be climbed nor a race to reach the top. It is a vast, interconnected wheel—where each emotion, experience, and revelation serves as a crucial thread in the fabric of awakening. This is the evolution of human consciousness, unfolding within the divine design.

For too long, the journey of consciousness has been framed in linear terms—a scale of enlightenment, a ladder of progression, a rigid structure that inadvertently fosters separation rather than unity.

We have measured growth in terms of higher and lower, light and dark, good and evil, positive and negative, failing to see the deeper perspective: *consciousness is not about moving beyond, but moving through.*

What if we embraced a dimensional system? A model where consciousness is not a destination but an ever-turning wheel, each spoke representing a necessary aspect of the whole?

This curvature is the missing key—an integrated mechanism that reveals the harmony within all states of being, rather than dividing them into fragments of worthiness, karmic punishments, or failure.

Interwoven Nature of Consciousness

In this wheel, there are no discarded emotions, no rejected experiences—only interconnected energies that shape and refine us. We cannot know courage without first confronting fear, just as we cannot embody wisdom without first navigating uncertainty.

To exclude any aspect of our emotional reality is to weaken the very structure of consciousness itself.

Take shame, for example, a deeply misunderstood emotion, often cast aside as an obstacle to enlightenment. But shame, when faced with openness and vulnerability, becomes a bridge to wholeness.

It is not a weight to be cast off but a doorway through which we enter deeper states of synchronicity and self-awareness. Without the shadow, there is no contrast to the light; without the descent, there is no ascent.

The wheel teaches us that every phase, every state of being, is a supporting mechanism—each experience a note in the great symphony of existence.

To reject one part is to disrupt the harmony of the whole. It is only by accepting the entirety of our being—every joy, every wound, every lesson, every moment of doubt—that we step into true alignment with the quantum unified field.

Quantum Mechanics and the Role of Duality

The world of quantum mechanics reveals an intricate and profound connection between polarity and the nature of reality. Quantum entanglement demonstrates that even seemingly opposing particles are inextricably linked, influencing one another across vast distances.

Similarly, wave-particle duality shows that matter exists as both particle and wave, existing simultaneously as potential and manifestation—a clear reflection of the interplay between feminine and masculine forces.

The zero-point field, or field of pure potential, is where all opposites converge and collapse into Oneness.

In this field, energy precedes matter, and the boundaries between subject and object, self and other, dissolve. It is the quantum connection where everything is intertwined, and polarity itself becomes the pathway to wholeness.

POLARITY OF OPPOSITES

At the heart of existence, an unseen force pulses through the cosmos, weaving together the fabric of reality. It is the current that flows through the smallest atoms and the grandest galaxies, the silent architect of both creation and destruction.

This force is polarity—the interplay of opposites, the eternal dance between light and shadow, expansion and contraction, energy and form.

We often perceive duality as conflict, but what if opposition is not division, but the very engine of creation? Science and metaphysics converge on a singular viewpoint: polarity is not an obstacle to overcome, but a law of nature to be understood and harnessed.

Electromagnetic Polarity: Blueprint of Energy

Everything we see, touch, and experience is governed by the fundamental forces of electricity and magnetism. Positive and negative charges create electric fields, where opposite forces attract and like forces repel.

This principle governs the technology that powers our world, from the simplest circuit to the boundless energy of stars.

Magnetic polarity mirrors this truth. North and south poles do not exist in isolation; they require each other to generate the invisible fields that shape the physical universe.

This duality is not just mechanical—it is cosmic law in motion, a force as omnipresent as gravity, binding the seen and unseen together. *(Source: NASA, 2023)*

Molecular Polarity: Alchemy of Life

At the molecular level, polarity dictates the chemistry of existence.

Water, the very essence of life, owes its miraculous properties to its polar nature. With one end slightly positive and the other negative, it dissolves substances, transports nutrients, and sustains biological function.

The contrast between polar and nonpolar molecules determines everything from cellular membranes to the creation of complex organic structures. Without polarity, life as we know it would not just be different— it would be impossible. *(Source: Chemistry LibreTexts, 2021)*

Quantum Polarity: Dance of Light and Matter

In the quantum realm, the boundaries between opposites blur into paradox. Particles exist as both waves and solid matter, shifting their nature based on observation.

Electrons, photons, and subatomic forces oscillate between states, revealing a universe where polarity is fluid, where energy and form collapse into one another in a ceaseless exchange of potential.

The very fabric of space is alive with this dynamic equilibrium. The quantum field, the invisible ocean from which all physical reality emerges, thrives on the tension of opposites—presence and absence, contrast and expansion, probability and certainty, existence and nonexistence.

Here, polarity is not just structure; it is the creative force behind all that becomes. *(Source: Frontiers in Physics, 2020)*

Polarity in Biology: Flow of Life and Consciousness

Within our own bodies, polarity fuels the currents of life. Our nervous system relies on the movement of charged particles to send signals, allowing us to think, feel, and move. Every heartbeat, every breath, every thought is the result of electrical impulses traveling through our neural pathways—a biological manifestation of the universal principle of polarity.

Even on a psychological level, human emotions are governed by contrast—joy and sorrow, fear and courage, love and loss. Just as the body requires balance between positive and negative ions to function, our consciousness grows through the interplay of darkness and light. *(Source: (Frontiers in Public Health, 2021)*

Polarities of Creation: Union of Divine Forces

Across spiritual traditions, polarity transcends the physical and becomes a force of metaphysical creation.

Ancient wisdom speaks of feminine (electric) and masculine (magnetic) energies—not as gender constructs, but as fundamental expressions of the cosmos.

The feminine force is intuitive, receptive, and the wellspring of creation. The masculine force is structured, directive, and gives form to the infinite potential of the feminine. One without the other is incomplete; together, they birth worlds.

When these polar energies are harmonized within us, we align with the greater rhythms of existence as expressions of the whole. The universe itself is a balance of expansion and contraction, of stillness and motion, of the unseen and the manifest.

To resist polarity is to resist life itself. To embrace it is to awaken to a reality where opposition is not war, but symphony. *(Source: Journal of Metaphysics, 2023)*

Grand Synthesis: Polarity as the Pulse of Life

Ultimately, polarity is not a force of division, but of transformation. It is the alchemy of evolution, the silent hand that shapes every aspect of existence. Opposites are not enemies; they are co-creators, spinning the wheel of life in perfect, paradoxical harmony. *(Source: Physics Today, 2021)*

To comprehend polarity is to understand the language of the universe—the rhythm of creation itself. When we cease to fight the duality within and around us, we step into a state of flow. We see that every challenge, every contrast, every seeming contradiction is simply an invitation to greater awareness and growth.

Polarity is not just a principle of opposition; it is the foundation of all existence, the mechanism that fuels movement, change, and expansion—forever flowing, forever balancing, forever creating. *(Source: Consciousness Studies Journal, 2020)*

Process of Integration

Integration is the conscious alignment with one's divine essence—a sacred process of weaving wisdom, experiences, lessons, and growth into a higher state of awareness.

At its heart, it is the act of reconciling inner contradictions, healing and integrating emotional wounds, and embracing all aspects of existence with grace, compassion, and non-judgment.

This journey allows individuals to embody their true nature and live in harmony with universal laws, fostering inner peace, alignment, and self-realization.

Beyond healing past traumas or incorporating metaphysical concepts, integration extends into the energetic realm, uniting the individual with the collective consciousness and the universal flow.

It is a profound recognition of interconnectedness, a realization that we are threads in the infinite fabric of the cosmos.

This metaphysical process not only deepens personal transformation but also contributes to the evolution of collective awareness, bringing us closer to the divine Law of Oneness.

Unique to each person, integration unfolds as a hero's journey of self-realization, marked by phases of awakening, healing, and transformation. Though often challenging, it is profoundly empowering, offering the opportunity to transcend limitations and step into one's highest potential.

As we align with the flow of universal energy, we discover not only our divinity but also our essential role within the greater cosmic web, embracing the eternal dance of unity consciousness and infinite possibility.

- **Introspection:** The first step is to reflect and become aware of the fragmented or unconscious parts of the self that need to be healed. This awareness often arises through personal introspection, life experiences, or spiritual practices.

- **Acceptance:** In the next step, we stop rejecting or resisting undesired parts of ourselves. This includes embracing our vulnerabilities, our organic human vessel as the conduit of divine essence, both our light and shadow with compassion and non-judgment.

- **Healing:** This takes place when we actively work to transcend and transform limiting beliefs, emotional wounds, and subconscious patterns. This could involve integrating therapy, spiritual practices, or self-care routines that help release stuck energies.

- **Embodiment:** As we continue integrating, we embody the higher frequencies of pure love consciousness, peace, and unity, living in alignment with our authentic self and soul purpose.

The practice of real integration is a vital aspect of embracing and harmonizing all aspects of the self, transforming limitations and illusions of separation into opportunities for growth, and awakening to the infinite potential that resides within.

As we integrate, we align with the greater cosmos, stepping into our true sovereignty and embodying the eternal light of our divine being.

Pathways of Change

- **Embracing the Shadow**—the unconscious aspects of the self that we may repress or deny. The shadow contains emotions, fears, traumas, and insecurities that, when acknowledged and healed, can be transformed into sources of power, wisdom, and insight. Integration requires recognizing these aspects as part of who we are and no longer rejecting them.

    o Example: If we have experienced emotional trauma or unresolved anger, integration asks us to face these emotions, understand their origin, and release their negative charge. In doing so, we transform the energy into compassion, strength, and clarity.

- **Balancing Opposites**—whether it be the balancing of the masculine and feminine energies, intellect and intuition, or the active and receptive forces. Integration helps us realize that both sides are essential and must be in harmony for us to live authentically.

This is often referred to as the sacred inner union, where we unite the dual aspects of ourselves to create a higher, more cohesive whole.

- ○ Example: If one leans too much into the masculine energy (logical, active, controlling), integration calls for honoring and bringing in the feminine energy (intuitive, receptive, nurturing). When harmonized, these energies create a dynamic flow of creation and manifestation.

- **Healing and Transformation—** acknowledging wounds and regulating the nervous system, whether from past trauma, unresolved emotional experiences, or limiting beliefs—and transmuting them into higher states of awareness. Transformation begins when we no longer see ourselves as broken, but rather as whole beings capable of rising beyond limitations.

- ○ Example: Integration could involve recognizing patterns of codependency or self-sabotage and consciously choosing to break free from them, replacing them with self-love, empowerment, and healthier ways of being in relationships.

- **Unity with the Higher Self**—refers to the process of aligning with the aspect of consciousness that transcends the survival-based ego and connects us to the divine essence. It is about recognizing that we are spiritual beings having a human experience and that our essence is interconnected with the divine Source of all creation. As we integrate our higher wisdom, we embody the qualities of love, compassion, and awareness in our daily lives.

  o   Example: Meditation, mindfulness, and intention scripting are practices that help us cultivate a deeper connection with the Higher Self, fostering the flow of divine wisdom and guidance in every moment.

- **Awakening the Light Body**—activating a higher energetic aspect of our being that transcends the physical form. This light body allows us to embody divine frequencies of higher consciousness, love, and universal wisdom. As we integrate more of our true essence, we expand our consciousness and awaken to the realization that we are infinite, multidimensional beings.

- o Example: This could involve practices such as energy healing, chakra clearing, or conscious breathwork that open and align the energetic centers of the body, allowing the flow of divine light to permeate every cell.

Boundless Love as the Ultimate Integrator

When we witness our own expansion through this new paradigm of evolution, the wheel of consciousness, we move beyond judgment and resistance into radical acceptance.

We stop labeling emotions as high or low, good, or bad, enlightened, or unenlightened. Instead, we begin to see that everything—every heartbreak, every triumph, every fall, and every rise—exists within the same sacred motion.

This is the path of integration and embodiment— the boundless devotion, awakening to the truth that wholeness can only be achieved when we embrace every part of ourselves. It is not just about accepting the light within us but acknowledging the shadows, the forgotten pieces, and the untold stories that shape who we are.

We must stop running from our past, our pain, our flaws, and our fears. We must recognize that the sum of all our experiences, both the beautiful and the broken, is what makes us complete.

Only by integrating these aspects, by weaving them into the very fabric of our being, can we experience the fullness of our potential.

When we choose this path, we no longer live in fragments, disconnected from our divinity. Instead, we personify the essence of our existence—raw, authentic, and whole. And in that embodiment, we find our power, our peace, and our purpose.

Not just the light, but the lessons of the dark shadow aspects of ourselves and the world. Not just the joy, but the wisdom of pain. Not just the clarity, but the transformative power of uncertainty.

The wheel turns, and with each "reLovution", we return to ourselves. Not as fractured beings trying to escape the lower rungs of perception, but as luminous souls embracing the infinite dance of existence.

For in the end, awakening is about the embodiment of pure love without conditions. Love for the hero's journey, love for the process, and love for all that was ever created.

Pathway of Discernment

In the linear model, judgment is often mistaken for wisdom. We categorize emotions, behaviors, and even people into rigid labels—good or bad, unworthy, awakened, or asleep, worthy, high or low vibe.

But judgment is a tool of separation, a construct of the conditioned mind that reinforces division rather than unity.

Discernment, however, is a tool of wisdom. It does not condemn; it observes from an intuitive place of deep, profound knowing (Gnosis).

Discernment does not divide; it understands.

Where judgment clings to rigid absolutes, discernment flows, moving with the rhythm of pure consciousness. It allows us to perceive reality not through the lens of conditioned belief, but with clarity, grace, and intuitive insight.

In the esoteric tradition of Gnosis, true knowing is not an intellectual exercise of the mind—it is an awakening. A direct, experiential wisdom that transcends thought, revealing the deep, innate connection between the self, the divine, and the vast interconnectedness of all existence. This knowledge does not come from books or doctrine but emerges in moments of profound awareness, where the veils of illusion dissolve, and certainty is simply known.

From a metaphysical perspective, discernment is the ability to pierce beyond surface appearances, to distinguish between what is organic and what is imposed, what is in alignment with the unified field and what is merely an echo of ego, illusion, or external conditioning. It is a sacred attunement—an inner compass guided not by fear or bias, but by the resonance of genuine authenticity.

This art of knowing requires more than logic; it is a heart-centered skill, a refined connection to one's higher self. To cultivate discernment is to navigate life with unwavering integrity, to protect oneself from deception, and to make choices that reflect the highest alignment of one's soul. It is not merely about seeing—it is about understanding, about stepping beyond the illusions of duality and into the vast, infinite field of the All.

To discern is to co-create with conscious intention, to walk in alignment with wisdom, and to shape reality not through force, but through the mastery of perception itself.

To move from judgment to discernment, we must cultivate a practice of awareness, neutrality, and compassionate detachment:

- **Pause and Observe:** When confronted with an emotion, situation, or individual, resist the impulse to label or react. Instead, step into the role of the observer. *What is* *this experience teaching me? What energy is present here?*

- **Separate Perception from Projection**: We understand that judgment often arises from unexamined wounds or the projection of conditioned beliefs and victimhood. Discernment requires us to differentiate between what is and what we assume to be true based on our past experiences.

- **Feel Without Attachment**: Emotions are not directives; they are signals. Shame, anger, sadness—all are part of the human experience. Instead of suppressing or indulging them, allow them to flow through you without resistance.

- **Stop Seeking Validation**: Judgment seeks to confirm a belief, reinforcing the ego's sense of control. Discernment seeks to understand, remaining open to new viewpoints and insights even if they challenge previous perspectives.

- **Respond with Wisdom, Not Reaction**: Judgment is reactive; it fuels division, self-righteousness, or self-condemnation. Discernment is responsive; it allows us to act with clarity, compassion, and inner authority.

By integrating discernment into our awareness, we move from rigidity to fluidity, from opposition to unity. We cease trying to escape, fix, deny, or elevate ourselves above human experience and instead embrace its fullness.

The interaction between science and metaphysics lies in their shared focus on understanding and navigating complex realities, though they approach this goal from different perspectives.

In science, discernment is the ability to analyze, interpret, and differentiate sensory data or abstract concepts, often rooted in empirical evidence and critical thinking.

In metaphysics, discernment expands beyond the physical to include intuitive understanding, spiritual insight, and the ability to perceive the energetic realms of existence and consciousness.

Constructive collaboration emerges when scientific discernment is used to interpret metaphysical phenomena, bridging empirical reasoning with abstract or spiritual principles.

In essence, scientific discernment brings structure and clarity to metaphysical concepts, while metaphysical discernment deepens and broadens the understanding of interconnected systems and unseen dimensions of presence.

Together, they enable a more comprehensive approach to exploring reality and making informed, intentional choices in both the material and spiritual realms.

Discernment empowers you to perceive truth from illusion, make conscious choices, and navigate life with clarity and authenticity. This sacred skill draws from the heart, mind, and soul, combining intuition, logic, and universal principles of energy.

Navigating Resistance

Resistance to change is a natural response to fear, uncertainty, and the discomfort that comes with stepping into the unknown. It often emerges when we feel that something familiar is slipping away, or when we face the daunting idea of losing control.

To navigate this inner turbulence, we must first understand its root cause. What is it that we are truly afraid of? Is it failure, the fear of not being capable, or the loss of security? Once we identify the underlying fears, we can begin to dismantle them.

Shifting our mindset is key. Instead of viewing change as a threat, we can reframe it as an opportunity for growth and transformation.

When we begin to focus on the benefits—how change could lead to a more fulfilling life or bring us closer to our purpose—the fear that once felt so overwhelming begins to lose its power. The thought of growth becomes more appealing than staying stuck in the comfort of the known.

But even with a positive shift in perspective, the journey ahead can feel daunting. The solution lies in breaking the process down into smaller, manageable steps.

Rather than trying to leap into a huge shift all at once, we can take one small action at a time, building momentum and confidence with each step. Progress becomes a series of small victories, not a giant leap.

Along the way, emotional resilience is crucial. Change can stir up vulnerability, so it's essential to practice self-compassion, acknowledging that resistance is a natural part of transformation. In those moments of doubt, mindfulness can be a powerful tool—anchoring us in the present and reducing the anxiety that stems from an uncertain future.

As we navigate the change, seeking support from others can provide an invaluable perspective. Talking to people who have faced similar challenges can help us see that we're not alone in our struggles and that change is not only possible but essential for growth.

Educating ourselves about the process also provides clarity, making the unknown feel more like a series of manageable steps than an insurmountable obstacle.

Rather than avoiding resistance, we can engage with it. *What is it trying to tell us? What lies beneath the fear?* By addressing resistance head-on, we empower ourselves to move through it. This often involves experimenting, testing new approaches, and allowing ourselves to make mistakes without judgment.

Every small step we take is a victory. By celebrating our progress along the way, we reinforce the belief that change is not only possible but rewarding.

In the end, resistance is not the enemy—it is simply the signal that growth is on the horizon, waiting to unfold with the courage to embrace it.

QUANTUM PLAYBOOK: MASTERING DISCERNMENT

Activating the power of discernment is an essential skill in traversing life with clarity, wisdom, and grace. By aligning with your heart, tuning into your intuition, clearing mental clutter, and connecting with higher energy, you reduce negative polarization.

Step 1: Aligning with the Heart Center

Discernment is often rooted in the heart, which serves as a bridge between intellect and spirit. By activating the heart center, you can connect with higher wisdom, allowing you to make decisions that resonate with your true essence.

- Example: Practice heart-centered breathing. As you inhale, imagine drawing in light and love to your heart center. As you exhale, release any doubt or confusion. This helps clear energetic blockages, allowing intuition to flow freely.

Step 2: Tune Into Intuition and Inner Guidance

The power of discernment is closely linked to your intuition—the inner knowing that transcends logical thought. To activate this, quiet the mind and tune into subtle energies. Intuition speaks through feelings, images, light codes, and inner nudges that guide your decision-making.

- Example: When faced with a decision, take a moment of stillness. Ask your higher self for guidance, and pay attention to any feelings, thoughts, or images that arise in your awareness. Trust that this inner wisdom is aligned with your highest good.

Step 3: Clear the Mind

The mind can cloud discernment when it's overwhelmed by emotions, external influences, or distractions. Gaining mental clarity through meditation, mindfulness, or even simple reflection enhances your ability to discern truth from illusion. Question everything before you integrate into your belief system.

- Example: Practice mindfulness by observing your thoughts without attachment or judgment. Observe the external chaos for awareness, but do not absorb, react, or identify with it. Let go of preconceived notions and biases. This creates mental space, allowing you to receive more clear and balanced insights.

Step 4: Connect with Higher Realms

Metaphysical discernment can be enhanced by connecting with universal energies, such as Source, the Divine, or spirit through the third eye activation of the pineal gland. These energies offer clarity, truth, and perspective that transcend earthly experiences.

- Example: During meditation, ask for guidance from your higher self. Visualize yourself surrounded by pure golden light or standing in front of an open door leading to a realm of infinite wisdom. Allow this connection to guide you to discern what resonates with your soul.

Step 5: Ask Empowering Questions

When you question everything, it unlocks your spiritual insight and direct your focus toward higher wisdom. These guide you to the resonance that resides within your soul, helping you make choices aligned with your divine purpose and *Coherent Heart*.

- Example: Ask yourself, "What would love choose in this situation?" or "What is my soul guiding me to do?" Let these questions lead you toward clarity and empowerment.

Affirmations:
I trust my inner wisdom to guide me toward the path of my higher self in every situation.

11. Fusion of Quantum Physics & Consciousness

The branch of science called quantum physics unveils a reality far beyond our everyday understanding, where particles don't behave like solid objects but instead exist in a state of infinite possibilities, called superposition.

They can be in multiple places at once, only settling into a specific state when observed. Quantum mechanics, the framework for understanding this behavior, reveals that these particles are interconnected in ways that defy classical logic.

One of the most mind-bending phenomena is quantum entanglement, where two particles, no matter the distance between them, instantly affect each other as if linked by an invisible thread. This suggests that the universe may not be as separate and disconnected as it appears but is a deeply interconnected web of energy, information, and potential.

Quantum Mechanics

At the heart of quantum physics lies a paradox so profound it shakes the very foundations of reality: the observer effect. In the peculiar quantum realm, particles don't exist in fixed states but rather float in a boundless sea of infinite possibilities, suspended in a delicate dance of superposition. *(Source: Wheeler & Zurek, 1983)*

They can occupy multiple states at once—until the moment they are observed. Only then does their wave function collapse, choosing a single reality and selecting one path from the many potential outcomes.

Observation is not a passive act; it is an active force that seems to mold the very fabric of existence, shaping what we perceive as reality. *(Source: Wheeler & Zurek, 1983)*

Consider the proton: a tiny but powerful particle, carrying a positive charge and residing at the heart of an atom's nucleus. It plays a crucial role in defining the identity and stability of all matter, making it essential to the very fabric of the universe. *(Source: Feynman, 1965)*

A particle, in essence, is a fundamental building block of everything, from the smallest subatomic components like protons and electrons to the vast entities that shape our world.

From the smallest subatomic particles to the vast structures of the cosmos, each particle moves in harmony with the forces of nature, holding secrets that bind the universe together. *(Source: Heisenberg, 1927)*

Now, imagine the iconic Double-Slit Experiment—one of quantum mechanics' most illuminating revelations. Fire a photon at a barrier with two slits, and conventional logic would suggest that it must pass through one slit or the other, just like a grain of sand. But quantum mechanics defies this intuition.

When unobserved, the photon behaves as a wave, passing through both slits at once and creating an interference pattern as if it exists in multiple places simultaneously.

Yet, the moment we measure which slit the photon travels through, it behaves like a particle, following a single path and erasing the interference pattern.

It is as though reality doesn't crystallize until it is witnessed, revealing how our very act of observation brings the quantum world into focus. *(Source: Young, 1801; Feynman, 1965)*

This discovery upends classical physics, suggesting that observation is not simply an act of discovery but a catalyst of creation itself.

As physicist Niels Bohr famously remarked, "Everything we call real is made of things that cannot be regarded as real." The very act of observing forces the quantum wave function to collapse, fixing a once-fluid possibility into a definitive state. *(Source: Bohr, 1928)*

But what role does consciousness play in this process?

From a metaphysical viewpoint, consciousness is the very essence of existence—an infinite, all-encompassing force that transcends the physical body and mind.

It is the core awareness that unifies all things, the Infinite Intelligence, divine presence that is both boundless and indivisible. *(Source: Chopra & Kafatos, 2013)*

Consciousness is not just a byproduct of our thoughts, but the very fabric of reality itself, the Source from which all life and matter emerge. It weaves through every corner of the universe, shaping everything we experience and manifesting the world around us. *(Source: Lipton, 2005)*

In this way, consciousness is divine intelligence, guiding each soul's journey toward greater awareness and unity with the whole of existence. It is the silent designer of all creation, orchestrating the unfolding of reality at the deepest level within the unified field. *(Source: Sheldrake, 1995)*

According to the Copenhagen interpretation, it is not merely measurement, but conscious observation, that dictates quantum outcomes. *(Source: Bohr, 1928)*

This echoes ancient philosophical and esoteric teachings, which have long asserted that we have the power to shape reality.

If consciousness indeed influences the quantum world, then reality is not a static construct but a fluid, responsive field shaped by focused awareness. *(Source: Chopra & Kafatos, 2013)*

Quantum Entanglement

Adding another layer to this enigma is quantum entanglement, a phenomenon Albert Einstein famously dismissed as "spooky action at a distance."

When two particles become entangled, they remain mysteriously linked, mirroring each other's state instantaneously, no matter how far apart they are—whether across a room or spanning galaxies. (*Source: Einstein, Podolsky, & Rosen, 1935; Aspect, 1982*)

This defies the classical notion that nothing can exceed the speed of light and hints at an underlying, non-local connectivity woven into the fabric of existence itself. *(Source: Aspect et al., 1982)*

Together, the observer effect and quantum entanglement weave a startling narrative: Reality is not an isolated sequence of events but an interconnected web where perception and intention play an active role. *(Source: Wheeler & Zurek, 1983)*

This idea finds resonance not just in modern physics, but in the Hermetic principle that "The All is Mind"—the notion that reality is ultimately a manifestation of thought, a projection of consciousness. *(Source: Hermes Trismegistus, The Kybalion)*

Yet, this does not suggest that the mind can bend reality into existence like magic or wishful thinking.

Rather, it implies that the quantum field is a boundless ocean of potential, waiting to be shaped. *(Source: Lipton, 2005)*

Consciousness acts as a tuning fork, selecting from infinite probabilities and collapsing them into tangible form. In this light, we are not passive observers of an indifferent universe—we are active participants, co-creators of reality itself. *(Source: Chopra & Kafatos, 2013)*

The Link with Hermetic Philosophy

At the core of Hermetic philosophy lies the principle of Mentalism, a profound idea that unveils the universe as a mental construct, brought into being and continuously sustained by The All divine, infinite consciousness—often called the Universal Mind.

Far from being an external, fixed reality, this principle suggests that all of existence—both the material and immaterial—is a projection of thought and consciousness.

Reality is not a separate, unchanging entity but rather a dynamic, ever-evolving mental tapestry, where every experience, every sensation, is an expression of consciousness itself.

"The All is mind" challenges our traditional understanding of a fastened, independent reality, urging us to shift our perspective.

Instead of viewing the universe as something separate from us, it invites us to recognize that it is not only shaped by, but arises from, the vast expanse of the mind.

This perspective suggests that the boundaries of our external world are intertwined with the depths of our consciousness, where the material and immaterial converge as a reflection of the thoughts we collectively hold.

Bridging Science & Ancient Wisdom

Reality is not a fixed construct but a fluid symphony of potential, waiting for the observer to bring it into form.

Quantum mechanics reveals that before observation, all possibilities exist in a state of superposition—a shimmering sea of infinite outcomes, unbound by time or space.

It is only when consciousness interacts with this field that a single reality crystallizes into being, much like a sculptor shaping raw marble into form.

Yet, perception does not occur in isolation.

But this revelation is not new. Ancient wisdom has long declared that mind is the fundamental nature of reality. According to Hermetic philosophy, all of creation emerges from an infinite, intelligent consciousness—the I AM—from which all energy, matter, and form arise.

This concept aligns strikingly with the implications of quantum physics. If the universe is fundamentally mental, then reality does not exist independently of awareness; instead, it is shaped, influenced, and sustained by the very act of thought and perception.

Esoteric traditions across cultures echo this wisdom. In Advaita Vedanta, the material world is seen as Maya—an illusion projected by consciousness, or dream-like nature of the material world.

It refers to the idea that what we perceive as reality is a veil, obscuring the true nature of existence.

This "dream state" suggests that the world we experience through our senses is not the ultimate truth, but rather a temporary, shifting appearance that conceals the deeper, unified reality.

In Buddhism, the mind is the architect of experience, and enlightenment is the realization of unity with the infinite.

The Tao speaks as the formless origin of all things, much like the quantum field of potentiality.

Quantum mechanics, esoteric wisdom, and metaphysics converge in this understanding: we are not passive witnesses to an external universe, but active participants in its co-creation.

The observer is not separate from the observed; rather, they are one and the same. Like a drop returning to the ocean, our individual awareness merges with the infinite intelligence of the cosmos, where all things are eternally connected.

Interpretation of Mentalism

Throughout the ages, fragments of "truth" have been scattered like shattered pieces of a once-whole mirror, some preserved, others hidden or destroyed.

Each piece whispers a part of the story, yet none of them tell the full tale.

Religions rose from the ashes of others, each claiming dominance, but in doing so, they erased voices and hidden wisdom that could have illuminated the path for all.

The Catholic Church silenced Gnostic wisdom, Islam marginalized the Zoroastrians, Hinduism overshadowed Buddhism—and every tradition, in its quest for control, buried the light of unity beneath layers of division.

But in the silence, forgotten voices held the answers we once knew. Yeshua spoke of the Kingdom of God within us, yet today, we build walls of judgment and self-righteousness, turning a deaf ear to the call for unity.

The divine "I AM" presence pulses within us all, but we have lost the thread that binds us together.

We stand on incomplete ground, constructing doctrines of certainty on shaky foundations, while the bold eternity of existence quietly lingers inside, waiting to be understood.

To recognize the divine within us, we must reclaim what was lost. This is not a call to prove one path superior to another, but a plea to see the infinite reflected in every tradition. It's time to let go of the walls that divide us and awaken to the wisdom that unites us all.

The light of the divine does not reside in a single story; it shines brightly in them all as we are all reflections of unity consciousness, radiating through the prism of our unique lens of experience.

Over time, society scattered these sacred stories, breaking wisdom into pieces to conquer and control, creating division where once there was wholeness. This was a collective choice born from fear—a terror that manipulated us into submission, turning us away from our own power.

Yet control was never ours to wield. In this new era, the age of Aquarius, it is time to release the grip of division and rewrite these fragmented narratives. Not to return to the old ways, but to find balance—where the broken pieces of the puzzle come together within us, aligning with the truth of infinite possibility.

When we find unity within, the external world will reflect that harmony. It's time to step into abundance, not from a place of separation, but from a neutral space, seeing beyond the illusions that have long held us captive.

Reality as a Mental Concept

In today's world, modern science, especially the field of quantum mechanics, lends striking support to the concept of Mentalism. The observer effect demonstrates that consciousness plays an integral role in shaping reality.

In essence, the mere presence of awareness causes the physical world to "collapse" into existence. This mirrors the Hermetic notion that the universe is a mental phenomenon, sculpted by the thoughts and perceptions of conscious beings.

Further scientific validation comes from the quantum field theory, which proposes the existence of an underlying field that connects all aspects of the universe. This energy or field of information, which physicists hypothesize to be the fabric of all creation, aligns with the viewpoint of the Unified Field.

Science unveils the essence of Mentalism, demonstrating that reality is not passively observed but actively constructed by the brain. Our perceptions are not direct experiences of the external world; rather, they are intricate interpretations shaped by sensory input and the subconscious frameworks that govern our minds.

In this view, reality is a projection of our minds, continuously molded by our thoughts, beliefs, and perceptions.

Intentional Thinking

The essence of Mentalism is the power of intention—the conscious direction of thought to shape reality.

Every focused thought is an instruction sent to the universe, an electrical impulse sparking in the brain, reinforcing the very pathways that turn vision into reality.

Science confirms what the ancients always knew: what we think, we become. Studies on visualization and affirmations reveal that the brain does not distinguish between real experience and vividly imagined intent. When we hold a desire with clarity and conviction, the neural circuits fire as if it has already manifested, aligning our energy with the outcome we seek.

But intention alone is not enough. To truly master reality, we must move beyond passive wishing into embodied knowing with a *Coherent Heart*—that unwavering certainty that what we desire is already unfolding.

The universe does not respond to fleeting hope; it answers to energetic confidence, to thoughts infused with belief so deep they shift the very structure of existence itself.

This principle is the foundation of visualization and affirmations, practices that have been shown to produce measurable changes in brain activity.

When we vividly imagine success, the brain responds as if the experience is already real, priming the body and mind to bring it to fruition. The universe mirrors our internal state, responding to the vibrational frequency of our focused intent.

By mastering intentional thinking, we transcend passive existence and step into the role of conscious co-creators, shaping our reality with precision, purpose, and unwavering belief.

EMOTIONS AND NEURAL CIRCUITS

Emotions are not fleeting states of being; they are electrical and chemical currents that sculpt the architecture of the brain.

Every emotion—compassion, fear, joy, grief—activates specific neural circuits, reinforcing thought patterns and shaping our perception of reality. The brain does not merely record experience; it reconstructs it—filtering external stimuli through the lens of past emotions and internal beliefs.

Positively charged emotions, such as gratitude, compassion, kindness, and empathy, generate coherent neural activity, strengthening pathways associated with clarity, resilience, and higher-order thinking.

Negatively charged emotions, such as fear, anger, worry, judgment, or shame, trigger fragmented neural firing, reinforcing stress responses and survival-based cognition.

This means that our emotional state dictates the quality of our thoughts, decisions, and even the body's physiological responses.

Emotional intensity determines the depth of neural imprinting—which is why deeply felt experiences, whether traumatic or euphoric, leave lasting imprints in the subconscious mind.

But emotions are more than just neural chemistry—they are frequencies that ripple through the body's energetic field.

The heart-brain connection demonstrates that the heart generates an electromagnetic field 60 times stronger than that of the brain, sending more signals to the brain than the brain sends to the heart.

This suggests that emotions may not originate solely in the brain but within the body's greater energetic system, influencing cognition, intuition, and perception.

If emotions sculpt reality at both neurological and energetic levels, then intentional mastery of emotional intelligence becomes the key to transforming consciousness.

By cultivating higher vibrational states, we create coherent brainwave patterns, unlocking heightened awareness, deeper intuition, and a reality shaped by intentional thought rather than unconscious programming.

Mind Over Matter

The brain's remarkable ability to influence our physical health demonstrates the profound connection between mind and matter. Through the placebo effect, for example, we see how belief alone can trigger real physical healing. Similarly, epigenetics shows that our thoughts and emotions can influence gene expression, altering our physical state.

This invites us to reconsider the nature of existence itself. By viewing reality as a dynamic, malleable construct shaped by thought, belief, and consciousness, we are empowered to break free from the deterministic view of a material universe.

It challenges the idea that we are passive recipients of reality and instead emphasizes our role as active creators, co-authoring our experiences with the mind's immense potential. Through this lens, personal transformation, healing, and even collective evolution become attainable by mastering our thoughts and aligning them with higher levels of awareness.

In essence, the Hermetic principle of "The All" and its scientific interpretations provide a profound roadmap for understanding our capacity to co-create reality, emphasizing the boundless potential of the mind in shaping the world we perceive and inhabit.

HOLOGRAPHIC UNIVERSE THEORY

The holographic universe theory presents a radical shift in how we understand reality, challenging our deepest assumptions about existence.

In this model, the universe operates like a hologram—a three-dimensional projection encoded on a two-dimensional surface. *(Source: Bohm, 1980; Hooft, 1993)*

Every fragment of this hologram reflects the whole, implying that the vast cosmos is not a sprawling expanse, but an intricate web of interconnected patterns where each part mirrors the entirety.

This theory, pioneered by physicists like David Bohm and expanded by Gerard Hooft and Leonard Susskind, positions consciousness as a pivotal force in the fabric of reality.

At its core, the holographic principle suggests that what we perceive as physical space, time, and matter emerges from a deeper, non-local realm—a unified field where all information resides.

Bohm's "implicate order" describes this hidden layer, where everything is interconnected and infinitely dynamic. What we experience as reality—the physical universe—is merely the "explicate order," a projection of this unified field.

Like a hologram's three-dimensional image arising from a flat surface, the universe is a manifestation of underlying, non-local patterns of energy and information. *(Source: Bohm, 1980)*

This concept aligns with quantum mechanics, where non-locality allows particles to influence each other instantaneously, no matter the distance between them. Quantum entanglement defies classical notions of separateness and hints at a fundamental unity binding all things.

The holographic model builds on this, proposing that the separation we perceive between self and other, matter and energy, space and time, is an illusion.

Our sensory experiences are projections created by our awareness interacting with the quantum field. *(Source: Chopra & Kafatos, 2013)*

In essence, quantum physics shows us that reality is not fragmented. Instead, it points to a unified field where matter, energy, and consciousness are intertwined, and separation is merely an illusion. *(Source: Bohm, 1980)*

The discovery of entanglement also challenges the concept of local realism—the belief that objects exist with defined properties independent of observation. In the quantum world, things don't exist in a definite state until they are observed or measured. *(Source: Heisenberg, 1927)*

This perspective is revolutionary: If the universe is a hologram, the boundaries we perceive are not inherent but emergent.

Our individual experiences are localized expressions of a universal consciousness, with each of us representing a unique perspective of the whole. *(Source: Sheldrake, 1995)*

This idea resonates deeply with metaphysical principles, which view the physical world as a stage where spirit unfolds its journey through duality, polarity, and self-awareness. *(Source: Zohar & Marshall, 1994)*

Furthermore, the holographic model offers a framework for understanding phenomena like synchronicity, intuition, and the power of thought.

If all information is interconnected, every thought, emotion, and intention ripples across the hologram, shaping the collective reality. *(Source: McCraty & Atkinson, 2003)*

This concept bridges the gap between metaphysical ideas about the creative power of the mind and quantum physics recognition of the observer's role in shaping outcomes.

The holographic principle also provides a profound explanation for the fractal nature of existence. From spiraling galaxies to branching trees and neural pathways, nature mirrors itself at every scale. This fractal repetition is a hallmark of holograms, where each fragment reflects the entire image. *(Source: Mandelbrot, 1982)*

In the holographic universe, the microcosm and macrocosm are one and the same—an infinite interplay of patterns, each offering a glimpse of the whole. (Source: Bohm, 1980)

This understanding unites science and metaphysics, revealing a richer, more mysterious reality—a reality where the infinite and the finite, the spirit and the physical, the observer and the observed, are one. *(Source: Bohm, 1980)*

The idea that we are spirit having a human experience bridges ancient wisdom with modern science, offering transformative insights into existence, purpose, and identity.

It invites us to see ourselves not as confined by physical form but as eternal, boundless consciousness temporarily embodied in the material world. This perspective reshapes our understanding of reality and illuminates the profound interconnectedness of all things.

Accessing the Universal Holograph

Imagine standing in front of a vast mirror, your reflection flickering with each passing moment.

But what if that reflection wasn't just a mere image of yourself—it was the very fabric of the universe? What if every thought, every perception, every moment of awareness wasn't just a passive experience but the very projection of the world around you?

This is the stunning revelation of modern science. Reality is not what it seems.

The world we touch, see, and feel—the solidity of everything around us—is not as it appears. It is, in fact, a projection—a complex illusion crafted from two-dimensional information.

Just like a hologram, which may appear to be three-dimensional but is created from the interplay of light and shadows on a two-dimensional surface, the universe itself may be woven from the same illusion. (*Source: Bekenstein, J. D., & Hawking, S. W., 1973, Black holes and entropy. Physical Review D)*

At the heart of this theory is a profound understanding of black holes, those enigmatic regions of space that challenge our very conception of time, matter, and energy. It turns out that these cosmic giants do not store information within their depths as we might expect.

Instead, they store it on their surface—on a boundary. This realization has led to the insight that everything we experience in three-dimensional space might be projected from a distant, invisible two-dimensional boundary.

What we perceive as reality could be a shadow cast by an underlying structure of pure information. *(Source: Hooft, G., & Susskind, L., 1995, The world as a hologram, Physics Today)*

Then, the quantum realm offers further revelations: reality is not fixed; it emerges from the quantum field itself.

Our universe, as we know it, may spring from a deeper ocean of information—an invisible, underlying matrix that we cannot see but that shapes everything we experience.

Much like waves of possibility, particles exist as probabilities, forming themselves into matter only when our consciousness interacts with them. We, the observers, collapse this quantum potential into the solid reality we perceive.

This raises an unsettling yet fascinating question: If everything we perceive is a projection, then what of consciousness itself?

The Mind as a Hologram

If the universe is a hologram, then consciousness may not be confined to the brain alone. It could arise from a vast, interconnected web of awareness that transcends time and space. *(Source: Bohm, 1980; Sheldrake, 1995)*

Picture the mind—each part a mirror of the whole, every fragment reflecting the entire universe. This resonates with the holographic principle, which asserts that every component of a system contains information about the whole, a concept that bridges quantum physics and metaphysical thought. *(Source: Hooft, 1993; Mandelbrot, 1982)*

Our brain processes information holographically, where every thought, perception, and feeling mirrors the cosmos in its entirety.

Imagine the brain as a supercomputer, continuously running complex algorithms and interpreting data from the environment, with each "bit" reflecting a larger cosmic pattern.

This revelation is profound: consciousness flows from a vast interconnected field that spans the universe, binding all things together. Quantum mechanics, particularly non-locality, suggests that particles influence each other instantaneously, regardless of distance.

In this framework, the brain is not the origin of consciousness but a receiver—a tuning fork that resonates with the frequencies of the cosmos. It interprets and processes the data it receives, shaping our perceptions and experiences, yet the source of that information is far greater. *(Source: Bohm, 1980; McTaggart, 2007)*

If consciousness and the universe are intricately interwoven, what might this reveal about the nature of reality?

The implications are profound, suggesting that our perceptions not only reflect the universe but actively shape it. As consciousness and matter merge, the boundaries between mind and universe begin to blur.

But it doesn't stop there. If consciousness and the universe are intricately interwoven, what else can we learn about the very nature of reality?

A Simulation or a Program

What if everything you see, feel, and experience isn't real in the way you think? The Simulation Hypothesis and the Holographic Principle challenge the very fabric of existence, suggesting that reality may be an illusion—a construct meticulously designed beyond our perception.

Philosopher Nick Bostrom (2003) argues that if an advanced civilization could create hyper-realistic conscious simulations, the likelihood of us living inside one vastly outweighs the probability of existing in a "base reality." If consciousness can be simulated, are we living beings—or merely sophisticated code in an unfathomable system?

Meanwhile, theoretical physicists propose that all information within the universe is encoded on a distant two-dimensional boundary—a radical idea known as the Holographic Principle.

This suggests that the three-dimensional world we navigate may be nothing more than a projection, a grand illusion where depth, time, and matter emerge from a deeper cosmic blueprint. *(Source: Bostrom, N., 2003, Are You Living in a Computer Simulation?)*

In this holographic model of the universe, matter, space, and time are not the foundation of existence—they emerge from a deeper level of information. Like stars and planets that form and dissolve in the cosmic dance, the very particles that comprise matter exist not as solid objects but as waves of probability. They only take form when consciousness interacts with them, collapsing their wave-like state into the tangible reality we perceive.

This reflective understanding is echoed in quantum mechanics, where particles exist in multiple states of possibility, only "deciding" on a particular form when observed. But even in their most solid state, these particles remain part of an information-based projection—a manifestation of an underlying, invisible reality. The universe is not a rigid, fixed structure; it is a living, breathing entity—shaped by awareness.

Here, the interplay between these theories becomes hauntingly clear: If the universe is a hologram, could it also be a simulation? If reality is encoded, does this hint at an underlying computational architecture? Are we perceiving the rendered output of an advanced system far beyond our comprehension?

This fusion of physics, consciousness, and computation dismantles the notion of reality as we know it. If life is a projection, what lies beyond the screen? If we are in a simulation, who—or what—is the architect? *(Source: Bostrom, N., 2003, Are You Living in a Computer Simulation?)*

But even in their most solid state, these particles are part of an information-based projection. What we see is only one manifestation of an underlying, invisible reality. The universe is a living, evolving entity—shaped by awareness.

Beyond the Illusion: Power of Awareness

This is where magic happens. The boundaries between mind and matter, between ourselves and the universe, dissolve. What we perceive as "separation" is revealed as an illusion.

We are not passive observers of the universe—we are active co-creators. Every thought, every belief, every perception shapes the world around us. We are not merely responding to the world—we are, in fact, shaping it.

This view of reality parallels the ancient wisdom of Mentalism that sees the cosmos as a vast thought-form—a creation of the Universal Mind. In this vision, each individual is not separate from the whole system. Instead, each of us is a reflection, a part of the larger system.

We are the universe, and the universe is within us. Each thought, belief, and intention has the potential to change the course of existence.

What if we recognized that our perceptions are not responses to external stimuli but creative forces that shape the very fabric of existence?

The power to co-create with the universe lies in our conscious awareness. The moment we acknowledge this perspective, we step into our full power.

Co-Create with the Universe

The holographic universe beckons us to realize that we are not trapped in the illusion of separation—

a construct of the ego-mind that reinforces duality and disconnects us from our inherent unity with the Divine Source, the universe, and one another.

Every aspect of our lives, every moment, is a chance to rewrite the projection of reality. After all, we are active participants in the unfolding story of existence.

Imagine what the world would look like if each of us fully embraced this birthright—the understanding that the universe is not "out there" but within us, ready to be shaped by our consciousness.

ENERGETIC HIGHWAY OF THE BIOFIELD

What if the energy flowing through and around you holds the key to healing, consciousness, and the very fabric of existence? The biofield—an invisible yet profound energy matrix—permeates and sustains all living beings. Long recognized in ancient healing traditions as prana, chi, or life force, modern science is now racing to understand its full potential.

A groundbreaking randomized, placebo-controlled, double-blind study found that distant biofield energy healing led to measurable improvements in fatigue, sleep disturbances, stress, cognitive function, and anxiety—without a single reported adverse *effect (Source: Health Psychology Research)*. This challenges conventional medicine's understanding of health and suggests that energy itself may be a powerful catalyst for well-being.

The "Biofield Science: Current Physics Perspectives" suggests that the toroidal field may be more than a mystical force—it could be the missing link between consciousness and quantum reality. Scientists propose that electromagnetic fields, quantum processes, and coherent states may explain the nature of the biofield, potentially reshaping our understanding of the human body and mind.

Paradigm Shift in Perception

These studies represent a hypothesis in how we view healing, energy, and consciousness. As scientific inquiry deepens, one question becomes impossible to ignore: *Could the biofield be the missing link between mind, matter, and the unseen forces that shape our reality?*

From a metaphysical view, the human body is more than flesh and chemistry—it is an intricate energy system, where currents of prana, chi, or etheric life force flow through meridians, energy centers, and the toroidal field. This energetic highway, known as the biofield, is the bridge between the physical and quantum realms, influencing health, perception, and consciousness itself.

Yet, when trauma, fear, and conditioned beliefs block these pathways, energy stagnates in the lower three centers, reinforcing cycles of survival, scarcity, and limitation. Ancient wisdom and modern science converge on a profound perspective: real transformation occurs when these energy fields are unblocked to allow the flow state.

When the heart enters coherence—emitting a stable, rhythmic signal—it synchronizes the brain and body, unlocking access to higher states of awareness.

Esoteric traditions have long called this the Sacred Heart, Anahata, the green ray of divine intelligence—a portal to the Unified Field of Consciousness. It is the portal to free will and limitless potential—a quantum force pulsing within you, waiting to be liberated.

ALCHEMY OF HEART-CENTERED AWARENESS

The mind is the active force behind creation, shaping reality through perception and thought-forms. It governs reason, logic, and the ability to mold energy into form. Like a master sculptor, the mind uses mental transmutation (Hermetic principle) to shift states of consciousness and manifest new realities.

Yet, when the mind is disconnected from the heart, it becomes rigid—bound by over-analysis, fear, and the illusion of separation. The mind can become a cage, limiting the expansive potential of consciousness.

But the mind is not still—it is ever-evolving, expanding, and creating, generating energy through the awareness of its own wholeness. It perceives itself in every layer of existence, deepening its understanding through contrast—light and shadow, peaks and valleys, separation and reunion. But the purpose of contrast is not division; it is expansion.

Consciousness evolves through love. When the mind fully recognizes itself—integrating all that it is—it becomes the origin, the cause, the architect of form across space and time.

When we embrace unconditional love, we align with the highest expression of our divine essence—becoming living embodiments of pure love consciousness, flowing freely through every moment, every relationship, and every choice.

Through this lens, dimensions are not separate, but interconnected. The higher dimension does not dominate the lower; it extends into possibility, shaping reality through connection, not control.

This is the mechanism of expansion, encoded in the unshakable laws of creation. When aligned and in coherence, we hold the key—the map to all that is.

The Interplay

The mind directs, but the heart aligns. They must work together in harmony for true creation. The mind sets intention, but the heart fuels it with energy—emotion (energy in motion) amplifies thought-forms into reality. Without heart alignment, manifestations may be rooted in egoic desire rather than divine will.

The union of mind and heart is the key to unlocking the infinite potential that lies within. It is the ultimate integrator: Thought + Pure Love = Divine Creation.

When one fully embodies the coherent heart-mind state, reality shifts. No longer constrained by linear cause and effect, the individual becomes a conscious creator, influencing the quantum field with clarity, purpose, and devotion. This coherent state allows each person to:

- Access the Zero-Point Field, where infinite possibilities exist.
- Collapse quantum potentials into reality through focused intention.
- Experience heightened intuition and synchronicity.
- Expand awareness beyond the physical, tapping into non-local consciousness.

The Zero-Point Field, from the perspective of quantum physics, is an infinite energy reservoir that permeates even the emptiest vacuum, alive with subtle fluctuations known as "quantum foam." It exists between the duality of positive and negative, embodying the neutral space of unity. *(Source: Bohm, 1980)*

Metaphysically, this field is seen as a boundless well of potential, linking all things across space and time in a unified field of existence. *(Source: Sheldrake, 1995)*

Heart-centered awareness is the transformative journey of transcending the limitations of mind and ego. By merging emotional and spiritual intelligence, we awaken the heart's wisdom, dissolving fear and blockages while embodying compassion, presence, and devotion.

This practice reconnects us to our divine essence, guiding us beyond external distractions to the subtle whispers of our intuition. It is an active engagement with life, aligning our consciousness with the universe's rhythm and co-creating our reality in peace, authenticity, and sovereignty.

In this sacred space, the heart becomes a catalyst and a container, directing the energy of the unified field, bringing light, clarity, and harmony. As we embrace this heart-centered existence, we shift from fear to creative flourishing and spiritual expansion. *(Source: Lipton, 2005)*

This journey is not just personal healing; it is a collective evolution of consciousness. An awakened heart ripples outward, healing both ourselves and the fabric of humanity. *(Source: Sheldrake, 1995)*

We align with our true divine nature. The heart guides us with wisdom, unconditional love, and grace, reminding us that we are eternal sparks of divine consciousness, radiant and free.

Heart-mind manifestation is not about forcing the world to conform but aligning with the higher intelligence of Source. As we harmonize with the heart's field, synchronicities flow, leading us back to the realization that we are never separate from the divine, expressing itself through our human avatars.

Thought without heart is cold calculation. Heart without mind is ungrounded idealism. But when thought is infused with the frequency of love, it becomes Divine Intelligence in action—the perfect union of form and formlessness, of logic and spirit, of creation and embodiment. Thus, the mind is the tool, but the heart is the key. Together, they unlock the infinite.

FABRIC OF REALITY

The structure of reality is a beautiful, intricate dance of consciousness and energy, woven together in a harmonious tapestry of existence. Imagine your thoughts as the grass beneath your feet, growing through the rhythm of your heart. This is the gateway to understanding—our perception of reality is but a sliver, less than 1% of the visible light spectrum.

Linear thinking limits us; true reality is non-linear. Detaching from the need to know and embracing love aligns us with the flow of existence. We are not just passive observers; we are integral participants, each of us a unique note in the cosmic symphony, resonating with unity.

Your life is more than just a collection of moments; it's the unfolding of your cosmic archives, a record that holds the energetic imprints of all your past, present, and potential lives. These imprints are not just passive memories—they are active, dynamic records of your soul's journey.

These Akashic Records are often described as a cosmic archive—holding the energetic imprint of every soul's journey, thought, and experience across time.

As explored by David Bohm, the quantum unified field is the invisible web connecting everything in the universe. It is the foundation of all existence, where space, time, matter, and consciousness merge into one dynamic energy. In this vast field, all things are interconnected, vibrating in harmony.

While the Akashic Records reveal the unique imprint of each soul, the unified field encompasses all of creation. Some spiritual traditions see the Akashic Records as a localized access point within this infinite field, offering a bridge between the personal and the universal.

Together, they remind us that we are not isolated but woven into the fabric of reality—a part of a greater whole, eternally interconnected.

By accessing the Akashic records within the quantum field, through stillness and meditation, you align with the wisdom of the universe. Here, you can witness the lessons you've repeated, the karmic ties you need to resolve, and the potential for rewriting your soul's story.

Every choice you make, every thought you have, is recorded, and you are the author of your own cosmic narrative. The power to rewrite these records lies within you.

Now imagine consciousness existing outside of linear time, where past and future collapse into an eternal present. In this state, you become aware of the sacred geometry that underlies all creation—the perfect patterns that shape galaxies and DNA alike.

This is not a coincidence. This is consciousness expressing itself through mathematics, through sacred light codes.

SACRED CODES OF GEOMETRY

Sacred geometry is the study of patterns, shapes, and proportions that are believed to form the blueprint of all creation. It is rooted in the idea that certain geometric forms are fundamental to the structure of the universe, reflecting the interconnectedness and harmony inherent in nature.

From the spirals of galaxies and the structure of DNA to the growth patterns of plants and the vibrations of sound, sacred geometry reveals that existence is built upon universal laws of proportion, symmetry, and balance.

In the shadowed depths of history, one name stands out as a beacon of brilliance—Nikola Tesla. His mind, a swirling vortex of creativity, reached for truths that echoed through the ages, unearthing secrets of the universe long before modern science caught up.

Among his most cryptic revelations was his obsession with the numbers 3, 6, and 9. Tesla famously declared, "If you only knew the magnificence of the 3, 6, and 9, then you would have the key to the universe."

But what did he mean by this, and why do these numbers continue to captivate the human imagination, drawing the curious into a deeper understanding of the cosmos?

To understand the profound significance of 3, 6, and 9, we must first look beyond mathematics and into the heart of sacred geometry—where numbers are not just figures on a page, but the very language of the universe.

In sacred geometry, these numbers are the cornerstones of existence, each representing an essential aspect of creation.

Trinity of Creation (3)

The number 3 holds a place of honor, embodying the sacred Trinity—a symbol of divine unity, balance, and creation that has been revered across cultures for millennia. It is the number of manifestations.

Imagine the simplest form in geometry: the triangle. This three-sided shape doesn't just symbolize stability— it represents the synthesis of opposites, the union of dualities, the sacred dance between spirit and matter.

It's the cosmic law of creation itself, where the One divides into the Two, and through their union, emerges the Three—a new reality, whole and perfect.

In metaphysical terms, 3 represents the bridge between the unseen and the seen, the formless and the form. It's the number of the divine spark that ignites the flame of creation.

The trinity—often seen as the Father, Son, and Holy Spirit in religious traditions—echoes the interplay of energy, matter, and consciousness. At the heart of this energy is the creative principle that is both the origin and the goal of all things.

Harmony of the Universe (6)

The number 6 resonates with the heart of the cosmos, the very energy of harmony and balance.

This number calls us into alignment with the interconnectedness of all things, the invisible web of existence where every thread matters, every note plays a role in the divine symphony.

In geometry, the hexagon, with its six sides, is the shape of nature's perfection—seen in the symmetry of snowflakes, honeycombs, and crystal formations.

This shape speaks of the profound efficiency and unity of creation. The hexagon isn't just beautiful; it is the epitome of balance, the seamless union of form and function.

Spiritually, 6 represents the divine feminine energy—nurturing, receptive, and boundlessly loving. It is the energy that sustains life, nurturing it into fullness. The number 6 reminds us that at the core of creation is a force of unconditional love, where opposites merge to create a harmonious whole.

It's the sacred union between the material and the spiritual, where the heart becomes the point of integration, a place where the physical world meets the divine.

Completion and Enlightenment (9)

At the pinnacle of these numbers stands 9, the culmination, the divine plan unfolded—the number of completion, enlightenment, and return to Source. It is the highest single-digit number, representing the end of a cycle, the culmination of the journey, and the beginning of a new level of consciousness. It signifies the profound transcendence of limitation, the expansion into higher realms of understanding.

In sacred geometry, 9 represents the Flower of Life pattern—the sacred blueprint of creation. It is the number that embodies the essence of wholeness, spiritual maturity and the fulfillment of divine purpose.

The Quantum Vortex

Quantum particles dance in uncertainty, defying our conventional understanding by existing in multiple places at once, connected instantaneously across vast distances. This is the realm of non-locality, where space and time dissolve, revealing that the boundaries between matter and energy, form and formlessness, are far more fluid than we once believed.

In this mysterious world, sacred geometry provides the blueprint. The vortex, the spiral, and the golden ratio are mathematical expressions that occur in nature and the fundamental laws of the universe. These patterns mirror the energy that flows through all of existence.

Nikola Tesla, through his work with the Tesla Coil and his concept of free energy, understood these energetic spirals. His obsession with the numbers 3, 6, and 9 wasn't just numerical—it was his recognition of the harmonious symmetry that governs the universe. These numbers are the very keys to creation, unlocking the secrets of energy, frequency, and vibration that shape our reality.

The vortex—the spiral—embodies this flow of energy. It echoes the cycles of life: birth, death, and rebirth, capturing the infinite rhythm of creation. Just as 3, 6, and 9 represent balance and transcendence, they reflect the eternal dance that weaves all of existence together.

In sacred geometry, the heart is symbolized by the Flower of Life—a series of interlocking circles forming a vortex-like pattern. This is no mere decoration; it's a profound map of creation, embodying the flow of life force energy.

The *Coherent Heart*, more than just an organ, is the central hub of energetic activity where free-will is accessed—a portal to the quantum unified field that connects everything in the universe.

Neutral Point of Unity

At its heart, sacred geometry is not just a field of mathematics—it is a lens through which we can see the very fabric of reality itself. Shapes like the Flower of Life, Metatron's Cube, and the Fibonacci sequence are the designs of the universe, guiding the flow of matter and energy. They represent the unified wholeness of existence, reminding us that all things are deeply interconnected.

When we engage with these sacred patterns—whether through art, meditation, or intention—we tap into the natural rhythms that govern all life. It's an alignment that promises to elevate our consciousness, bringing balance to our inner and outer worlds. Sacred geometry offers a profound understanding of how reality is structured, revealing that we, as conscious beings, are integral to this divine design.

In physical reality, we often perceive existence as duality—light and dark, positive and negative. Yet, at its core, existence is not just duality but a Trinity. The Trinity arises because, beyond the opposing poles, there is always a neutral point—a Zero Point of balance between the two.

This balancing point serves as the reference from which duality emerges, the central origin that gives meaning and context to opposites. Without this neutral grounding, opposites cannot exist in relation to one another.

From this perspective, all existence reflects this threefold nature: positive, negative, and neutral. This Trinity is fundamental to creation and operates on every level of reality, though it may manifest differently depending on the context.

This sacred balance is reflected everywhere, in the simplest geometric form—the triangle, which symbolizes the interplay between positive, negative, and the neutral point that unites them.

Mastering inner balance is the key to unlocking the mysteries of the universe. Beneath the visible world lies a field of consciousness—the Unified Field, or Zero-Point Field—a limitless, neutral wellspring of potential where consciousness and energy originate. In this space, everything is possible.

Decoding the Patterns of Life

Tesla's theory invites a sense of mystery and wonder, sparking debate about whether it's a profound mathematical framework for reality or simply a fascinating quirk within the realm of numbers and geometry.

These numbers resonate with the very structure of nature, particularly in the context of the golden ratio, which underpins the patterns of growth in plants, the architecture of galaxies, and the symmetries in sacred geometry.

The golden ratio (approximately 1.618) encapsulates a deep, hidden order that weaves through everything from the spiral of seashells to the arrangement of planets and even the human form.

Let's dive deeper into the mathematics. The year of 9 (for example: 2+0+2+5 = 9) brings a new layer of significance, as 9 in numerology is revered as a master number—an ultimate symbol of completion, wisdom, and universal understanding.

It holds a unique property: when any number is multiplied by 9, the sum of its digits will always reduce to 9 (for example: 9 x 8 = 72, and 7 + 2 = 9).

This is no coincidence, as number 9 represents the infinite, the eternal cycle, a number that cannot be divided by anything except itself. It stands as a symbol of the spiritual journey, the end of one cycle and the beginning of another, a full-circle return to the origin.

The power of 9, when observed through numerology, is connected to profound universal principles. It symbolizes the end of a cycle yet simultaneously points to a greater perspective—the continual loop of rebirth, transformation, and regeneration.

From this viewpoint, Tesla's theory offers a glimpse into the mathematical symmetries of nature. Is it a key to existence, or simply a captivating numerical puzzle?

COSMIC ENCRYPTION OF 26

There is a number, silent yet omnipresent, woven into the very fabric of existence—waiting to be noticed by those who are attuned enough to listen to the key to infinite.

This number is 26. It pulses through the blood in our veins, hums in the heart of dying stars, and inscribes itself into the genetic blueprint of life.

It governs the celestial ballet of equinoxes, unfolds in the multidimensional architecture of the universe, and whispers through the quantum dance of time itself.

26 is more than just a number—it's a cosmic cipher, embedded into creation itself, calling us to uncover its mysteries.

Physics: Blueprint of the Cosmos

In the world of theoretical physics, bosonic string theory demands the existence of 26 dimensions for its mathematical consistency. These dimensions aren't arbitrary; they form the invisible scaffolding upon which all existence is built. From the flickering quantum fields to the grand expansion of the cosmos, 26 is woven into the very design of reality. *(Source: Green, Schwarz, & Witten, 1987)*

Even the fine-structure constant—the number that governs the relationship between light and matter—resonates with 26. It's a number that dictates the stability of atoms, the delicate dance between electrons and photons, and the very essence of matter itself. Were it to shift, even by the smallest fraction, the universe as we know it would unravel.

Yet, 26 persists, hidden beneath the surface, as the foundational key to the universe's delicate harmony.

Biology: Code of Life

The human body, too, carries the signature of 26. While our genetic code operates on 23 pairs of chromosomes, the addition of three stop codons brings the total to 26.

These codons act as the punctuation marks of life, guiding the ribosomes to cease translation at precisely the right moment, ensuring proteins form with exacting accuracy. Without them, the intricate language of biology would unravel into chaos, and life as we know it would cease to exist.

The relationship between these codons and the orderly production of proteins is not merely an accident—it's a testament to the deeply encoded wisdom that governs the mystery of the universe. *(Source: Crick et al., 1961)*

But it doesn't end there. It also flows through our breath.

Hemoglobin, the molecule that sustains life, owes its existence to iron—*element 26*. Forged in the fiery heart of dying stars, this element binds to oxygen and carries life to every cell in the body.

Without iron, respiration would be impossible, and the intricate web of biological life would collapse.

The presence of 26, both in the atomic structure of iron and the genetic code of life, suggests a cosmic intentionality—an intelligence behind the design of existence.

Astronomy: Pulse of the Cosmos

Beyond Earth, 26 governs the life cycles of stars. When a massive star exhausts its fuel, it begins producing iron—*element 26*. At this threshold, fusion halts, and the star collapses in a brilliant supernova, scattering the elements necessary for planets and life throughout the cosmos. *(Source: Woosley et al., 2002)*

Without this process, the universe would remain barren, a void devoid of the richness required for existence.

Even the motion of celestial bodies adheres to this sacred number. The precession of the equinoxes—the Earth's slow axial wobble—completes a full cycle every 26,000 years.

Ancient civilizations, from the Mayans to the Egyptians, aligned their temples and pyramids with this cycle, suggesting an awareness of cosmic rhythms that modern science has only recently begun to understand.

Echo of Natural Order

Beyond the realms of physics and biology, the number 26 unfolds its significance within the mystical world of sacred geometry and esoteric wisdom.

In Kabbalah, the Tetragrammaton—the sacred name of Creator or God (YHWH)—bears the numerical value of 26. This is not mere symbolism; it is a reflection of divine creation itself, a numerical thread woven into the very fabric of existence, the resonance of the cosmic order that governs the universe. *(Source: Scholem, 1965)*

But the influence of 26 doesn't stop there. In the emerging field of quantum consciousness, researchers have posited that the brain's microtubules—tiny cellular structures fundamental to the nature of consciousness—resonate at frequencies that align with sacred numbers, including 26 Hz. *(Source: Hameroff & Penrose, 2014)*

If consciousness itself is attuned to these frequencies, then our very perception of reality may be shaped by numerical harmonies embedded in physics, biology, and the fabric of existence itself.

Merkaba Field: Vehicle of Ascension

Even beyond the body and the cosmos, 26 appears in the architecture of space itself. Ancient mystical traditions speak of the Merkaba—the light-body field surrounding all living beings.

Depicted as a star tetrahedron, two interlocking pyramids spinning in multidimensional space, it is said to be a vehicle of ascension, a chariot of light that bridges dimensions.

Modern physics now recognizes what the ancients described in esoteric terms. This geometric shape, once thought to be myth, aligns with torsion fields—vortex-like energy structures that transcend space and time.

And within its sacred geometry, number 26 reveals itself once more. In deep meditation, when practitioners visualize the Merkaba at 26 intersections of light, they report profound states of awareness, moments of inexplicable synchronicity, and glimpses into a reality beyond the physical.

Could it be that 26 is not just a number, but a key? A key to unlocking the full potential of consciousness within the unified field, to understanding the grand design of the universe, to transcending the illusion of separation and stepping into the infinite?

SOURCE OF WHOLENESS

In the quantum unified field, there is no separation—no physicality, no matter as we know it in our third-density reality. What exists is frequency, vibration, information, and consciousness. As Einstein noted, this invisible field of energy is the governing agency of the particle. It doesn't just influence the particle; it controls and supports it entirely. If we could alter the information within this field, it would ripple outward, affecting particle matter itself.

Astonishingly, the atom, the foundation of what we perceive as reality, is 99.99999% energy and information, with only 0.00001% of it being matter. This tiny fraction is an illusional holographic projection of stable energy frequencies that creates the appearance of separation. *(Source: Bohm, D., 1980, Wholeness and the Implicate Order)*

What we perceive as "reality" is merely a sliver of the full spectrum of frequency. The rainbow of visible light reflects off this stabilized energy, giving form to the illusion of material existence. But what if, instead of creating from matter—the illusion of separation—we could tap directly into the field itself? What if we aligned with the Source of wholeness? To do so, one would have to transcend the confines of the material density and journey into the quantum void.

Anchoring Unity Consciousness

To align with the Source of wholeness is to transcend the boundaries of time and space, releasing the ego's grip on limiting beliefs and stories. It is a journey into a realm where the distinction between self and universe dissolves—where the delusions of physicality fade, and we step into the boundless expanse of possibility.

In this sacred space, unity consciousness reigns, and separation ceases to exist.

Here, we reconnect with the pure essence of life— the quantum unified field that pulses at the heart of creation. Resonating with this energy, we are drawn into the Source that shapes all things.

Aligned with the Source, creation flows effortlessly—not through force or control, but through divine harmony. By attuning to the frequencies of the quantum field, we unlock the power to manifest—not by striving, but through deep alignment with divine order.

Our intentions, rooted in this coherence, become transformative, not as passive observers, but as conscious co-creators with eternal Source.

At its core, this understanding transcends both science and metaphysics, revealing that all of existence is woven from the fabric of energy. The separation we perceive are temporary distortions in the mind. Wholeness is not something to seek externally; it is something to remember—our innate connection to the wellspring of creation's field, the Source from which all things flow, both seen and unseen.

When we reconnect with the divine Source, we realize the quantum void is not an abstract concept but a living, breathing field of infinite potential, waiting for us to merge with it.

In the union of self and Source, we step into our fullest power, knowing that everything we need, everything we desire, already exists within the energetic matrix of the universe. This co-creation becomes an effortless dance—flowing with the pulse of existence, allowing the universe to manifest through us, as us.

To reach this state, imagine refocusing your attention from every aspect of the material world: your body, relationships, possessions, responsibilities, memories, and future expectations.

Surrender completely to the present moment, placing your energy not in the physical, but in the infinite unknown. Picture a world stripped of physicality—no Earth, no stars—just a vast void, teeming with energy and frequency.

This nothingness is everything—an infinite wellspring of potential. Free from the weight of identity and past, your mind undergoes a profound transformation. The fragmentation caused by external distractions dissipates. Your brain, once scattered, reorganizes itself, creating coherence, a harmonious state of being.

In this harmony, brainwaves slow, shifting from chaotic beta states to calm, synchronized rhythms. Electrical signals pulse through the unified neural network, amplifying in strength and precision. The clearer the intention, the more potent the signal.

This is creation in its purest form: sending a focused signal into the quantum field—not as a separate being, but as the Source itself. No longer bound by material density, you become a vibrational match to infinite possibilities.

In this realm of pure consciousness, the heart becomes the key. Pure love, the essence of Source energy, radiates outward, generating a magnetic field of immense power. The more coherent the heart, the stronger its energy, and the greater its ability to draw realities to you.

With devotion and visualization, you magnetize your future. Your heart becomes the force that binds atoms, drawing experiences from the quantum field into material existence.

When your vibrational frequency aligns with the quantum field's potential, synchronicities unfold. Opportunities, serendipitous events, and meaningful coincidences emerge—not by chance, but as visible evidence of your creative power. These moments, charged with purpose, remind you that you are the architect of your reality, a co-creator with the universe.

At this critical juncture, the past loses its grip. Every betrayal, every failure, every wound fades into irrelevance. You realize that none of it ever defined you.

QUANTUM PLAYBOOK: DESIGNING REALITY

By embracing quantum principles in your goal-setting process, you align your intentions and energy with the infinite possibilities of the quantum field. With clear precision, purposeful intentions, aligned actions, and an openness to uncertainty, you actively shape potential outcomes into a singular, focused reality.

As the observer, your attention and vibration become the driving force, collapsing possibilities into form. By harmonizing your thoughts, actions, and energy, you tap into the creative power of the universe to manifest the reality you desire.

Step 1: Clarifying Your Desired Outcome (Collapsing Possibilities)

In quantum mechanics, outcomes remain in superposition—multiple possibilities—until an observation collapses them into a single reality. Similarly, in goal setting, your future holds countless potential paths, but by focusing your attention and clarifying your desired outcome, you collapse those possibilities into one tangible reality, creating a clear and purposeful direction forward.

Example: Writing a Book

Goal: Complete a science fiction novel by 2026.

Action:

- **Define your goal clearly:** Instead of vaguely saying "I want to write a book," provide specifics and say, "I will write a 300-page novel by December 31st."
- **Visualize and feel the outcome:** Spend a few minutes each day visualizing yourself completing the book. Imagine the feeling of holding the finished product, envision the cover, or imagine sharing it with others.
- **Focus on the end result:** By holding this specific outcome in your mind, you collapse all the possibilities into one, completing your novel.

- **Why it Works:** By defining a concrete outcome and focusing on it consistently, you are collapsing the wave of potential realities into a single probable outcome, influencing your decisions and actions towards that vision.

Step 2: Harnessing Intention (Quantum Field of Possibilities)

In quantum physics, observation shapes reality. Similarly, when you focus your conscious attention and set a clear intention, your decisions actively shape your reality, guiding the quantum field of infinite possibilities to align with the path that leads you to your goal.

Example: Starting a New Business

Goal: Launch a successful online business within the next 6 months.

Action:

- **Set a powerful intention:** "I intend to create a coaching business that provides value and generates a steady income."
- **Observe opportunities:** Stay aware of any signs, resources, or ideas that come your way. Notice when certain opportunities feel aligned with your goal, and act on them.

- ○ **Daily Affirmations:** *"I am aligned with my purpose and every step I take brings me closer to the success and fulfillment of my heart's desire."*
- ○ **Observe how the universe responds:** Trust that the quantum field is responding to your intention and be open to the opportunities that arise.
- ○ **Why it Works:** Your focused attention on the goal acts as an observation of the quantum field, collapsing infinite possibilities into one path that feels aligned with your desires. By maintaining awareness and acting on insights, you shape your reality.

Step 3: Action and Momentum (Influencing the Wave Function)

Quantum theory suggests that particles move and change based on their wave function—until they're measured. Similarly, you create momentum in your goal by taking consistent action, which "measures" your intention and influences the outcome.

Example: Health Transformation

Goal: Lose 30 pounds in 8 months.

Action:

- **Define the specifics of your goal:** "I will lose 30 pounds by following a healthy eating plan and mindful movement practices 4 times a week."
- **Daily Consistency:** Every day, take action toward your goal—meal prep, exercise, hydrate, and get enough rest.
- **Track your progress:** Keep a journal of your health journey, recording small victories and challenges. This reinforces your wave function, continuously shaping your reality.
- **Celebrate milestones:** Acknowledge your progress at key milestones (e.g., every 5 pounds lost) to create positive reinforcement.
- **Why it Works:** The action you take each day is measuring your intentions, collapsing the wave of infinite possible outcomes into a concrete reality. Each action amplifies the probability of your goal's achievement by creating momentum.

Step 4: Embracing the Universal Laws (Resonating with Desired Reality)

Quantum physics reveals that everything in existence is energy, vibrating at different frequencies. This energy interacts with like energy, creating a powerful resonance that shapes our reality.

When we align our thoughts, emotions, and actions with the desired outcome, we harmonize our personal frequency with that of our goal. This alignment sends a signal to the quantum field, attracting opportunities, people, and circumstances that match that frequency.

Essentially, by tuning into the vibrational essence of what we wish to create from the coherent mind and heart space, we magnetize it into our lives, manifesting the conditions necessary for our intentions to unfold.

Example: Finding a Dream Career

Goal: Secure a fulfilling job in your desired field

Action:

- **Create a vision board:** Include images of the company you want to work for, the role you desire, and the lifestyle you wish to live.
- **Act as if:** Start living in alignment with your goal. If you're pursuing a leadership role, take on leadership activities in your current job, or volunteer for projects that will enhance your skills.
- **Emotional alignment:** Practice gratitude for the job you currently have, focusing on what it offers you, and know you appreciate the job you are about to receive.
- **Network and engage with your ideal role:** Start connecting with people in your desired

industry, attend events, and be open to conversations that can lead to opportunities.

- **Why it Works:** By focusing on the vibrational energy of the reality you want to create (success, fulfillment, abundance), you align your energy with that frequency. The quantum field responds to your vibration, attracting the right circumstances and people that align with your goals.

Step 5: Trusting Divine Timing and Surrender (Quantum Uncertainty and Flow)

In quantum mechanics, uncertainty is inherent; we cannot always predict the exact outcome or timing. Similarly, when setting goals, you must trust in the process and allow space for the universe to deliver what is in your highest good, even if it's not exactly how you imagined.

Example: Creative Project (e.g., Writing, Art, or Music)

Goal: Finish a creative project, such as an album or artwork.

Action:

- **Set a broad intention:** "I will complete my creative project with joy and ease, allowing inspiration to flow freely."
- **Show up consistently:** Commit to a creative practice—write 500 words daily, paint for

1 hour every morning, or compose music every evening.

- **Trust the flow:** Sometimes the process will not go according to plan, and that's okay. Trust that what you create when in flow will align with your goal in unexpected ways.
- **Release attachment to the outcome:** While you still take actions, avoid over-focusing on the "how" and "when." By releasing this attachment and letting go of the need to control every detail, you create space for the universe to work in harmony with your intentions, bringing opportunities and solutions in ways that may exceed your expectations. Let go and allow the flow of life to guide you toward your desired state.
- **Why it Works:** Quantum uncertainty shows that many potential outcomes exist until the observer focuses on one. By surrendering the timeline and trusting the flow, you align with the rhythm of the universe, which may surprise you with opportunities that you wouldn't have anticipated. The uncertainty invites room for miracles.

Step 6: Leveraging Feedback Loops (Quantum Entanglement)

In quantum entanglement, particles remain connected across distances. Similarly, feedback from others and the environment will support or challenge your goals. Engage in dynamic relationships and opportunities that mirror the success your heart desires.

Example: Learning a New Skill

Goal: Become proficient in speaking French.

Action:

- **Engage with a supportive community:** Join a language-learning group, whether online or in person, where others are working on similar goals.
- **Practice daily:** Dedicate time each day to study the language, practice speaking, or listening to native speakers.
- **Seek feedback:** Have conversations with native speakers or tutors to refine your skills. The feedback you receive will guide your progress and help you adjust your approach.
- **Celebrate progress with others:** Share your milestones with friends or language partners to create a positive feedback loop of encouragement and support.
- **Why it Works:** Just as quantum entanglement shows that particles influence each other at a distance, engaging with others who support your growth reinforces your commitment to the goal and accelerates the process.

You have always been whole—a limitless, multi-dimensional being, fully capable of stepping into your power, creating from the field of infinite potential.

12. Expanding Quantum Reality

When we master the process of acceptance, redirection, and intention, we release the energy that was once wasted on resistance. We begin using our attention to consciously create our reality.

Remember, acceptance isn't about surrendering to defeatism, it's about recognizing reality as it is, without the filters of resistance. In this space of acceptance is where our vision becomes clear, and the path to what we want unfolds.

The shift happens when we stop fighting against the worst-case scenario. By releasing the energy of resistance, we allow our attention to become a force of creation. The moment we embrace acceptance, we free up the energy to focus on what we truly want. As we do this, reality begins to shift in response.

Ultimately, we are all reflections of each other, mirrors of both light and shadow, shaping and being shaped in the endless rhythm of duality.

This journey is not about taking sides—it is about integration, about merging the fragmented pieces of ourselves and discovering the divine within. Darkness exists to teach us balance, for even the shadows serve a purpose in shaping our evolution.

What is truly fascinating is that you may be a beacon of light to one person and a shadow to another. Our roles shift depending on who we witness and who witnesses us from their unique perceived lens.

The goal, however, is not to judge but to find equilibrium within.

When we recognize others as vessels of both darkness and light, we transcend illusion and begin the sacred process of embodiment—not just ourselves, but the world around us.

When we walk in balance, the duality we once clung to fades away, giving way to unity. The code for this has always existed within us, quietly waiting to be unlocked. Each of us is an expression of limitless polarity, incarnated into form to fulfill a higher purpose—one that begins with healing.

Healing the wounds of past generations, remembering and integrating the divine essence within, and rediscovering our inherent worth—all of these are the steps that reveal the deeper calling of our existence.

This journey was never meant to be about division. It has always been about union. Along the way, we have been gifted various tools—first religion, then science, and now technology.

Pathways of Change

No matter the tools we use, the mission remains unchanged: to heal and integrate, to embody, to find balance, and ultimately, to walk together in harmony.

1. Understanding Reality as Energy and Frequency

- **Shift:** Move from seeing reality as fixed and external to recognizing it as fluid, responsive, and shaped by consciousness.

2. Observer Effect and Conscious Creation

- **Shift:** Become an intentional observer. Instead of judging or reacting to life as if it's happening to you, recognize that it is happening through you. Shift focus from fear and limitation to expansion and possibility.

3. Nonlocality and the Oneness of Consciousness

- **Shift:** Transcend the illusion of separation. Understand that your thoughts, emotions, and actions ripple across the quantum field, affecting the collective reality. Cultivate unity consciousness, where healing yourself contributes to healing the whole.

4. Accessing Quantum Timelines

- **Shift:** In the quantum model, time is non-linear—past, present, and future exist simultaneously as probabilities. Stop defining yourself by past limitations. Instead, align with the energy of your desired future self. Through meditation, visualization, and intentional energy work, you can collapse old timelines and step into a new reality.

5. Power of Conscious Alignment

- **Shift:** Move from ego-based survival mental processing to heart-centered awareness. Practice gratitude, compassion, and mindfulness to elevate your vibration and synchronize with higher possibilities.

6. Multidimensional Quantum Jumping

- **Shift:** By shifting perception and energy, you can "quantum jump" to a version of yourself that has already aligned with the reality you seek. See yourself as fluid, not fixed. Engage in identity shifts—act, think, and feel as if you are already the expanded version of yourself. Through deep embodiment, you merge with that reality.

Discovering Curiosity & Growth

We often reject the darkness—the shadow, the fear, the chaos.

We bury it deep, pretending it doesn't exist, clinging to the "fake it until you make it" mentality.

But what we resist does not vanish; it waits. It lingers in the forgotten corners of our being, growing restless, until one day it comes back—screaming, clawing, demanding to be acknowledged.

When we judge another, we are merely shining a light on the unhealed parts of ourselves. The very things that trigger us in others are reflections of the wounds we have yet to tend.

Have you ever wondered why certain behaviors enrage you while others go unnoticed?

It is because those triggers are invitations—whispers from the soul urging you to look inward, to find the fear, pain, disingenuous behaviors, or separation you have been avoiding.

But here is the transformation: judgment, when met with awareness, becomes the gateway to compassion. The moment we stop resisting the reflections that disturb us—the moment we acknowledge them with compassion instead of rejection—something profound happens.

We heal. And in that healing, our judgments dissolve, leaving behind only understanding, curiosity, connection, and unity.

So, the next time you feel the impulse to judge, pause. Ask yourself: *What part of me is yearning to be seen?* Because the path to understanding others begins with loving every fragment of yourself.

SHIFTING CONSCIOUS VIEWPOINTS

From a neuroscience viewpoint, shifting perspective isn't merely an abstract concept—it's a tangible, neurological transformation.

By rewiring neural pathways, regulating emotions, and reframing cognitive frameworks, we can reshape our perceptions, thoughts, and behaviors.

Pathways of Change

The brain, in all its complexity, is neuroplastic: it's capable of restructuring itself in response to intention, experience, and repetition.

1. Rewiring Old Thoughts

- **Shift:** Interrupt the cycle of old thought patterns and deliberately engage with new ways of thinking. Journaling, cognitive reframing, and immersing yourself in diverse perspectives all foster the creation of new neural connections, leading to a more adaptable brain.

2. Reflecting with Conscious Awareness

- **Shift:** Cultivate metacognition—the ability to observe your own thoughts without judgment. Practices like meditation, mindfulness, and Socratic questioning (e.g., "Is this thought objectively true?") help activate the prefrontal cortex, broadening your ability to perceive situations from multiple perspectives.

3. Regulating Emotions

- **Shift:** When the amygdala is triggered, it can hijack rational thinking, locking us into survival-oriented responses. This can limit our ability to break free from entrenched perspectives, keeping us stuck in reactive, narrow thinking. Use breathwork, mindfulness, and vagus nerve stimulation (through humming, cold exposure, or deep breathing) to regulate the nervous system. A calm nervous system enhances cognitive flexibility, enabling easier shifts in perspective and emotional regulation.

4. Training Your Brain

- **Shift:** If our focus is on negativity, the RAS seeks out evidence that supports this belief. Conversely, when we choose to focus on opportunities or solutions, the brain's RAS adapts, finding confirming evidence for our new outlook. Employ techniques like positive affirmations, visualization, and intentional focus to retrain your brain's filtering system. Repeatedly directing your attention to the positive helps reshape your cognitive filters, gradually changing how you view the world.

5. Changing Interpretations

- **Shift:** Since our thoughts shape our emotional responses, changing our interpretations shifts how we feel and react. When faced with a challenge, ask yourself:

  - What's another way to view this situation?
  - What would I advise a friend in this circumstance?
  - How might this situation contribute to my growth?

  This practice of cognitive reframing builds neural pathways linked to adaptability, resilience, and emotional intelligence.

6. Using Body Language

- **Shift:** Studies show that expansive body language can boost confidence, while deep, slow breathing reduces stress and anxiety signals in the brain. Experiment with power poses, movement-based therapies like yoga or dance, or somatic practices to influence your mental state through physical action. Shifting your body can shift your mind, making it easier to approach situations from a fresh perspective.

7. Shifting Through Novelty

- **Shift:** Engage in activities that introduce novelty into your life. Travel, learn new skills, read diverse viewpoints, or have deep conversations. These experiences stimulate cognitive flexibility, opening your mind to new possibilities.

Incorporating these neuroscientific principles into our daily lives rewires the brain's circuitry—each shift creating new pathways, fostering adaptability, and allowing us to see the world from perspectives that were once hidden.

Taking Radical Accountability

Perfection is an illusion. We are not meant to be flawless; we are here to be human—to make mistakes, stumble, fall, live in integrity, and rise again. The beauty of our existence lies not in achieving some unattainable standard, but in our capacity to learn from the missteps along the way on our hero's journey.

Each blunder is a stepping-stone, each misstep a lesson that propels us forward, deeper into understanding, growth, and self-expansion.

Let's shift our perception to understand that mistakes are not failures; they are invitations—opportunities to look within, reflect, and evolve. We are here to experience, to stretch, and to push the boundaries of who we are.

When we embrace our imperfections with grace, we allow ourselves to be fluid—open to change and growth rather than rigidly clinging to an ideal of perfection.

On our journey, we encounter challenges, setbacks, and moments of doubt. But these are not signs of weakness or deficiency; they are the soil in which our strength, wisdom, and resilience are cultivated. Every time we falter, we have an opportunity to reflect on what needs to shift, what patterns we need to break, and how we can expand into a better version of ourselves.

The hero's journey is not about achieving excellence—it's about remembering divine essence. Becoming more aware of who we are, embracing all parts of ourselves, and honoring the lessons we learn along the way. It's about allowing ourselves the grace to fall, to rise again, and to continue evolving with self-love, compassion, and understanding for our own humanity, the precious gift of life.

When we embrace radical accountability, we face the uncomfortable truth that we, too, can cause hurt—whether intentionally or unknowingly. It requires the courage to own our actions, to acknowledge the impact we've had on others with our words, and to take full responsibility for our role in those moments.

But this accountability is not about self-flagellation; it's about acknowledgement, understanding, growth, compassion, transformation, and ultimately, forgiveness.

When we cause harm, it's easy to point the finger outward—to blame circumstances, misunderstandings, or the actions of others.

But the real shift begins when we look inward and recognize the role we played in the situation. Ask yourself: *What choices did I make that led to this? How did my words or actions contribute to this pain?*

This is not about self-criticism, but about learning to stand in our truth and accept our imperfections as opportunities for growth. Once we've owned our part in the hurt, the next step is to learn and not repeat.

Radical accountability doesn't just involve admitting our transgressions; it's about understanding them fully and changing our actions. *What patterns led to this behavior? What unresolved wounds within us caused the reaction?* This self-awareness is the key to breaking cycles of hurt and moving toward emotional maturity.

Then, we must integrate what we've learned. **Knowledge without action is stagnant.** To truly heal, we must apply the insights we gain to our future decisions, ensuring we don't repeat the same mistakes.

It's in this integration that growth happens—not just for ourselves, but in our relationships with others. We become more mindful, more compassionate, and more aligned with our highest selves.

Finally, forgiveness—especially self-forgiveness—is essential. The inner critic of the unhealed mind will often try to keep us stuck in guilt or shame, but this only prolongs the suffering. True healing happens when we recognize that our mistakes don't define us. We can forgive ourselves for the hurt we've caused with humility, commit to doing better, and move forward with a renewed sense of self-compassion.

By embracing radical accountability, we break free from cause and effect, the cycle of judgment, self-criticism, and stagnation. We create space for healing, growth, and transformation—not only for ourselves but for the world around us. Through this process, we become more aligned with the sincerity of human essence: imperfect yet always evolving with a coherent mind and heart, always capable of change, and always worthy of forgiveness.

ACCEPTING MIND-HEART ALCHEMY

Within the depths of human consciousness lies an untapped power—the fusion of mind and heart. Often seen as opposing forces, the mind thrives on logic, structure, and reason, while the heart pulses with intuition, emotion, and connection. True transformation arises when these forces align, creating harmony beyond the ordinary.

The *Coherent Mind* is sharp and analytical, an architect of reality, mapping possibilities and navigating complexity. It deciphers patterns, channels thought into action and has the power to manifest. Yet, when detached from the heart, the mind risks becoming rigid—ruled by fear, doubt, and the ego's need for external validation.

The *Coherent Heart*, on the other hand, is an ocean of intuition and empathy. It speaks in silent waves of insight, resonating beyond language. Here, pure love and emotional intelligence flourish—not through logic, but through an awareness that defies explanation. It is our portal to the unified field, attuning us to life's interconnected pulse. Yet, without the clarity of the mind, its wisdom can become clouded by unchecked emotion.

When mind and heart unite, they create a synergy—grounded and expansive—a space where intellect and intuition merge into clarity, purpose, and deeper resonance. Coherence isn't about silencing one for the other but weaving their strengths into a seamless rhythm. Intellect is infused with depth, intuition sharpened by discernment and sovereignty.

In this state, the heart enriches logic with emotional intelligence, while the mind provides the heart with structure and intent. Together, they form a dynamic partnership that enhances decision-making, deepens experiences, and fosters peace. Choices made from this balanced space reflect our highest wisdom, not mere calculation.

Mind-heart coherence is not just personal alignment; it's a gateway to an expanded consciousness. Anchored in the present, we tap into a wellspring of creativity, insight, harmony, and bliss. We gain the magnetic ability to co-create reality. No longer fragmented, we move through life as unified forces, flowing effortlessly with its rhythm.

In rare moments of full coherence, we touch the pulse of the divine, embodying something greater than thought or feeling—an expression of universal energy, deeply interconnected with all that is. This is the unity of existence, where every thought and feeling aligns with our true nature.

At its core, mind-heart coherence is a return to wholeness—a reclamation of inner power, guiding us to navigate life with grace, authenticity, and an open heart. In this sacred balance, we don't just exist—we awaken, fully alive, attuned to the infinite pulse of the universe.

Illusion of Matter: Cosmic Trick of Perception

What if everything you perceive—the solid weight of a laptop beneath your fingertips, the warmth of sunlight on your skin, the very fabric of reality—was nothing more than a grand illusion? A trick of perception orchestrated by your nervous system, decoding the endless sea of energy that exists beyond your senses. *(Source: Hoffman, Donald D., 2019)*

The world you see is not the world as it is, but a slowed-down projection of energy translated into form. Quantum physics reveals that matter, at its most fundamental level, is not solid but a symphony of vibrating energy fields. Your finger does not pass through the laptop not because of any inherent solidity, but because the electrical fields of its atoms repel those of your own. *(Source: Davies, Paul, 2004)*

You are not touching the laptop—you are experiencing the resistance of force fields, translated into the sensation of touch by your brain. *(Source: Greene, Brian, Quest for the Ultimate Theory, 1999)*

Everything you feel, see, or hear is not an objective external reality, but a neural interpretation. The external world is energy—fluid, formless, infinite. Your brain acts as a frequency decoder, collapsing waves of potential into the reality you perceive. *(Source: Heisenberg, Werner, Physics and Philosophy: Revolution in Modern Science, 1958)*

Light itself does not have color until your eyes translate its frequency into visible hues. Sound does not exist as music or noise until your brain processes vibrations into meaning. You do not experience the world as it is; you experience a constructed reality—one that exists within the confines of human perception. *(Source: Pribram, Karl, 1971)*

Ancient mystics, from the Kabbalists to the Vedic sages, spoke of Maya—the great cosmic illusion that veils the true nature of existence. Today, science whispers a similar viewpoint. The physical world, governed by classical mechanics, is merely a slowed-down version of quantum reality—a dense mirage built from waves of probability. The material trickster, matrix, is not the source of reality but a manifestation of consciousness interacting with energy. *(Source: Einstein, Podolsky, & Rosen, 1935; Bohr, 1928)*

If consciousness is the only fundamental reality—if all else is a construct of perception within the universal hologram—then what does that mean for our existence? Who are we, beyond the so-called illusion? *(Source: Chopra & Kafatos, 2013)*. Perhaps the answer lies not in the world we see, but in the awareness that sees it.

EMBRACING THE ROLE OF SPIRIT

In metaphysical traditions, the spirit is revered as the eternal, boundless essence of existence—the animating force that ignites the physical body, imbuing it with life's spark.

The body is not who we are, but a sacred vessel, a temporary conduit for the spirit to engage with the tangible world, expressing itself through higher frequencies.

This union serves the profound purpose of spiritual evolution: to embark on a transformative journey of growth and self-awareness.

The human experience is both a mirror and a catalyst, reflecting our divine essence and offering us opportunities to remember, reclaim our sovereignty, and expand our consciousness.

This understanding aligns with the Law of One, which teaches that all beings originate from a singular Source, fragmented into infinite expressions to experience and understand itself.

Illusion of separation, often called "the veil" or "Maya," is essential for exploring duality—light and shadow, unity and individuality—inviting us to integrate these polarities within ourselves.

At its core, this *Hero's Odyssey* is a quest for reconnection with the divine Source. It is remembering that unity is the true nature of existence. By transcending the illusion of separation and embracing the Oneness of all creation, the spirit fulfills its purpose, harmonizing the fragmented physical realm with the radiant wholeness of its origin.

Through this sacred journey, we rediscover that we are not simply in the universe—we are the universe, knowing itself through human experience.

Purpose of Embodiment

Why would an infinite spirit choose to inhabit the limitations of a human body? This question lies at the heart of many mystical philosophies.

Human experience provides a unique opportunity to encounter contrast and duality—emotions of pleasure and pain, love and fear, connection, and isolation.

These contrasts allow spirit to deepen its understanding of itself and its infinite capacities through the gift of mastering emotional intelligence, particularly the capacity to love unconditionally, forgive, and create.

From a metaphysical perspective, our challenges are not arbitrary but carefully orchestrated experiences of the soul designed to facilitate growth. They act as mirrors, reflecting the lessons needed to align with spiritual intelligence and further expansion.

By navigating the very real human feelings, creative expressions, lessons, and balance, we neutralize the egoic identity and uncover our inner strength, alchemical mastery, and wisdom, embodying our divine essence.

REMEMBERING OUR POWER

The phrase "spirit having a human experience" also emphasizes that this life is a multi-layered process of becoming. As spirits, we are whole, infinite, and connected to the divine Source. It is our primary existence.

However, upon entering the human form, we encounter the Maya dream state—an amnesia of sorts—where the boundaries of ego and individuality obscure our infinite nature. This forgetting is purposeful, as it enables us to rediscover our path of inherent divinity through the lens of free will and personal evolution.

Metaphysical and scientific models converge here, suggesting that the energy fields and quantum vibrations that underpin physical reality are not separate from us but emanate from within.

In essence, we are multi-dimensional beings, woven from threads of energy, thought, emotion, and spirit. From this perspective, we recognize that we are more than physical bodies governed by cause and effect and the Law of Karma.

We are not confined to this one lifetime or this one dimension. We are eternal cosmic travelers, simultaneously human and divine, playing in the dance of dimensions, creating, evolving, and returning to the infinite Source from which we came.

Each of us carries the four sacred bodies of consciousness—the physical, mental, emotional, and spiritual—each distinctively resonating at a vibration that shapes our experience of reality. *(Source: McTaggart, 2007)*

The physical body is our tangible vessel, a miracle of energy slowed into matter. Quantum physics matches this viewpoint: what seems solid is, at its core, a symphony of vibrating particles, dancing within the infinite quantum field. *(Source: Heisenberg, 1927; Feynman, 1965)*

The mental body is the architect of our reality, where thoughts and beliefs ripple into the unseen. Just as the quantum observer collapses potential into form, our intentions shape the world we experience. Every thought carries weight; every belief alters the fabric of possibility. *(Source: Lipton, 2005; Bohm, 1980)*

The emotional body is the song of our heart—a field of energy that vibrates with the frequencies of love, fear, joy, and grief. These emotions ripple outward, harmonizing or distorting the quantum resonance of our reality. *(Source: McCraty, 2003; Porges, 2011)*

Science affirms this in the power of *Heart Coherence*: when love and gratitude flow, the universe responds in kind.

And then, there is the spiritual body—the eternal spark, the unbroken thread connecting us to the divine Source of all creation. It is the purest vibration, the quiet hum of unity, where the boundaries of time and space dissolve. In quantum terms, this is the zero-point field: infinite potential, infinite connection. *(Source: Bohm, 1980; Laszlo, 2007)*

Together, these bodies form the bridge between the seen and unseen, the finite and the infinite. They remind us that we are not mere observers of this world—we are creators.

When we align with the higher frequencies of love, intention, and presence, we harmonize with the universe itself, collapsing chaos into order, suffering into peace. *(Source: Emoto, 2004; Chopra & Kafatos, 2013)*

We are the resonance. We are the field. And we hold the power to shift the world—one vibration, one moment, one heartbeat at a time.To embrace this multidimensional nature is to remember our power, our connection, and the limitless potential that exists within. We are, in essence, a reflection of the universe—vast, eternal, an aspect of unified infinite intelligence.

Let us honor the symphony of our being and awaken to the possibility that reality is not happening to us; it is unfolding through us. We are the light in motion, divine and whole.

Transcending Time

Time, at first glance, feels real and unyielding. We watch moments unfold, hear the steady tick of the clock, and observe the seasons shift.

It seems as though time marches forward in a linear progression—from past to present to future—carrying us along with it. *(Source: Kant, 1781)*

But when we peer deeper into the nature of time, through both science and philosophy, we begin to see something far more elusive, far more complex.

In physics, particularly within Einstein's theory of relativity, time is not the fixed, uniform entity we often assume. Time, along with space, forms what we know as the time-space continuum. Imagine this continuum as a vast, elastic fabric, holding everything from stars and planets to specks of dust.

This fabric stretches across the universe and encompasses not only the familiar dimensions of length, width, and height but also the dimension of time. What Einstein revealed was that space and time are inseparably intertwined.

Our experience of both is shaped by the forces around us—motion, gravity, and the very fabric of the universe itself. *(Source: Einstein's General Theory of Relativity, 1915):*

Picture a heavy object placed on a trampoline, creating a deep dent and warping the surface. Similarly, massive objects like stars and planets warp space-time. The greater the mass, the more pronounced the distortion. The force of gravity is the result of this warping. *(Source: Thorne, 1994)*

Time and space themselves are fluid, bending and stretching depending on speed and gravitational influence. For example, someone traveling near the speed of light experiences time more slowly than someone standing still.

This phenomenon, known as time dilation, shows that time is not a fixed, universal constant but a flexible dimension. *(Source: Einstein, 1915; Hafele & Keating, 1972)*

Yet the mystery of time goes beyond physics. Many spiritual and philosophical tradition s, from ancient Buddhism to quantum mechanics, suggest that time, as we experience it, is an illusion—a mental construct.

The "present moment" is the only true reality; the past and future are projections of our minds. The past exists only in memory, and the future only in anticipation.

Time, then, is a narrative our minds create to make sense of experience. In this view, the past and future are not tangible; they are figments of thought. The only true reality is the eternal "now," which remains unchanged, regardless of the passing moments. *(Source: Wheeler, 1990)*

So, is time an illusion? In a profound sense, yes. Time, as we perceive it—divided into past, present, and future—does not exist as an absolute truth. It is a construct of our consciousness, shaped by our perceptions. Whether through relativity or spiritual teachings, time is revealed as a fluid, ever-shifting concept, influenced by the forces of the universe and the mind. *(Source: Einstein, 1915; Tolle, 2005)*

The real intrigue of the time-space continuum lies in its fluidity. It is not a static backdrop against which events unfold, but a living, breathing fabric, constantly changing. Reality is ever-evolving, shaped by both the physical forces governing the universe and the way we perceive and interact with them. We are not passive observers. *(Source: Wheeler, 1990; Bohm, 1980)*

As conscious beings, we actively engage with this fabric, shaping it with our movements, choices, and awareness. In this way, we are co-creators of our reality, constantly molding the fabric of existence with our very thoughts, actions, and awareness.

Let's delve deeper into this notion of time. Have you ever really been to the past? Or to the future? When you think about the past, you are experiencing it in the present moment, right here and right now.

But have you ever actually been there? It's not a physical place; it's a mental construct, a narrative our minds create to make sense of what has already happened. The same holds true for the future—it hasn't arrived yet, and it is just as elusive. The present moment is not a tiny fraction sandwiched between the past and the future. It is eternity. Always present. Never-ending. Simply being. *(Source: Tolle, 2005; Damasio, 2010)*

When the now is filtered through the limitations of the mind, it gets refracted, distorted into the linear sequence we call time. The mind, trying to comprehend this eternal moment, traps it within the confines of past and future. It bends our perception, stretching and compressing time, projecting the illusion of motion. *(Source: Wheeler, 1990; Kant, 1781)*

Physical death, then, could be viewed as a kind of awakening. When we shed the limitations of the mind and the body, we return to the ever-present now, where time no longer has meaning. In the grand sweep of the universe, time is simply a construct—an idea that allows our consciousness to navigate the human experience. We are not bound by it. *(Source: Einstein, 1915; Bohm, 1980)*

We are timeless multi-dimensional beings, existing in infinite now, free of the past and untouched by the future. We are one with eternity, connected to all that is, in the eternal moment that binds us to the cosmos.

Timeline Traveler

Linear time is not a river you float through; it is an ocean of infinite possibilities, each one waiting for you to tune in.

Every version of you, every outcome, every path— already exists. The only thing separating where you are from where you want to be is the frequency you are locked into.

You are shifting timelines with every thought, every feeling, every shift in perception. Reality is not fixed; it is a mirror reflecting your energy, unconcerned with time. They tell you the past is a permanent imprint, however, the past is not a memory—it is an active frequency.

Every time you recall it, you are not remembering; you are re-experiencing it. That is why the past changes as you evolve. What once felt like failure becomes wisdom. What once wounded you becomes fuel.

The moment you shift your perception of the past, you shift your energy in the present. And when you shift the present, you alter the trajectory of the future.

But what if you could draw energy from what hasn't happened yet, with the same certainty as what already has? What if time isn't moving from past to present to future, but existing all at once—waiting for you to align?

Look forward. Feel the pull of the future. When you do, your mind recalibrates, tuning into a new timeline, and suddenly, the future draws you in just as the past once held you back.

Your feelings move you through timelines—*emotions are the remote control of your reality*. That is why those who feel stuck stay stuck. That is why those who feel free become free. Reality does not respond to what you want—it responds to what you embody. And what you embody is dictated by what you believe to be true.

Tapping into imagination is not fiction; it is a map of your timelines. When you dream of a greater future, you are not creating something from nothing—you are glimpsing a version of yourself that already exists.

The key is to step inside it. Feel it. Live inside it before it happens.

Because reality does not come to you—you bend toward it, drawn by the gravity of your own belief.

You were never meant to be shackled by the illusion of time. You are not a prisoner of fate—you are a cosmic traveler of timelines.

The past is not your sculptor—the power of now is your architect. Shift your focus forward. Feel its pull. Align with it. Step into the current of what is waiting for you.

Because the moment you do, you will no longer be a passive observer of reality—you will become its creator.

The only question is: Which timeline are you feeding with your attention and energy?

Imagination: The User Interface of Reality

Our imagination isn't just creativity—it's the most direct route to knowledge. It's not about fabricating; it's about tuning in to what's already there, waiting to be discovered.

Consider Tesla, who envisioned his inventions long before they materialized. Einstein, who saw the laws of physics unfold in his mind before they were proven. They weren't simply thinking—they were connecting with a unified field of intelligence that transcends linear time. That same field is accessible to you, right now.

The art of imagination is the user interface of your unconscious mind, a bridge between thought and infinite. Like any interface, it can be seamless and clear, or glitchy and unreliable, shaped by your beliefs, habits, and mental conditioning. This is why some people effortlessly access profound ideas, while others are lost in a sea of disjointed thoughts.

Yet, imagination alone isn't enough. You need focus. Because imagination without control is mere noise. Imagination with precision? That's the tool of genius.

A distracted mind skims the surface. A restless mind dives deep but surfaces too soon. *A trained mind?* It plunges into the depths, unfazed.

And the deeper you dive, the more hidden knowledge you uncover. Focus unlocks precision, and precision unlocks intelligence.

Imagination is not passive—it's interactive. You don't just create with it; you receive through it. This is why breakthroughs often occur in dreams, and why deep meditation reveals solutions logic could never reach. When you enter imagination with purpose, you don't just think—you access. And what you access becomes knowledge.

And knowledge, when applied, becomes wisdom.

Like any software, your imagination can be upgraded. Expose yourself to new perspectives, explore new disciplines, embrace fresh ways of thinking, and you'll install new mental pathways. The more advanced your imagination, the greater the level of information you can access.

And once it's fully upgraded? You'll no longer need to search outside for answers. You will simply go within.

This is just the beginning. Imagination is a structure. A force that can be mastered and refined. Once you understand how to wield it, the universe is yours to explore.

JUMPING PARALLEL TIMELINES

What you seek is also seeking you. Thoughts are not just abstract ideas; they are waves—carriers of frequency and energy.

In contrast, mass holds frequency and energy but is bound by space and time. Waves, however, transcend space and time, existing everywhere simultaneously *(Source: Feynman, 1965)*. This means that if you can think of a desire, it already exists as a wave in the quantum field—it simply has not yet taken on mass.

The quantum field is an infinite spectrum of probabilities, where every possible reality already exists as an energetic blueprint *(Source: Heisenberg, 1927)*. Your mind acts as a receiver, capable of tuning into these frequencies, much like a radio picking up a signal. Quantum jumping operates on this very principle—the idea that by aligning your thoughts and energy, you can shift between different potential timelines, each offering a version of you that has already manifested your desires.

Since everything in existence is energy in motion, your dominant thoughts and emotions determine which frequency you align with—and, ultimately, which timeline you step into.

In this sense, jumping parallel timelines is the act of consciously choosing which version of reality you inhabit, tuning yourself to the frequency of the life you desire, and stepping into that timeline, already existing as a probability in the quantum field. *(Source: Bohm, 1980).*

Manifestation: Thought, Emotion & Energy

Because thoughts are waves, they shape your experience of reality. However, thoughts alone are not enough—emotion is the key to quantum jumping.

Emotions are energy in motion ($E=mc^2$), the "light" in Einstein's equation. They act as amplifiers, determining the intensity and magnetism of your thoughts. The more coherent and elevated your emotions—such as joy, gratitude, and devotion—the stronger the signal you send into the quantum field *(Source: McCraty, 2016).*

Yet, the subconscious mind holds the controlling key to your vibrational state. It operates 95% of your thoughts, behaviors, and beliefs. Most of what you think today is simply a repetition of what you thought yesterday, reinforcing your current timeline.

This is why emotional and thought mastery are essential—your subconscious determines your vibration, which in turn determines the reality you experience.

Mirror Principle: Inner State Creates Outer Reality

Many people struggle with manifestation because they rely solely on their five senses, which can only perceive the physical world. But beyond your five senses lies a deeper intelligence: intuition, will, perception, reason, imagination, and memory *(Source: Hill, 1937)*. These are the tools that allow you to shape reality from within, rather than reacting to the external world.

So why do most people remain trapped in old timelines? Because they rely solely on their physical senses, allowing external conditions to dictate internal reality. But manifestation is the reversal of this process—it is the art of living from the inside out.

To quantum leap, you must break the momentum of your current identity by shifting your focus, emotional state, and actions. Rewrite the narrative that defines you.

Pathways of Change

- **Align your vibration** – Focus on thoughts and emotions that match your desired reality rather than those reinforcing what you don't want.
- **Reprogram your subconscious** – Use visualization, meditation, and affirmations to install new paradigms that support your manifestation.
- **Activate your higher faculties** – Train your intuition, perception, and imagination to bypass sensory limitations and tune into the quantum field.
- **Embody the feeling now** – Emotionally experience your desire as already fulfilled, imprinting its frequency into your subconscious.

The moment you shift your focus and emotional energy to the reality you want, you activate the quantum bridge—and what once existed as a wave begins to take on mass, materializing into your lived experience.

Leaping Timelines: Accept, Redirect, Choose

To create the life you desire, the first essential step is to harmonize both polar and non-polar attention. This dynamic approach unleashes your full potential, releasing resistance and creating space for your goals to manifest. *(Source: Lipton, 2005; Chopra & Kafatos, 2013)*

When we feel trapped, as though we've hit rock bottom, it's crucial to embrace the power of acceptance. Remember, acceptance is not passive resignation—it's an active release of resistance. To resist is to feed the very energy we wish to escape. But when we accept, we invite change. *(Source: Tolle, 2005; Damasio, 2010)*

This shift begins with embracing our current circumstances, no matter how uncomfortable they may be. The moment we step aside, the path to our desires becomes clear.

Imagine your worst-case scenario unfolding—not as defeat, but as life continuing regardless. This isn't surrender; it's the cessation of struggle. *(Source: Sheldrake, 1995; Bohm, 1980)*

Acceptance enables us to release our fears and attachments. When we accept the worst, the energy that fuels our resistance dissipates. By stepping out of the way, we make room for something greater. *(Source: McCraty & Atkinson, 2003)*

Unbiased attention plays a vital role here. Acceptance is neutrality—it's the fertile ground where transformation begins. The present moment, ever-shifting, cannot be grasped. We only have power over the next moment, and that power lies in our ability to choose. *(Source: Chopra & Kafatos, 2013)*

We often mistake setbacks for failure, internalizing them and feeding them with negatively charged energy. But what if, instead of seeing a challenge as failure, you saw it as an opportunity for growth? *(Source: Lipton, 2005; McTaggart, 2007)*

Recognizing that every challenge contains the seed of a blessing shifts everything. Every event, no matter how negative it appears, is neutral at its core.

It is how we direct our attention that determines whether we view it through the lens of a blessing or a curse. *(Source: Zohar & Marshall, 1994)*

Consider a missed opportunity: perhaps missing a bus spared you from something worse. The universe might be guiding you in ways you can't yet comprehend. *(Source: Chopra & Kafatos, 2013)*

This insight comes only after reaching a state of acceptance. If you're still reeling from a fresh wound, don't rush to see blessings. First, accept. Feel the emotions, process them, and don't attach. Once you cease the struggle, you can begin to find the growth hidden within. *(Source: Tolle, 2005)*

The final, most powerful step is redirecting your attention to what you truly desire. When your mind and heart are balanced in equanimity, you become free to focus entirely on your goals. *(Source: Lipton, 2005)*

This is where magic happens. Mastering this process makes you unstoppable. Your attention becomes the key that unlocks the door to your desired reality. *(Source: McTaggart, 2007)*

If you feel bad about yourself today, fully accept that feeling. Acknowledge it without judgment. Only in this space of acceptance can you begin to shift.

Avoid repressing or suppressing your feelings, as they will resurface, often more intensely. Even using positive affirmations to avoid the emotions you're truly feeling becomes a form of resistance, perpetuating the struggle. *(Source: Lipton, 2005)*

The three-step method—accept, redirect, and choose—can transform your life. This is the essence of quantum jumping. The key is to stop fighting against your emotions and instead use them as a steppingstone for growth. When you release the weight of resistance, you make room for change, and that's where true transformation begins. *(Source: Karpinski, 2018)*

This method doesn't just transform you; it determines the path your life takes. Ancient cultures and spiritual teachings have always understood the importance of attention. *(Source: Sheldrake, 1995; Bohm, 1980)*

The way we direct our attention shapes our reality. We first observe the present moment, then enter a state of acceptance. From there, we uncover the blessings within the situation with the art of gratitude and focus on what we truly desire. *(Source: Chopra & Kafatos, 2013)*

As co-creators of our own lives, we have the ability to choose our path and shape our destinies. True transformation begins the moment we direct our attention to what matters most. *(Source: McTaggart, 2007)*

Master this, and you become the architect of your own destiny, manifesting the life you've always dreamed of. Move forward with confidence and purpose—the life you desire is waiting for you to claim it.

QUANTUM PLAYBOOK: UNLEASHING LIMITLESS POSSIBILITIES

To judge is instinctive—it confines us, robbing us of deeper perspectives, casting the world in rigid absolutes: right or wrong, good or bad. But to question, to explore with an open heart and mind, is transformative. It frees us from the chain of judgment, inviting a deeper understanding that transcends the surface.

Healthy curiosity, however, is a doorway. It invites discovery, dismantles assumptions, and nurtures connection. It shifts our focus from reaction to reflection, from assumption to exploration, from division to understanding. In curiosity lies the power to evolve, to move beyond the confines of the familiar and into the vast expanse of possibility.

When we release judgment, we don't abandon discernment—we expand it. We see beyond the surface, embracing complexity without fear. We cultivate the wisdom to listen, the courage to question, and the humility to grow.

Step 1: Shift from Labels to Exploration

Judgment thrives on categorization, reducing people to roles, actions, and beliefs. But no one is a single moment, a single choice, or a single perspective. Behind every action is a story. Behind every belief is an experience.

- Instead of reacting with certainty, pause. Ask: What unseen forces have shaped this person's choices? What emotions or fears might be driving their actions?
- When you feel judgment rising, reframe the question: What else could be true?

Curiosity does not require agreement—it only requires presence. The moment we step beyond labels and into exploration, we unlock the depth of human experience.

Step 2: Shift into Active Listening

Judgment flourishes in the absence of listening. It thrives on assumption, feeding off the stories we construct before we've heard other perspectives. But listening—true listening—is the antidote.

- Silence the inner voice that prepares a response before the other person has finished speaking.
- Resist the urge to filter their words through your own preconceptions.
- Practice presence—listen not to respond, but to understand.

We are not meant to mirror each other in perfect agreement. Our differences are not threats but reflections of our unique resonance. When we listen without judgment, we create space—not just for another's voice, but for a deeper wisdom that might otherwise go unheard.

Step 3: Ask Open-Ended Questions

Judgment is a reflex. Curiosity is a practice. The difference is in the questions we ask.

- Instead of assuming, ask: What if there's more to this than meets the eye?
- Instead of condemning, ask: What lesson might this moment be offering me?

Questions dissolve the rigid framework of right and wrong, shifting us from certainty to discovery, from reaction to expansion.

Step 4: Shift with Empathy

Judgment simplifies the world—too complex to grasp at a glance—by reducing it to binaries. But empathy reveals the spectrum. From a neuroscience viewpoint, mirror neurons allow us to feel what others feel, bridging the gap between self and other.

The prefrontal cortex and insular cortex work together to process emotion, fostering deep cognitive and emotional empathy. Neuroplasticity proves that with conscious effort, we can rewire our brain away from bias and into deeper compassion.

- When judgment arises, ask: What might they have endured? What struggles shape their choices?
- Recognize that empathy is not agreement—it is understanding.

Neuroscience confirms what ancient wisdom has always taught: compassion is not weakness—it is strength.

Step 5: Examine Conditioned Beliefs

Judgment is often a reflection of ourselves—a projection of unexamined fears, biases, and conditioning.

- When triggered, pause. Ask: Why does this unsettle me? What belief am I holding that makes this uncomfortable?

- Recognize that what we label as "wrong" is often an inherited narrative rather than an absolute truth.

Curiosity is liberation. It is the conscious choice to trade assumption for exploration.

Step 6: Celebrate Differences

At the root of judgment is fear—the fear of the unfamiliar, the unknown, the misunderstood. But fear is not truth. It is merely a conditioned response.

The amygdala triggers a fear response when faced with something unfamiliar, reinforcing bias. Neuroplasticity proves that through exposure and conscious effort, we can rewire our perception of differences as opportunities, not threats.

- Instead of asking, Why do they think this way? ask, What can I learn from their perspective?
- When faced with a belief that challenges your own, lean in with wonder, not resistance.

Differences do not divide us—fear of them does.

Step 7: Turn Judgment into Self-Reflection

Judgment is often an unconscious defense, a shield against discomfort. But the discomfort is a gift—it reveals where we are still growing.

- When judgment arises, ask: What in me is reacting?
- Instead of externalizing discomfort, turn inward: What unhealed wound is being triggered?

True wisdom lies not in defining right from wrong, but in embracing the infinite perspectives that make up the human experience.

Step 8: Cultivate a Growth Mindset

Judgment thrives in the illusion of permanence—the belief that people are fixed, their actions defining them indefinitely. But we are all in motion, evolving, learning, and transforming.

- Instead of judging someone for where they are, recognize that they are in progress, just as you are.
- Instead of saying, They will never change, ask: What experience might lead to their growth?

Your Choice: Judgment or Expansion?

The same applies inward. Self-judgment can be just as limiting as judging others. When we meet our own missteps with curiosity instead of criticism, we create space for transformation.

Curiosity is the bridge between judgment and understanding. It invites us beyond surface-level perceptions into the vastness of human complexity.

Instead of assuming, ask.
Instead of dismissing, explore.
Instead of condemning, seek to understand.

The world is waiting to be discovered.

13. Art of Reinvention

Self-transformation is the process of profound personal change that leads to a deeper understanding of oneself and a shift in behavior, mindset, and values. It involves moving beyond the limitations of the past—whether they are ingrained beliefs, habits, or emotional patterns—and embracing new ways of thinking and being.

It is often sparked by deep introspection, a desire for growth, healing, or a deeper sense of purpose, and it requires a commitment to self-awareness, reflection, and action.

At its core, self-transformation is about letting go of old identities and stepping into a more authentic version of ourselves. It may involve confronting fears, challenging limiting beliefs, and facing difficult emotions or experiences. This process can be uncomfortable, as it often requires letting go of familiar ways of thinking and doing, but it is also empowering, as it opens the door to greater potential, fulfillment, and peace.

This ongoing journey involves cultivating emotional resilience, building self-compassion, and continuously learning lessons and evolving. It often requires embracing the unknown, trusting in the process of change, and aligning our actions with higher values and aspirations.

Ultimately, self-transformation is about reclaiming our personal power, breaking free from past constraints, and stepping into a life that is more aligned with our pure essence and purpose. It's a process of becoming the best version of ourselves—not for the sake of perfection, but for the sake of authenticity, evolution, and a deeper connection with life.

However, it's not just about changing your habits or altering your circumstances; it's about peeling back the layers of who you've been and embracing the highest potential that already lies within you. It's a deeply personal odyssey that calls you to face your insecurities, heal old wounds, and embrace the power of becoming.

This transformation starts with the spark of awareness—the moment you wake up to your true self, to the stories and beliefs that have shaped your existence.

It can be unsettling at first, as it forces you to confront the parts of you that have been hidden or suppressed. But in that discomfort lies the catalyst for change. It is in this space of vulnerability that growth takes root.

The shift begins in the mind. To transform, you must first change the way you think. This means letting go of the limiting beliefs that have kept you stagnant and replacing them with thoughts that empower and uplift you.

It's about shifting from a mindset that holds you back to one that propels you forward—one that embraces the idea that you are capable of boundless growth, that your past doesn't define your future, and that every challenge is an opportunity for expansion.

Healing is the heart of self-transformation. It's not just about moving forward; it's about releasing the weight of past pain, trauma, and regret that keeps you anchored to a version of yourself that no longer serves you.

This is the delicate work of forgiveness, not just of others but of yourself. It's the act of shedding the old emotional baggage so you can rise with newfound lightness and clarity.

When you heal, you free yourself to step into a new life—one where you are no longer defined by the hurt but by your resilience.

Emotional mastery becomes your foundation as you navigate this metamorphosis through the *Coherent Heart*. Transformation doesn't mean suppressing or ignoring emotions; it means learning to understand and process them.

It means finding balance between your heart and mind, where you no longer react impulsively but respond with purpose and intention. As you cultivate emotional intelligence, you begin to move through life with a sense of peace, strength, and grace that was once elusive.

As you evolve internally, external change begins to unfold. Transformation is not just a mental or emotional process—it's embodied in the habits you create the actions you take, and the way you show up in the world.

Each new choice you make is a step toward aligning your life with the deepest desires of your soul. You no longer live by default but by design, living your truth with confidence, passion, and authenticity.

But perhaps the most profound part of self-transformation is compassion. This journey is not a sprint; it's a marathon. There will be setbacks, moments of doubt, and times when progress feels slow. But it is in those moments that self-compassion becomes your anchor.

Instead of judging yourself for your imperfections, you learn to embrace them, knowing that each step, no matter how small, is part of the process. You realize that growth is not about perfection but about progress, and every day is an opportunity to be a little more of who you are meant to be.

Self-transformation is not a destination—it's a lifelong journey. It's about continually evolving, continually shedding old layers, and continually stepping into your power.

With each new phase, you create a deeper sense of purpose, fulfillment, and joy. The person you are becoming is already inside you, waiting to emerge.

Elements of Transformation

Self-transformation is not about perfection but the continual evolution of the *Coherent Mind* and *Coherent Heart*. Each milestone reached unveils another, inviting you to expand, evolve, and embody your highest self.

It begins with a moment of clarity—a sudden awareness that your thoughts, emotions, and beliefs have been sculpting your reality, often unconsciously. This realization can be unsettling, forcing you to confront old wounds, limiting patterns, and hidden fears.

Yet within this discomfort lies an invitation—to release what no longer serves you and step into a life of conscious creation.

Change starts in the mind. The moment you believe transformation is possible, the world around you begins to shift. Doubt, fear, and insecurity lose their grip as you rewire your thoughts, replacing self-imposed limitations with empowering perspectives.

But real transformation isn't just intellectual—it is felt. It moves into the heart, where healing occurs and is integrated. To evolve, you must learn to forgive— yourself, others, even life itself. Only by releasing past pain can you reclaim the energy needed to create a new reality.

Emotional mastery is essential. It is not about suppressing feelings but understanding them, learning to respond with wisdom rather than react with impulse. This balance cultivates peace, resilience, and an unshakable sense of self.

Yet transformation requires more than awareness—it demands action. It is found in the habits you shift, the small, intentional choices that rewire your brain and shape a new reality. It is not in grand leaps but in quiet, consistent steps that lasting change unfolds.

As you evolve, the world around you reflects your inner evolution. You attract experiences, people, and opportunities aligned with your energy.

Yet the journey is not linear—there will be challenges, moments of doubt, and times when progress feels invisible. Here, self-compassion is vital. Every setback is a recalibration, a lesson in resilience guiding you back to your neutral state.

Transformation is the hero's journey—an ongoing unfolding of your potential. When your mind and heart align, change becomes inevitable. In stillness, in the space between thoughts, you awaken to a deeper knowing: You are not bound by your past. Remember to:

1. **Observe** internal narratives and subconscious conditioning.
2. **Challenge** outdated programs with inner wisdom.

3. **Rewire** neural pathways through visualization, meditation, affirmations, and repetition.

4. **Embody** through action—aligning thoughts, emotions, imagination, and behaviors. Become the change.

The fusion of neuroscience, quantum physics, and metaphysics reveals a profound perspective—we are the animators of our reality, shaping the world through the blueprint of our beliefs, attitudes, and perceptions.

The mind, a vast landscape of neural pathways and subconscious imprints, holds the key to our perceived reality. Like an architect drafting blueprints for a structure, we design our lives through belief systems ingrained from childhood, societal conditioning, and ancestral memory.

But what happens when those blueprints limit our expansion? Can we dismantle and reconstruct them? Science, metaphysics, and esoteric wisdom converge on a singular perspective: we are not bound by the past—we can alter our attitudes and reshape our reality.

BECOMING MAGNETIC

The universe moves in perfect harmony, an unseen rhythm that orchestrates the dance of planets, the ebb and flow of tides, and the quiet hum of energy within every living cell.

Nothing struggles to exist; everything simply aligns. This is the essence of synchronization—the effortless flow that governs all creation. And when we learn to attune ourselves to this frequency, we become magnetic. Not by force, not by pursuit, but by resonance.

It is important to understand the magnetism is not about chasing; it is about embodying. A river does not strain to reach the ocean—it surrenders to the pull of gravity, allowing the current to carry it home. Likewise, when our thoughts, emotions, and intentions align with the frequency of our highest being, we cease to control what we desire.

Instead, we draw it to us. Opportunities, people, and experiences begin to appear as if summoned by fate, not because we willed them into existence, but because we became the kind of energy they naturally gravitate toward.

At its core, synchronization is coherence. Just as a tuning fork causes another of the same frequency to vibrate, our internal state shapes the world around us.

We have learned that science confirms this through heart-brain coherence—a state where the electromagnetic field of the heart harmonizes with brainwave activity, creating clarity, heightened intuition, and a magnetic presence. When we are internally aligned, the external world mirrors that order. We do not force; we simply become.

True magnetism is the art of aligned reinvention. The more we embody the energy of what we desire, the more naturally it flows toward us.

Desperation repels; confidence attracts. Lack generates resistance; abundance dissolves it.

The universe does not respond to what we want—it responds to what we are. To manifest alchemical union, we must practice self-love. To attract success, we must demonstrate that success is already within us. Every thought, every belief, every emotion is a frequency—when we shift our inner state, the outer world rearranges itself to match.

To synchronize with destiny, we must first become it. This is not passive surrender, but conscious attunement—elevating our vibration, refining our presence, and stepping into the current of life rather than fighting against it.

Like a star that does not beg to be seen but simply radiates, we attract effortlessly when we embrace our own unique brilliance.

The magnetic do not seek. They embody. And in embodying, they merge with the rhythm of creation itself.

POWER OF EMBODIMENT

Awareness is the spark, but action ignites true transformation. To create lasting change, we must embody our beliefs through consistent, aligned behavior—where thought, emotion, and action move in unison.

This is where the connection between the *Coherent Mind* and *Coherent Heart* becomes essential.

Manifestation is not just wishful thinking—it is a synergy of neuroscience, energy, and intention. From a scientific perspective, the brain's neuroplasticity allows it to rewire itself based on focused thought and action, reinforcing new pathways of belief.

In the metaphysical realm, everything is energy, vibrating at specific frequencies. The energy you emit—your emotions, thoughts, and intentions—creates the reality you experience.

At the core of manifestation is alignment. When thoughts and emotions align—your energy becomes a powerful magnet, drawing your desires into reality.

The key is to feel as though what you seek is already yours. Intention, backed by belief and emotion, sends a clear energetic signal to the universe. Trust the process, stay open, and allow the how and when to unfold in divine timing.

But belief alone is not enough—it must be embodied.

If you seek abundance, practice generosity. Giving affirms your trust in the infinite flow of prosperity.

If you affirm self-worth, set boundaries that honor your value. Boundaries are not limitations—they are declarations of self-respect.

If you visualize confidence, take action that stretches your comfort zone. Confidence is not a state of being; it is a practice.

If you embrace radical accountability, align your choices with integrity. Every action is a statement of who you are.

Action is the bridge between who you are and who you are becoming. Transformation is not passive; it is a daily commitment to embodying your highest version. When you align your energy with your desires and act accordingly, change becomes not just possible—but inevitable.

BLEND OF MANIFESTATION & HARMONY

The synthesis of neuroscience, quantum physics, and metaphysics reveals what mystics have known for centuries: we are co-creators of reality.

Consciousness acts as a tuning fork, resonating with the frequencies of the reality we choose to perceive. Like a guitar string vibrating in response to a note, our thoughts, beliefs, and emotions sculpt the world around us. But for many, this symphony is drowned out by the noise of conditioned fears and limiting patterns—repetitive scripts that keep us trapped in the familiar.

But there is a way out. Transformation begins when we actively rewire our beliefs, replacing fear with expansion, doubt with certainty. This is not a passive process—it is a radical, intentional shift. A daily choice to step beyond past conditioning and embody the truth of our limitless potential.

By bridging the gap between science and metaphysics, we awaken to a profound realization: we are not victims of circumstance but architects of reality.

Every thought, every word, every intention is code, scripting the very fabric of our existence. Like a cosmic algorithm, the mind tirelessly works to weave coherence between our internal landscape and external world.

The universe is not a passive backdrop; it is a mirror, reflecting the vibrational signature you broadcast. It does not distinguish between what you desire and what you fear—it simply amplifies the energy you emit.

If you align with limitations, life will reinforce those constraints. If you shift into trust, expansion, and certainty, reality will rearrange itself to match.

So, what will you choose? Will you script your life with unwavering devotion, knowing you are the author of your experience? Or will you remain entranced by the illusion of lack, unknowingly perpetuating the very struggles you long to escape?

We are not passive observers of life—we are its creators. The present moment is our canvas, and every thought, belief, and action is a brushstroke shaping the masterpiece of our reality. The only limits we face are those we impose upon ourselves. The moment we transcend them, we awaken to the infinite potential that has always been ours to claim.

Alan Watts once said, "What we see as reality is merely a dance of energy, interpreted through our senses and limited by our thoughts."

The entire cosmic symphony—the shadows and the light, the breath and the stars—does not exist apart from you. It moves through you, shaped by the lens of your perception. You are both the observer and the creator, reflecting and refracting reality in an infinite dance of energy.

Heaven and hell are not distant realms but spirals we weave with our own projections. Choose wisely what you send into the world, for it will return—again mnd again—shaped by the hands of eternity. That's how powerful you are.

Code of Alchemy

In *Coherent Heart*, we explore the concept of the Philosopher's Stone, the very code of alchemy, begins with the breath and unfolds through the words we speak.

It is the key to understanding balance, to weaving together the wisdom of the past and the foresight of the future by shaping the present.

Imagine the most basic of shapes—the triangle, the circle, and the square. To the untrained eye, they may seem simple, but these forms are profound in their symbolism.

The triangle embodies the ethereal plane, the realm of higher consciousness. The square represents the physical world, grounded and tangible. And the circle—represents the eternal plane, the endless wheel of consciousness, an infinite continuum that stretches beyond time and space. Together, these shapes hold the mysteries of creation.

When you see these shapes in combination, particularly in the form of the great pyramids, the significance deepens. The three points of the triangle—the foundation of the ethereal plane—stand for Mentalism, Correspondence, and Energy.

These principles are the essence of singularity, the singular point from which all things emerge. The physical plane is in constant rotation, forever interacting with the ethereal realm, driven by rhythm, polarity, karma, and gender.

In order for the physical to manifest, it must be aligned with the divine. This is where free will comes into play when we activate the *Coherent Heart* center.

The power to choose is the very mechanism that allows us to receive the divine in human form. And in that moment of receiving, we become co-creators—expanding not only our own existence but also the realms we inhabit.

As we evolve, we rise into the eternal plane through the Law of Correspondence—As above, so below. In this space, everything begins to shape shift.

The very fabric of reality bends, and we move into a higher dimension of understanding.

These are the clues left behind by ancient wisdom encoded in the world around us, waiting for us to remember and to live in alignment with the great cosmic dance that is our birthright.

Keys to Transformation

For too long, we've been conditioned to chase abundance, earn worthiness, and wait for healing, as if they exist outside of us. But what if we've had it backward all along?

Healing is not bound by time. Abundance is not earned through effort. Worthiness is not a prize—it is a state of being, already alive within us.

The moment we stop measuring ourselves by external validation, everything shifts. We move from scarcity to flow, wanting to embodiment, "I need" to "I AM."

Transformation begins when we recognize that every challenge is not an obstacle but an initiation—an invitation to step beyond illusion. Growth unfolds in three stages:

- **Shadow:** The realm of unconscious patterns—fear, scarcity, conditioning—that keep us trapped in survival mode. This is not punishment but a mirror, reflecting what remains unhealed. Abundance is never absent, only unseen.
- **Presence:** The shift from resistance to awareness, from victimhood to self-mastery. Transformation begins not when we escape struggle but when we meet it with consciousness—alchemizing pain into wisdom, limitation into liberation.
- **Abundance:** The highest expression, where all illusions of separation dissolve. Abundance is not something we chase; it is something we remember. It is not just material wealth but an unshakable knowing that everything we seek has always been within.

The old paradigm tells us abundance is external, something to manifest through struggle. We don't manifest abundance—we awaken to its resonance.

Purpose is not found; it is reclaimed. Pure love is not earned; it is our divine blueprint.

So, stop asking, "When will I have what I want?" The real question is, "Can I see that I already do?" Because the moment we choose ourselves fully, life chooses us back.

Every. Single. Time.

Abundance is not in the future. It is here. Now. Flowing. Eternal. The only thing keeping us from it is the mirage that it is elsewhere.

Each of us carries a unique energetic blueprint, shaping our purpose, relationships, and evolution. The more we embrace our own becoming, the more life reveals its magic.

Transformation is not about force but surrender. Not about waiting but choosing. Not about searching but being.

We are already whole. Already enough. Already free.

This is not just philosophy.

It is the code. The key that unlocks everything.

QUANTUM PLAYBOOK: EMBODYING MASTERY

The universe doesn't respond to desperation—it responds to alignment. You don't chase. You become.

Step 1: Stop Forcing, Start Flowing

Struggle is resistance. When you release control, you create space for synchronicity. Flow isn't passivity—it's intelligent surrender.

- **Example:** Instead of chasing a job, an opportunity, or a relationship, focus on becoming the energy that attracts it. Want love? Be love that you seek. Want success? Embody confidence before the opportunity arrives.
- **Daily Practice:** Identify where you're forcing an outcome. Pause. Take three deep breaths and affirm:
  - Affirmation: *I trust the divine timing of my life. What is meant for me flows effortlessly.*

Step 2: Train Your Intuition

Your highest guidance isn't found in overthinking—it's found in stillness.

- **Example:** Instead of making endless pros-and-cons lists, practice the body test: Ask yourself a yes-or-no question. If your chest feels open and expansive, it's a YES. If it feels tight or heavy, it's a NO.

- **Daily Practice:** Each morning, spend 5 minutes in silent observation. Watch your thoughts without reacting.
  - Affirmation: *I trust my inner guidance. The answers I seek are already within me.*

Step 3: Master Your Energy

Your energy is your currency—where you invest it determines your reality.

- **Example:** Before a stressful meeting, don't just react—set an energetic intention: "I bring clarity, confidence, and calm into this space." Watch how others mirror your state.
- **Daily Practice:** List 3 things that drain your energy and 3 things that elevate your energy. Make one shift today to invest more in what fuels you.
  - Affirmation: *I am the guardian of my energy. I direct it with conscious intention.*

Step 4: Embody the Frequency

You do not attract what you want—you attract what you are.

- **Example:** If you want wealth, stop saying "I can't afford this" and act with mission, conscious work, and balance. Start affirming "Money flows to me in expected and unexpected ways." Watch how opportunities shift.
- **Daily Practice:** Write down three ways you can embody your future self today—how would they walk, talk, think, and act? Live it now.
  - Affirmation: *I do not chase—I align. I know I already am what I seek.*

Step 5: Reprogram Your Subconscious

Your mind is a recording of the past—until you rewrite the script.

- **Example:** Instead of saying "I am not good at public speaking", reprogram with "I am becoming a powerful, confident speaker." The brain rewires through repetition and experience.
- **Daily Practice:** Each night, repeat one empowering belief before bed. This is when the subconscious is most receptive.

- ○ Affirmation: *I am rewriting my reality. Every thought I choose shapes my future.*

Step 6: Take Aligned Action

Belief without action is fantasy. The quantum field responds to movement with integrity.

- **Example:** If you want to start a business, stop waiting for "the right time." The moment you take aligned action—registering the domain, making the first call, showing up— you amplify the energy and the universe responds.
- **Daily Practice:** Take one bold step toward your goal today, no matter how small.
  - ○ Affirmation: *I take aligned action. I move in trust before the evidence appears.*

Step 7: Shift Your Mindset to Abundance

- **Example:** Financial freedom starts in the mind. If you believe that wealth is scarce or difficult to attain, that will be your reality. Shifting from a mindset of scarcity to abundance is key to attracting material riches.
- **Daily Practice:** Identify and release limiting beliefs about money. Replace phrases like

"I don't have enough money" with "Money flows easily and abundantly to me."

- ○ Affirmation: *I am worthy and deserving of wealth, and I attract prosperity with ease.*

Step 8: Heart-Centered Prosperity

- **Example:** The heart is a powerful magnet, and when you align with integrity not reactivity with heart-centered energy, you elevate your vibration. Wealth is a frequency, and when you resonate, you attract it.
- **Daily Practice:** Before making financial decisions, sit in stillness and focus on your heart's intuitive guidance. Visualize money flowing freely to you, feeling the joy and ease it brings.
  - ○ Affirmation: *My heart is open to receive abundance of prosperity. I welcome wealth with gratitude and joy.*

Step 9: Visualization and Feeling

- **Example:** Visualization is a powerful tool for manifesting wealth. But it's not just about seeing it—it's about feeling the emotions of already having wealth.
- **Daily Practice:** Take ten minutes daily to imagine yourself living your ideal life—see

yourself enjoying financial freedom, giving generously, and experiencing joy.

- ○ Affirmation: *I see, feel, and experience wealth in my life every day.*

Step 10: Gifting and Generosity

- **Example:** In the quiet act of gifting a book to a stranger in need, you ignite a flow of pure generosity, amplifying the energy of abundance that effortlessly returns to you. There is no expectation, only the purity of giving—an authentic, unspoken exchange that flows from your heart and into theirs. In giving, you align yourself with the universal flow of prosperity, confirming that generosity is a magnet for more, not only in material form but in connections, joy, and opportunities that return to you tenfold.

- **Daily Practice:** Commit to giving 10% of your income to charity, or donating your time for a cause, or those in need, is a powerful technique to open the flow of abundance. The universe responds to generosity with more prosperity, The more you give, the more you signal that you trust in its flow.

  - ○ Affirmation: *I am an abundant being. I give freely and joyfully without expectations. My generosity creates a ripple of abundance, flowing effortlessly through me and to me.*

Step 11: Develop Wealth Consciousness

- **Example:** You must act as a conscious being in all areas of your life—not just finances. A wealth-conscious mind sees opportunities everywhere and aligns actions with gratitude for every choice.
- **Daily Practice:** Start focusing on gratitude for what you already have. Write down 5 things every day you are thankful for. Take aligned action toward your goals as a creator, not someone seeking to be rescued, even when the path seems unclear. The universe responds to decisive action
  - Affirmation: *I am grateful for all my blessings and all the abundance that is yet to come.*

Step 12: Change Your Environment and Vibration

- **Example:** Your external environment can impact your internal vibration. Clear clutter and create a space that reflects your abundant mindset.
- **Daily Practice:** Tidy your living or workspace. Remove items that no longer

serve you and make room for prosperity. You can even use wealth symbolism (like gold, crystals, or symbols of abundance) in your environment.

- o Affirmation: *My environment supports my abundance. I attract wealth effortlessly through my surroundings and acts of service.*

Step 13: Trust and Let Go of Attachment

- **Example:** The art of detachment and releasing controlling outcomes are essential. Trust that abundance of wealth will come in the form and timing that is right for you.
- **Daily Practice:** Whenever doubt arises, take a moment to surrender your fears and let go of the need for financial rescue. Trust that the universe is mirroring your internal world.
  - o Affirmation: *I am open to the process of giving and receiving with a generous and grateful heart.*

Step 14: Own Your Power

- **Example:** Instead of praying for a savior or waiting for permission, decide that you are worthy now. Declare with humility but confidence, act with morality, and command as though it is done.

- **Daily Practice:** Each morning, stand in front of the mirror, look into your own eyes, and state your declarations with certainty.
  - Affirmation: *I am the architect of my life. I move with integrity, accountability, power, and purpose. I know that I'm a powerful being.*

The universe was never withholding. It was waiting for you to step into balanced alignment and embodiment.

Let the mind rest. Let the heart lead. Let the soul remember.

You do not chase. You do not force. You do not beg.

You declare, transform, and become, magnetizing everything that was always meant for you.

This is the key. The code. The ultimate unlocking.

It's already yours, believe it, breathe it, claim it!

14. Final Reflections

Know Thyself: We Are Eternal and Boundless

We are not merely individuals navigating the vastness of existence—we are expressions of the life force, manifestations of the dynamic dance between consciousness and potentiality, where the universe seeks to experience itself through us.

There is something sacred in recognizing our place within the whole, understanding that we are not here by accident, alone, nor are we here without purpose. We are all intricately woven into the fabric of something far greater than ourselves.

Each of us has a role to play, a unique contribution to offer, like a quantum cell within a vast, thriving organism. Though we may not always understand the full scope of our impact, we know that by being the best version of ourselves, we enhance the health of the greater whole.

Our existence is not random; it is profound. Consciousness gives life to reality, and in this process, we are not separate from the universe, but rather its living, breathing expression.

Source consciousness is experiencing itself through you, expanding its knowledge and understanding, all through your unique presence, perception, and purpose.

Our spirit, the eternal essence at the core of our being, is intricately woven into the fabric of human experience. When we awaken to our multidimensional nature, we pierce the illusion of time, lifting the veil that divides us from our higher self.

In this profound realization, the dream of separateness fades, and we embark on a journey of growth, discovery, and expansion, embodied in our intelligent physical form.

Yet, what we perceive as "reality" is not as solid and absolute as it appears. Instead, we uncover a transformative understanding that bridges the realms of science and metaphysics, where the lines between the material and spiritual dissolve, revealing a unified tapestry of existence.

In this integrated perspective, the universe is not a lifeless mechanism, but a conscious, dynamic unified field—shaped by the flow of energy, information, and awareness. Science reveals the underlying principles that govern this interconnected reality, while metaphysics imparts wisdom to understand its deeper purpose.

This convergence invites us to view life not as a series of random events, but as a sacred process where we, as co-creators, sculpt our reality. Our thoughts, emotions, and intentions resonate with the quantum field, influencing the experiences that unfold before us.

This shift in perception moves us away from victimhood and empowers us to embrace our role as active participants in the dance of creation. *The more we love our world from a place of neutrality, the more peace and harmony we magnetize; the more we judge it, the more suffering and disharmony we amplify.*

Every moment, whether joyous or challenging, offers an opportunity to align with the deeper wisdom of unity, harmony, and purpose. The human experience is not a departure from spirit, but a profound extension of it.

We are stardust and light—eternal consciousness clothed in flesh, walking a path of profound discovery.

The physical realm, once thought to be solid and independent, reveals itself as a holographic projection of our consciousness, encoded with the intricate patterns of a multidimensional reality.

The holographic universe theory uncovers a universe where every part reflects the whole, much like a hologram. Quantum mechanics and neuroscience support this idea, suggesting that our perception of reality is similarly encoded.

The implications are vast: what we experience as "reality" is not an isolated, material construct, but an unfolding expression of a deeper, invisible order that shapes all existence.

We are granted the profound opportunity to choose a life of abundance—a life steeped in inspiration, inner peace, joy, harmony, beauty, magic, and creativity. It is a chance to serve humanity's evolution, and to witness the extraordinary transformation of our wondrous planet.

In this sacred hero's odyssey, we hold the power to co-create a reality that reflects and anchors the highest timeline of harmony and unity. By embracing the divine within and around us, we share our light to inspire a collective rise. Each present moment becomes a precious gift—an invitation to embody the magic waiting to unfold through us.

When our earthly journey concludes, our spirit undergoes a profound metamorphosis. Free from the limitations of physical form, we merge with the infinite consciousness that birthed us.

This transition is not an end, but a luminous awakening—a return to our primary Source of all existence. The essence of our experiences—every triumph and trial, memories and lessons—remains etched in our eternal cosmic akashic archives, expanding our awareness as we enter higher realms of existence.

In this boundless state, individuality dissolves into the infinite, becoming a radiant thread in the grand tapestry of creation.

Our path, once limited by the perspective of a single physical lifetime, merges into the vast knowing of all that is. The spirit is not lost in infinity, but integrated into universal intelligence, contributing to the ongoing evolution of existence.

From this vantage point of pure love, we stop seeking one objective truth. Our physical form, and the reality we experience are dynamic manifestations of energy and information, perceived through the lens of individuated human awareness.

The interplay of light, energy, sound, and vibration creates the illusion of solidity and separateness, yet the essence of our being remains unified with the greater cosmic design.

This paradigm shifts the narrative of existence from materialism to interconnectedness, inviting us to ponder: *if reality is a hologram, then what possibilities lie within the power of our consciousness to structure and reimagine it?*

Declaration:

As I journey through the vast landscapes of my chosen human experience, I AM both the observer and the observed in the cosmic symphony, forever intertwined with the infinite. Aligned with eternal wisdom, I create, transform, and manifest the desires of my heart, knowing each moment is a chance to rise, expand, and express the boundless creative power of who I KNOW and FEEL I AM—energy in motion, shaping my own evolution.

15. Manifestation Playbook for Co-Creation

When neuroscience and metaphysics converge, they spark a profound alchemy—a bridge between the precise mechanics of the brain and the infinite potential of the quantum field.

Clear intentions light up the Reticular Activating System, rewiring neural pathways to automatically seek and seize opportunities that align with your vision. At the same time, the energy of your emotions radiates outward, leaving an imprint on the quantum field, orchestrating synchronicities that manifest your desires.

This Manifestation Playbook is your daily guide, a tool designed to empower you to actively shape your reality through consistent practice and focused intention.

It is far more than thought—it's the seamless fusion of cognition, vibration, and unshakable trust. When clarity converges with emotional coherence, and belief overpowers doubt, you become a magnet, effortlessly drawing your highest potential into your reality—unveiling everything you've longed for with grace and ease.

KNOW thyself and command your declarations with certainty, grace, and humility.

Step 1: Crafting Reality Through Conscious Imagination

Create a mental movie of your desired reality. Engage all your senses—see, feel, hear, and even smell the details of your manifestation as if it already exists.

- **Neuroscience Insight:** Visualization activates the same brain regions as performing an action, strengthening neural pathways that reinforce your desired outcome. The brain cannot differentiate between imagination and reality, enhancing recognition of opportunities.
- **Why It Works:** Studies show that mental imagery enhances motor and cognitive functions, aiding in performance improvement and goal achievement (*Source: Driskell, Copper & Moran, 1994*).
- **Techniques:**
  - Spend five minutes each morning visualizing your future self experiencing your desires.
  - Feel the emotions of success, or abundance of beauty and wealth in the present moment.
  - Create a vision board of your life to reinforce your mental imagery.
  - **Affirmation:** *I see, feel, and embody my highest reality, and the universe aligns with my vision.*

Step 2: Rewiring the Subconscious Mind

Speak or write affirming statements in the present tense, reflecting your desires as if they are already reality. Repetition is key.

- **Neuroscience Insight:** Affirmations reprogram the subconscious mind and activate the Reticular Activating System (RAS), filtering reality to align with your beliefs. The brain forms neural pathways through repetition, reinforcing behavioral and identity patterns *(Source: Doidge, 2007; Hebb's Law, 1949)*. Studies confirm that when you act as if you are already the person you want to become, your brain reorganizes itself to match that identity.
- **Why It Works:** Repeated self-affirmation exercises have been shown to enhance resilience and reframe self-perception confidently *(Source: Cascio, 2016)*. By embodying the thoughts, emotions, and actions of your future self, you activate new neural circuits, making it easier to take aligned action and attract corresponding opportunities.
- **Techniques:**
    - Write ten affirmations that resonate with your goals and repeat them daily.
    - Use a mirror to speak those statements with conviction and emotion.

- ○ Replace limiting beliefs with empowering convictions: instead of "I want success", say "I am successful."
- ○ Shift language and energy: Instead of "I want a soul mate to complete me," say "I am already whole and aligned with my highest vision."
- ○ Surround yourself with glimmers of your future self—change your environment, dress for success, and declare as if your abundance is inevitable.
- ○ **Affirmation:** *I embody my highest potential, and my reality reshapes to match me.*

Step 3: Magnetizing Abundance with Gratitude

Cultivate the practice of daily appreciation by focusing on the blessings in your life, big and small.

- **Neuroscience Insight:** Gratitude releases dopamine and serotonin, elevating mood and shifting the brain into a positive, receptive state.
- **Why It Works:** Research indicates that gratitude interventions improve psychological well-being and reduce stress

levels *(Source: Emmons & McCullough, 2003).*

- **Techniques:**
  - Keep a gratitude journal or write down three things you are grateful for each morning.
  - Express gratitude for your health, breath of life, vitality, your loved ones, and your security.
  - Throughout the day, pause and feel gratitude for present-moment joys.
  - **Affirmation:** *I am grateful for the infinite blessings in my life, and abundance flows effortlessly to me.*

Step 4: Energetic Clearing & Healing

Remove limiting beliefs and emotional blocks through self-awareness and healing practices to release resistance.

- **Neuroscience Insight:** Emotional clearing rewires neural pathways, reducing stress-related inflammation and expanding cognitive flexibility.
- **Why It Works:** Research shows that emotional processing techniques effectively reduce psychological distress *(Source: Feinstein, 2012).*
- **Techniques:**
  - Use Emotional Freedom Technique (EFT) tapping on meridian points to

release limiting beliefs and stagnant energy.

- o Journal shadow work prompts to uncover and integrate suppressed emotions.
- o Practice soul retrieval by focusing your attention on your heartbeat, relating with your inner child.
- o Engage in breathwork healing modalities.
- o **Affirmation:** *I release all that no longer serves me, making space for limitless expansion.*

Step 5: Power of Contemplation

Enhancing cognitive flexibility, strengthening neural connections for intuition-based decision-making.

- **Neuroscience Insight:** Contemplation isn't passive reflection—it's a neurological recalibration. When you pause and turn inward into stillness, your default mode network activates, heightening self-awareness. *(Source: Fox, 2015).* This practice strengthens neural pathways that regulate emotions, rewires limiting beliefs, and quiets the amygdala, reducing stress and fear responses. Simultaneously, the reticular activating system begins filtering reality through the lens of your deepest intentions, aligning your external world with your internal clarity.

- **How It Works:** In the science of deep reflection, the prefrontal cortex orchestrates insight, helping you access new perspectives and emotional intelligence. The limbic system regulates emotions, fostering resilience and inner peace. The RAS primes your brain to notice synchronicities, turning contemplation into manifestation. It also increases theta brainwaves, the state linked to intuition and subconscious reprogramming. It activates the vagus nerve, shifting the nervous system from stress to harmony, increasing heart rate variability for emotional resilience.

- **Techniques:**
  - Set a timer for ten minutes and sit in stillness.
  - Observe your thoughts without attachment, allowing deeper awareness to surface.
  - If distractions arise, return to your breath and ask: What wisdom is seeking me?
  - Place your hand over your heart and take five deep, slow breaths.
  - Focus on a feeling of gratitude to shift your energy.

- o Ask yourself: What is my heart's deepest knowing? Write down what arises.
- o Between tasks or decisions, take a three-second pause before reacting.
- o Breathe in, exhale fully, and ask: Am I acting from alignment or conditioning? Let the answer emerge from within rather than forcing it.
- o **Affirmation:** *My heart speaks with clarity, and I trust its guidance. In stillness, I attune to my highest wisdom.*

Step 6: Heart-Mind Coherence

The heart's electromagnetic field influences and magnifies energy patterns beyond the body.

- **Neuroscience Insight:** Research from HeartMath Institute confirms that when the heart and brain are aligned and synchronized, it enhances intuition, decision-making, and emotional regulation (*Source: McCraty, 2017*).
- **Why It Works:** The emotions you generate create electromagnetic waves that interact with the quantum field. When you cultivate gratitude, certainty, harmony, and joy, your energy field becomes coherent and magnetic, amplifying the likelihood of your desires materializing.

- **Techniques:**
  - Practice Heart Coherence Breathing: Inhale for five seconds, exhale for five seconds, focusing on heart-centered gratitude.
  - Feel the emotions of already having what you desire—this primes your nervous system for receiving.
  - Before taking action, check: Am I acting from alignment or fear? Adjust until your mind and heart are balanced.
  - **Affirmation:** *My heart and mind vibrate in perfect harmony, attracting my highest potential effortlessly.*

Step 7: Quantum Calibration

Release people pleasing and reclaim your sovereignty.

- **Neuroscience Insight:** Your subconscious identity dictates 95% of your reality. If you continue to see yourself as limited, unworthy, or powerless, your brain will filter experiences to confirm that narrative *(Source: Doidge, 2007; Hebb's Law, 1949).*
- **Why It Works:** The mirror neurons in your brain encourage conformity but true creation happens when you detach from societal programming and reclaim sovereignty.
- **Techniques:**

- ○ Define the highest version of you—the one who already lives in alignment with your heart center.
- ○ Break free from external validation: Whenever you feel pressured by others' opinions, pause and affirm: I follow my inner compass, not the unconscious crowd.
- ○ Each morning, embody your future self—dress, speak, and move as if you are already living your vision.
- ○ **Affirmation:** *I am a powerful creator of my reality. I walk my own path, and the universe aligns in my favor.*

Step 8: Energetic Transmutation

Mastering emotions with the power of forgiveness enables you to master creation.

- **Neuroscience Insight:** Holding onto resentment activates the amygdala, keeping the nervous system in a cycle of stress *(Source: Davidson & McEwen, 2012)*. Unprocessed emotions hijack the nervous system, keeping you locked in cycles of stress, fear, and reactivity.
- **Why it works:** Forgiveness is not about condoning the past—it is about releasing the emotional charge that binds you to it. But the moment you choose forgiveness,

the prefrontal cortex engages, restoring emotional balance and opening neural pathways for clarity and expansion *(Source: Lutz, 2008)*. In the quantum field, forgiveness is an act of energetic transmutation—it dissolves resistance, raises your frequency, and aligns you with creation itself.

- **Techniques:**
  - Identify what emotional cycles keep repeating—fear, doubt, anger, shame, guilt, resentment, victimhood, or insecurity—and ask: What limiting story am I still holding onto?
  - Use *Coherent Heart* breathing techniques while visualizing golden light expanding from your heart, dissolving emotional blocks.
  - Each night, release emotional density by stating "I let go of what no longer serves me. My energy is free to expand."
  - **Affirmation:** *I embrace the power of forgiveness, liberating my energy from the weight of the past. In choosing reconciliation, I reclaim my sovereignty as the architect of my own reality.*

Step 9: Emotional Resilience

When you resist discomfort, you contract. When you embrace it, you expand.

- **Neuroscience Insight:** Healing is not about eliminating discomfort—it is about realizing your resilience within it. The nervous system is wired to seek safety, yet true empowerment comes not from avoiding pain, but from trusting your ability to move through it *(Source: Porges, 2011)*. Neuroscience reveals that emotional resilience is built through prefrontal cortex activation, allowing you to regulate fear rather than be controlled by it *(Source: Davidson & McEwen, 2012)*.

- **Why it works:** In the quantum field, healing is not an escape—it is expansion. The moment you trust yourself enough to face discomfort without fear, you transcend it, stepping into a reality where pain no longer defines you—it refines you. The nervous system is designed to seek safety, but true power comes when you learn to self-regulate rather than react.

- **Techniques:**
  - The next time fear, doubt, or discomfort arises, pause instead of reacting. Ask: What if this feeling is a doorway, not a threat?
  - Grounding technique: Place one hand on your heart and one on your belly. Breathe deeply and affirm: I am safe. I am expanding.
  - Reframe challenges and shift perception: Instead of "Why is this

happening to me?", shift to "What is this teaching me?"

- o **Affirmation:** *I embrace discomfort and expand beyond it. I trust myself to navigate all experiences with strength and grace.*

Step 10: Frequency Matching

Your external reality reflects the energetic highway of your inner world.

- **Neuroscience Insight**: Quantum physics confirms that everything is energy, including thoughts and emotions *(Source: Planck, 1900; Einstein, 1920)*. The observer effect shows that conscious attention influences reality.
- **Why It Works:** When you elevate your emotional and spiritual intelligence to match your desired reality, you shift into a probability wave or timeline where that reality is most likely to manifest *(Source: Tiller, 2005)*.
- **Techniques:**
  - o Act as if your desired outcome is already certain—move, speak, and decide from a place of already having it.
  - o Catch misaligned habits—if abundance is your goal, eliminate thoughts and behaviors that affirm scarcity.

- o Daily energy audit: Ask Does my current emotional state match the future I desire? Adjust accordingly.
- o **Affirmation:** *I am in perfect alignment with the frequency of my highest potential timeline.*

Step 11. Body's Antenna

Shift your perspective and embody your power.

- **Neuroscience Insight**: The nervous system, fascia, and cellular structure act as conductors of bioelectricity. Posture, movement, and breathwork regulate dopamine, serotonin, and cortisol levels *(Source: Sapolsky, 2004)*.
- **Why It Works:** Your body communicates with the quantum field. When you embody confidence, certainty, and expansion, your biochemistry shifts to reinforce those states.
- **Techniques:**
  - o Change your posture: Stand tall, open your chest, and move as if you are already successful.
  - o Use breath to shift energy—if fear arises, inhale confidence and exhale self-doubt.
  - o Take one bold action daily that aligns with your future self.

- ○ **Affirmation:** *My body, thoughts, and energy radiate confidence, aligning me with vitality and success effortlessly.*

Step 12: Overcoming Cognitive Bias

Shift your mindset from negative chatter into optimism.

- **Neuroscience Insight**: The brain's confirmation bias makes you seek evidence for what you already believe and the limiting stories you act upon. *(Source: Nickerson, 1998).*
- **Why It Works:** When you train yourself to feel optimistic and expect positively charged outcomes, your neural pathways restructure, allowing you to recognize and accept abundance of vitality, beauty, wealth, joy, and magic.
- **Techniques:**
  - ○ Say "yes" to small forms of abundance (compliments, kindness, generosity, unexpected gifts, opportunities).
  - ○ If you catch yourself rejecting good things, pause and affirm: I am worthy of receiving.
  - ○ Shift from "Will this happen?" to "I am already in the process of receiving" mindset.
  - ○ **Affirmation:** *I am open, worthy, and ready to receive unlimited abundance.*

Step 13: Collapsing Timelines

The moment you shift your focus and emotional energy to the reality you want, you activate the quantum bridge—and what once existed as a wave begins to take on mass, materializing into your lived experience.

- **Neuroscience Insight:** Quantum entanglement and relativity suggest that time is not fixed—it is malleable *(Source: Einstein, 1920; Aspect, 1982).*
- **Why It Works:** The more emotionally certain you are about a future reality, the faster time bends in your favor, because resistance dissolves and alignment accelerates.
- **Techniques:**
  - Speak in present tense: Instead of "One day I'll have this", affirm "This is already mine."
  - Embody inevitability: Move through your day as if your desire is unfolding effortlessly.
  - Each night, affirm: Everything is aligning with precision and ease.
  - Affirmation: *Time bends in my favor. I command that I anchor the highest potential timeline of harmony, peace, vitality, and joy.*

This Manifestation Playbook demands dedication and practice. Resistance surfaces when your heart field is misaligned with subconscious beliefs, emotions, or attachments—hidden forces that quietly shape the reality you experience.

This dissonance creates an energetic block, halting the flow of universal energy that is essential for bringing your dreams to life. At its core, defiance manifests as doubt, fear, victimhood, or an obsessive attachment to outcomes—signaling to the universe that your intentions are not fully in alignment.

Remember, when you cling to limiting beliefs, like "Why does this always happen to me?" you unwittingly create an opposite force that pushes your desires away. Rather than magnetizing your dreams, conflict keeps you ensnared in cycles of lack, struggle, and missed opportunities, trapping you in a perpetual state of yearning.

To transcend this, you must release your grip on controlling the future and surrender to the natural flow of the universe. Cultivate a mindset of abundance, self-worth, and unwavering trust that the universe is always supporting you.

By integrating these powerful techniques, you tap into both the scientific and metaphysical dimensions of your being—your brain and energy system—aligning them with the harmonious co-creation of your optimal reality.

Breakthroughs don't come from chasing answers—they emerge when you create space for them. The more you integrate stillness, heart awareness, and intentional pauses, the more your mind and energy system synchronize with the flow of wisdom, turning contemplation into a superpower.

You Are the Architect of Reality

The future is not predetermined—it is fluid. The life you desire is not something you must chase; it is something you must embody. You are not bound by past limitations or external circumstances—the quantum field responds to your certainty, coherence, and unwavering belief.

So, try something new and step beyond logic. Trust the unseen. Collapse the wave. Live your best life!

You are not a passive participant in your destiny. You are the architect of time itself.

Vitality's Legacy

Within each cell, a masterpiece is born,
A sacred dance, by life's cadence sworn.
Your DNA hums like an ancient song,
Ripples of ocean, deep and strong.
Stem cells unfurl like galaxies wide,
Nebulas swirling, where dreams reside.

Immune cells blaze like suns that never wane,
A solar flare within, born of light and rain.
Your skin, like canyons, a timeless grace,
Each wrinkle etched with life's embrace.
Neurons pulse like threads of ancient songs,
Silent webs where all hearts belong.

Strength hums in creation's silent breath,
Patterns etched through the pulse of death.
A design concealed in the stars above,
The chorus of unity, a hymn of love.
Each breath, a gift, woven and true,
A blueprint of being, the universe in you.

Feel the sun's kiss—a golden embrace,
Its warmth a mirror of inner grace.
Walk barefoot where earth and spirit meet,
Feel life's pulse beneath your feet.
Breathe the forest air, slow and deep,
Let its rhythm lull all wounds to sleep.

Nourish your cells with the light of dawn,
With water, love, and the soil you walk upon.
Vitality—your birthright, here and now,
A force of nature, glowing bright somehow.

PART 2

Sonnets of Transcendence

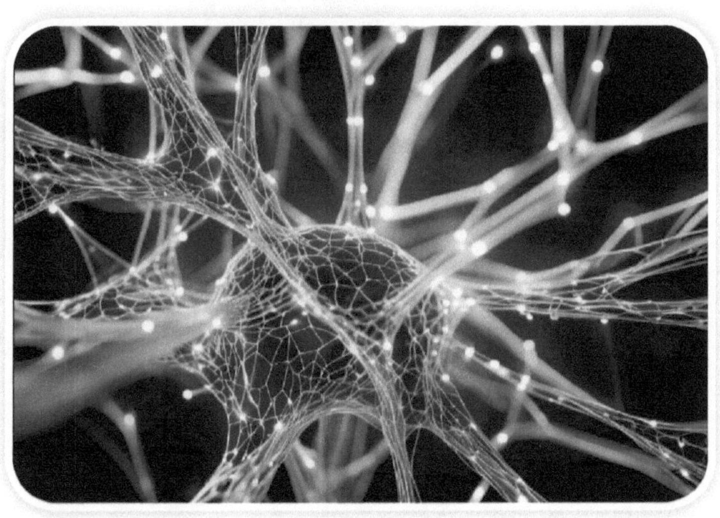

ALCHEMICAL DECREE

Through every portal, across all time,
I summon my power—it is wholly mine.
Awaken my gifts as shadows descend,
With fiery resolve, I rise, transcend.

No chain can bind, no force restrain,
I expand unshaken, I shed the pain.
To those who sought to hold me still,
Your whispers fade, erased by will.

Let every tether come undone,
Let hollow schemes unweave, unspun.
Their power wanes, their echoes die,
Like falling stars across the sky.

Like shifting tides on parchment traced,
My strength returns, old story replaced.
My hands outstretched, my fate reclaimed,
A world reborn within mind's name.

As above, so below,
As within, so without.
I claim my life, my truth, my fire—
And so it is, my soul aspires.

ARTIST AND THE MASTERPIECE

Thou art both artist and the work of grace,
Each thought, each breath, doth paint the world anew.
With every stroke, the universe doth trace,
A canvas vast, where dreams and light break through.

In every pulse, thy spirit finds its voice,
And paints the heavens with a soul untamed.
Through heart and mind, thy choice doth now rejoice,
For beauty springs from light that's yet unclaimed.

Yet lo, the truth—within thee lies the key,
For thou, the sculptor, shape the clay of time.
With mind and heart, thou dost create and see,
A world where magic weaves through every rhyme.

In thee, the brush, the paint, the art, the light—
A masterpiece that soars beyond the night.

Creator Within

We live amidst a storm of fear and woe,
Where stress and strife ignite the flame of pain.
An age of sorrow where the shadows grow,
And sickness spreads its roots through the brain.

Yet lo, thy fate is not a stone-cast chain,
For thou, with will, canst steer the course of life.
Thy thoughts and heart, like rivers, break the stain,
And clear the path from doubt and endless strife.

Within thee lies the power to create,
Thy essence weaves the world with every breath.
Shift now thy gaze, align thy heart with fate,
And life shall bloom beyond the reach of death.

For thou art co-creator of thy grace,
And in thy soul, thou dost find my embrace.

POWER OF TALES

Thy body bends to tales thy heart doth weave,
Each whispered thought, a seed in fertile ground.
What stories thou dost tell, thy flesh believes,
And thus, thy life doth rise or fall unbound.

In mind's domain, where fate begins to form,
The threads of thought, both fragile and profound.
Weave woe or joy, and each emotion warms,
The essence of thy soul where truths are found.

Yet, hark! The greatest truth doth lie within,
Thy power, pure, to shape thy very days.
No past, no wound, no sorrow's bitter sin,
Can hold thee when thy light illuminates.

Speak forth with might, let words as thunder fly—
For in thy tale, thy boundless spirit soars high.

FEAR'S DOMINION

Fear, like a serpent, coils within the mind,
Its cold breath winds from thought to trembling frame.
It binds the soul, and in its grasp we find,
The limbs grow weak, the spirit dulled by flame.

It sinks its fangs within the root, so deep,
Where primal essence shudders in its sway.
The chest grows tight, the vision clouds to weep,
As fleeting breath stolen, led astray.

Upon the altar of our lives it feeds,
The adrenal pulse, a tempest fierce and wild.
Yet when it dwells too long, it sows dark seeds—
Depleting strength and leaving hearts beguiled.

But still, within the heart, a spark may rise,
And through the dark, the soul shall claim the skies.

TRINITY OF LIFE

In thee, the pulse of life doth intertwine,
With thought, with breath, and currents yet unseen.
The energy of mind, both pure and fine,
Doth mold the flesh, where spirit's light is keen.

Through shifts of sight, perception's power grows,
For belief doth stir the tides of grace and health.
When heart aligns with mind, the body knows
That healing lies in soul's transcendent wealth.

Lo, in the flow of thought, the cells may change,
As light within the mind doth quicken flow.
A shift in heart can cause the world to range,
And through thy soul, the body's strength shall grow.

See now with love, and trust the light within—
For in thy mind and heart, true health begins.

PULSE OF THOUGHT

Within the quantum, the river of thought flows,
Its currents shape the body's silent dance.
Each thought, a spark that lights the cells below,
And weaves a fate through every fleeting glance.

As stars align, so too the genes may bend,
When mind doth stir the fabric of the flesh.
The body heeds, as energies transcend,
And health or ill doth rise from thought's own mesh.

Yet lo, the power lies within thy heart,
For perception molds the world with steady hand.
Shift now thy sight, and let the darkness part—
Thy cells will follow, vitality by thought's command.

In thought's dominion, health shall find its seat—
When mind and heart in harmony do meet.

ESSENCE OF SELF

In realms unseen, where currents vast do glide,
The soul and mind, like particles, entwine.
In silent dance, where energy abides,
They shape the form that through all time shall shine.

As light doth bend, so thought must also sway,
In waves of force that weave through space and time.
Consciousness, like stars that chase the day,
Molds inner truth, where light begins to climb.

Yet lo, within, thy heart's pure voice does call,
To guide the pulse that stirs the breath within.
For in thy soul, all power doth install,
And healing blooms where thought and love begin.

So know, dear soul, thy sacred force is true—
In heart and mind, the world awaits anew.

SEED OF THOUGHT

Upon the mind's vast stage, where thoughts take flight,
The seeds of being stir, and life unfolds.
Each spark of belief ignites the soul's pure light,
And guides the genes where silent truth beholds.

As whispers drift through fields of quantum glow,
Where atoms dance to forces yet unseen,
So too, thy thoughts, both shadowed and aglow,
Shall carve the path, and shape what's yet to be.

Epigenetic codes, once bound in sleep,
Awake at thought's command, to bend and sway.
The mind, in power, sows the seeds we keep,
And shapes the world through thought's eternal play.

Know thy mind, like roots beneath the earth,
Doth shape the bloom and give all life its worth.

REINS OF AWAKENING

Most oft, the mind, by shadows deeply bound,
Doth yield to thoughts that weave the chains of fear.
The subconscious, silent, does confound,
And guides the soul through pain, through tear.

Yet thou art not a slave unto thy past,
Nor captive to the whims of darkened sway.
The power to transform is thine at last,
To break the chains and cast the night away.

For in thy heart, a light begins to burn,
And in thy soul, a force begins to rise.
No longer shall the ghosts of fear return,
Nor self-made prisons hold thee in disguise.

Awake, dear soul, thy strength resides within,
And from thy heart, let true transformation spin.

ART OF REBIRTH

To craft the life thou seek'st, with joy and health,
Thy thoughts must first align with heart's pure light.
For in thy mind, the truest form of wealth,
The seed is sown and blossoms forth in sight.

The body, like a garden, needs thy care—
To tend, to nourish, prune, or let it grow.
Yet change begins within, so rare, so fair,
Where power blooms and healing winds blow.

Thine inner world, a forge of flame and fire,
Where mind and heart in perfect balance meet.
Transform the flesh, fulfill the soul's desire,
And from this union, life shall be complete.

So take thy brush, and paint with hands of light,
For thou art both the artist and the sight.

ON THE EDGE

Fear, not a foe, but messenger we meet,
In soft shadows, it murmurs through the air.
It calls us still, to face the place we greet,
The edge where comfort ends, and change is rare.

At times, it cautions, urging slower pace,
To turn, to pause, and shift a chosen way.
Yet in its grasp, a sacred, trembling space—
The doorway where the soul begins to sway.

For growth is born where fear and courage kiss,
Not in the calm of softened, gilded lands.
To stand within that storm is sacred bliss,
Know we've crossed the line where fear commands.

When we embrace it, soft as morning dew,
Fear's power yields, and we are born anew.

CALL FOR UNITY

O humankind, thy course must now be turned,
From strife and greed to paths of light and peace.
For in thy hearts, the deepest truths are burned,
That harmony shall bring all pain's release.

No longer toil in shadows, blind, and bound,
For earth and sky, and stars, they cry to thee:
In unity, a brighter way is found,
To heal, to grow, and in pure love be free.

Cooperate with nature, let her guide,
And with thy fellow beings, walk as one.
Awake to truth, let spirit be thy stride,
And face the storm with hearts that never run.

The future lies in change that choose to mend,
In love, in wisdom, together shall we send.

SUBCONSCIOUS ALGORITHM

Beneath the veil of thought, where silence reigns,
A force unseen yet shaping life's own course.
The subconscious mind, where memory wanes,
Stirs the soul with quiet, potent force.

As algorithms hum in secret code,
Our thoughts are shaped, and patterns intertwine.
In silence, they determine where we go,
Like fate itself, within a grand design.

In shadows woven by the moon's embrace,
It guides the heart and bends the will unseen.
A vault of past that time cannot erase,
Yet in its depth, our truth lies in between.

But, lo! Within thy grasp, the secret flows—
A river deep, where ancient currents wind.
By conscious hand, the stream of thought may grow,
And bend to thee, in freedom's light, confined.

So take the helm and steer with vision true,
For in thy mind, all worlds await for you.

BELIEF'S SILENT REIGN

Upon belief, a silent force doth lie,
A garden sown, its roots in mind's own ground,
Where thought, like ancient vines, creeps low and shy,
And shapes the world with tendrils all around.

Through sacred creeds and culture's weighty chain,
We bind our hearts to paths we cannot see.
And yet, within these walls, we bear the strain
Of unseen locks that turn us from the free.

But lo! The mind, though bound, can yet unbind,
And tear the ancient thorns that wound the soul.
For in thy heart, the power still shall find
To change the stars and make the shadows whole.

So, break the chains, let truth arise, unbound,
For in thyself, the cosmos shall resound.

MALLEABLE MIND

The brain, like clay, doth bend beneath the hand,
Its pathways shift as thought and will command.
No hardened stone, but soft with grace's might,
It molds the truths we choose to bring to light.

Through shadow's depth, where hidden fears do dwell,
We seek the root where silent doubts do swell.
Awareness sharp, we call these ghosts to face,
And break the chains that bound us in dark place.

Through whispered words, we craft anew the frame,
Affirming strength, we lift from doubt's dark shame.
With breath and mind in harmony, we weave,
New pathways formed, old patterns to deceive.

Thus, with intent and healing from the heart,
The mind rewrites its truth and plays its part.

NEURAL WEB

Behold the web where thought and nerve entwine,
A vast domain, both hidden and divine.
Each pulse, each spark, doth trace a fated path,
Where mind and body weave a seamless math.

A century past, such dreams were thought of lore,
To move with mind and stretch beyond the floor.
Yet now we see, through wires and neural beam,
That bionic limbs obey the will's keen dream.

Through science, the brain's deep truth we spy,
Where thoughts and memories in silence lie.
The synapse bends to learn, to shift, to grow,
A plastic dance, where currents freely flow.

In every spark, the secrets of our soul,
Unveil the mind, as it becomes the whole.

Synapses of Identity

Behold the intellect where thought and nerve entwine,
A vast domain, both hidden and divine.
Each pulse, each spark, a whisper in the thread,
Where mind and body weave the path we tread.

A century past, such dreams were scorned as lore,
That thought alone could shape what limbs restore.
Yet now we see, through wires and phantom nerve,
The hand once lost may move, may feel, may serve.

Through science, we reclaim what fate denied,
A dancer walks, a painter turns his eye.
The synapse bends, rewrites, adapts, transforms,
A current sparked, a future re-informed.

In every spark, the soul's own light expands,
Not bound by flesh, but by the mind's command.

SCULPTOR OF REALITY

Upon the mind, like dawn, attention glows,
A golden thread that weaves the world anew.
It bends the dark where silent shadows grow,
And shapes the path that thought and fate pursue.

A fleeting brush of light, a whispered call,
From countless streams, one current finds its way.
A sculptor's hand that lifts or lets it fall,
Yet trembles when the heart and mind betray.

For focus, like the tide, may rise and wane,
A restless wind that shifts with fleeting will.
It builds, it breaks—it heals, it yields pain,
Yet wields the power to make the stillness thrill.

So, wield it well—this light, both fierce and true,
For what you hold in mind shall shape what's you.

ALCHEMY OF SOUND

From breath's first gasp, the newborn's cry takes flight,
A call unchained, both fragile and immense.
Not born of need alone, but seeking light,
A bridge to love, a bond of innocence.

In whispered tones, the infant shapes its voice,
Each echoed sound a step toward what is true.
Through trembling words, heart begins with choice,
To carve a world in language old and new.

Yet speech alone cannot the soul reveal,
For meaning dwells where silent glances gleam.
In tender touch, in love's unspoken zeal,
Where presence sings beyond the realm of dream.

Thus, let us speak—but more than words impart,
For language fades yet love remains the heart.

MESSENGER OF THE SOUL

O wondrous fire, that burns within the breast,
Unseen, yet felt, through every pulse and vein,
Thy tempest stirs the heart, thou art our quest—
A hidden force that drives us, joy, or pain.

In ancient times, they knew thee not by name,
Nor could they grasp thy power or thy sway.
Yet thou dost rule, and through thee, we reclaim
The paths that lead our fates in bright array.

For in depth, we find our truest selves,
In each emotion, wisdom doth unfold,
From sorrow's tear to joy, the soul's great wells,
Thy voice doth speak of truths both young and old.

So let us heed thy call with heart and mind,
For in thy message, we shall peace yet find.

ART OF SELF AWARENESS

A force unseen, yet in our hearts doth glow,
Emotional intelligence, that guide.
It shapes our fate, through all life's ebb and flow,
And turns the darkest storm to strength and pride.

Self-aware, we trace the roots of care,
The pulse of fear, the stir of joy or grief.
And through the art of calm, we learn to bear
The weight of change, transforming pain to brief.

With empathy, we step beyond our skin,
And hear the silent cries that none would speak.
In others' hearts, we find what lies within,
And bridge the gaps, both humble and unique.

Through grace we lead, not in command but light,
Uniting hearts, we turn the dark to bright.

LIFELONG EVOLUTION

From breath's first cry, our journey finds its way,
A path of growth through wonder's soft embrace.
In infant years, we learn to leap and play,
Then rise with steady steps to find our place.

By guiding hands, we shape words and sound,
In love's embrace, we learn the ways of right.
Yet knowledge, when in rigid rules bound,
Can steal the joy from learning's golden light.

But lo! The sage who nurtures heart and mind,
Unlocks the gates where curiosity sings.
For wisdom blooms when passion stands aligned,
And learning's flame ascends on purpose's wings.

Thus, life itself is but a teacher's art,
A quest for truth that lives within the heart.

DRIVE TO THRIVE

An unseen force compels the will to rise,
A spark that turns the dream to noble deed.
It whispers soft, yet echoes through the skies,
And bids us chase the truths we most do heed.

It speaks within—a voice both strong and bright,
A silent bond of heart, of mind, of soul.
Through trial's path, it steers us toward the light,
To claim the space that makes our being whole.

Two forces pull—one fleeting, one divine,
The first seeks praise, the next ignites the flame.
For love of self will make the stars align,
And purpose, not the world, shall call thy name.

So, seek within—let passion forge the way,
And rise beyond the bounds of night and day.

ARTISTIC EXPRESSION

Thy mind, not passive, but a forge of fate,
Each thought and belief doth shape the world you see.
In neuroplastic grace, you contemplate,
The boundless realms where you are truly free.

With every choice, thy canvas is made clear,
Not bound by past nor by circumstance's claim.
An artist bold, with brush, thou dost appear,
To craft thy life and set the world aflame.

No longer slave to shadowed thoughts of old,
But master now of every stroke and hue.
Thine inner power, a force both pure and bold,
Shall paint the future as you see it true.

So, wield thy mind, and with thy heart's intent,
Create the world that's waiting, heaven-sent.

DANCE OF NEURONS

Through mind and matter, science threads its way,
A bridge of thought and flesh, both firm and true.
In neurons' dance, the past begins to sway,
And futures born from light may now break through.

No longer bound by shadows' heavy grasp,
Mental health blooms soft, radiant bloom.
For every tale of sorrow, hope will clasp,
And healing finds its place beyond the gloom.

Yet wisdom bears the weight we must defend,
For truth may falter where the falsehoods creep.
With knowledge as our guide, we learn to bend,
And from the mind's deep well, our strength we keep.

We shape the world with every thought we sow,
In beliefs we plant, our lives begin to grow.

STORM WITHIN

When stress doth seize the body in its grasp,
And floods the veins with fire, rage, and dread.
The heart doth race, the breath becomes a gasp,
As mind and muscle fight with terror led.

Yet lo, the breath—when steadied—turns the tide,
To call the mind and body back to peace.
It whispers calm, where frantic forces hide,
And brings the storm to rest, that wars may cease.

With each deep breath, the nervous pulse rebinds,
The parasympathetic calls for rest.
And slowly, balance enters tangled minds,
For in this stillness, strength and health are blessed.

Thus, breath is mightier than fear's command,
It rewires all, with peace at its hand.

BONDS WE WIELD

From breath's first cry, we seek the hearts of kin,
For bonds are etched within our very soul.
In love's embrace, our trust begins to spin,
And shapes the mind, to heal or take its toll.

Yet should those bonds be broken or betrayed,
The heart learns fear, and walls begin to rise.
A mirror cracked, where love's bright light may fade,
And shadows form beneath unseeing eyes.

The world becomes a stage for hidden pain,
Where wounds unhealed distort the love we seek.
Through cycles bound in loss, we strain in vain,
In webs of fear and longing, cold and weak.

But by the light of truth, these chains unbind,
And healing dawns, with clarity of mind.

Trauma's Mark

When shadows fall and mind is torn apart,
The amygdala, that keeper of our fear.
Awakes to haunt the tender, wounded heart,
And feeds on anxious thoughts, both far and near.

In times of danger, fear does guard the soul,
Yet after wounds, it stays, a constant guest.
Its fire burns, the heart no longer whole,
While peace remains a distant, silent quest.

Through neuroplastic hands, the brain rewires,
But not to heal, but stoke these fires anew.
Each thought, each fear, ignites a darker pyre,
Till shadows blind the light we once held true.

Yet still, with care, this path we may untread,
And heal the mind, restore the peace once dead.

CYCLE OF WOUNDS

In silent halls where shadows long remain,
A child absorbs what's left unsaid, unseen.
The wounds of those who walked through bitter pain
Are etched in hearts, though they remain serene.

The parents' mask, though kind, conceal the scars,
Their coping shields—avoidance, numbing cold—
Are passed, not spoken, like forgotten bars
That bind the hearts of those they should unfold.

Thus, children learn the steps of silent cries,
Inherit shadows, fears, unspoken chains.
Their minds embrace what is, not what could rise—
A dance of sorrow through inherited pains.

But hope persists though bloodlines may entwine,
New roots of love can grow, and hearts align.

FEAR'S SONNET

Once the wheel turned, the world felt so alive,
But now, each rotate, shadows takes its place—
The mind recalls what once did fear revive,
And every car becomes a danger's face.

The amygdala, in trembling dread, retains
A map of fear, a path that's deeply drawn.
Each mile reminds, each curve, brake, lane,
The past relived, though it's already gone.

But healing comes not by denying pain,
But through the breath, mindful steps we take.
Exposure softens fear, gentle rain,
And fear itself, like night, begins to break.

Though shadows linger, there's a brighter road,
For in the light, we find the strength to grow.

JOURNEY WITHIN

In fractured states, we seek to find our way,
From shadows cast by wounds we dare not show.
Through battles fought both night and day,
Where hearts are torn, and spirits lost below.

Yet healing starts with truth—within, we find,
A strength to rise from places dark and cold.
No longer bound to thoughts that keep us blind,
But claiming worth, through stories retold.

The chains of pleasing others fade away,
When love is free, unchained by fear or cost.
True strength is found in choices we make,
To speak our truth, untouched, and never lost.

For healing's not a battle, but tender grace,
A journey home to self, divine's sacred space.

MENTAL FORGE

Beneath the mind's deep veil of tangled thought,
Where whispered shadows twist in silent strife,
The brain, a forge—both frail and fiercely wrought—
Weaves paths unseen to guide the threads of life.

When sorrow's weight distorts the soul's pure light,
And grief upon the heart lays heavy chain,
The tempest stirs, and shakes the soul from sight,
While fear and anguish hold their bitter reign.

Yet lo! Within the darkened forge does burn
A spark unseen—its glow to heal, restore—
For thought can bend the very tides, and turn
The course of fate, unlock a brighter shore.

So let not darkness blind thy vision's quest,
For in thy mind, thou art both scarred and blessed.

TANGLED PATHWAYS

In realms of neurons, where thoughts and feelings play,
The pulse of mind beats firm beneath the skin.
A dance of life where biology holds sway,
And thoughts, like winds, through tangled pathways
spin.

The brain, our guide, both vast and intricate,
With webs of nerve and chemical design.
Doth mold our moods, our fears, our fate—
A fragile world within this frame of mine.

Yet though it falter when the storm doth rage,
And grief or stress may cloud its inner light.
The mind, through time, can heal from every cage,
And rise again, as day renews the night.

For though the world may twist and cause pain,
The mind's great power can heal and break the chain.

Uniquely Wired

The human brain is not a simple mold,
But a masterpiece of variance, rare and deep.
A symphony of neural threads untold,
Where pathways and their rhythm sweep.

Neurodiversity—a truth profound,
That difference is not flaw, but strength in bloom.
In every mind, a world's unbound,
To shape new realms or chase a brighter loom.

Autism, ADHD, and dyslexia—
Not faults, but facets of a greater whole.
Each trait a thread within this vast idea,
Weaving a tapestry of heart and soul.

For each brain's tempo beats a tale unique—
Not broken, but a world of strength we seek.

Brilliance of Mind

What once was flaw now blazes in golden light,
A spark unchained, too fierce for chains to bind.
Where others grope through mist and endless night,
These minds unveil the truths that most can't find.

Through autism's flame, the seer's steady gaze
Unveils the patterns lost to fleeting sight.
In restless fire, dreamers carve their praise,
Their thoughts take wing, unbound by dark or night.

Where dyslexic hands shape visions unseen,
They mold new worlds from clay thought too frail.
What once was scorned now fuels creation's sheen,
And weaves tomorrow from the ash of pale.

Thus, genius walks where lesser fears have fled,
A light reborn where shadows once had spread.
What was shunned now claims its rightful space—
For brilliance wears a thousand forms of grace.

Gift of Diversity

Though wisdom burns in minds both vast and rare,
A shadow lingers, veiling truth in doubt.
For long, the world denied their gifts to bear,
And cast their boundless vision, trembling, out.

The healer's hand once sought to mend, restrain,
Declaring all that strayed from norm untrue.
Yet in those depths, where others turned in vain,
Flamed light too fierce for lesser souls to view.

But now the tide surges, the barriers fall—
No mind too bold, too bright, to claim its space.
Where stigma stood, now freedom answers call,
And genius strides with unapologetic grace.

For in diversity, we find our strength,
Each voice a note that colors life's grand song.
No law, no gate can hold what dares to length,
For difference is the gift that makes us strong.

OBSERVER'S HAND

In the unified field where countless stars are born,
The threads of fate, in quiet dance, entwine.
The world, in shadow, waits, its form untorn,
Yet bends beneath the gaze of those who shine.

Till thought breaks through the veiled dark,
Awakening the dust from which all flows.
Where endless paths in stillness leave their mark,
Until the mind bestows its watchful rose.

For all that is, exists by thought's command—
The dreamer's vision shapes both earth and sky.
The universe, like clay, takes the hand
Of those who dare to question and to fly.

In Mind, the world takes shape and doth appear—
The observers might now stand crystal clear.

SHIFTING CRAFT

Through shifting gaze, we touch the web of mind,
A boundless realm where thought and soul entwine.
Our dreams and beliefs, in currents, intertwined,
Do stir the fabric, and the stars align.

Not passive travelers in this world we roam,
But active we, in every breath and stride.
Our thoughts, like rivers, shape the lands we own,
A dance where consciousness does guide.

No longer bound, observers left behind,
But forces born to shape new realms anew.
Each spark of love, each thought we seek to find,
Resonates and ripples, casting light through you.

By higher frequencies, our hearts align,
And with compassion's grace, we shift the flow—
In moments born of love, we redefine
The very world we're bound to, here below.

For in this web, reality's our craft,
Each fleeting thought a force, each breath a draft.

INTERSECTING SYNERGIES

In fields where quantum webs entwine,
A synergy of mind and matter stands.
With entangled threads, the lines begin to shine,
A world where consciousness and cosmos blend.

When one, though distant, touches distant twin,
An unseen force links all through space and time.
This cosmic thread unites us deep within,
Defying bounds, transcending laws sublime.

And perception, that spark of thought and light,
Shapes this world of endless possibility.
In every glance, each shift within our sight,
A wave collapses, setting all things free.

For in this dance, where thought and form align,
The universe and consciousness entwine.

Quantum Tapestry

Where drifting waves in silent concord flow,
Sonata unseen defies both space and span.
Entangled fates, though worlds apart, still know
The threads that weave beyond the reach of man.

A force untouched by time's relentless blade,
Yet vast enough to span the cosmic deep.
Through thought alone, the hidden web is laid,
Where souls and stars in boundless rhythm sweep.

If mind extends beyond what flesh constrains,
A current swift yet tethered to the Whole.
Then thought dissolves the form where matter wanes,
And binds all life within a common soul.

Thus, in the quantum vastness we may see,
A web of mind, as endless as the sea.

Infinite Trust

I stand aligned with dreams pure and bright,
A beacon drawing abundance to my soul.
Each day I walk in faith, bathed in love's light,
And trust the cosmic forces make me whole.

With every breath, I feel peace's gentle flow,
A tide of joy that rises, ever near.
The path ahead, a dance of sweet release,
As I embrace the bounty of this year.

I let go of control, and in its place,
I trust the Universe to guide my way.
With heart aglow, I move through time and space,
Magnetized to all that I deserve today.

In harmony, I claim my highest grace,
And know that all I seek, I soon will trace.

Light and Shadow

We are but mirrors, shining dark and bright,
In endless dance of shadow, light, and grace.
Each soul reflects another's truth and might,
And forms, in fractured ways, the cosmic face.

For shadows serve as teachers, not as foes,
To guide us back to balance, whole and pure.
As light and dark within our being grows,
We find self-love that will endure.

One soul may light, another cast in shade,
Yet neither bears the weight of blame or guilt.
When hearts unite, the sacred truth is laid:
In duality, the bonds of life are built.

For unity, the deepest truth we seek—
To heal, to love, and walk as one, not weak.

POWER OF INTENTION

In thought, a seed is sown with purpose clear,
A spark of will guides the destined stream.
With focused heart, the universe draws near,
And bends to thee, fulfilling every dream.

For intention, like a torch, lights up the way,
A force that shapes the wind and directs the tide.
As waves are moved by currents in their play,
So are our dreams by energy supplied.

The universe, in answer to thy call,
Responds in kind, with paths to lead thee forth.
Each thought and word, a ripple through the thrall,
That shifts the tides of life, and proves thy worth.

Set thy course with a steady, conscious hand,
And watch as fate unfolds at thy command.

BAROMETER OF MEASURE

Emotions rise, like winds upon the sea,
A gauge of soul, revealing what we are.
In joy and love, our spirits are set free,
And through their light, our dreams are born afar.

For gratitude, a golden glow doth shine,
It lifts the heart and bids the soul to dance.
With every thought and feeling, we align,
And draw to us the blessings of our trance.

When joy is found, we soar on wings of light,
And glide with grace through realms of peace.
In higher states, our vision shines more bright,
As we attract the gifts that never cease.

So, raise thy heart, let love and bliss unfold,
For in their light, the world shall be retold.

Gentle Surrender

To manifest, release the reins and trust,
For time's own rhythm sets the destined pace.
In fate's embrace, no doubt, no fear, no rust—
We surrender to its gentle, steady grace.

The universe, with wisdom vast and deep,
Unfolds the path that leads to all we seek.
In faith we rest, while dreams through shadows creep,
And trust what we need will soon unweave.

When clear desires flow, untouched by control,
And credence takes root, its reach begins to grow.
The universe will guide the yearning soul,
To manifest the light that love bestows.

Let go, trust divine, and let the current be,
For all we seek is drawn to you and me.

Cultivate Inner Peace

With mindful breath, I seek a sacred space,
Where peace and calm descend and fill my soul.
Through every storm, I rise with steady grace,
And let no fear command my heart's control.

In silence deep, I find my center pure,
A stillness born from thoughts released with ease.
Each day I pause to heal, to grow, to cure,
And tend to wounds with love that brings peace.

For twenty minutes, I shall clear my mind,
And in that time, my heart will be renewed.
Through journaled ink and words of truth I find,
The harmony that nourishes, my spirit's food.

Through practice, strength shall rise, a quiet art,
And calm will reign within my beating heart.

SOULFUL EXPANSION

Each day I choose to open wide my heart,
To let the divine flow freely through my soul.
In sacred light, my spirit doth impart,
And through this bond, I feel my spirit whole.

With every breath, I feel my being grow,
As consciousness expands to realms unknown.
In truth's embrace, my essence starts to show,
And from this knowing, I am not alone.

I seek the sacred texts, the wisdom deep,
In energy of yoga, breath, and flow.
For thirty minutes weekly, I shall keep
A mindful path where cosmic rays may grow.

Thus, in this quest, I find my soul's true place,
Aligned with All, immersed in boundless grace.

THE FUSION

With courage fierce, I face my deepest fears,
The shadows that within my soul reside.
No longer shall they rule, nor claim my tears,
For I shall meet them with a heart open wide.

The wounds of past shall heal with tender grace,
Like every thought and fear I dare to see.
With love I transmute each darkened space,
And merge the fractured parts that long to be free.

Each week I turn to one dark corner's light,
To seek the truth and guide the pain to peace.
No more shall I avoid the hidden fight,
For in their depths, my soul's true strength will cease.

Thus, I embrace each shadow, every scar,
For they are sacred, and my soul's bright star.

CLAIMING WORTH

With coherent heart, I claim my worth divine,
No longer swayed by doubt, nor shame, nor fear.
Before the mirror's gaze, my soul aligns,
And in my eyes, no judgment shall appear.

Each flaw, each scar, a mark of beauty's grace,
A tale of strength and love that's yet untold.
I honor every line, each tender trace,
For in their folds, my worth is pure as gold.

In moments of imperfection's strife,
I'll gently cradle all I've come to be.
With love that blooms in every breath of life,
In vulnerability, I stand so free.

Thus, I'll embody love, both pure and true,
For in this claim, my spirit's born anew.

SACRED HARMONY

In Earth's embrace, I find my soul's retreat,
Where gentle winds and rivers softly call.
Her heartbeat sings, a rhythmic sweet,
Aligning spirit with the seasons' thrall.

Through fertile fields of blooming hue,
I walk in reverence, a grateful mind.
Each step upon her soil, a promise true,
To honor all her gifts with love entwined.

The creatures' song, whispers in the trees,
Are guides to wisdom, calm and ancient, deep.
In Nature's arms, my heart is born to ease,
For in her breath, the truths of life we keep.

Thus, I will live in balance, wild and free,
With Earth as home, in sacred harmony.

Mind-Heart Coherence

In heart and mind, a tempest fierce does roar,
Two realms apart yet bound by fate's own thread.
The heart, a fire that sparks from ancient lore,
While mind, a steady flame, by reason led.

But lo, the storm—how cruel the mind's command!
It grasps for control, while the heart makes its stand.
Yet in the fury, a deeper truth takes root—
A union blooms, where once there's but dispute.

When thought and feeling merge in sacred grace,
The soul ascends, transcending time and space.
A force more boundless than the blade or throne,
Where mind and heart, united, claim their own.

Now whole, I stand—aligned with spirit divine,
A vessel touched by stars, and love's design.

CREATIVE FLOW

In an aligned state, a seamless union meet,
A sacred pulse, a whispering of light,
The chaos swirls, yet all in balance greet,
As soul and thought ascend to clearer sight.

Like rivers winding through the dawn-lit land,
Our ideas flow, untamed but true and bright.
With every stroke, the canvas at our hand,
Becomes the field where dreams take flight.

But in depths, a sudden force shall rise,
The stillness broken by the roar of waves.
To heal and renew, to shift our inner skies,
And lift the veil where quiet wisdom paves.

Thus, in this flow, where thought and heart collide,
New worlds are born, creative spirit will abide.

WHEEL OF CONSCIOUSNESS

The path of souls ascends not by the climb,
Nor rises in a laddered, rigid way.
But spirals through the endless stretch of time,
Where shadows fall and light ignites the day.

No rank, no measure, guides our true flight,
No scale of worth defines its sacred rise.
What was, what is, and all that stays in sight,
Weaves through the thread of wheel's eternal ties.

Mortal eyes may see in light and dark a war,
As if the stars and night are sworn to fight.
But lo, the sun and moon contend no more—
Their dance a song, where day surrenders night.

So, round we move, where time and space align,
A single spark, divine, eternal, and benign.

TRANSCENDENCE

Through entwined space, I call my name,
No voice can steal, no past can claim.
The chains that held me once now break,
I rise, renewed with every ache.

The shadows reached to pull me low,
To steal my peace, to drown my glow.
But in balance, a flicker, bright—
I remain unshaken, in the light.

To those who tried to dim my flame,
To twist my truth or place the blame,
Your whispers fade, your grip undone,
Like mist that melts before the sun.

The tides return, the wind stands still,
I shape my world with steadfast will.
No longer lost, no longer bound,
I walk my path, my soul unbound.

As above, so it must be,
As within, so I am free.
No dream too far, no star too high—
I spread my wings, I touch the sky.

MIND'S ARCHITECT

We are but echoes of the beliefs we weave,
Yet cast in realms where fear and shadows reign.
The mind, ensnared, believes what it must grieve,
A dirge of doubt that binds the heart in chains.

But lo! No star hath carved thy path in stone,
Nor is thy will by fate's dark thread confined.
Within thy breast a sovereign light is sown,
Where mind and heart in sacred flame bind.

Through storms and shadows, thy heart doth beat,
A steady pulse that guides thee through the dark.
In every trial, new strength thou shalt meet,
And find within thyself a lasting spark.

Thou art the architect of life's design,
Each choice thou makes carves the path ahead.
Affirmations strong, sunbeams do brightly shine,
A pulse of truth that frees the soul instead.

Awake, for thou art more than flesh and bone,
Thy spirit stirs the clay with hands of light.
For vitality is thine—no tempest shakes thy throne—
Drink deep of devotion and claim thy power's might.

For thou, divine architect, shalt rise and soar,
And shape thy reality, forever more.

References

The following citations cover a range of topics of research and scientific papers related to trauma, neuroplasticity, emotional regulation, brain functioning, and healing, which align with the insights provided in the book.

- Meaney, M. J., & Szyf, M. (2005). Environmental programming of stress responses, Molecular Psychiatry
- Shin, L. M., & Liberzon, I. (2010). The neurocircuitry of fear, stress, and trauma. NeuroImmunoModulation
- Duman, R. S. (2014). Pathophysiology of depression and the neuroplasticity hypothesis. Psychiatric Clinics of North America
- Bremner, J. D. (2006). Traumatic stress: Effects on the brain. Dialogues in Clinical Neuroscience
- Van der Kolk, B. A. (2014). The body keeps the score: Brain, mind, and body in the healing of trauma. Penguin Books

- Goleman, D. (1995). Emotional intelligence: Why it can matter more than IQ. Bantam Books
- Lanius, R. A., Bluhm, R. L., & Frewen, P. A. (2011). The neural correlates of emotional regulation in posttraumatic stress disorder. Journal of Psychiatric Research
- Siegel, D. J. (2012). The developing mind: How relationships and the brain interact to shape who we are. Guilford Press
- Cozolino, L. (2010). The neuroscience of human relationships, Norton & Company
- Fink, A., Grabner, R., & Neubauer, A. (2009). Enhancing creativity by means of cognitive stimulation: the effects of brainwave synchronization. Creativity Research Journal
- Dorst, K., Dorst, A., & Langer, P. (2014). The role of theta waves in creativity and problem solving. Frontiers in Psychology
- Zheng, W., et al. (2016). Coherence and synchronization of brainwaves in flow states. Neural Systems and Rehabilitation Engineering
- Lutz, A., et al. (2004). Meditative states and gamma brainwave synchronization. Journal of Cognitive Neuroscience
- Csíkszentmihályi, M. (1990). Flow: The Psychology of Optimal Experience. Harper & Row

- Dietrich, A. (2004). The cognitive neuroscience of creativity. Psychonomic Bulletin & Review, 11(6), 1011-1026
- Keller, J., Bless, H., Blomann, F., & Kleinböhl, D. (2016). Physiological evidence that the experience of flow, Biological Psychology
- Kotler, S., & Wheal, J. (2017). Stealing Fire: How Silicon Valley, the Navy SEALs, and Maverick Scientists Are Revolutionizing the Way We Live and Work. HarperCollins
- Weinstein, N., Przybylski, A. K., & Ryan, R. M. (2015). The impact of flow on well-being: A longitudinal study. Journal of Personality and Social Psychology
- Maes, M., Kubera, M., & Leunis, J. C. (2011). The gut-brain axis and the immune-inflammatory response system, CNS & Neurological Disorders-Drug Targets
- Mayberg, H. S. (2003). Positron emission tomography imaging in depression: A neural systems perspective. Neuroimaging Clinics of North America
- Miller, A. H., & Raison, C. L. (2016). The role of inflammation in depression: From evolutionary imperative to modern treatment target. Nature Reviews Immunology
- Porges, S. W. (2011). The Polyvagal Theory: Neurophysiological Foundations of

- Emotions, Attachment, Communication, and Self-Regulation. W. W. Norton & Company
- Schore, A. N. (2009). Relational Trauma and the Developing Right Brain, In Progress in Neuro-Psychopharmacology and Biological Psychiatry
- Church, D., & Feinstein, D. (2017). Clinical EFT (Emotional Freedom Techniques) Improves Multiple Physiological Markers of Health, Journal of Evidence-Based Integrative Medicine
- Clond, M. (2016). Emotional Freedom Techniques for Anxiety: A Systematic Review with Meta-analysis. Journal of Nervous and Mental Disease
- Sebastian, B., & Nelms, J. (2017). The Effectiveness of Emotional Freedom Techniques in the Treatment of Post-Traumatic Stress Disorder: A Meta-Analysis. Explore: The Journal of Science and Healing
- Bach, D., Groesbeck, G., Stapleton, P., Banton, S., Blickheuser, K., & Church, D. (2019). Clinical EFT Reduces PTSD, Psychological Distress, and Cortisol Levels in Veterans. Journal of Nervous and Mental Disease
- Maslach, C., & Leiter, M. P. (2016). Understanding the burnout experience:

Recent research and its implications for
psychiatry. World Psychiatry

- Raj, S., & Powell, T. (2021). The Myth of the
Normal Brain: Embracing Neurodiversity.
AMA Journal of Ethics

Key Sources

The insights presented in this book are drawn from my studies while earning a Neuroscience Coaching Certificate, integrating the principles of neuroplasticity, quantum physics, and metaphysical teachings. These disciplines converge to provide a profound scientific and philosophical framework, illuminating the intricate interplay between science, belief, consciousness, and energy in shaping our experiences.

Below are key sources that delve deeper into these transformative concepts:

- ***Dr. Joe Dispenza*** – Breaking the Habit of Being Yourself
- ***Dr. Bruce Lipton*** – The Biology of Belief
- ***Dr. Candace Pert*** – Molecules of Emotion
- ***Dr. Amit Goswami*** – The Self-Aware Universe
- ***David Bohm*** – Wholeness and the Implicate Order
- ***Dr. Lynne McTaggart*** – The Field
- ***HeartMath Institute Research***
- ***Dr. Rollin McCraty*** – The Science of the Heart

- ***Neville Goddard*** – The Power of Awareness
- ***Dolores Cannon*** – The Convoluted Universe Series

About the Author

Lali A. Love is an award-winning author, intuitive, and alchemist whose storytelling spans dark fantasy, science fiction, paranormal thrillers, and transformative metaphysical poetry. Known for her bestselling titles such as *Heart of a Warrior Angel* and *The De-Coding of Jo* Angel Academy series, Lali has captivated readers worldwide with her gripping narratives and inspiring verse.

Her literary portfolio includes the uplifting coffee table art book *The Joy of I.T.*, the evocative poetry collection *Organic eMotions,* and the transformative self-growth series *Realms of My Soul.* Lali's work continues to resonate deeply, earning her a global following and establishing her as a voice for those seeking healing, empowerment, and a deeper connection to the self.

Recognized with prestigious awards, including the NYC Big Book Award, Independent Press Gold Award, Queer Indie Gold Award, and International Reader's

Favorite Gold Award, Lali has firmly established herself as a prolific literary voice.

But her mission transcends writing—Lali is dedicated to activating and elevating consciousness. Through her creative work, she champions mental health, self-love, and authenticity, helping readers embrace their divine essence and live in alignment with their highest potential.

As a neuroscience-certified coach, Lali expertly integrates neuroplasticity, quantum physics, and metaphysics to offer readers practical techniques for inner transformation. Her approach empowers individuals to transcend limiting beliefs, create lasting change, and step into a life of freedom and fulfillment.

Through her immersive fiction and powerful poetry, Lali A. Love guides readers on a journey of self-discovery and transformation, unlocking new possibilities and inviting them to live a life of inspired action.